We Have Lost The President

A Funny English Comedy-Thriller-Mystery

by Paul Mathews

We Have Lost series
Book 1

Paperback version first published in 2020

Copyright © Paul Mathews 2020

Paul Mathews has asserted his right under the Copyright, Designs and Patents Act 1988 to be identified as the author of this work.

All the characters in this book are fictitious, and any resemblance to actual persons, living or dead, is purely coincidental.

All rights reserved. Except for brief quotations in critical articles or reviews, no part of this publication may be reproduced, stored in a retrieval system, or transmitted in any form or by any means, electronic, mechanical, photocopying, recording, or otherwise, without the prior permission of the copyright owner.

ISBN: 9798656156943

Cover illustration by Alex Storer
www.thelightdream.net

The name's Pond. Howie Pond.

Chapter 1

Howie Pond was not a happy man. He'd been dragged out of bed and into Buckingham Palace by an early morning bleep. In the frantic rush to squeeze into his best suit and leave his south London pod, he'd forgotten to grab any breakfast. The palace canteen didn't open until 7.00am. And, despite its extravagance, the White Drawing Room, in which he now stood, didn't contain a coffee machine. The Royal Family probably took it with them, he thought to himself. A last act of defiance before they fled to Florida, all those years ago. 'Let them drink instant!' he imagined the king screaming, as he sprinted to his escape helicopter, clutching a gold-plated espresso maker.

He squinted at his bleeper. It was still installing software he didn't want and refusing access to his e-comms. Howie heaved a huge sigh. He hated technology – or 'Tech', as everyone insisted on calling it these days. Yes. Tech with a capital 'T' – the marketing slogan of a firm that had gone bust with a capital 'B' years ago, taking billions of pounds of British Government money with it. Today's Tech didn't deserve a capital 'T'. It hardly merited a small 't'.

Another minute passed. The bleeper was still in its own little world of digital self-improvement. Howie wanted to hurl it against the wall. But he couldn't risk damaging it. This 4cm-by-8cm messaging device was all he had to communicate with when he didn't have access to an e-terminal. Sometimes he wished the hackers had done a better job eleven years ago, when they deep-hacked voice comms, the internet and much of the equipment that relied on them. Mobile phones, landlines, laptops, tablets – they were all rendered useless in one deadly strike. But to Howie's great annoyance, the hackers had completely ignored these bloody bleepers. The British people had been stuck with them ever since. Those hackers had a sick sense of humour.

He'd had enough of this machine's nonsense. He took it firmly in hand and pressed hard on a random button. The bleeper buzzed in disapproval and flashed a message on its screen:

I'm BUSY at the moment. Please WAIT.

'Humans are busier than machines,' he grumbled to himself. He pressed another button to make his point, even harder this time. Another bleep. Another message:

As I just informed you, I'm BUSY. Please STOP pushing my buttons. I'll tell you when I'm READY.

Howie was just about to throw the bleeper on the floor and stamp on it, when it played its annoying welcome jingle. The display reset:

Good morning, Howard. It is 06:15 on Tuesday, April >>DATE ERROR<< 2044.

Howie hated Tuesdays. Even more than people, or defective Tech, that called him Howard. He clicked the bleeper's status button:

You are currently AVAILABLE. You have 352 UNREAD e-comms. Long live the Republic!

He pressed the bleeper's update button and lifted the device to his lips. 'Status is super-busy. Not available. Acknowledge.' The bleeper bleeped. The display reset:

You are AVAILABLE all day. You have 354 UNREAD e-comms. Remember – Republicans deliver, Democrats dither!

Howie growled. It didn't matter if he was super-busy, mega-busy or super-mega-busy. His bleeper didn't care. It wanted him available for crisis and disaster twenty-four hours a day, seven days a week – like he was some sort of government superhero. Got a communications problem no one else can solve? Bleep Super Howie. Any time of day or night. He'll drop everything and come flying to the rescue.

As he shoved the bleeper in his pocket, the head of the National Security and Intelligence Service, Martha Blake, appeared in the doorway. Howie straightened his tie. It was one from before the revolution, but still presentable. Then he tried to smooth the wrinkles in his non-crease suit. They wouldn't budge. He gave up and sat back in his chair. He wasn't normally so fussed about his appearance at work. But he always felt underdressed when he met Martha. Her black trouser suits were so stylish and her white blouses so dazzling, they must have been imported from the New States. And it didn't matter what hour of the day or night it was, her flame-red hair always burned brightly – like a warning sign to anyone who was thinking of making her life difficult.

Martha moved inside the room and shut the door. 'Apologies for summoning you to the palace at this hour, Howie. I've been here since half past five, if that's any consolation.'

'We are the Republic's humble servants. Whenever the call comes, we must obey,' replied Howie, stifling a yawn.

'I'm sorry that my e-comm was so vague. But I had to tell you this face-to-face.' She swallowed hard. 'I'm afraid it's not good news.'

Of course it wasn't good news. It was a Tuesday. All the major catastrophes he'd dealt with in his career – the Tech meltdowns, the data leaks, the coffee droughts – had dropped into his lap on a Tuesday. Usually because no one bothered to read their e-comms on a Monday.

'What's the story?' asked Howie, rubbing his eyes.

Martha swallowed again, harder than before. She sat down on the leather sofa opposite, leaned back and pushed a hand through her hair. 'It's big.'

'Let me guess. One of the vice presidents has lost their briefcase again?'

'No, it's not the VPs, for a change.'

'A civil servant has left top-secret papers on a park bench?'

'Not this week. As far as I know.'

'The First Lady, then? She's got another self-help book coming out this week. My press office still hasn't seen it.' Howie put his head in his hands. 'Oh, no. Don't tell me it's got photos of the president doing yoga poses again?'

Martha shook her head. 'That book is the least of our worries. It's worse than that.' She puffed out her cheeks. 'Much worse.'

Howie couldn't imagine anything worse than the media circus surrounding the First Lady's books. They were a nightmare. Packed with inappropriate insights into the president's daily routine, the stories went on for weeks. 'Okay,' he sighed. 'Tell me what's happened.'

'We have lost the president,' announced Martha, the tension in her voice giving the words an unnatural rhythm. 'Lost. As in, we can't find him.'

For a second, Howie thought Martha had just told him that they'd lost the president. He chuckled at the idea. President Jan Polak going missing? It was a ridiculous concept. It would be like the sun not rising in the morning.

'It's no laughing matter, Howie. We can't locate the president. He didn't turn up to his office this morning. He's not in his official quarters. And no one has seen him since last night.'

He hadn't been hearing things. 'There must be some mistake, Martha. He'll be around the palace somewhere.'

'Believe me, Howie, he's vanished. And he's not answering his bleeper.'

That was odd. The president and his bleeper were inseparable. As Howie leant forward to rest his chin on his hand

and consider this development, he felt something move inside his jacket pocket. Reaching inside, he pulled out a small, pink envelope. Both he and Martha recoiled from it. It was far too bright for that time of the morning.

'Is that for me?' she asked, after what seemed a minute, but was actually five seconds.

Howie looked at the envelope and saw his name on the front in capital letters. 'No. It's for me.'

'Then open it,' ordered Martha. 'It could be a message from ... I don't know, kidnappers.'

Howie ripped open the envelope. Inside, he found a card. The cover made him take a breath. There was no writing – just a photo of bundles of $100 bills. Maybe this really was a ransom demand. He felt a lump in his throat.

'Is there a message inside?' asked Martha. Every muscle in her face tensed.

Howie opened the card. Every muscle in his face relaxed.

'Who is it from, Howie? Hackers? Royalists? Some crazed Democrat? Read it out to me!'

Howie cleared his throat. 'Congratulations, birthday boy. Forty-two today. You may be old, but you look like a million dollars ...' He sensed an inappropriate punchline, but it was too late to back out now. '... all green and wrinkly.' He might have managed a laugh, had the circumstances been different.

'There's also my girlfriend Britt's signature,' Howie continued, unsure why he was doing so. 'And I think those are ... kisses.' He could feel his cheeks turning the same shade of pink as the envelope.

Martha pondered this news for several seconds. 'Your girlfriend didn't say anything about a ransom demand?'

Howie shook his head, just in case she wasn't joking. A knock on a door saved him from further embarrassment.

Martha raised a finger. 'One moment. It'll be about the Code Red crisis plan. I can't access the damn thing. Would you believe it?'

Howie would believe it. Tech was as unreliable as the people who designed it.

'Come in!' shouted Martha.

Kaia-Liisa Saar, the president's chief private secretary, popped her head round the door. 'Apologies for disturbing you, but I can't access the crisis plan. I'm just getting a message that says there's a network problem. It's probably better if you speak with the Tech people yourself.'

Martha groaned. 'Alright. I'll pop round in a moment.'

Kaia-Liisa nodded and closed the door behind her.

'So we're really at Code Red?' asked Howie. 'It's not a test exercise?'

'No. Only a fool would organise one of those so close to Independence Day. And anyway, you and I would have been notified in advance.'

Martha was right. But Howie still couldn't quite believe the president had gone missing. 'Maybe Jan has popped back to Poland and forgotten to tell us? A family bereavement or something?'

Martha shook her head. 'Jan has no family left in Poland. His parents are dead. He has no uncles, aunts or cousins. And his grandparents died years ago. To my knowledge, he hasn't returned there since he became president.'

'Fair enough. But what about business interests?'

'He has none. Here, in Poland or anywhere else. And you know Jan. He would've told us if he was unexpectedly jetting off to the place of his birth. Or anywhere else.'

As Howie nodded, his body trembled. It wasn't just the lack of sleep, food and caffeine. It was the horrible realisation that this must be for real. They really had lost the president.

Martha clasped her hands. 'Let's not waste any more time playing guessing games. Here are the logistics. I'm going to be working from Jan's private office. It means I can monitor what comes in. Kaia-Liisa is very good. She's on top of all Jan's business.'

Howie shuffled in his chair. 'What have you told her?'

'Only that the president is working on urgent state business away from the office. And that he's unavailable and uncontactable until further notice. I also told her I'm reviewing the Code Red crisis plan at Jan's request. And there will be meetings on it during that process. Meetings that don't require a private secretary to be present.'

'Good stuff. The fewer people who know the full story, the better.'

Martha got up and moved to the door. 'I'd better contact the Tech team.' Just before she left the room, she turned and smiled apologetically. 'Oh, and for what it's worth … happy birthday, Howie.'

Howie didn't respond. He didn't celebrate birthdays. He'd never seen the attraction of celebrating being one year nearer the grave. But this year, Britt had broken with protocol and sent him a card. Whatever lopsided logic had led her to do so, he was grateful for the reminder. Because the cosmic alignment of his birthday and a Tuesday were the equivalent of a solar eclipse for the Ancient Greeks – a sign the gods were seriously pissed off and looking to kick his mortal backside. At least the Greeks had goats to sacrifice. He just had his career.

He remembered a previous birthday that had fallen on the second working day of the week. It had been eleven years earlier – Tuesday, 12 April 2033. It was the day he'd been thinking about a few minutes ago. The day when hackers brought the country to a standstill and the previous government banned all internet and phone access to avoid further attacks – a ban still in place today. A day when Howie had to answer a multitude of media questions with no idea what the hell was going on. A dark day for him, the former president and his Democratic government. Modern historians had christened it 'The day the internet died'. Smart-arse journalists called it 'Net Loss Day'. What would the media call today, if they found out the president was missing? 'Pres Loss Day', or something equally stupid. Howie would have to make sure the media never got the opportunity to write that, or any other, headline.

That would be tricky. Especially once all the loose-tongued vice presidents were informed of the situation.

Howie felt his bleeper buzz in his pocket. It usually only vibrated if it was a message from someone on his priority senders' list. He quickly pulled it out, praying that it was a message from the president – one that contained a perfectly reasonable explanation for his unexpected absence. But it wasn't. It was a service message from his bloody bleeper:

Hello again, Howard. Just checking you're STILL there. UNREAD e-comms don't READ themselves, you know! You have 359 of them. And you are AVAILABLE, so there's really no excuse for ignoring them.

Howie didn't have to explain himself to a machine. He flicked the bleeper's off switch and shoved it back in his trouser pocket. If the world needed saving in the next hour or so, another superhero could do it. One who didn't have three hundred and fifty-nine unread e-comms.

He heard a scream of frustration from the corridor. Seconds later, Martha crashed through the door, her red hair flailing behind her.

'We no longer have a Tech team!' she shouted. 'The Americans have poached them. They all resigned on Friday evening.'

'How can they do that?'

'Because we forgot to put a notice period in their contracts!' Martha's eyeballs cartwheeled. 'They were the only human beings who knew how to outwit these maddening machines. And they could walk out the door whenever they wanted. Can you believe it?!'

Howie could believe it. His guess was the VP in charge of Tech had left contractual notice periods to the VP in charge of commercial. The VP in charge of commercial had assumed that kind of thing was for the VP in charge of human resources. And the VP in charge of human resources had been one hundred per cent confident the VP for Tech would have it all covered.

Martha slumped onto the sofa opposite. 'We're at the mercy of the auto-techs now!' She caught her breath. 'I was here last week, and got stuck in a broken lift with one of the charmless little dustbins. It refused to diagnose the problem for the first forty-five minutes. And do you know why? Because it was on its "break".'

No one liked the auto-techs. They were half the size of humans. But twice as unhelpful. They just seemed to glide around, doing their own thing – occasionally firing a laser into your iris to check who you were. They were Tech with a small 't' – in every sense. The only person who received consistently good service from them was the president – a deliberate ploy by the manufacturers, Howie suspected. Their only other fan was the vice president for Tech, Ivan Bonn. He'd promised that the auto-techs would totally transform government Tech. That was five years ago. Everyone was still waiting.

Howie's stomach rumbled. He really needed his breakfast. More importantly, so did his cat, Indie-Day. She went berserk if she wasn't fed by seven o'clock – all extended claws and swinging paws – and he'd just bought an uber-modern synth-leather sofa. Britt was off for the rest of the week, so she'd be comatose until at least midday. He needed to get back to his pod.

'We've got a Code Red crisis meeting in just over an hour, and no crisis plan,' announced Martha. She looked Howie in the eye. 'You've written crisis plans before. Could you knock one together for me by half seven? Just an outline. You're so good at this kind of thing.'

The problem with being so dependable, Howie often told himself, is that everyone starts to depend on you. He couldn't afford to let that happen. Not with luxury furniture at stake.

'You know exactly what to do in a crisis, Martha. You're already doing it. I bet you've already got the security team combing the place.'

'Yes, I have. Bogdan and his team are conducting a room-by-room search of the palace. But the problem is there are nearly eight hundred rooms in this place. We have to search every one of them for clues. What if nothing turns up?'

'Don't worry. Every room is covered by cameras.' Howie looked at a small lens in the ceiling above them. Something wasn't right. 'Where's the red light?'

'The cameras failed at eleven o'clock last night.'

'What? All of them?'

'Yes. And the system's memory has been wiped. I've got Ivan Bonn looking into what happened. He'll give us an update at the meeting.'

'Okay. So, you've got Bogdan and Ivan on the case. That's your crisis plan.' He crossed his fingers and imagined a five-egg omelette.

Martha leaned towards him. 'It would look better if it was all written down, though, don't you think?'

The prospects of Howie eating breakfast and saving his furniture weren't looking good. He would have to think fast. 'Look, crisis plans are more trouble than they're worth. They're discussed, drafted, redrafted, finalised, printed off – if the printers are working – and by that time, the crisis has spiralled out of control.'

Martha nodded. Howie was impressed with himself. He hadn't drunk any coffee and he was still managing to talk sense. He continued. 'This is a national security matter. You're in charge here, Martha. This is your chance to do whatever you want. Maybe something different?' What was the title of that tedious management course he'd been sent on last week? Ah, yes. 'Extraordinary situations call for radical solutions.'

Martha looked Howie straight in the eyes. He waited for her to thank him politely for his views, tell him she needed a crisis plan on her desk in an hour's time, and he would be writing it. She stood up. 'You're right. A plan will just constrain us. Perhaps a radical solution is what's needed.'

Howie sank back into the sofa and smiled. Job done.

'Just one favour to ask,' added Martha. 'Could you say something at the crisis meeting about how we present this to the media and the wider world? You know the sort of thing – politely tell them not to open their big mouths and that we'll handle everything.'

Giving media advice to a room full of vice presidents – most of whom didn't even read a newspaper – wasn't his favourite task. But it was a small price to pay for his temporary freedom.

'No problem. Now, if you'll excuse me, I need to pop back to my pod.' He paused to think for a plausible excuse. 'In the rush, I left my bleeper behind.'

'Of course. One can't be without one's bleeper. Especially when we're at Code Red.'

Howie's stomach gurgled in anticipation. He and the cat would be breakfasting together. And his new synth-leather sofa wouldn't have a claw mark on it.

'My driver will take you back home. He'll wait outside and bring you straight back here. You'll only need to pop in for a few minutes, won't you?'

'Erm, yeah. Just a few minutes,' mumbled Howie, trying not to sound like a man whose breakfast dreams had just been shattered.

'Good. I'll walk you to the car. I could do with some fresh air. I'll need it, if I'm going to be radical.'

Howie got to his feet. At least the cat won't go hungry, he thought, as they made their way outside.

Chapter 2

Britt twisted her head towards the bedside unit. The rest of her body stayed glued to the mattress. She rubbed her eyes and tried to read the numbers on the e-alarm. It was six fifty-something in the morning. An unfamiliar time for her. Especially on a day off.

Indie-Day meowed from behind the bedroom door. Britt buried her face in the pillow and hauled the duvet over her head. There was no Howie underneath it. She remembered now. The early morning bleep. The scramble for clean underwear. The frantic search for his 'stupid, bloody bleeper'. It must have been urgent.

The duvet was providing no protection from the cat's cries for attention, which were starting to sound more threatening. But she'd only had three hours' sleep and her energy levels were too low for cat feeding.

She stared up at the ceiling and replayed in her head, one more time, yesterday's conversation with George, her editor at *The Republican* newspaper. She could remember it word for word:

'Sit down, Britt, this won't take long.'
'I'll stand, if you don't mind. I prefer to stand when I receive bad news.'
'Why do you assume it's going to be bad news?'
'Because you always give me bad news in your office on Monday afternoons. And this is your office. And it's Monday afternoon. You often call the bad news "good news". But I'm a

journalist. I know the difference.' She flashed a half-second smile.

George delivered the bad news. 'Two of the features team were involved in a nasty car crash on Fulham High Street yesterday. Thankfully, they'll survive. But they're going to be on long-term sick leave.' He peered over the top of his glasses. 'It means we're seriously short-staffed in that section.'

Britt didn't like the sound of this.

'So I've made a decision,' announced George.

She stood motionless – like a condemned criminal waiting for the hangman's trapdoor to open beneath her feet.

'I'm taking you off the news desk, Britt, and putting you on features.'

She gave an enormous sigh. Features were her worst nightmare.

'Lifestyle features,' added George.

Scrap that last thought. Lifestyle features were her worst nightmare. 'You mean all that crap that sells advertising and no one reads?'

'Our sub-editors read it. And that's good enough for me. You start next Monday. Take the rest of the week off. Call it a reward for all your hard work on news.'

Britt walked to George's desk and leaned forward. 'I'd rather you fired me than have to write that crap.'

George jolted back in his seat. With his grey suit and whiskers, he reminded her of a trapped mouse. Howie often complimented Britt on her cats' eyes, and she fixed them on George – in the same way she'd seen Indie-Day focus on small rodents.

'You're a very good journalist,' croaked George. 'I have no intention of firing you.'

Britt leaned back from the desk. 'Then keep me on news – where I belong.'

'Look, Britt, lifestyle features aren't so bad. They —'

'They remind people of the lives they're not living. This isn't America, George. Anyone with a lifestyle packed their bags for the New States fifteen years ago.'

'Not everyone.' George breathed in noisily through his nose. 'I stayed.'

Britt checked herself, mid-outrage. Amerigration was still a raw subject for many of the Republic's citizens. Millions of Britain's brightest had left for the rebranded United States, just a few months after Britain's 2029 revolution. Millions more had had their applications rejected. Any insinuation that George hadn't met the Americans' criteria could get her fired. And despite her earlier bullishness, she didn't really want to lose her job. That meant there was only one option. She'd have to strain every fibre in her body and be diplomatic. She took a deep breath.

'You thought you could make a difference by staying here. Just like I want to make a difference. But I can't make a difference on features. I just can't. I can only make a difference on news.'

She wasn't sure where all that 'make a difference' rubbish had come from. But it sounded sincere. She attempted a warm smile. But failed. Forget facial expressions. Maybe he would see her point of view? See her well-reasoned argument in all its logical glory. It was clear to her. She was in the right. He was just being a dick.

George got up, keeping his eyes fixed on Britt. They stared at each other, arms by their sides – like two gunslingers in one of those old-world westerns that Howie liked to watch. She felt the muscles in the back of her neck tense, as he opened his mouth.

'No. I'm sorry. You've been on news for some time now and this will be a good development opportunity for you.'

The words were like a shot to her heart. So much for diplomacy. Time to return fire.

'Don't talk crap, George.' Her finger was pointing like a mini Smith & Wesson. 'We both know why you've asked me and not one of the others.'

'And why's that?'

'Because my stuff is political. You don't want me digging up anything before the election.'

George crossed his arms. 'We are *The Republican* newspaper. And, in case you hadn't noticed, a Republican government has been in power for the last ten years.'

'Yes. But we're editorial. Not advertising.'

It was George's turn to draw his finger and point it at her. 'Just listen to me, for once. Our readers do not want to hear about the Republicans' failings in the run-up to a presidential election. After the election, we'll take a more critical view. But not until then.'

Britt snorted her contempt.

'I'm sorry, Britt. But that's life. That's politics.'

'That's bollocks,' snapped Britt. It was her parting shot. George might have won this shoot-out. But he wasn't going to win the war.

Her thoughts returned to the here and now. The cat was still meowing. But the sound was different. It was softer and more welcoming. That could only mean one thing. Howie was back.

She heard the front door slide shut. Their 2030s prototype pod was so small, and the walls so thin, you could hear conversations in another room if you listened carefully. And with nothing else to do, she listened.

'Hello, pussycat. You must be starving.'

The cat knew the routine. It gave its standard response – a short, instructive meow.

'Come on, girl. I'll fix you some breakfast. But don't mention my birthday, okay?'

Howie's birthday. Yes. They had never celebrated birthdays before. But Britt would be thirty next week. And she had decided things were going to change. She'd seen an all-weather leather handbag in Oxford Street – an American import – and she'd decided she was going to hit her thirties in style. But Howie had probably found her birthday card by now and he'd be seriously pissed off. For now, it would be safer for her to stay in the sanctuary of the bedroom.

Britt settled herself under the duvet, with one ear on what was going on in the kitchen. Howie often confided in the cat. By listening in, she might discover how bad his mood was.

She heard Howie's voice. 'I bet you're wondering why I had to leave so early, eh, girl? Well, we've got a Code Red crisis on at the palace.'

This sounded interesting. Britt lifted herself on one elbow and turned her ear to the door.

Howie sighed. 'Let's just say, I'm not the only one who's done a disappearing act this morning.'

This was more than interesting. This could be a potential news story. Britt sprang from the bed, rushed to the door and pressed her ear to it, so she wouldn't miss anything. Then she remembered. She didn't write news stories any more. But wait. What was to stop her investigating it? George had given her the rest of the week off. This could be the story that saved her from features. A shiver of hope shot up her spine.

Then Howie spoke again. 'Hang on, where's your bowl? And your dry food? They're usually in here. Someone's moved them.'

Britt swore under her breath. She'd reorganised the kitchen units last night. And Howie had got back so late, she didn't have time to give him the guided tour.

'Where are they? I'm not going to have time to feed myself at this rate!'

Howie had to find them quickly, she thought, or he'd lose his conversational thread with the cat.

'For king's sake!' he cursed. 'Everything's going missing this morning.'

Britt wanted to burst out of the bedroom and shout: 'Dry food – here! Bowl – there! Now keep talking!' But that wasn't going to work.

'They've got security searching the palace,' continued Howie. 'Though that lot couldn't find a fart in a vacuum.'

16

Cupboards clattered. Bowls banged. Cutlery clanged.

'Ah, there they are!' roared Howie. 'Hallelujah!'

Make that two hallelujahs. Now feed the cat and finish your story.

Indie-Day meowed her impatience.

'Alright. It's coming, girl!'

Britt hoped what was coming was the name. She needed a name. Say the name, Howie.

'There you go. Make that disappear. Now I've got to try and find —'

Time froze. Britt's whole body tensed in expectation. It was coming. The name was coming. Time thawed. And then it happened – a car horn blared from the street below.

'Bloody hell,' groaned Howie. 'It's me that's got to disappear now.'

Britt felt like she'd been zapped with 50,000 volts. Her muscles paralysed. Her mind scrambled. Her hopes frazzled.

Howie sighed. 'Looks like no breakfast for me. I don't know what time I'll be back this evening, Indie-Day. Sleeping Beauty in there will have to feed you, if it's late.'

A few seconds later, Britt heard the front door slide shut. The noise jump-started her body. She could feel the stress hormones surging through her veins and her heart thumping in her ears. She needed to lie down.

Britt collapsed on the bed and stared at the grey walls for inspiration. She couldn't find any. She didn't have the name. And the headline 'Someone has gone missing, but we've no idea who it is' wasn't going to excite George or any other editor.

She imagined writing a lifestyle feature on interior decorating. She got two sentences in and started to feel nauseous.

Britt sat on the edge of the bed. She couldn't just give up. She had to think. Who might have gone missing? Howie worked with hundreds of people. Who did he rant about the most? That was easy. The vice presidents. One of them had probably blundered, on a bigger scale than usual, and gone into hiding.

Yes. It must be one of them. But she'd have to find out which one.

She cleared her head. She needed an information source. She guessed Howie wouldn't be returning to the pod again, so she'd have to find someone else. No one came to mind. None of her normal contacts were that well-connected. She would have to find a new one.

Who would be close to all this? Who would know what was going on? And who would be stupid enough to tell a complete stranger?

Forget the police. Yes, they were dumb. But her contacts there had stopped returning her bleeps since her December front-page story on cop corruption. A civil servant, maybe? Someone in the private or press offices? Not a bad idea. Though they'd be at work until the end of the day.

So who?

Then she remembered something Howie had mentioned, minutes before. The Buckingham Palace security team. They were clueless, according to him. If she could track one of them down, maybe she could get some more information? But how would she do that?

She tried to remember if she'd written anything about palace security. She hadn't. But a colleague had, a couple of weeks ago. A security guy had been on his way out of the palace after his night shift when a tourist's bag was snatched. He'd chased and caught the thief. That was around eight o'clock. If Britt hung around Buckingham Palace at that time, she might be able to intercept one of the night-shift security team as they were leaving.

Britt jumped from her bed. A quick water-spray and she could be there in half an hour. She opened her wardrobe and grabbed the first dress she saw. Then she stopped. And realised. She could be recognised.

For a start, there was Howie. He worked at the palace. It wasn't impossible his eagle eyes might spot her loitering outside. Then there were the police officers outside the gates.

Always bored and looking for someone to harass, they might recognise 'that bloody journalist' and throw her in a police van for the day. And there were all those colleagues of Howie's she'd met, socially and professionally. They knew who she was and what she did for a living.

She would have to disguise herself. Nothing too extravagant. She wasn't going to turn up dressed as the Queen, demanding the reinstatement of the monarchy. No. She would pretend she was a tourist and dress appropriately. Raincoat, scarf, sunglasses, guidebook – that should be enough.

Britt opened the wardrobe and began preparing her costume. This is going to be fun, she thought. A fancy-dress party for one. With a prize at the end of it – her old job on the news desk.

Chapter 3

Howie sat back and admired the grandeur of Buckingham Palace's State Dining Room. The fireplace, chandeliers, curtains and portraits were exactly the same as when the Royal Family were here. And whatever you thought about the royals, they really knew a thing or two about interior decoration. The lavish surroundings somehow made meetings here more bearable. But the room's majestic magic wasn't going to work this morning. There was one simple reason – it was full of vice presidents. Every one of them was either slouched or slumped on the oak dining table that stretched out before him. A few were fiddling with their personalised digi-pens while staring blankly at digi-pads. Most looked more ready for a long nap than a crisis meeting. For many of them, their main contribution would be the muddy footprints they'd just planted on the red carpet. Howie scanned the faces. None of them belonged to the president's twin brother, Vice President for Defence Oskar Polak. That was strange. He was never late for anything.

Then Howie remembered. Oskar was at a two-day defence summit in Paris. It was probably a blessing. Meetings ran more smoothly when he wasn't around.

Martha Blake stood up and addressed the room. 'Welcome everyone. Thank you for attending this Code Red crisis meeting at such short notice. For those who don't know me, my name is Martha Blake, and I'm head of the National Security and Intelligence Service.'

Those who knew Martha were already exchanging worried glances. Her appearance at meetings was never good news for the politicians.

'Apologies for the secrecy on the bleeper, but you had to hear this in the most secure way possible. And that, as always, is face-to-face.' She gestured to a stony-faced man, sat on her left. 'This is the head of Palace security, Bogdan Bogdanowic.'

Bogdan greeted the table with a grunt. Howie knew him well. Getting the facts out of him was about as easy as extracting sharks' teeth.

'And, of course, you all know Howie Pond – the president's official spokesperson, head of comms and number-one communications expert.'

Howie nodded in acknowledgement. Then he quickly added a 'Good morning' and a smile, to emphasise his communication credentials. Nobody responded.

'So why are we all here?' asked Martha. 'There's no easy way to say this. So I'll just go ahead and say it.' She took a deep breath. 'We have lost the president.'

A chatter of concern went around the table. Martha allowed the room to settle and then continued. 'No one has seen or heard from him since eleven o'clock last night, when he finished work in his office in the palace and headed towards his private rooms. We currently have very little intelligence. But I'm working on that.'

Some poor soul, in a secret basement somewhere, is trying to make sense of this mess, thought Howie. Rather them than me.

'And there was a problem with the security cameras,' continued Martha. 'Bogdan has more details.'

Martha sat down. Then Bogdan stood up, with the frightened expression you'd expect from a man whose team had just lost a president. He reluctantly delivered his report in a deadpan voice. 'Security cameras in palace malfunction at 11.00pm last night. All two hundred and fifty. CAMS – Central Automated Monitoring System – should alert security team. But didn't.'

Howie had briefed the media on CAMS last year, after the multi-million-pound contract was leaked to the *Daily Democrat* newspaper. 'It's a small price to pay for guaranteeing the president's security,' Howie had explained. He hoped the words wouldn't come back to bite him on the backside.

Bogdan loosened his tie. 'CAMS is hundred per cent automated. Physical checks did not reveal problem until 5.00am today.' He tightened his tie. 'During six-hour window, president disappear. My security officers see and hear nothing.' Then he gripped his tie, as if hanging on for dear life.

It was time for Howie to do a bit of digging. 'So what were your security team doing between eleven and five, Bogdan? It's the first question the media will ask.'

Bogdan didn't look at Howie. 'They were in palace. At strategic locations.'

'But no one was outside his bedroom?' asked Howie. 'Because that'll be the media's second question.'

Bogdan kept staring straight ahead. 'No. CAMS is designed to stop anyone getting that far. But my team search president's bedroom and other rooms. And gardens.' He turned and stared at Howie. 'And to answer media's third question – so far, we find nothing.' He sat down, tugging at his collar, as if it was a noose around his neck.

The vice president for homeland security, Daisy Gray, jumped from her seat. 'It's Independence Day on Thursday!' she shouted. 'Jan needs to be here. He's got to be here. So he can announce he's standing for president again. It's in the constitution.' She took a gulp of air. 'What do we tell the citizens? And the Americans? They love him. They don't want anyone else running the country. It'll be chaos. Oh my God, there'll be another revolution!'

Martha intervened before Daisy could take another breath. 'We'll discuss external communications shortly. Until then, as Jan would say, let's keep calm and carry on.'

Excellent advice. Keep calm and carry on – the president's campaign slogan. One that had helped him sweep to power in 2034, after the collapse of the online world. And helped him gain re-election five years later, when there wasn't even a crisis to keep calm about. But Daisy was right – if Jan Polak wasn't here at eleven o'clock on Thursday morning to announce he'd be running for a third term, as everyone expected, one of the vice presidents would be taking his place. On second thoughts, blind panic did seem a perfectly rational response.

Daisy was trembling with fear. 'Stay calm? How the bloody hell can we stay calm?! Jan's our shining light. Our golden boy. Our election-winning machine.' She looked round the table at her colleagues for moral support. There wasn't any. Maybe they were already thinking what Howie was thinking. With no Jan Polak, one of them would have to run for president. After ten seconds of silence, Daisy sat down, muttering to herself.

Martha tried not to sound concerned. 'We keep calm and, above all else, we keep this Code Red confidential. The more people who know, the more chance the news will leak out. And for that reason, I'm not informing, or involving, the police at this stage.'

Howie breathed a sigh of relief. He didn't like informing, or involving, the police at any stage. They leaked like a church roof in a monsoon.

Daisy sprang up again, like a crazed jack-in-the-box. 'That's insane! If the president doesn't turn up here, the police are our only hope of finding him. They're the eyes and ears of London. We have to tell them. I'm vice president for homeland security. I've got a duty to tell them.'

Martha deployed her best diplomatic voice. 'Vice President Gray, I understand your concern. But there is nothing in the constitution that requires you to do that.'

'Okay, it's not in the constitution,' blurted Daisy. 'But I have professional relationships to maintain. Don't they count for anything?'

Martha was firmer this time. 'Not when the president goes missing.'

Daisy thought for a second. 'I know. We'll compromise. I'm meeting the chief of police for dinner at The Savoy at eight o'clock tonight. Freddie is discreet. He won't breathe a word to anyone. He could help us.'

Howie looked at Martha. He could tell this conversation was straining even her powers of diplomacy.

'If and when the time comes to inform the police, I shall do it,' declared Martha. 'Until then, I would suggest everyone keeps contact with the police to an absolute minimum. Including dinner with the chief of police at The Savoy.'

Daisy sank back into her box without another word. Martha turned to Ivan Bonn. 'Now, Ivan, you're looking into why the cameras failed.'

Ivan jolted upright, as if suddenly woken from a nightmare. 'What? Oh, yes. Camera failure. Looking into it. Not personally. Don't do actual Tech. My team does. Well, they did. They all left on Friday.'

Martha sighed. 'So no one is working on it?'

'Not a human. An auto-tech. He's on it. Diagnosing what happened. System failure or system hack. He's salvaging data. Recent records.'

Martha grimaced. 'An auto-tech?'

'Yes. Name's Brian. Helpful little chap.'

There was a helpful auto-tech? That was news to Howie. It must be a new model. Either that or something had gone wrong with its programming.

'Seems a bit of a coincidence – the Tech team disappearing, then this happening,' bellowed a grey suit from the end of the table.

'America pays better,' explained Ivan. 'They got Tech. Internet. Mobiles. Laptops. Billion-dollar budgets. We don't.'

'Maybe the president went with them?' muttered a different grey suit.

Martha gritted her teeth. 'I believe the Americans already have a president. So that vacancy is already filled. Now, if we could just focus —'

'Could he have been kidnapped?' interrupted a dark grey suit. 'Or assassinated?'

She waved her hands. 'Please. It is pointless speculating until the search of the palace is complete and we know what happened with the security cameras.'

'Could he really be dead?' shouted the darkest grey suit in the room.

Martha raised her voice. 'We haven't found a body. So we must assume he's alive. Unless anyone here knows any different?'

The room went quiet.

Martha turned her gaze towards Howie. 'Now, our comms guru will advise on what you should, or shouldn't, be saying to the media and everyone else about this.'

Before Howie could leave his seat, Bogdan stood up and spoke. 'Can I leave? I not deal with media. Need to get back to my team.'

Martha nodded. 'Of course. Bleep me if you find anything.'

Bogdan headed for the nearest exit. As Howie watched him leave the room, he wondered if they'd heard the full story. Time would tell.

Howie stood up. The vice presidents started to talk amongst themselves. He coughed to get the room's attention. It didn't have any effect. He clapped his hands together and shouted 'Okay, ladies and gents.' Still no response. He tried waiting for them to settle. Even more conversations started.

'Vice presidents!' shouted Martha. The room instantly fell silent. 'Howie is going to talk to you. So please, listen.'

Howie began his presentation. 'Don't worry, this won't take too long.' The vice presidents were like bleepers. They could only handle small packets of information. Otherwise they overloaded and malfunctioned. 'It's very simple. If someone asks you where the president is – staff, journalists, external contacts, whoever – you say nothing. You send journalists to me, and non-media to Kaia-Liisa in the president's private office. But you, vice presidents, should make no comment at all.'

Howie paused, anticipating the usual interruption from someone who thought they knew better than he did. It didn't come. That was odd. Maybe the vice presidents were finally trusting his judgement? Highly unlikely. But not impossible. He continued. 'Let's be clear. If the media get hold of this story, there will be public hysteria. It'll be worse than Net Loss Day. We can't afford to let that happen. Not with Independence Day just two days away. And that is why you say nothing.'

The vice presidents sat staring at him, with open mouths and expressions of wonder. It seemed like he was getting through to them. After ten years of trying, his advice was finally being listened to and accepted, without complaint or criticism. It was a strange feeling. A pleasant feeling. He congratulated himself and decided to move on to a different matter, before they changed their minds. 'One more thing. The president has media interviews scheduled today. We can cancel the Republican-supporting media, no problem – they won't kick up a fuss. But not the *Daily Democrat*. Their editor gets very upset if we agree to something then pull out at the last minute. And we don't want them giving us a hard time in such a sensitive week.' He looked around the room. 'So if we can't give them Jan, we'll have to offer them someone else to interview.'

Daisy stood up and grinned. 'I don't think that'll be a problem.'

Howie couldn't believe it. 'That's good to know, Daisy. Thanks.' He'd never known cooperation like it from this lot. He half-wondered if they'd been smoking something illegal.

The room started to applaud. It was extraordinary. He didn't know what to do. So he bowed and enjoyed the moment. 'Thank you, ladies and gents.'

Daisy ran towards him, arms outstretched and shouted 'Mr President!'

The vice presidents had called Howie a lot of things over the years. Mainly behind his back. Sometimes to his face. But he'd never been called 'Mr President' before. Whatever Daisy had been smoking, it was strong stuff. He braced himself for a bear hug. But he didn't get one.

Daisy ran past him. 'We're saved!' she shouted. 'I knew you'd be back. Long live the president!'

Howie looked behind. There were three men. Two male vice presidents, whose names always escaped him, either side of a man who looked very much like the president, wearing his trademark royal-blue suit and black leather shoes.

Daisy threw her arms around the new arrival and started sobbing with joy. A granite suit cheered. A charcoal suit whooped. Even more applause. Howie stood there, feeling like a man who'd arrived at the wrong office party.

Martha stood up. 'You had us all worried, Jan.'

'Sorry to disappoint you,' the man replied. 'But I'm not Jan. I'm Oskar.'

The applause stopped – as if the boss had just knocked on the door and told everyone to get back to work.

Daisy unwound herself from Oskar. She stepped back and examined him. 'Are you sure you're not Jan? You're wearing his suit.'

'I am Oskar and these are my clothes,' sneered the man. 'One is allowed to make the same purchases as one's brother.'

This was definitely Oskar. His lack of charm was unmistakeable. Daisy mumbled an apology and retreated to her seat, shoulders hunched like a scolded cat.

Martha turned to Oskar. 'I was informed by your private office that you were still in Paris today – at the defence summit.'

'I flew home after Monday's business was concluded. Today is just a talking shop.' Oskar gestured to his two colleagues to find him a chair, which they did without speaking. 'I forgot to turn my bleeper on this morning. That's why I'm late.'

The first meeting you've ever been late for, thought Howie.

Oskar's two companions brought him a chair and stood one on each side, like Roman bodyguards. Oskar settled into his seat and turned to Howie. 'Now why can't my brother do his media interviews? Because I'm certainly not doing them.'

Martha clasped her hands. 'We have a problem, Vice President Polak.'

'Why do you people always present me with problems and not solutions?' asked Oskar, in a weary tone.

Martha was used to dealing with Oskar, so didn't take offence. 'This isn't just any old problem. Your brother disappeared overnight. We have no idea where he is, why he's gone or when he'll be back. We've got security searching the palace. But nothing's turned up yet.' She paused, waiting for a reaction from Oskar. There wasn't one. 'That is why the president can't undertake interviews, or anything else in his diary, until we find him.'

Oskar yawned. 'Is that it?'

Martha nodded. Everyone waited. Oskar looked around the table and smiled to himself. After a few more seconds of silence, he turned back to Martha and spoke. 'So, my brother disappears for a few hours, and the Republic is thrown into crisis?' He laughed in that dry, humourless way that always annoyed Howie. 'We're like some sort of ancient civilisation that can't function without its great leader. I'm sure even emperors and pharaohs had the occasional day off.'

'They didn't have national newspapers to worry about,' replied Howie.

'We worry too much about newspapers. It's not newspapers who'll vote for the next president, is it? It's the citizens.'

'Citizens read newspapers.'

'Yes, Mr Pond, but how many?'

'About seventy-five per cent, now there's no internet. Print media is king now.'

'We're not a monarchy any more,' scoffed Oskar.

Howie knew he mustn't lose his cool. Only vice presidents were allowed to do that in meetings. 'We can't just ignore the media.'

'Then you deal with them,' snapped Oskar. 'That's what you're paid to do. And I'll do what I'm paid to do. And that's deal with matters of state.'

Howie wanted to carry on the argument, but it would be pointless. Oskar wasn't going to back down in front of the other vice presidents.

'So what are you saying about your brother's disappearance, Oskar?' asked Martha. 'That it's nothing to worry about?'

Oskar leaned back in his seat. 'When we were boys, he would disappear for hours. Sometimes he would tell our mother where he was going. Sometimes he wouldn't. He just left.' He thought for a second. 'I remember he once got as far as Warsaw after jumping on a train. He even tried to fly to Australia, using our father's passport.'

With Oskar as a twin brother, it was understandable Jan might have wanted a bit of space. And the other side of the world didn't sound unreasonable.

'So you think he'll show up soon?' enquired Martha, not sounding convinced.

'Jan always did come back.' Oskar looked at his watch. 'Eventually.'

Martha's tone was becoming more urgent. 'But you have no idea where your brother might be now?'

'None whatsoever. We may be twins. But we're not telepathic.'

Howie joined in again. 'He's got to be somewhere.'

Oskar stood up. 'Yes. And I'm sorry, but I've got to be somewhere, too. So I shall leave all of this to you competent people.' His two companions moved his chair back to allow him to leave.

'Could it possibly wait?' asked Martha, in a polite but firm tone. It was one that anyone else would have responded to by sitting down, shutting up and apologising for their rudeness. But not Oskar.

The president's twin brother looked down his nose. 'It's a matter of state.'

'Very well. But be aware – this is Code Red confidential. We are not informing, or involving, the police. This is just the domain of the National Security and Intelligence Service for now.'

'That's fine,' Oskar replied, as if confirming how much milk he wanted in his tea.

'I shall bleep you if there are any developments.'

'You do that.'

'You definitely can't do the *Daily Democrat* interview at five o'clock?' asked Howie.

'Certainly not! Firstly, my diary is full. And secondly, in my opinion, I think you should cancel all Jan's interviews. Especially the *Daily Democrat*. They can go to hell, as far as I'm concerned.'

Howie smiled. 'They're always quite complimentary about Jan.'

'But not about me, Mr Pond. Now, I'm late already. And so are my two colleagues, who are attending to the same business as I am.'

Howie would love to know what that business was. But it wasn't his place to ask.

Oskar nodded the faintest of goodbyes. Then he and his two-man entourage marched out of the room.

Howie sighed. 'So who's going to do the *Daily Democrat* interview? We need someone.'

'Do we, though?' asked Daisy. 'You heard what Oskar said.'

'Yes, we do. What are the main opposition-supporting newspaper going to say if, two days before the big day, we can't find one vice president to give them an interview? They'll say we're running scared.' He gestured towards the vice presidents. 'There are fifty of you. You've all been media trained. One of you can do it.' There was no response from any of them. 'Oh, come on – one of you!'

An arm shot up in the air. It belonged to Zayn Winner, an actor-turned-politician mainly known for appearing in a series of low-budget science-fiction movies in the 2030s. *Alien Invasion, Alien Mutation, Alien Vacation* – Howie had seen them all. And they were all bloody awful.

'I can do it!' shouted Zayn, with a cheesy grin.

The assembled vice presidents, as one, turned their heads to their silver-suited colleague and raised their eyebrows.

Howie wasn't sure about this. Zayn was a good guy. A bad actor, but a good guy. He could play a role, learn lines, put on a performance. But he didn't always stick to the script. In fact, not sticking to scripts was why he no longer made movies. Zayn would need a lot of directing. Howie would rather cast someone else in the role. 'Any more volunteers?' he asked. There weren't. All vice-presidential hands were firmly under the table.

'Looks like it's you and me, buddy!' boomed Zayn, with both thumbs up. 'The dream team!'

'Th-th-that's fantastic, Zayn,' stuttered Howie, trying to sound pleased, but failing. 'Grab me for a chat later.'

Martha turned to Howie, an apologetic look in her eyes. 'You'd better meet up straight after this meeting. Because Howie is going to be doing a little job for me.'

Howie didn't like the sound of this. In the language of central government, little jobs were always big jobs. And big jobs – well, if you were asked to do a big job, you were in real trouble.

'Actually,' added Martha, 'I'd be lying if I said it was a little job. It's a big job.'

Howie was in real trouble.

'This is an extraordinary situation,' continued Martha. 'And extraordinary situations call for radical solutions.'

A radical solution? This was getting worse. When Howie had suggested a radical solution to Martha, he hadn't actually expected her to come up with one. Or to be part of that radical solution. Howie didn't do radical. He did same-old, tried and tested. Martha knew that.

She fixed her gaze on Howie, like a hawk who'd just spotted a field mouse. 'Under emergency powers granted to me in such Code Red situations, I'm creating a new special investigator role in my organisation. They will deal only with Code Red crises such as this.' Martha took a deep breath. 'And Howie will be filling that role.'

Howie didn't respond. He couldn't. His tongue was paralysed. And by the looks on the faces of the vice presidents, so were theirs.

'Howie's investigation will complement, and be independent of, security operations, Tech investigations and normal intelligence channels. Howie has worked side by side with the president for the last ten years and developed a unique relationship with him. I believe he can provide the insight we need to solve this crisis and get Jan back here before Thursday morning.'

'Can you do that?' asked Daisy. 'I mean, don't we all have to vote on it?'

Howie felt a rush of relief. The vice presidents could never agree on anything. That's why Jan took all the key decisions. Their indecision could be his salvation.

Martha's reply was firm. 'No. This is an operational matter. It's not for politicians to decide.'

Relief was replaced by realisation. And then resignation.

'So what exactly will Howie be doing?' enquired Daisy. It was the question Howie would have asked, had his tongue been working properly.

'He'll be gathering intelligence from the president's closest contacts. And be reporting directly to me.'

Howie tried to move his tongue. But only succeeded in looking like he was blowing a raspberry at the entire room.

'I thought stunned silence might be your reaction to my announcement, Howie. But you know Jan better than anyone. Maybe better than Oskar. Certainly better than my intelligence team – they'll be working in the background, but you'll be on the front line.'

Howie retracted his tongue. That was all he could manage for the moment.

'Oh. And you'll still be head of comms, by the way. At least, if it's anything to do with the president. Your deputies can deal with the rest.'

Howie's tongue was finally working again. 'I'm … I'm not sure I can be a special investigator and head of comms.'

Martha's face was filled with a confidence that Howie didn't have right now. 'You can do it, Howie. It's essential you do it. I know you can do it.'

He looked at the vice presidents. Their faces spoke as one – 'He can't do it.'

Howie took a deep breath and responded. 'I'll do it.'

Chapter 4

Britt ran up the concrete steps that led from Charing Cross Station Metro to the centre of Trafalgar Square. She might make it to the palace for eight o'clock, if she hurried.

Then she saw it. Several megatons of traffic. All nose-to-tail, thanks to the miracle of anti-bump Tech. Hundreds of cars, taxis, vans, lorries and buses – nosing forward, millimetre by millimetre, like a rush-hour glacier.

Britt dashed to the nearest pedestrian crossing. It was completely impassable. So were all the others she could see. Crowds had formed around each one. There were tourists taking photos with their sunglass-cams, frustrated workers sending bleeps, and gleeful schoolkids playing games. What was going on? She looked around for someone in authority. There was no one. They were probably stuck in traffic.

'Lights screwed up, half hour ago. They're stuck on red,' explained a large American man next to her. He chuckled. 'Would never happen in the New States, that's for sure!' He was right. Even if it did, it would be fixed in minutes.

Britt considered her options. There was no point trying a different station exit. Whichever one she took, she needed to cross a road. And another Metro trip wasn't a good idea. It would waste time and probably end in similar chaos. No. She'd have to wait for a fault line to appear in the solid block of vehicles and escape through the crack. But the way things looked, the next ice age might come sooner.

'Where you headed, ma'am?' asked the American.

'Nowhere at the moment,' replied Britt. She was undercover. Complete strangers didn't need to know her business.

'I'm sightseeing. Though if this traffic don't budge, I'm gonna have to make do with old Nelson on his column!'

Britt looked up at the statue of Lord Nelson, far above her.

The American chuckled. 'Guess his navy got in similar tight spots. Surrounded by the enemy. But old Nelson could always see a way out. Even with one eye!'

Lord Nelson was the only authority figure currently in Trafalgar Square. So Britt followed his eye line. He was looking straight down The Mall, where she was heading. The traffic in that direction was a solid mass. It didn't even seem to be moving any more.

Then three Italian supercars caught her eye. Side by side. Red, white and blue. They were the new flatcars she'd heard about. Low-level, squarish and almost completely horizontal, they were only half a metre high. They were probably headed for a motor show. Or a celebrity's driveway. But they were going nowhere at the moment.

Britt turned to the American. 'You know much about cars?'

'Sure do. We got the best in the world back home.'

She pointed at the nearest flatcar. 'What would happen if I jumped on one of those?'

He burst out laughing. 'I'd say the driver would kick your ass!'

Only if they could get out of the vehicle fast enough, thought Britt. She was quick on her feet. After years of undercover reporting, she'd learnt to be. She could be halfway up The Mall by the time the drivers had squeezed out of their low-level driving seats.

'Could it take a person's weight?' asked Britt.

'A person like me? No way, José! But a person like you, ma'am? Well, I'd say so.' The American smiled. 'I know what you're thinking. You'd be crazy to do it. But to quote Lord Nelson, desperate affairs require desperate measures!'

The American was right. Lord Nelson was right. She'd already taken desperate measures once today by dressing up as a tourist in search of a story. It was time to take some more. Time to show the traffic who was boss. Time for a pedestrian fightback. Time to try and jump across three Italian flatcars without causing major injury, death or, even worse, getting arrested.

Britt glanced down at her shoes. They were walking boots. They should give her enough grip. Jumping in them wouldn't wreck her feet. But they might not be so kind to the Italian flatcars. She didn't care. Her career was on the line.

In the distance, she heard Big Ben start to chime the tuneless melody that preceded its hourly bongs. That meant it was almost eight. She was running late.

Britt took a deep breath. Could she do it? Could she make it to the other side of Trafalgar Square in one piece? It would be dangerous. It was certainly stupid. But she had no other option. She had to do it.

The American grinned. 'If you're gonna do it, then go and do it!'

Britt had made up her mind. She was going to do it.

She checked her run-up. The distance looked about right for a quick burst of speed and a one-footed take-off. She checked the traffic hadn't started moving. It hadn't. She checked there were no tourists, commuters or schoolkids in her way. There weren't. She checked there was no chewing gum or dog mess on the pavement. There was. But not in her path.

Britt took another deep breath. She glanced at the American. He grinned and mouthed 'Go!' Then she pushed off and ran at the nearest flatcar. As she took the first step, Big Ben chimed the first of its eight bongs. She took another four steps and jumped a metre into the air – her arms thrust above her head like a rush-hour long-jumper.

She landed with a thud on the first flatcar, right on the second bong. The sound of metal straining under the impact was louder than she expected. Tourists' heads turned. She heard the flatcar's male driver scream at her in Italian. She didn't speak Italian. Even if she could, she wouldn't have apologised. Drive a normal car – then you wouldn't have this problem. She took a step forward. The car's blue surface was shiny but firm. Her boots were doing the job. She could do this.

On the third bong, she looked back to see if she had caused any damage. There were two boot-sized dents where she had landed. Shallow but noticeable. Criminal damage or accidental damage? Who cares? It wouldn't matter if they didn't catch her.

On the fourth bong, she started running at the second flatcar. Its female driver was already screaming and waving her hands, in anticipation of her arrival. More people were starting to notice what was happening. But who cared? Her adrenaline was pumping. She was starting to have fun. And it wasn't Britt Pointer doing this. It was a tourist. One who, if apprehended, would explain that people did this all the time in her country.

She jumped and landed on the fifth bong. She could feel the car's white metal skin give way, as her boots smacked into it. She didn't bother to check the damage. Instead, she looked back at the American. He whooped and punched the air. But it wasn't over yet.

On the sixth bong, she started to run at the third and final flatcar. Its male driver was shouting louder than the other two drivers put together. More trapped pedestrians stopped to watch, as well as other stranded motorists.

Britt jumped on the seventh bong. Fuelled by adrenaline, she rose higher than before. A tourist's sunglass-cam flashed. The bright light distracted her. She took her eyes off the landing zone. Before she could refocus her attention, her boots had hit the flatcar's red bonnet. It wasn't a clean landing. Her left foot slipped. She tried to keep her balance for a couple of seconds. But there was only ever going to be one winner – gravity.

She smacked sideways onto the windscreen. Big Ben struck its eighth and final bong at the moment of impact. Her left shoulder hit the glass with her full weight. The windscreen cracked. But it didn't shatter. There were gasps from the spectators. Screams from the driver. Groans from Britt. That hurt.

She stumbled to her feet and leapt off the car. Her boots hit the solid concrete and her knees gave way. She put out her hands to break her fall. Her palms slapped the pavement. More pain. But it was forgotten a second later, when she stood up. And she realised. She'd done it.

Britt half-expected an extra bong from Big Ben to mark her achievement. Instead, the crowds of stranded pedestrians started to applaud. The screams of the three Italian drivers were now drowned out by cheers and whistles from the crowd. Britt glanced up at Lord Nelson. He seemed to be waving at her. Oh, great. Now she was seeing things. Maybe she'd banged her head? She felt her skull. No lumps or bumps. She checked her hand. No blood. She looked again at the statue. She saw now. It was a pigeon on Nelson's hand, stretching its wings. The stretch turned into a rapid flutter. Lord Nelson was no longer waving. He was shooing her away.

A voice rang out from the crowd. It was the American. 'If you're gonna get going, get going!'

The American was right. Lord Nelson was right. The driver of the red flatcar was trying to extract himself from his vehicle. A police foot patrol could appear at any moment. Once they'd been alerted, they could send up one of their helicopters. Then there would be no escape. She couldn't stay here a second longer.

Britt sprinted towards Admiralty Arch, which straddled the entrance to The Mall. Once she had passed through it, the Italians and everyone else in Trafalgar Square would lose sight of her.

Half a minute later, Britt was through the arches and onto The Mall. A sign announced the road was closed to traffic from today, in preparation for Thursday's Independence Day celebrations. That was good news. But the pavements on both sides of the road were clogged with people. That was bad news.

Britt didn't have time to stop. A quick decision was needed. Run along St James' Park on the left? Or alongside the procession of stone buildings on the right? They both looked as busy as each other. Hold on. Maybe there was a third option? There were piles of barriers dumped by the roadside. But no workmen. They were probably having breakfast. And no police patrols either. They were probably having breakfast, too. It meant she could run straight down The Mall without fear of workmen, police or Italian flatcars chasing her.

She manoeuvred round a line of ineffective traffic cones and entered The Mall. The reddish tint of the road surface reminded her of an athletics track. She'd been a good four-hundred-metre runner at school. But the palace was at least twice that distance away. And her walking boots were great for jumping on flatcars, but weren't so great for sprinting.

Britt looked along the length of The Mall. A short distance ahead, a stream of tourists, workers, dogs and their owners were crossing the road. More obstacles in her path. This was no longer a sprint. More like a steeplechase.

She didn't slow down. Why should she? The traffic lights were on green. Okay, the road was closed and she wasn't a motor vehicle. But she was moving faster than most London traffic ever managed. Yes. That was it. The roles had reversed. She was now traffic. And she wasn't going to stop for any pedestrians.

'Out of my way!' she honked, as she approached them.

The people in her path scattered and shouted warnings to each other. A Yorkshire terrier panicked and ran in front of her. She leapt over it and carried on running. Nothing was going to stop her today. Nothing with two legs, four legs or four wheels.

The trees, plants and wildlife of the park on her left-hand side flew past in a blur. The St James' Park pelicans screeched wildly, as if urging her to the finishing line. She lifted her head and ran on.

Britt was soon halfway up The Mall. But her adrenaline levels were dropping and she was starting to feel her injuries. Her left shoulder throbbed. Her legs ached. Her hands stung. But she didn't stop. She couldn't afford to. She had security staff to intercept.

A minute later, Britt was racing towards a second line of pedestrians.

'Move, move, move!' she hooted. But the family of German tourists she was heading towards were busy studying a map. She tried to squeeze past sideways, but her right shoulder slammed into the father and she bounced off his solid frame. Then she collided with a skinny youth in a white overall, carrying a tray of doughnuts which spilled onto the road. Dogs barked as they lurched towards the unexpected treats. Their owners barked at the dogs not to eat them. Then the owners barked at Britt. But she didn't bark back. She was already gone.

Not far now until the big roundabout at the end of The Mall and the finish line of Buckingham Palace. But then yet more pedestrians appeared ahead of her. Six women with identical dogs – clones, probably. The animals were very large, very noisy and very interested in the sweaty, panting human who was sprinting towards them.

She decided to shout 'Coming through!' and hope the humans could keep their canines under control. Five did. One didn't. The angry animal lunged at her. Britt twisted herself sideways in mid-stride. But the dog was already airborne and had her left leg in its sights. She waited for the crunch of teeth on bone. But it didn't come. The owner yanked the lead just in time, and the dog flew back with a yelp. The other dogs snarled at her. Britt snarled back. They backed off. They knew a pack leader when they saw one.

Britt looked behind her. No one was chasing her. No humans. No dogs. No cars. She was on the home straight. The palace's ornate black and gold iron gates were coming into focus now. But there were three of them – a main central gate and two smaller ones either side of it. She hadn't had time to do any research. Which one should she head towards?

She could see a large number of sky-blue uniforms standing by the central gate. Loitering around there would soon get her noticed. And she had only ever seen the president's car come through that gate, so it was unlikely staff would use it. No. They would use one of the side gates. The left one was nearest, with no police guarding it. She headed there.

Britt didn't want to attract any police attention. So as she arrived at the large roundabout outside the palace, she eased up her pace. Her body began to protest. She could hardly breathe. Her lungs were on fire. Her legs were like jelly. It was cardiovascular payback time.

She stumbled towards the railings and collapsed onto them. She was gasping like a freshly caught fish. Wet with sweat. Aching everywhere. But she was here.

After a minute of recovery, Britt composed herself and put on her sunglasses. The lenses were huge. They had to be – they were part of her disguise. She checked her bleeper. It was 8.07am. The night shift should be leaving any time now. If they hadn't already.

She wasn't alone. There were a few dozen tourists wandering around. But she didn't look out of place. Still short of breath, she took a small guidebook from her pocket and pretended to be taking in her surroundings. Half an eye on the gates and half an eye on the police. Nothing much was happening.

Something better happen soon. Or this time next week, she could be writing a lifestyle feature on ten great things to do in London. Britt shuddered. It wasn't something she even wanted to think about.

Chapter 5

Howie was back in the White Drawing Room, waiting for Martha to arrive with some official documents. The crisis meeting was over. Howie's acceptance of the role of special investigator had left the room stunned. Even more stunned, it seemed, than the news of the president's disappearance. Without the usual barrage of dumb questions from the vice presidents, the meeting had finished in record time. That suited Howie. He was going to need as much time as possible to help solve this missing-president mystery.

He finished his second cup of espresso. But his later-than-normal caffeine injection wasn't settling him as much as it should. His mouth still felt dry and he had butterflies in his stomach. It was clearly an attack of nerves. And he knew why. It was because he was about to sign up for the National Security and Intelligence Service – the organisation whose job it was to protect the president, the Republic and all its citizens from domestic and foreign aggression.

But, he had to admit, he was also quite excited.

Howie loved watching those old-world films with that stylish secret agent. What was his name? Ah, yes. How could he forget the trademark introduction? 'The name's Bond. James Bond.' Howie often fantasised about being a secret agent in particularly dull meetings – during which, in his fantasy world, he'd dealt with dozens of awkward civil servants with a well-aimed tranquiliser dart to the neck. Or, in the worst cases, by pushing a button to release an imaginary trapdoor from underneath their uncooperative arses.

His mind wandered even further. Several actors had played the part of 007. Thankfully Zayn Winner hadn't been one of them. Howie would make a better job of it. Then a thought struck him. Maybe he could play the role? But for real, not in a movie. His nerves faded as he imagined himself in a dinner jacket, playing roulette in a foreign casino surrounded by mysterious strangers with exotic names and heavily accented English.

He stood up and turned to the large mirror hanging above the fireplace. He straightened his crooked tie. Adopted an enigmatic smile. Sucked in his belly. Pushed out his pectorals. And stared at his reflection. He couldn't resist it. 'The name's Pond. Howie Pond.'

'Glad you can remember your name, Howie,' interrupted Martha as she entered the room clutching a file. 'Because I shall need your signature on these pieces of paper.'

Howie spun round. 'I was, erm, just practising my introduction.'

'I know what you were doing. And sorry to disappoint you, but we're not going to be calling you 007, 008 or 00 anything.'

Howie tried to stop himself frowning. But he failed. 'Oh, right.'

'You won't have a licence to kill or an Aston Martin. If you're lucky, you may get the opportunity to order a Martini that's shaken not stirred, but please, stay sober unless alcohol consumption is entirely necessary. Now sit down and listen.'

Howie did as he was told. Martha sat down opposite him, took five documents from her file and handed them to him. 'Right. Sign that to confirm your new special investigator role. Sign this pledge to defend the Republic's national security at all costs, while keeping expenses to a minimum.' She handed him a bundle of cash. 'Two thousand pounds. Cash always comes in handy in our line of work. You'll need to sign for that, too. And sign this for your credit card. It's limit-free. But go easy.'

'Am I getting any electronic gadgets?'

'No, no, no. We have a very tight budget. Miniature cameras, briefcase transmitters, exploding watches – all things of the past.'

Howie couldn't imagine James Bond putting up with this kind of austerity. He would probably defect to the Russians. 'What's the last piece of paper I've got to sign?'

'Oh, that. Nothing important. Just some additional terms and conditions of employment.'

Martha hadn't mentioned these before. 'What additional conditions?'

'Don't worry. It's mainly to do with what happens if you die on the job. How we dispose of your body, possessions, et cetera.'

Howie looked horrified. 'What about my cat? Is she going to be disposed of?'

'If she's working for the Russians, yes. Otherwise, no.'

'What about my girlfriend?'

'The same applies.'

'No. I meant what will you tell her if I, you know …'

'Die?'

'Yes.' Howie never liked acknowledging his own mortality. Especially not on his birthday.

Martha sighed. 'I'll tell her she's got to look after your cat. Is that enough for you?'

Yes, that probably was enough.

'Look, Howie, don't worry. The additional conditions are for the James Bonds of this world. Not the Howie Ponds. But Human Resources insist you sign all of them. You know what they're like. I'm sure even James Bond had to deal with HR. They just didn't show it in the films.'

Howie wasn't going to let HR get in the way of things, so he signed the forms. Martha handed him a card.

'Here's the credit card. It's in your name. That's because you're not undercover. Remember, you're information-gathering. Putting together the pieces of a jigsaw. You're not saving the world from an evil genius with a nuclear warhead.'

She paused. 'Well, at least we don't think that's the case – at the moment.'

That was reassuring. Howie had been hoping the situation would have become clearer in the last hour or so. 'There's still no intelligence about what happened?' he asked.

'Zero. But you're going to change that.' Martha handed Howie a second card. 'Now, this is your security service ID card, should you need it. Don't go flashing it around. It's not for getting to the front of the queue in supermarkets. It's for emergencies. For example, if the police start bothering you.'

'Why would they do that?'

'You'll find people summon the police for all sorts of reasons. Sometimes very senior people. That's when you use the ID card. Just remember, the police know nothing about the president's disappearance. And that's how it should stay.'

'Okay. Where do you want me to start?'

'The First Lady. As you know, she and the president live separate lives. She has a townhouse in Blackfriars. They meet at weekends. So she won't know about this yet.' Martha paused. 'Or at least, she shouldn't.'

Howie was taken aback. 'You think she could have something to do with this?'

'At this stage, I don't think we can rule out anyone who's close to Jan.'

That wasn't many people. 'What about Oskar? He didn't seem too worried about his brother's disappearance.'

'No, he didn't. But you leave Oskar to me. You concentrate on the First Lady.'

'So we're focusing on friends and family?'

'Yes. They're the first place to look for answers when somebody disappears.'

'What about his enemies?'

Martha raised her eyebrows. 'Enemies? Name me some names.'

Howie tried to think of one. He couldn't.

'You see? You can't. He's one of the most popular politicians ever to have walked the earth. Two landslide victories. A third awaiting him in the summer, if he reappears in time.'

Howie nodded. 'Okay, not enemies. How about people who might just be resentful or jealous?'

'Yes. And that brings us back to friends and family.'

Howie understood. And a terrible realisation engulfed him. They only had two days to resolve this. The Democrats still had several weeks to nominate their candidate for the 2044 presidential race. But presidents, and their vice presidents, were required to know their minds on Independence Day. Then Howie had an idea. 'Is there anything in the constitution that allows Thursday's announcement to be postponed? We could say ... I don't know ... Jan is ill or something.'

'I already made a quick check. Whoever drafted the constitution didn't have a government lawyer with them. I couldn't find any escape clauses.'

Howie remembered telling the media, at one of his first ever briefings, that the country's finest minds had crafted the constitution. He also remembered the Republic's first president telling him it had been cobbled together in a Westminster bar the night after he came to power. There had been a lawyer there. But he'd mixed champagne and vodka. Then collapsed unconscious in the ladies' toilets.

Martha continued. 'Let's not leave this to lawyers. Practical action is what's needed. You inform the First Lady of what's happened. See how she reacts. See what she says. See where that takes you.'

'And I'll find out about her book, while I'm there.'

'If you have the time, yes. You and I will keep in touch via our bleepers.'

Howie went to get up.

Martha waved her finger. 'Not so fast. First, have that quick chat with Zayn about the *Daily Democrat* interview.'

Howie sighed. Chats with Zayn were never quick.

Martha got up and began walking to the door. 'He's waiting in the corridor. I'll send him in.'

'He never listens to me. Maybe you could stay and drill some sense into him?'

'I can't, I'm afraid. I have my regular monthly meeting with the American ambassador, this morning. Most unfortunate timing.'

'Can't you cancel it?'

Martha stopped by the door. 'And risk the Americans getting suspicious? No. If they find out, it'll make things more complicated. They'll want to get involved. We don't want that.' She took a breath. 'Best of luck, Howie. Have a good day. And stay in touch.'

'Don't worry,' replied Howie, feeling like he was saying goodbye to his Mum before his first day at school. 'I will.'

Howie watched as Martha left the room. Zayn burst through the door a few seconds later. 'Here he is, the new James Bond!' Zayn dived into the sofa opposite and landed with a thump. 'Does that make me Miss Moneypenny?'

'Come on, Zayn, be serious for once in your life.'

'I caught it all, buddy. I heard you. "The name's Pond. Howie Pond." Priceless. I nearly wet myself.' Zayn didn't stop for breath. 'Hey, where do you think Jan the man is, huh? Overslept at a lady friend's place, maybe? Let's face it, the ladies love that man – even more than me!'

'Come on. We both know Jan is a man dedicated to his work. And he's a married man. He's far too smart to have an affair. Especially with an election on the horizon.'

'Maybe so.' Zayn winked. 'Or maybe not. Anyway, 006-and-a-half are you going to brief me on my mission or what?'

'Yes. The *Daily Democrat* journalist is a woman called —'

'Oh, sorry,' interrupted Zayn. 'Before we do boring detail, I've had an idea.'

Countless movie directors must have heard those words on the first day of filming. Howie would do what they'd probably done – listen to Zayn for thirty seconds and then politely tell him to shut up and follow directions.

'I played the American president in *Alien Invasion*, *Alien Mutation* and *Alien Vacation*. You've seen them, right?' Zayn slapped Howie's knee. 'Sure you seen them! I thought I could use that energy. You know, ride that vibe, in the interview.'

Howie didn't want to ask. But he had to. 'What do you mean, ride that vibe?'

'We talk about the election like we're talking about the aliens. It's us versus them. Republicans versus Democrats. Matter versus anti-matter. A war of the worlds.'

'No, Zayn, I don't want you to —'

'I throw in a few one-liners to lighten it up a bit. A few jokes about the First Lady coming from Mars.'

Howie's tone was more serious now. 'No, you don't do that. You never do that.'

'You're right. Not Mars. Somewhere colder. Neptune maybe.'

'No!' shouted Howie. 'You stick to the government script: lots done, lots still to do; democracy works, Democrats don't; Jan's the man, he's got a plan. And no jokes.'

'Ah, come on, Howie! There's not enough laughter in politics. I can bring a whole new dimension to it. A fun, fifth dimension. That'll work with the alien theme.'

Howie scowled and crossed his arms. At least Zayn couldn't interrupt body language. But it seemed even non-verbal communication was lost on him.

Zayn became more animated. 'Believe me, comedy is my thing. I've got a natural talent for it. Did you see me in *I Married a Robot*?'

Howie thought for a second. 'That was a comedy?'

'I was nominated for an award for that performance!'

'You probably nominated yourself.'

'Okay. I did nominate myself. But it still counts.' Zayn attempted a serious face but succeeded only in looking like he had trapped wind. 'Listen, Howie. Trust me. Let me do the interview my way. I'll be funny. And the journalist is going to love it.'

For all the wrong reasons. 'Sorry. We're doing it my way.'

'But Howie —'

'I want to be falling asleep in that interview, you're so dull.'

'Okay,' sighed Zayn. 'We'll do it your way.' He rolled his eyes. 'The boring way.'

'Good. The journalist is Mina Pritti. You know her?'

'Never heard of her,' muttered Zayn, with a sulky shake of the head.

'She's sharp. So watch what you say.'

'I have done interviews before.'

'Not when the president's just gone missing, you haven't. Just be natural. Don't talk about Jan, unless you absolutely have to.'

Zayn slouched on the sofa. 'So what can I talk about? The weather? Or is that too controversial?'

'You talk about the government's ten-year record. And its future plans. Spend today learning that government script. That's all I want to hear.'

'Jeez. By the sound of it, we're all going to be asleep in this interview.'

'That's the best-case scenario. But I've got a feeling Mina is going to be wide awake. And you need to be, too. I'll be sitting in, so you're not on your own.'

'You don't have to babysit me.'

'Yes, I do. That's my job.'

'As well as saving the world? You've got a lot on your plate, 006-and-a-half.'

'Just listen. The interview is at five. I'll bleep Mina and tell her the president is tied up on official business and you're standing in. You and I will meet here fifteen minutes before. Understood?'

Zayn pulled a face, like a teenager who'd just been told to tidy his room.

'I'll take that as a "yes".'

'Can I go now?' mumbled Zayn.

'Yes, you can. See you at a quarter to five in your office.'

Zayn got up and skulked out of the room, without saying goodbye.

Despite his clear instructions, Howie had a feeling the *Daily Democrat* interview wasn't going to go smoothly. But he couldn't waste time worrying about it. He had a lost president to find.

Chapter 6

Britt lifted the giant sunglasses from her nose and checked the time on her bleeper. It was 9.15am. This wasn't going to plan. She'd been loitering outside Buckingham Palace for over an hour now. But there was still no sign of anyone, or anything, leaving through the gates.

The lack of movement was strange. Especially at this time of the morning. Perhaps the palace was in security lockdown? If so, she could have a long wait. And the longer she stuck around, the more likely she was to draw attention to herself. There were only so many times she could study her guidebook and admire the railings, before a police officer made their way over and started asking awkward questions.

Britt decided the best form of defence was attack. She would approach the police before they came to her. Charm them, disarm them and then farm them for info. To achieve this, she would pretend she was an American. Police officers loved to show off to American tourists. Everyone knew that.

She looked over at the main gate, where a dozen police officers were standing in pairs. The nearest couple were two middle-aged men sharing a joke. Maybe they were laughing at her – the dumb tourist looking for the history of the Buckingham Palace railings in her guidebook? So what if they were? It could work to her advantage. Britt pushed her sunglasses back into place and marched towards the gate.

She waved as she approached. 'Hi there, officers,' she shouted, in her best American accent. 'Can I ask you boys in sky blue a few questions?'

The first officer, taller than his colleague, responded. 'Is it about those railings, madam? Because you were looking at them for so long, we thought you were going to try and saw them off.' He chuckled and clapped his hands, applauding himself.

The short officer gave a schoolboy grin. 'If you are going to steal them, could you wait until we're on our tea break? Then one of the young 'uns can chase after you!'

Two middle-aged men who thought they were funny. Brilliant. She knew exactly what to do. 'Your English humour kills me!' shrieked Britt. 'They don't always get it back home in the New States. But I'm crazy about it. You two should be on the digi-screen!'

The tall officer straightened his cap. 'I've often said, when the two of us joined up it was law enforcement's gain and light entertainment's loss.'

The short officer patted his colleague's arm. 'We're a double act, me and him. Twenty-odd years we've worked together.'

The officers beamed at each other – like two newlyweds at the altar – and spoke as one. 'Yes. Twenty very odd years!'

Britt grinned. She wasn't smiling at them. She was smiling at her incredible good fortune. This would be easy. She would win these two officers' trust just by laughing at their terrible jokes. Not only that, they were experienced enough to know who, and what, came through those gates. Britt threw her hands up in the air. 'Oh my God, you're so funny! I can see it's my lucky day!'

The tall officer pointed at her face. 'I'm surprised you can see anything in those sunglasses, madam. Why don't you remove them? You'll get a better look at the railings then.'

'And we can check you're not one of America's most wanted!' sniggered his sidekick, before they both collapsed into giggles.

Britt had to keep her sunglasses on. If she didn't, the officers might realise she was 'that bloody journalist'. But it was so cloudy, there was no real reason to wear them. She would have to think fast. 'I have very sensitive retinas. It's genetic.'

The officers stopped laughing.

She continued. 'So those questions. First up, is the president home today?'

The tall officer pointed towards the flag fluttering from a pole on the palace roof – the familiar flying duck silhouetted against a sky-blue background. 'Of course, madam. The duck of freedom always flies when the president is resident.'

'He's definitely inside?'

'Oh yeah, he's definitely inside,' confirmed the short officer. 'And I'll tell you something else …'

This could be vital security information. She braced herself.

'We are … definitely outside.'

Both officers roared with laughter. Britt swore under her breath. Then she joined in the laughter. 'You guys are such kidders!' She let them catch their breath, before firing off some more questions. 'So I'm guessing there are police outside, working the usual eight-hour shift pattern? And security inside, working twelve-hour shifts with an early morning handover? It's just I haven't seen any security guys coming or going since I been here. It's so weird.'

The officers looked at each other, wrinkled their noses, and turned back to Britt. They weren't smiling now. She realised she'd blundered. They weren't questions any tourist would ask. Even an American tourist. She would have to try and recover the situation. 'I mean, erm …' What did she mean? If she messed this up, she could end up in the back of a police van. And this time next week, she'd be writing lifestyle features. Think, Britt. If you're not a tourist, who are you? Then it came to her. ' … I mean, that's how it works in the New States. I'm in presidential security, back home in Washington. We're reviewing everything. Gates, security, police. That's why I'm in London – to see the ambassador.'

She looked at the officers' faces. Their noses were still wrinkled. Then the tall one spoke. 'Actually, we do the occasional extra shift outside the American embassy.'

'Lovely bloke, that ambassador,' added the short one. 'Now, what was his name?'

They both glared at Britt, like impatient quiz show hosts. Her mind went blank for a second. She knew the answer. In fact, she'd interviewed the ambassador last year. But under pressure, she just couldn't remember his name.

'I just call him Mr Ambassador,' laughed Britt. She looked at the officers' faces. For once, they weren't laughing.

She dredged her memory banks. What headline had she used for the article? Something about him shaking British society. Shaking. Shaker. Stackshaker. That was it.

'Clinton Stackshaker!' she shouted in relief, as the details of the interview came flooding back to her. 'Such a great guy. Six kids! His nanny, Ella, should get a congressional medal of honour.' She looked in her bag. 'Now. Where's my ID?' She rummaged for a few seconds. 'Oh, fudge. I think I left it at the hotel.'

The officers looked at each other, stony-faced. The tall one nodded to the short one. The short one nodded to the tall one. Then they turned to Britt. This was it. They were delivering their verdict.

The officers beamed smiles of relief.

'Thank goodness you said that, madam. For a moment, you sounded like one of those journalists who pretend they're someone they're not and then pump us for top-secret information.'

'Three of our mates lost their jobs because of a bloody journalist. But me and him aren't stupid. We know a reporter when we see one.'

Now she had avoided a trip in a police van, Britt knew what to do. 'Don't worry, guys. I can find out this stuff from Clinton Stackshaker. It's no big deal. I'll just tell him you two boys in light blue couldn't help me. It'll mean more work for him. But I'm sure he'll under—'

'Hang on,' interrupted the short officer. 'We don't wanna put Mr Stackshaker to any inconvenience.' He looked at his colleague. 'I reckon we can run through one or two details, don't you?'

The tall officer nodded. 'I don't see why not. As long as they don't end up on the front page of a newspaper!'

The officers slapped each other on the back and snorted with laughter.

'You boys are hilarious!' squealed Britt, while making a note of the officers' ID numbers.

'It's like you said,' confirmed the tall officer. 'We police the streets, while security look after everything inside the palace. This main gate is for VIPs.' He then gestured towards where Britt had been standing. 'That side gate is for security staff. The other one is for deliveries.'

The short officer scratched his head. 'But you're right. Night shift are usually well gone by now.' He turned to his colleague. 'Here, you don't think anything's happened, do you?'

The tall officer shook his head. 'Impossible. We'd have been told about it.'

It was obvious the pair were clueless about the missing person. And probably most other things. But there could be a nugget of information here, if she dug a bit further. 'Actually, it's security we're focusing on in our review. You guys know anything else about that?'

The short officer looked over Britt's shoulder. 'Hang on. There's Herbert Bogdanowic – the security guy. He's your expert.'

Britt turned around. A young blonde man wearing headphones was leaving the palace grounds via the left-hand gate.

The tall officer drew close to Britt and spoke in a hushed voice. 'And don't say I told you this, but that young man's uncle is the head of Palace security – Bogdan Bogdanowic.'

'Oi, Herbert!' yelled the short officer. Herbert carried on walking, so he yelled even louder. 'Hey, Herbie!' Still no response. 'He couldn't hear a bomb go off with those things in his ears. I'll go and get him for you.' Just as he was about to make his way over, a bleeper buzzed in his pocket. 'Excuse me for a second. Duty calls.' He took the bleeper out, pressed a button and read a message.

Britt wanted to leave the two officers and intercept Herbert herself, but maybe the message was about whoever was missing? It was worth sticking around to find out.

'Anything I should know about?' asked the tall officer.

The short officer showed him the bleeper. They both furrowed their brows, looked at Britt, read the message again and stared at her.

After a few seconds, the tall officer spoke. 'You weren't in the vicinity of Trafalgar Square this morning, by any chance, madam? Around eight o'clock? Only a female matching your description used some Italian supercars as a pedestrian crossing.'

Britt swore silently. This was all she needed. She was meant to be the hunter. Not the hunted. More quick thinking was required. She put on her best innocent face. 'Me? No. I came through St James' Park.'

The officers carried on staring. Britt needed a detail. She thought back to her sprint past the park this morning. 'To see the pelicans,' she blurted. 'And don't they screech! You guys could probably hear them.'

Britt waited for a few seconds. Then the tall officer put his hand on his chest. 'Forgive us, madam. It was stupid to even consider that a person with your responsibilities would abuse Italian supercars in such a reckless manner.'

'I knew it weren't you,' added the short officer. 'How many criminals wanna chit-chat with the boys in sky blue, eh?' He turned to his colleague. 'We don't go to their dinner parties, do we?'

'Not without a search warrant.'

The pair chuckled. Britt turned round. Herbert was striding towards St James' Park. She didn't want him to get too far ahead of her. She might lose him in the crowds.

'It's been great talking with you guys,' gushed Britt. 'Now, I don't want to put you to any more trouble. So I'm just gonna go introduce myself to Herbert over there, before he disappears.' Britt waved her goodbyes before they had a chance to protest. Then she ran towards Herbert, as fast as her aching legs could carry her.

As she ran, she wondered what role she should play with Herbert to maximise her chances of extracting information from him. Should she try being a tourist again? Or a new Palace co-worker, who'd just clocked off the night shift, like him? Or one of the girls in sky blue? That could land her in jail. She didn't have much time to make up her mind.

Then an idea came to her. If Herbert thought she already knew something, she could just ask him to confirm the details. The American security persona she'd just used would work perfectly for that – a stranger from the New States. Someone who knew something, but not everything. Someone who was operating off-grid. Someone who was offering help to a man in trouble. It was perfect.

Britt realised she'd lost sight of her prey behind a small crowd of tourists. For a few seconds he was gone. But then his distinctive mop of blonde hair and bright red headphones popped into view again. She locked on to her target, zeroed in and was soon walking right behind him. Britt tapped him on the shoulder and he spun round.

'Excuse me,' asked Britt in her American accent. 'Are you Herbert Bogdanowic?'

Herbert looked surprised. Then confused. Then worried. He took off his headphones. 'Yeah, that's me.'

'Could we talk? Privately?' She lowered her voice. 'About security matters.'

'What do you mean?'

She whispered in his ear. 'I mean in Buckingham Palace.'

Herbert's face turned pale. 'Are you secret service or something?'

'Not over here. But I work security for the president of the New States. And I'm here to help you.'

'Help me?'

She looked around to check no one was within earshot. 'With your Code Red situation.'

Herbert didn't look convinced that he should be talking to her. Britt continued. 'It's a situation I'm sure your uncle Bogdan, head of Palace security, is aware of.'

His mouth dropped.

'I don't want to say any more in the open,' she whispered. 'We're not even supposed to know anything yet. The Americans, I mean.'

Herbert seemed dazed. After a few seconds he mumbled a question. 'Who are you?'

Britt didn't want to use her own name. But she hadn't come ready with an alternative one. How dumb of her. Even more quick thinking was required. Nothing sensible came to mind. Then a pelican screeched. And something not very sensible came to mind. 'I'm Pellie Cann.'

'Pellie ... Cann?' asked Herbert, as if he'd misheard.

'Yeah. Just like the bird.'

Herbert nodded unsurely. 'Pellie Cann. Right.' He looked as if he needed more convincing.

Britt launched into a gabbled explanation. 'My parents were nuts about pelicans. My mom ate nothing but mackerel for her entire pregnancy. I think she was hoping I'd be a pelican! But they got me instead. And they gave me this dumb name. And now, every time I introduce myself, I have to tell them about my crazy folks.' She paused and then pretended to be on the verge of tears. 'But they're no longer with us.'

Herbert bowed his head. 'I'm sorry.'

'Don't be. They were probably reincarnated as pelicans.' She pointed towards the lake. 'That was probably mom screeching at me just now. Because I left my ID in the hotel. It's an hour away from here. You want me to go back and get it?'

'No, no. I can't hang around.'

'So let's grab some breakfast, Herbert. Then I can explain everything.'

'Okay. There's a pub about ten minutes' walk from here. They do a good breakfast. It's called the Grafton Arms.'

Britt smiled. 'Then let's go get some breakfast.'

Chapter 7

Howie glanced at the government car's e-speedo. It briefly flirted with the five-kilometres-per-hour marker. Then it fell back to zero as the driver braked. Welcome to central-London gridlock.

It was his own fault. He should have left the palace earlier. Instead, he'd spent an hour trying to access the president's electronic diary with Kaia-Liisa. But the same network problems that had plagued Martha that morning had prevented them from viewing it.

As a result, he was already running late for his nine-thirty appointment with the First Lady. To make matters worse, the traffic signals in Trafalgar Square weren't working and three sports cars were causing a blockage. Every now and then, a pedestrian would attempt to jump on the cars and cross the road. At which point, three annoyed-looking Italians on the pavement would scream and chase after them. It was truly bizarre.

Why were all these strange things happening today? Then he remembered. It was a Tuesday. And it was his birthday. And there was more of this to come.

Howie's backside was starting to get numb, so he shifted his position in the passenger seat. As he did so, his bleeper fell out of his trouser pocket. He picked it up and looked at its screen. It was completely blank. 'Useless bloody machine,' he muttered to himself, resisting the temptation to throw it out of the car window. And then he remembered. He'd switched it off in Martha's office and forgotten to turn it on again. He reluctantly pressed its start button. After playing its annoying welcome jingle, a message appeared:

Hello, Howard! It is 09:45 on Tuesday 12 April 2044.

The First Lady's security team had made clear she was leaving the house at ten o'clock. And she wasn't the kind of person who changed her plans for other people. He'd have less than fifteen minutes to tell her about her husband's disappearance. And find out about her new book – a task which normally took weeks. Even James Bond would struggle with that mission.

He clicked the bleeper's status button. Another message:

You are currently AVAILABLE. You have 399 UNREAD e-comms. Don't let them pile up now!

Howie told the bleeper where it could stick its advice and scanned his unread messages. Among the usual mass of admin, HR and 'copying you in for information' rubbish, something grabbed his attention. There were half a dozen e-comms from Maurice Skeets – the best-connected freelance journalist in London. They were all entitled 'Urgent – Story'. He read the most recent message:

Howie, this is big. No bullshit. It's about the president. Secret meetings. High-profile people. We need to talk. I'll be in the Two Chairmen at midday. Be there. Maurice.

This wasn't good news. In fact, whenever Maurice Skeets was onto a story, it always meant bad news. Very bad news. The last thing Howie needed was a big front-page story tomorrow, followed by dozens of media bids for a president who wasn't here. Even issuing a presidential statement would be impossible without Jan around to agree it.

Howie sighed. Why did it have to be this particular journalist? Anyone else, he could have batted off and dealt with another day. But he'd have to meet Maurice. His sources were always reliable.

The car started moving at a steady fifteen-kilometres-per-hour. The traffic was clearing at last. They would be there in a few minutes. After several unsuccessful attempts, Howie managed to type 'OK. Two Chairmen. Midday.' on the bleeper's tiny keypad and send the message to Maurice. Then he looked up. They were outside the First Lady's smart Blackfriars townhouse.

Howie told the driver to wait and jumped out of the car. He ran up the steps, pressed the intercom button and announced himself.

A glum-faced security woman answered the door. 'Morning, Mr Pond. The First Lady's in her study. Turn right at the end of the hall, second on the left.' She lowered her voice. 'She's not a happy bunny.'

That was no surprise. The First Lady was never a happy bunny when Howie was around.

He thanked the security officer, found the study and knocked on its door. A well-spoken voice shouted 'Enter!' and he pushed the door open. The First Lady was sitting behind an antique desk, dressed in a battleship-grey suit. The sun caught her gold jewellery as she swivelled her chair to face him. 'Ah, Mr Pond,' she drawled in her perfect English accent. 'I've been expecting you.'

It was the type of greeting James Bond received from super-villains hell-bent on world destruction. The only thing missing was a fluffy white cat. He double-checked that there wasn't one lurking in the oak bookcases, ready to pounce on him. There didn't seem to be. 'Good morning, First Lady. Apologies. I got held up in —'

'Can we get down to business?' She looked at a clock on the wall. 'You've got ten minutes.'

Howie sat down. 'I'll come straight to the point then. It's about your husband.'

'Yes,' she sighed. 'It's always about my husband.'

'This is serious. He's missing. No one's seen him since eleven o'clock last night. They're searching the palace and the grounds. But he hasn't turned up yet.'

The First Lady stared at Howie, unblinking, for several seconds. Then she spoke. 'And why are you telling me this, Mr Pond, and not the police?'

'The security service are leading on this. The police aren't aware. And that's the way we need to keep it, until the picture becomes clearer.'

The First Lady screwed up her face. 'Then why isn't a security person telling me?'

Howie sat up straight. 'As of today, I am a security person.'

'You?' sneered the First Lady. 'But you're just Jan's media mouthpiece.'

Howie ignored the insult. He'd been called much worse by journalists. And by vice presidents. 'The head of National Security, Martha Blake, has appointed me as a special investigator.' He flashed his new security service ID. 'I've been asked to help find your husband.'

The First Lady frowned. 'Oh. Well, he's not here, if that's what you're suggesting.'

'I wasn't suggesting anything. But seeing as you've mentioned it, can I ask if he was here last night?'

'He doesn't sleep here.' Her nostrils flared. 'Kings prefer their palaces.'

'You've no idea where he could be?'

'I'm his wife. Not his diary secretary.'

'When did you last see him?'

'Saturday – for lunch.' Her tone was becoming more irritated by the second.

'Did he say anything?'

'Yes. The wine was excellent.'

'Is that all?'

She thought for a moment. 'Oh, yes. The duck was overcooked.'

The First Lady was being as cooperative as usual. Howie ploughed on with more questions. 'It was just small talk then?'

'It was a conversation between a husband and his wife.'

'And what did you discuss?'

'That's private.'

'Yes. But if he told you anything that might help me —'

'Mr Pond,' she interrupted. 'If my husband told me anything that could help you locate him, I would inform you.' She placed her hands on the desk. 'But he didn't.'

'You've really no idea where he is?'

The First Lady's expression changed from one of irritation to boredom. 'I have no idea whatsoever.'

Howie decided to change the subject. 'Okay. While I'm here, tell me about your new book. I'm still dealing with the media. And you know how much the media love your books.'

A flicker of a smile swept across the First Lady's face. 'It's called *Finding the American in You*. It's published on Friday. And yes – I expect the media and everyone else to love it.'

Finding the American in You? It sounded a little different from her last two efforts – *Finding the Inner Me* and *Discovering the Outer You*. He'd need to find out more. 'Who's this book aimed at?'

The First Lady leaned back. 'It's for people over forty who aspire to a better life. But who are stuck on this side of the Atlantic.'

'Like the ones who missed out on Amerigration, you mean?'

'Those people.' She paused. 'And others who wanted to apply. But whose circumstances prevented them from doing so.'

Yes. While anyone with a British passport or permanent residency was eligible to apply, not everyone would have been in a position to drop everything and head across the Atlantic. Politicians wanting to become British president, for example. And their spouses.

'People like you, you mean?' asked Howie. He didn't have time to be diplomatic. He needed to know all the angles that the media might seize upon.

'Of course,' replied the First Lady, matter-of-factly. 'We had just married. My husband loved this country. He had the charisma, charm and intelligence to become president. He knew it. And all his political peers knew it.' She gestured towards a book on her desk. 'I wasn't a writer, back then. I worked in publishing.' She stopped for a second and looked thoughtful. 'We discussed it. We decided to stay here so Jan could pursue his political dreams. It wasn't a difficult decision.'

An idea was forming in Howie's mind – maybe the First Lady hadn't given up hope of an American exit? While the Amerigration programme was now history, the Americans did still consider applications from 'exceptional candidates'. The process was much tougher now – character checks, financial requirements and a senior-level American sponsor – but it was a question worth asking. 'Would you consider relocating to the New States at some point in the future?'

'It's never been an option, so I haven't given it any thought.' She leaned forward and furrowed her brow. 'But why are you asking me this?'

'The media might ask you when you launch the book, First Lady.'

'Oh, I see.' She thought for a second. 'Well, if they do ask me, I shall tell them to mind their own business.'

Howie doubted that would be the case. He'd learnt from bitter experience that the First Lady didn't hold back when it came to media interviews about her books. He took a deep breath. What he was about to say wouldn't go down well. 'I'll need to clear all your media bids for the foreseeable future. And that includes interviews about your new book.'

'We've had this conversation many times before, Mr Pond. This is not government business. This is my career. I don't see why —'

'With respect, everything you do is government business. So bleep me with the details when the bids start coming in. We want to keep media to an absolute minimum until we find Jan.' If looks could kill, Howie would already be dead. 'Please,' he urged. 'It's in the president's best interests.'

The First Lady sighed. 'Yes. My husband's best interests always take priority over mine.'

Howie glanced at the clock. It hadn't yet hit ten. There was time for a couple more questions. But what was he going to ask? Something that would give him a lead in his search for the president. Something that could be of real value. Then it came to him – something that Zayn had suggested. Was there another woman in the president's life? If so, the First Lady might know about it. Howie would ask. But he would have to be subtle. 'To go back to your husband, I was wondering if you knew of any close friendships that he might have formed recently. They could be male friendships … or female friendships.'

She shot straight back. 'You mean, is my husband is having an affair?'

Howie could feel himself blushing. 'Yes. That question.'

The First Lady narrowed her eyes. 'There is someone. I don't know for sure if it's an affair. But I'm fairly certain.'

Howie ignored his burning cheeks and carried on with the questions. 'And who's that?'

She picked up a stress ball on her desk and started to squeeze it. 'If I tell you, will I be informed if that person has proved to be a useful line of enquiry?'

Howie had no idea. He hadn't read all the terms and conditions of his new role. But he needed this information, so he would have to sound helpful. 'If I can do that, I will.'

She stared at him until the final second of his ten minutes had ticked away. Then she gave her answer. 'Alright. It's his personal trainer, Cherry Blush. She visits the palace twice a week.'

Howie knew the president had a personal trainer. But that was as far as his knowledge stretched. 'Do you know anything else about her?'

'She's twenty-seven and from London. She's based at the American Fitness gym in Canary Wharf.'

That was useful. In fact, it was a lot more information than he was expecting. 'How do you know all this?' he asked.

'Let's just say you're not the only one who's been doing a bit of detective work, Mr Pond.' She stood up. 'Message understood?'

Howie rose from his chair. 'Message understood.'

Chapter 8

Britt was in the Grafton Arms, waiting for Herbert the security guy to return from the bar. She had chosen a large table by the window, where they wouldn't be disturbed or overheard. It was a little too near the entrance for her liking, but it was only a small pub. And this shouldn't take long. She just needed to find out who had gone missing and when.

She checked her bleeper. It told her the time was just after ten. The short walk had turned into a half-hour trek as Herbert stopped to respond to urgent bleeps. He'd been so busy they had hardly spoken a word on their way here. But it hadn't been a problem. It reassured Britt that this young man knew exactly what was going on. And even if he didn't, his uncle definitely would.

She took in her surroundings. The pub's secret corners and snugs gave it a certain old-world charm. But it had one big disadvantage. It was a stone's throw from the Two Chairmen – Howie's favourite pub. Some of the regulars there might also be regulars here. And the last thing she needed was one of them popping in for breakfast and recognising her. She would have to be on her guard.

Britt slipped the sunglasses off her nose and scanned the dozen or so faces dotted around the pub. None of them were familiar. That was reassuring. She pushed the sunglasses back into place.

Herbert arrived carrying two tubes of orange juice. He handed one to Britt. 'Here you are, erm, Miss …'

'Cann,' she replied, in her undercover American accent. 'Pellie Cann.' It was the dumbest cover name she'd ever heard. But at least it was easy for her to remember.

Herbert sat down. 'Sorry I forgot your name. My brain is fried.'

'No problem. It must have been a real tough night for you.'

'You have no idea.'

'But I'm here to help you now.'

'Yes.' Herbert looked thoughtful for a few seconds. 'So how did you find me so quickly? I'd only just finished my shift.'

After the initial adrenaline rush of her unexpected offer for help, it was natural that he might have a few questions. There was no need to panic. In fact, the answer to this first question was easy. She would just tell the truth. 'Two police officers outside the palace gate identified you. I didn't catch their names. Officers 271 and 272. One tall, one short.'

Herbert nodded knowingly. 'Oh, those two? Yeah. That makes sense.' He sipped his juice. 'So you work in security in the New States?'

'Yeah. I work for the president in Washington.' Britt had never been to America. She was hoping Herbert hadn't either.

'I love the New States. But I've only been there once.'

She stayed calm. The chances were he went somewhere touristy. New York, Chicago or San Francisco. But not Washington. Please, not Washington. If he started asking her directions to the nearest McDonalds from the White House, she was screwed.

'My uncle got me a seven-day tourist visa. I stayed in Philadelphia all week. Loved it.'

Britt nodded. Thank goodness for that. It wasn't Washington. It was Philadelphia. Panic over. But hang on. Where was Philadelphia? What kind of city was it? Pellie Cann should know these things. But she had no idea. 'Oh, Philadelphia? That's fantastic! Heard so much about it. Never been there.'

Herbert raised his eyebrows. 'Really? Not even for work?'

Britt sensed that, for whatever reason, a presidential security guru ought to have been to Philadelphia. But it was too late to change her story now. 'No, really. It's crazy. I've never been.'

'Such a historic city. The Declaration of Independence and constitution were signed there. For the Old States, I mean. But still, I would have thought you'd have been there on a presidential visit? It's only a couple of hundred kilometres away.'

Britt sipped her juice. It gave her a few seconds to think. 'I operate from the White House. I don't do visits. I have people do that for me.'

Herbert twisted his lip. He was deep in thought again. Britt knew what he was thinking – 'Is this woman really an American intelligence officer?' Her answers to his questions had been pretty convincing. But there was the unlikely name, the lack of ID and her unorthodox approach in a public park. She could see why he was suspicious. He worked in security. He was probably used to people trying to bluff their way past him into restricted areas. Herbert would know a big hitter from a bullshitter. She mustn't underestimate him. No. She must keep answering his questions. Until he was convinced that Pellie Cann was telling the truth.

Herbert rested his elbows on the table and leaned towards her. 'So, why are you in London and not Washington?'

It was a good question. She wasn't Superwoman. She couldn't just fly across the Atlantic when a European leader didn't turn up for work. But she had an answer. 'I'm advising on security at the American Embassy in London. Americans like to bring in their own people. You know how it is.'

Herbert nodded. 'It's an interesting building, wouldn't you say?'

She sensed this was a final test. If someone claimed they were advising on security at an embassy, it was reasonable to expect them to know what the embassy looked like. He was pretty smart, this young man. But Britt had this covered. She'd conducted her interview with the ambassador at the embassy. It had come to her rescue again.

'That big white cube must be twenty-five years old now and it's showing its age,' she replied, with a breezy air of confidence. 'The ambassador's got the best deal on the top floor. But the rest of it needs a major refurb. And it might be riverside, but Nine Elms isn't exactly Mayfair. Well, what is, south of the river?'

Herbert smiled and held up his hands. 'Listen. I'm sorry about all the questions, Miss Cann. I had to be sure, you know.'

Britt screamed in triumph inside her head. She felt like a quiz show contestant who'd struggled in the first round, but just answered the £10,000,000 question. 'Hey, no problem. I'd do exactly the same in your shoes. Oh, and please, call me Pellie.'

Herbert smiled. 'You can call me Herbie. All my friends do.'

Britt smiled back. 'Sure thing, Herbie.'

'And sorry for taking all those bleeps on the way. But I had to. It was work.'

'Don't be silly. I can see Herbie is a man in demand.'

He sat back and made himself comfortable. 'Why don't you take your sunglasses off? This place is dark enough.'

There was no chance of that happening. Someone could walk in that door any minute who knew her. 'I have very sensitive retinas. It's genetic.'

'Oh, right. Well, the sunglasses really suit you ... Pellie.'

Britt beamed. 'Thank you! I love British guys. You're such gentlemen!' She grabbed her purse. 'How much do I owe you?'

'Nothing.' He leaned over and whispered. 'This gentleman knows the lady behind the bar. I got the drinks for free.'

'You naughty boy!' laughed Britt, patting his arm.

There was nothing wrong with a bit of light flirting. It was justified if it helped her achieve her goal. Anyway, Herbert was quite cute. His blonde hair and big brown eyes reminded her of the Labrador puppy she'd always wanted as a kid. But she was done with telling him what a good boy he was. Now it was time to start pulling on his lead.

Britt looked around to make sure no one could hear. 'Now, you got a situation at Buckingham Palace.'

'That's one way of describing it.'

'I know it's a Code Red.' She leaned in to him. 'That means we're not talking about the president's cat going missing.'

'No. We're not.'

'That's what I thought. Tell me more.'

'He hasn't got a cat. He's allergic to them. He's got a dog, though – a Labrador puppy.'

Me too, thought Britt. And her puppy wasn't playing ball. But she mustn't lose her patience.

'The dog is fine,' continued Herbert. 'We checked on him, this morning.'

Time to tug on Herbert's lead a bit harder. 'The president's pooch is safe and well. That's terrific news. But someone with two legs went walkies last night, huh?'

Herbert nodded. 'You know who, don't you?'

This was a tricky one. Should Britt say she knew? If she did, Herbert might ask her to confirm it. If she didn't, he might clam up. She would toss him a ball and see if he brought it back. 'It doesn't take a genius to work out that we're talking about a serious VIP here.'

'Yeah, we are. Only it's not just a very important person.'

He had picked up the ball. Finally. Now he just needed a bit of encouragement to bring it back to her.

'What do you mean?' asked Britt. 'Not just a VIP?'

'In this case,' whispered Herbert, 'the VIP is a very important …'

Just as her puppy was about to drop the ball at her feet, she heard the door behind her crash open and a deep Irish voice shouting, 'Good morning, Grafton Arms!'

The voice was familiar. Britt turned round to see who it was. His face was even more familiar.

'Don't worry about him,' laughed Herbert. 'It's only Conor O'Brean. He's harmless.'

Britt knew exactly who Conor was. And Conor knew exactly who Britt was. Not only was he a regular at the Two Chairmen, he was also one of Howie's press officers – one who knew her well. She spun back round and ducked down. But Conor was already bounding over.

'Don't believe a word this young fella tells you, madam! He's happily married with sixteen children and three ex-wives.' He giggled and ruffled Herbert's hair.

Herbert grinned and shook off Conor's attentions. Britt chuckled drily but didn't speak.

'You just finished your overnight duty, mate?' asked Herbert.

Conor saluted. 'Yes, sir! Officer O'Brean requesting permission to stand down, sir!'

'I just finished, too. I'm having breakfast then going home. But it's a working breakfast, if you know what I mean.'

Conor didn't know what he meant. Because he wasn't listening. Instead, he was reading the menu on the wall.

Britt leaned forward and whispered to Herbert. 'What did you mean about the VIP?'

Before Herbert could reply, Conor interrupted. 'I'll have the waffles,' he shouted to the barmaid. 'Medium-rare. And a tube of sugar water on the side – make it a litre.' Then he sat down beside them. 'Well, aren't you going to introduce me to your lady friend, Herbert?' He held out his hand. 'Conor O'Brean. It's a pleasure to make your acquaintance, madam.'

Britt smiled and shook Conor's hand. But she didn't say a word.

'You're not a nun, are you?' asked Conor. 'Have you taken the vow of silence? You poor thing. Having to listen to this young fella gibbering on all day. And do you have a name? Or don't you bother with names down at the convent? Maybe it's a nod of the head? Or a delicate sigh?'

Herbert saved Britt from further interrogation. 'Her name is Pellie Cann.'

Conor froze for a second. 'You're joking? Like the bird? You'll be telling me next you met her in St James' Park, with all the other pelicans!' He started giggling again.

Herbert smiled. 'Actually, I did.'

Conor exploded into laugher. He was like a hyena that was high on helium. 'I'm sorry,' he gasped. 'I'll just pop to the little boys' room and calm myself down. Then I'll be back to join you good citizens for breakfast.' He jumped up. Then convulsed with fits of laughter as he made his way to the toilet.

As soon as his friend was out of earshot, Herbert spoke. 'I'm sorry, Miss Cann. But I can't talk about the Code Red situation now that Conor is here. He's a press officer. They're like the unofficial secret service. They report back on everything they see and hear.'

'Let's go somewhere else then.' Britt didn't mean to sound desperate. But she couldn't help it.

'I wouldn't feel comfortable talking about it anywhere else. This pub is like a second home. And the security cameras haven't worked for years. What's spoken within these four walls never goes any further.'

'What about later this afternoon?' She was sounding more desperate by the second.

'Sorry. After the morning I've had, I'll be going straight home and crashing out for a few hours.'

Britt sighed and stared at the wall. There was a poster on it. It read 'Live Tonight – Super-Mega Electro Thrash! Starts 8.00pm'. It was her only hope. 'Are you free, this evening?'

'Yeah. I'm off now until Friday. Uncle's orders.'

'How about the gig here tonight? They'll be so much noise, no one will hear us having a private conversation.'

Herbert thought for a few seconds. 'I'll have to check with my girlfriend.'

What was there to check? She wasn't asking him out on a date. Couldn't he make a decision for himself? Then she remembered. He was a Labrador. He obeyed commands – he didn't give them. She decided to try some reverse psychology.

'Look, it's fine.' She stood up. 'If you don't want my help. We'll forget it.'

Herbert reacted immediately. 'No, no!' He checked no one was listening and then whispered. 'I screwed up. I need your help.'

The toilet door slammed shut. It was Conor. It was time for Britt to go. 'I'll see you here at eight, Herbie.'

Herbert nodded. There's a good boy, thought Britt, imagining patting him on the head. And she hurried out of the pub.

Chapter 9

Howie's government car turned a corner and his destination swung into view. The building's design was so chic and ultra-modern it could easily have been mistaken for an investment bank's headquarters. But the rows of people visible through its giant glass windows, frantically going nowhere on running machines, confirmed its true identity. This was a gym for the highest of high rollers – the Canary Wharf branch of American Fitness.

His car pulled up outside. He thanked the driver, told him to wait and stepped out. Howie checked his bleeper. It was 11.16am. It had taken more than an hour to get here from the First Lady's residence. It was time he had tried to spend usefully by checking his bleeper for updates from Martha Blake. But there hadn't been any. No ransom demand, no hostage video, no body discovered. That was good news, of course. But it would have been nice to have heard something. The only useful e-comm he'd received during the journey was from American Fitness, confirming that Cherry Blush, the president's personal trainer, was working today. But it also said she often worked off-site. He would just have to hope Cherry was in the building.

Howie stepped through the gym's grand entrance. The interior was just as high-class as its exterior. Whoever owned these places had serious money. The reception area's side walls were dominated by two larger-than-life posters. A beautiful, super-fit woman in her late twenties was excitedly lifting two dumbbells, without breaking sweat, and urging Londoners to 'Get American Fit!' He tutted. Everyone was obsessed with

America. Howie was quite happy to stay British unfit for the moment.

'Hello, sir. Are you a member?' asked a young woman behind the reception desk.

'No. I'd like to see Miss Cherry Blush, please.'

'I'm afraid Miss Blush is fully booked today, including some off-site visits. Would you like to leave a message?'

Howie didn't have time to leave messages. 'It's urgent. I need to see her now.'

'That won't be possible, sir. Only our Premium Club members can demand to see Miss Blush at their convenience.'

This reminded Howie of his last visit to his local medi-centre. On that occasion, he'd ended up paying £500 for a private appointment with a doctor. A doctor who had gone from being fully booked to being suddenly available – once he'd paid the fee. He wasn't planning on repeating that mistake here. 'What if I told you that it's a personal matter?'

The receptionist smiled. 'Then I would tell you that you should contact Miss Blush about that matter in her own personal time.'

Howie sighed. This woman obviously had experience of working in a doctor's surgery. 'Can you at least tell me where she is?'

'I'm afraid, for reasons of client confidentiality, I cannot provide you with that information. But it is available to our Premium Club members.'

This was going to be even harder than getting a medi-centre appointment. Howie thought about flashing his security service ID. But that wouldn't be a good idea. Firstly, he didn't want this receptionist knowing his true business. Cherry's colleagues probably knew the president was one of her clients, and he didn't want to arouse any suspicions. Secondly, for all he knew, Cherry could be involved in the president's disappearance. If she was, and this receptionist told her that a special investigator was asking after her, she might follow the president's example and disappear herself. No. He would have to do this the hard way. 'So how much is this Premium Club membership?'

'It's £50,000 pounds for the first year.'

Howie almost fainted. 'What about for one month?'

'It's £5,000. Payable by card. And there's Miss Blush's personal fee of £2,000 for unscheduled appointments. Payable in cash only.'

Seven thousand pounds? He could get fourteen doctor's appointments for that money. There was no way he was wasting £7,000 of taxpayers' money. It would be crazy.

But then he realised. If he wanted to locate Cherry quickly, what other choice did he have? He didn't know where she lived, or who her friends were or where she spent her spare time. And Martha Blake's people would have only done the most basic of checks on her when she was hired – assuming they even did that. They certainly wouldn't know anything about her daily movements.

Howie reluctantly handed over his newly acquired credit card. 'You win. One month's Premium Club membership. But I need it done quickly. And I need to see Miss Blush ASAP.'

'Certainly, sir. I can obtain all your personal details when I process the card.' She waved his card over a pay-terminal, glanced at its screen and returned it a few seconds later. 'Your membership fee has been processed.' She then pointed to a glass square on the counter. 'Scan your right hand, please.'

Howie did as he was told. A red laser beam scanned his palm in seconds.

'All done. Welcome to American Fitness, Mr Howard Pond.'

'Good. So where is Miss Blush? And when and where can I see her?'

The receptionist checked a digi-screen. 'You're in luck, Mr Pond. She's right here in the building. And she's suddenly become available for consultation.' She gave him the type of smile he'd only ever seen from successful bank robbers in old-world movies. 'Would you like to pay the £2,000 consultation fee and see her now?'

He wouldn't like to pay it. But he had no choice. He opened his wallet and handed over the £2,000 in cash that Martha had given him that morning. That hadn't lasted long.

The receptionist placed the money in a secure metal box. 'Thank you.'

Howie glared at her. He was a pretty streetwise guy. But he'd been stung for £7,000 in fees within a few minutes of stepping inside the building. Not even investment banks could get away with that.

The receptionist spoke into an intercom. 'New Premium Club member Howard Pond to see you, Miss Blush.'

'Thanks, honey!' trilled a voice from the intercom. 'Send him through!'

The receptionist turned to Howie. 'Miss Blush is in Room C, through the double doors. Just place your palm on the reader.'

Howie walked to the double doors and placed his right hand on another piece of square glass. A green laser scanned his palm. A series of security lights flashed. Then the electronic door slid open. He walked through and the door slid shut behind him. He was impressed. It was Tech that worked. That meant there wasn't just mega money behind this business. There was super-mega money.

He walked along the corridor, found Room C and knocked. The door opened and standing before him was the young woman from the posters in reception. She looked even more stunning in person. She flashed him a smile that could stop a train.

'Welcome to American Fitness!' she gushed, in a cheery London accent. 'Mr, erm … Sorry. I've forgotten your name already! What am I like?'

Howie sucked in his belly. 'The name's Pond.' He pushed out his pectorals. 'Howie Pond.' But he could only hold it for a couple of seconds, before he started coughing.

'That don't sound good. Let's get you in the warm.' She ushered him into her bright, modern consulting room. Howie regained his composure and sat down.

'Now, Mr Pond. You are a Premium Member. And I like to think I'm a premium personal trainer. Well, they put me on them posters, didn't they? You know, I always feel a bit funny when I walk through reception and see my face staring back at me. So weird. I'm much better in the flesh, don't you think? You don't have to answer that. It's just me having a bit of fun. Fitness should be fun, shouldn't it? And it is, with me. I wanted to make that clear. Now, you've literally just joined, yeah?'

Howie was astonished. She'd managed to say all that in a single breath. He paused a couple of seconds, to make sure she'd stopped talking. 'Yes, I've just joined.'

'Great. Now you plonk yourself down. Make your glutes comfortable – that's what we call your bum cheeks around here – and me and you are gonna talk fitness.' She looked around. 'Now where are my digi-wotsits?'

Howie watched, as she buzzed around the room. He could see why the First Lady had her suspicions. She could easily have been a model.

Cherry located her digi-pen and pad and turned them on. Then she sat down and began the session. 'So, the best way to start is if you tell me your personal goals.'

Howie only had one personal goal. And that was to find the president. But he wouldn't be informing Cherry that the nation's leader was missing.

'Then we'll take all your measurements,' she continued. 'Height, weight, muscle mass, blood pressure. All your vital bits and bobs. Then we'll work out a full programme for you.'

It was time to drop his bombshell. He showed his ID. 'Actually, I'm a special investigator for the National Security and Intelligence Service. I'm here because the president is one of your clients. I need to ask you a few questions.'

Her face dropped and her manner became less friendly. 'Is it about the business? Coz if it is, you need to speak to Maxim's people. Not me.'

'Maxim?' The name meant nothing to Howie.

'Viktor Maxim – the owner. He's Russian. And he's in town this week, as it happens. So go and hassle him. Not me.'

'No, it's not about the business. It's a …' What was it? He couldn't say what it was really about. His mind went blank.

Cherry filled the silence. 'Is it one of them random security checks?'

Thank goodness for that. 'Yes. It's one of those.'

'I see.' She paused. 'Are you gonna want your £2,000 back?'

Howie thought for a second. He had undoubtedly been conned. But he could turn it in his favour. He looked her in the eyes and spoke in a calm voice. 'If you cooperate, and answer my questions truthfully, I don't see any reason why I shouldn't compensate you for your valuable time.'

Cherry narrowed her eyes and puckered her lips. 'Alright, Mr Pond, I'll answer your questions.' She switched off her digi-pen and pad, dropped them on her desk and crossed her arms. 'So what you wanna know?'

Howie would have to tread carefully. He would start off with some background questioning, before turning to her relationship with the president. 'How long have you been the president's personal trainer?'

'About two years.'

'When and where do you meet up?'

'Twice a week – in his private rooms at the palace. Mondays and Wednesdays usually. Sometimes he cancels and we rearrange. But not often.'

'So you saw him yesterday?'

'Yeah.'

'A normal session, was it?'

'Yeah. Why shouldn't it be?'

'I was just asking. And it's Tuesday today, so you're seeing him tomorrow?'

'Unless I hear different, yeah.'

It was time to intensify the questioning. 'How did your professional relationship begin?'

'The president wanted to keep fit. I'm a personal trainer. It's not rocket science.'

This next question was a little delicate. He would have to phrase it carefully. 'You just provide fitness services? Rather than other ... professional services?'

Cherry gave him a filthy look. 'Yes. Dirty old men have to go somewhere else if they ask for extras. And that includes you, in case you were getting any ideas.'

Howie blushed. James Bond never had these problems when he was interrogating beautiful women. Bond would have deployed his devastating charm and good looks by now. Cherry would've already told him everything she knew. And she wouldn't have charged him £2,000 for the privilege. But he was Howie Pond. So he'd have to carry on with the questions. 'Did you and the president develop ... a relationship?'

'Course we did. Relationships are part of the job.'

Howie paused. 'Has it developed into a physical relationship?'

'Yeah. Very physical. He sweats buckets doing those press-ups.'

Howie wasn't sure whether Cherry was deliberately misunderstanding his question or just being a little bit slow. He would ask her again – very bluntly – and watch her reaction. 'What I mean is ... have you and the president become lovers at any time?' He held his breath.

Cherry paused, her face giving nothing away. Then she leaned forward and replied calmly, 'Do I look like the kind of girl who sleeps with married presidents?'

Howie could feel the hairs on the back of his neck standing up. His mouth felt dry. He swallowed hard. 'No. But appearances can be deceptive, Miss Blush. I just need a "yes" or "no" answer.'

'Then it's a "no" answer,' she replied firmly. 'I swear on my granny's life.'

Howie was a pretty good lie detector. He'd had a lot of experience dealing with truthful, and not so truthful, vice presidents and senior civil servants. There were lots of giveaway signs. But the eyes were the best barometer. And Cherry had maintained eye contact throughout their whole conversation. The First Lady may have had her suspicions but that's all they were. There was only one conclusion. Cherry Blush was telling the truth.

Howie nodded. 'I believe you. But I need to know if the president ever discusses his schedule with you? Where he's going, who he's meeting?'

Cherry shook her head. 'I'm his personal trainer. Not his personal secretary.'

The door flung open. A huge, shaven-headed man in a black security uniform stood in the doorway. He didn't look happy. 'Mr Maxim needs to see you, Miss Blush,' he grunted. 'He's in his office upstairs.'

'I'm with a client, Arnold. I won't be long.'

'He needs to see you right now,' Arnold growled. He smiled at Howie with all the warmth of a debt collector at a funeral. 'I hope that's alright with you, sir.'

Fortunately, Howie had finished his questioning. He was satisfied Cherry and the president hadn't been in a relationship. And she didn't seem to know anything that would be useful to his investigation. 'Of course. Give me one minute to wrap things up and we'll be right out.'

'I'll be back in here in sixty-one seconds, if you're not.' Arnold left the room, slamming the door behind him.

'Arnold is a really nice guy when you get to know him,' chirped Cherry. It was the first unconvincing thing Howie had heard her say. 'Now, about the £2,000 …'

'I won't be requesting its return. On condition that you don't mention our little chat to anyone.'

'No probs. So did I pass?'

'Pass what?'

'What do you think? The security check. That's what you said this was, yeah?'

'Oh, yes. Yes. You've passed.'

'Super-mega. I'd better shoot upstairs.'

It was also time for Howie to leave. And head for his meeting with Maurice Skeets. He exchanged goodbyes with Cherry, passed through security and headed outside to the car.

Once in the back seat, he instructed the driver. 'The Two Chairmen in St James' Park, please.'

As the car pulled away, Howie's stomach began to rumble and he felt a little light-headed. He had missed breakfast. And he never missed breakfast. His body might shut down if he skipped another meal. There was a simple solution. He would grab an early lunch at the pub. Yes. It's what James Bond would have done. It didn't matter if you were 007 or 006-and-a-half, a secret agent needed their lunch. He settled back into the soft, leather seat, shut his eyes and smiled to himself. Good old-fashioned pub food, here we come.

Chapter 10

Britt sat alone at a corner table in the Craven Cottage Café in Fulham, West London. The digital clock on the wall told her it was 11.45am. She gazed out of the window at her place of work – the impressive riverside offices of *The Republican*. She sighed and sipped her cup of tea. She should be working at those offices today. Instead, she was flying around, leaping on cars and pretending to be an American security officer. And so far, she had barely enough information for a small piece at the bottom of page sixty-eight, never mind a front-page article.

But if she wasn't at work, this café was the next-best place to be. It had served as her refuge from the office ever since she started working for the paper, seven years before. It was a place where she solved problems away from the distractions of bleepers, e-terminals and her colleagues. Sometimes she would spend a whole afternoon here, analysing facts and replaying conversations in her mind. And today she desperately needed to find some nugget of information among those brief words with Herbert in the pub – something that might give her a clue as to who was missing from Buckingham Palace.

Britt tried to remember every word of that Grafton Arms conversation. Most of it had been spent proving Pellie Cann's credentials. But Herbert had been about to say something to her, before they were interrupted by Conor O'Brean. What was it? Something very important? No. He was talking about a very important person. A VIP. But he said it wasn't 'just a VIP'. What did he mean?

She finished her chocolate muffin and went over the conversation again. What were Herbert's exact words? He had told her, 'In this case, the VIP is a very important —' And that was as far as he got. That missing word – what could it be? It must begin with the letter 'p'. That was all Britt could salvage. The smallest crumb of a clue. Smaller than the chocolate-muffin crumbs that now sat on the plate in front of her.

Was it a very important police officer? No. That would be a police matter, not a security situation for palace officials. What then? A private secretary? A physician, psychologist, psychiatrist? But would their disappearance really cause such a fuss? She didn't think so.

Then it came to her. Maybe 'p' stood for 'president'? It seemed a ridiculous idea at first. But, as each second passed, it seemed more believable. It would explain Howie rushing out of their pod in the early hours of the morning in a panic, as well as Herbert's nervousness. She caught her breath. That would be a story. A massive story. But only a story while the president was still missing. And it would need a lot of evidence before anyone took it seriously.

Britt remembered that one of her news-desk colleagues, Rosie Parker, was scheduled to interview the president this afternoon. Britt had wanted that interview herself. But George had surprised – and annoyed – her and everyone else by handing the assignment to Rosie. It was obvious why he'd chosen her. Rosie was a journalist who rarely troubled high-profile interviewees with difficult questions. But it didn't matter now. If there was no president, there could be no interview. Howie, or one of his press-office team, would have to cancel it. Maybe they had done it already? There was an easy way to find out. Britt would go to the office and ask Rosie right now.

She got up, left the café and made her way towards the offices of *The Republican*.

A few minutes later, Britt was back in the newsroom. Her colleagues were all too busy staring at e-terminals and tapping on keyboards to notice her unexpected arrival. All apart from Rosie, who was sitting at Britt's desk, flicking through a lifestyle magazine. Britt greeted her with as much enthusiasm as she could manage. 'Hi, Rosie.'

Rosie looked up, startled. 'Britt. I thought you were off until Monday.'

'I am.'

'Oh.' Rosie looked concerned. 'Everything alright?'

'Yes. Well, apart from the fact I'm on features from Monday.'

'I heard about that,' replied Rosie, with a false air of sympathy. 'You must be gutted.'

'Just a bit.'

Rosie's face lit up. 'On the plus side, George let me have your desk.' She pointed towards the far corner of the room. 'You'll be over there with the creatures from features.'

Britt gazed over at the features desk. It was only fifty metres away. And yet it was a whole different world. The lighting was dimmer. The desks smaller. The chairs bulkier. The faces ... well, she couldn't make out the faces. Just dark ovals bobbing behind e-terminals. Britt was lost for words.

As she often did, Rosie broke the silence. 'You're not here to hand in your resignation, are you?'

'No. I just popped in to say hello.'

Rosie looked disappointed. 'Oh, right.'

'You busy today?'

'I was. But not any more.'

'Why's that?'

'My interview with the president was binned.'

Britt smiled. Then she realised it was more appropriate to frown. 'No way. Did they say why?'

'No. I just got an e-comm from his media monkey.'

That must be Howie. 'What did it say?'

'Some rubbish about the president attending to important matters of state and that he'd get back to me when there was another window in the diary. But he couldn't say when that would be. Typical!'

That explanation was vague enough to back up Britt's theory.

Rosie continued. 'What's more important than getting your face on the front page of *The Republican*, the day before Independence Day, eh? He's supposed to be media-savvy.' She shook her head and sighed. 'You know, I'm not her biggest fan, but I bet that wife of his won't be cancelling her interviews tomorrow.'

'What interviews?'

'Publicity for her new book.'

Britt was a writer, not a reader, but everyone knew about the First Lady's books. They were always controversial. Howie hated them. If he ever saw them on display in bookshops, he'd turn them round so the customers couldn't see the front cover. Then an idea came to her. 'Where's George? I need to speak to him.'

'In his office. He's doing the quarterly returns. I wouldn't disturb him.'

Britt didn't reply. She didn't want to waste another second while the idea was fresh in her mind. She walked up to George's office and opened the door.

George was sitting at his desk, grimacing at some papers. He looked up as Britt closed the door behind her. 'Do you want to try that again – but this time knock on my door and wait for me to say "Come in"?'

Britt didn't have time for George's attempts at humour. 'I've got a proposal for you.'

George sat back in his chair. 'I told you. You're on leave. And when you come back, you're on features. Not news.'

'Fine. Then let me start on features today.'

George gave Britt a concerned look. 'Have you been taking illegal substances?'

'Rosie just told me today's interview with the president has been cancelled. We've got space to fill in tomorrow's paper.'

'Go on. I'm listening.'

'The First Lady has a new book coming out. She's doing media tomorrow. Let's get in first with an interview this afternoon. I'll write it up when I get back. You can run it tomorrow.'

George thought for a second. 'Sounds like a good idea. But it's no job for a newbie. One of the regular feature writers can do it.'

That wasn't what she wanted to hear. Britt needed that interview. She needed to come face-to-face with the First Lady today and ask her some searching questions. Questions that might give her a clue as to whether Jan Polak was a missing president or not. Britt stood tall. It was time to reveal to George that she was onto something. 'I won't just get you a feature. I'll get you a news story.'

His ears pricked up. 'A news story?'

'Yes.'

'Anything in particular?'

'Yes, I do have something in mind.'

'Run it past me.'

Britt wasn't going to give George the details at this early stage. He would just laugh and tell her not be so ridiculous. 'I'll tell you, once I've confirmed a few things.'

'But it involves the First Lady?'

Britt needed to be as vague as possible. 'It has some connection to her. But she's not the focus.'

'Who is then?'

Britt sometimes had to lie to her editor to get what she wanted. And this was one of those occasions. 'It's not focused on one person. There are lots of strands.'

'I see. Sounds complicated.'

'It is.'

George sat up in his chair. 'Okay, here's the deal. I'll fix that interview for this afternoon. I have a good relationship with the First Lady's publisher. It shouldn't be a problem – us getting an interview before everyone else does.'

Britt felt her stomach do a somersault of delight.

'We'll run it tomorrow as an exclusive,' continued George. 'So it needs to be good. And it needs to be friendly. Nothing negative about the book, the First Lady, the president, the Government or even the Democrats.'

Britt's heart skipped a beat at the mention of the president. But she remained outwardly calm. 'No problem.'

'I want the feature on my desk by seven o'clock tonight. And let's be clear. This is a features assignment I'm sending you on. If you mess it up, you can forget the news story.'

It was a hard bargain. But Britt was confident she could keep her side of it. 'It's a deal. I'm going home to do some preparation.' She also needed to grab a water-spray and have a lie down. Her body was aching all over.

'I'll bleep you the details of when and where it will be. Now get out of my office. And don't miss that deadline.'

Britt wasn't in the habit of missing deadlines. And this was one she definitely couldn't afford to miss.

Chapter 11

Howie's car pulled up outside the familiar black exterior of the Two Chairmen. This tiny side-street pub, hidden away from busy main roads and tourist attractions, was his usual place of sanctuary after a bad day at work. It was also the perfect spot to celebrate a good day in the office. And a place to unwind after a not-so-bad, not-so-good day. But occasionally, like today, it was a place of work.

With nowhere to park, and the palace not far away, the car moved off. The bongs of Big Ben told Howie it was midday. That meant he was on time for his meeting with Maurice Skeets. Howie walked into the pub and looked around. There was no sign of Maurice or anyone else.

'Hello, Howie,' beamed the barman. 'The usual, is it?'

Howie's usual was a pint of Guinness. Well, half a litre. Pints, gallons and all other imperial measurements had been banned after the revolution. Britain was metric now. But they still called half a litre 'a pint' in here. That was why he loved this old-world-style pub so much. But a pint, half litre or any other measure of alcoholic beverage probably wouldn't be a good idea right now. He was about to meet one of the country's top journalists. Not just that. After only four hours sleep, Howie's energy levels were already running low and alcohol wouldn't help. He also had to be on top of his game for the Zayn Winner interview with the *Daily Democrat* at five o'clock. And Martha Blake would want to see him for an update at some point. No. A pint of Guinness was out of the question.

'Just half a pint, please.' It was a fair compromise. No one ever got drunk on half a pint. And it was his birthday.

The barman looked puzzled. 'Did you say a half?'

'Yeah. And a steak-and-ale pie. With mashed potato and mushy peas.'

The barman grinned. 'Is that half a pie or a whole one? Because half pints don't really go with whole pies, do they?'

He was right. Those pies required a lot of fluid to wash them down. And Howie couldn't remember James Bond ever asking for half a glass of Château Mouton Rothschild with his whole lobster.

Howie smiled. 'Better make it a pint.'

'Sit yourself down, my old friend. I shall bring it over.'

Howie thanked the barman and sat down at a corner table at the back of the bar. The initial thrill of being in a pub during working hours had already worn off and he was beginning to feel nervous. He always did before meetings with Maurice. He was the type of journalist you didn't want sniffing round during a major crisis. Maurice could smell trouble a mile away. And he could smell bullshit from even further.

Howie took out his bleeper and read through all the messages from Maurice. Every one mentioned 'secret meetings' between the president and 'high-profile figures'. Maurice's information was usually accurate. Howie would have to listen to what he had to say. Then try and stall him. He couldn't afford to let any major stories about the president run while he was still missing.

Then something struck him. With Maurice's network of contacts, it was entirely possible that he might already know about the president's disappearance. The secret meetings story could be a fabrication – an excuse to get Howie alone and see his reaction to questions about the president's current whereabouts. Howie would have to be careful.

After a few minutes, the barman brought his pint of Guinness. Howie stared at the glass's inviting contents. The malted aroma hit his nose. He desperately wanted to take a mouthful. But a nagging voice in his head was telling him: 'It's Maurice Skeets. Don't take any chances.' So he didn't.

A moment later, Howie heard Maurice ordering a mineral water at the bar. He called to him. 'I'm over here.'

Maurice collected his drink, walked over and sat down opposite Howie. 'You drinking already, you bloody alcoholic? Bet you've ordered one of those dodgy pies as well, you greedy bastard.'

Howie maintained a dignified silence.

'That's a "No comment" is it? Course it is. It's Howie Pond I'm talking to.' Maurice cackled. 'Right, that's the chit-chat out of the way. Let's get down to business.'

Howie tried not to look worried. 'What's the story then, Maurice?'

'I got information – very reliable information – about meetings between his Royal Highness Jan Polak and three big players.'

'You won't be surprised to know that most of the people the president meets are big players.'

'I know that, you big prince. But these were all under the radar.'

'Talking generally, different situations and people require different degrees of discretion,' explained Howie, as he instinctively clicked into presidential spokesperson mode. 'But it would be inappropriate to discuss the details of those arrangements.'

'Maybe if I give you the names, you'll cut the bullshit and give me some proper answers, eh?'

'I can't promise anything.' Howie never did to journalists.

Maurice leaned forward and lowered his voice. 'Okay. First name is Sky Eastern. Chairwoman of Eastern Oil – an American multinational. They made bucketloads of cash from deep-sea drilling in the 2030s, while their competition went tits up.'

Howie nodded. He knew the company.

'Eastern Oil say they're all about clean energy now. You know, all that expensive synth-oil. But that's just corporate bullshit. They still got a big appetite for the black stuff.' Maurice glanced at Howie's pint of Guinness. 'Even bigger than your appetite for that black stuff.' He cackled again, louder this time. 'Eastern Oil want to do some tests in Republic waters – some drilling. I know that because I've seen a letter that's been circulating among their senior execs.' He sipped his water. 'They reckon there might be a big pocket of black stuff somewhere in British waters that they could exploit with their new Tech. If it's there, both the oil company and the Treasury would come out winners. But those tests need to be signed off at the highest level. We're talking Jan the man's approval.'

'A lot of things need presidential approval. So what?'

'You know how it is. The citizens want the new fuels. They don't like the old oil. They don't care about the economics of it. They care about the history. All those wars and stuff.'

'The public's views are always taken into consideration when major government decisions are made, Maurice.'

'Yeah. Then ignored. It's all about money. You know that. I know that.'

Maurice had only been here a minute or so, but Howie was already beginning to feel weary of his company. 'Get to the point.'

'Alright. Here's a scenario. Let's say the president has signed this all off. Officially or unofficially, it doesn't matter. My point is, if the media get hold of the story before an election, that's bad news for Jan the man. So he keeps it all hush-hush. Then he announces the test drilling after he's won a third term.'

Howie stared into his Guinness for inspiration. It had settled now. And so had his thoughts. It was clear what he had to do – bullshit for Britain. 'Decisions such as this require an awful lot of consideration. The president and vice presidents must be given the space to debate the issues freely, away from the public eye. Those meetings may take a variety of forms. But we would never discuss the details.'

'So you admit these meetings with Sky Eastern took place?'

'No. I have no knowledge of any such meetings.' That was true. It might change later. But for now it was true.

Maurice was getting agitated. That was a good sign. It meant he wasn't getting the answers he wanted.

'Let me rephrase that,' sneered Maurice. 'In general, does the president have secret meetings?'

'Not secret. Just not public.'

Maurice rolled his eyes. 'You don't half talk bollocks sometimes.'

Howie smiled. 'I hope that's clarified matters.'

Maurice frowned. 'No it hasn't. We'll leave Eastern Oil for now.' He took another sip of his water. 'Second name is Olga Frik. Chief executive of Auto-Tech Industries. They earn billions from contracts with the Republic. They make those annoying Tech robots.'

Yes, those robots were annoying. And that reminded Howie. One of them was investigating the failure of the Buckingham Palace security cameras. He would need to check up on that when he returned to the palace after lunch. 'The president meets with representatives of major government contractors from time to time. That's no secret.'

Maurice leaned forward. 'They met up for lunch.'

'That sounds nice.'

'A very long lunch.'

'That sounds very nice.'

'Is that all you've to got to bloody well say?'

Howie kept a straight face. 'I can repeat it for you, if you like.'

'You cheeky sod.' Maurice shook his head. 'Right. Name number three – Petra Putinov. She works for a big multinational. It's got interests in everything – food, drink, Tech, sport, leisure. Even engineering. That includes components used in military defence – rockets, missiles, that kind of thing. They supply the Republic with some gear. Nothing major. Just a few things.' He cocked his head. 'But maybe that's gonna change?'

Petra Putinov's name was more intriguing. It wouldn't be so easy to bat away questions about her. Howie thought for a second. 'But they've got a diverse portfolio of businesses?'

Maurice furrowed his brow. 'Yeah, but I'm talking about —'

'Well, there you are, Maurice. We're always looking to source the most competitively priced products for government. You'll have to come in for a briefing on our new procurement strategy when you have a spare afternoon.'

'I'd rather jump through a glass window,' growled Maurice.

Howie half-smiled. 'Make sure it's on the ground floor.'

Maurice rubbed his hands. 'So, come on. Enough of the bullshit. What's the story?'

'You tell me, Maurice. You're the journalist.'

Maurice paused. Then he sipped his water and lifted his glass. 'Cheers, my old friend.' He waited for Howie to do the same. He didn't. Maurice was trying to get him drunk. Which was a very good sign. He didn't have enough material to write a story yet. And that was how it was going to stay for the foreseeable future.

Howie shook his head. 'I'll have mine later. Once you've gone.'

Maurice glared at him. 'You unsociable bastard.'

Howie leaned back and stretched. 'Doesn't sound like much of a story to me, Maurice.' Then he let out an exaggerated yawn. 'In fact, it doesn't sound like a story at all.'

Maurice finished his water. 'I'm thinking it's something to do with oil. Some deal. If it's not oil, it's some big business action. Maybe there's presidential campaign funding involved?'

Howie didn't respond. He wasn't in the habit of helping journalists fill the gaps in their stories. Especially when they seemed to know a lot more than he did. Howie leaned forward. 'Have you ever thought of writing fiction, Maurice?'

'Ha, bloody ha. At least tell me one useful thing. Where is that big prince you work for this afternoon? I heard he binned a few interviews. Off to another secret meeting, is he?'

'He's at a location I can't disclose.' That was true. Howie couldn't disclose it because he had no idea what it was.

'Doing what?'

'Doing what presidents do.'

Maurice stood up. 'And you're doing what presidential spokespeople do – talk a load of bullshit and give journalists bugger all.'

Howie congratulated himself. He had given Maurice nothing of any use. It was the perfect outcome. He reached for his pint of Guinness, closed his eyes and savoured a large, celebratory gulp.

'I thought you weren't drinking in my presence, Pond?'

Howie opened his eyes. 'Oh, sorry, Maurice. Are you still here? I thought you'd gone.'

Maurice's lip curled. 'I'm gonna do some more digging on those meetings. I'm not giving up on this. There's something dodgy going on. And Maurice Skeets is on the case. So be warned.'

The barman arrived with Howie's food. 'One steak-and-ale pie with mash and mushy peas. Can I get you another drink to go with that?'

Howie looked at his glass. He'd managed to drink half a pint already. 'Yeah. Why not?' He was eating. The food would soak up the alcohol.

Maurice got up and walked to the door. Just before he left, he turned and shouted. 'Enjoy your pie, you unhelpful bastard.'

Howie smiled to himself. Not only had he been no help at all to Maurice, he'd gained the names of some serious big hitters that the president had apparently met with recently. They were all names he could give to Martha Blake for her team to do the relevant checks.

He began attacking his pie. As he chewed the first mouthful, he looked up at the pub's 1970s clock. It was just after quarter past twelve.

He downed what remained of his Guinness. That felt good. And another would be along in a minute. He could savour that one. He could go and sit by the fire in the little room upstairs after his lunch. It would be his birthday present to himself. He might even have time for a third pint of Guinness. He'd be back in the office by about one. Maybe one-thirty. With any luck, Martha's team would have found the president by then.

He smiled to himself. Yes. That sounded like a plan.

Chapter 12

Britt ran up the steps to the First Lady's residence, pressed the intercom button and announced herself. She looked at her bleeper. It was just after three. She was almost on time.

A bored-looking security woman answered the door. 'Can I help you?'

'Hello, I'm, erm …' She had to think for a second who she was. Was she Pellie Cann? No. She was definitely herself. 'I'm Britt Pointer – a journalist.'

The security woman eyed her suspiciously. 'We are expecting a journalist of that name. But you didn't seem one hundred per cent sure about it. Can I see some ID, please?'

It seemed Pellie could get away with having no ID, but Britt couldn't. She dug in her handbag for her ID. It wasn't in the side pocket where she normally kept it. 'One second. It's in here somewhere.'

The security guard sighed. 'No ID, no interview. Simple as that.'

Where was it? She always kept it in this bag. And now, today, when she needed it most, it had gone missing. She searched again. Still no joy.

'I'll bleep my editor. He can confirm who I am.'

'Bleep who you like. But if you don't have ID, you're not coming in.'

Britt wanted to give the security woman a hefty kick in the shins, push her to the floor and barge past her into the house. But she needed to avoid a police cell if she was to get her story. Instead, she made one final check in her bag.

Halfway through her search, she remembered. After yesterday's argument with George, in a moment of madness, she'd taken her ID card out of her bag and contemplated tossing it down a drain. Fortunately, she had come to her senses. But she hadn't put the card back in the bag. She'd put it in her jacket pocket. And that particular jacket was now hanging in her wardrobe. She cursed and felt a flush of panic. 'I left it at home.'

'No interview then.'

Britt couldn't afford to let the trail go cold here. She had to get past this woman somehow. 'I'm writing a feature for *The Republican*. You know – the newspaper?'

The security woman nodded. 'Yes. I read it every day. On my break.'

This sounded promising.

'It's a quality broadsheet,' continued the woman. 'Full of thought-provoking news, comment and features. It leans comfortably towards the current administration, but not in a sycophantic way. It's like a critical friend of the people.'

That was the kind of bollocks that George came out with. Britt felt herself grimace. She tried to reshape it into a warm smile. It didn't come off. She carried on. 'Then you'll have read articles by Britt Pointer.'

'Of course. And she doesn't mess around. She always goes straight for the jugular.'

That's exactly what Britt felt like doing with this woman. But she restrained herself.

'I'm on features now,' explained Britt, the words almost sticking in her throat. 'The one I'm working on is about the First Lady's new book.'

'Ah, yes. Self-help books. Don't read them myself. I'm more into the old-world classics – *Harry Potter*, *Fifty Shades of Grey*, that sort of thing.'

Britt had an idea. 'I could mention you in the feature.'

The woman looked confused. Then interested. 'Me?'

'Yes. I can paint a picture. I can say the First Lady surrounds herself with intelligent, well-read members of staff.'

The woman thought about her proposal. 'I've actually just finished writing my first novel. Maybe you could mention that?'

'Sure. What's it called?'

'Revenge of the Royals.'

'What's it about – very quickly?'

The security woman was more animated now. 'The Royal Family return from exile in Florida. They gather a people's army and storm the palace, capture the president and send him to the Tower of London. They restore a constitutional monarchy, exile the vice presidents to the Isle of Wight and bring back the internet, landlines and mobile phones.'

It wasn't a bad idea for a novel. It wasn't a bad idea, full stop. 'And you're publishing it yourself?'

'Oh, no. I've got a publisher lined up. A three-book deal. I'm quitting this job after the election. So I can focus on my writing.'

Britt realised that, if she played her cards right, this revelation could get her inside without her ID. 'Okay. Here's the deal. I ask you a few questions now. You give me a few answers. I'll give your book a mention in the feature.'

'You serious?'

'It's a great angle. You're a fantastic personality.' A little exaggeration never hurt anyone.

The woman smiled. 'You're definitely a journalist.'

Britt felt the relief surge through her. 'And you're definitely a novelist.'

'Yes, I am,' chuckled the woman. 'Come in, Ms Pointer.'

Britt stepped inside and the security woman closed the door behind her. After asking a few quick questions, Britt had all the information she needed. Then the woman directed Britt to the First Lady's study and they exchanged goodbyes. It was another victory rescued from the jaws of defeat.

As Britt stood outside the study door, about to knock, she realised how unprepared she was for this interview. Her preparations, back at the pod, had consisted of a double water-spray and a power nap that had lasted longer than planned. A lot longer. That had been followed by a frantic rush to get here on the Metro. Britt hadn't read any of the First Lady's books. And she had no idea what the new one was about. All she knew was the title, which George had given her. There was only one thing she could do – something she had perfected after a decade in frontline investigative journalism. She would have to make it up as she went along.

Britt knocked on the door. A regal voice from behind it beckoned her in and she entered. The First Lady was standing behind her desk, stacking several dozen books into adjacent piles. Britt introduced herself. 'Good afternoon, First Lady. I'm Britt Pointer from *The Republican*.'

The First Lady didn't look up. 'Please, sit down. I shall be with you in a moment.'

Britt sat down. After a few minutes, the First Lady had built a mini wall of books on one side of her desk. She turned and faced Britt. 'There – the perfect background for your photograph.'

The photo. Yes. Every feature journalist carried a camera. Correction. Every feature journalist except Britt. Some quick thinking was required. 'I was, erm … going to use a photo from our archives. You and the president. It will attract readers to the feature.'

The First Lady frowned. 'I would prefer a photo of myself and my books.'

It was time to launch into bullshit mode. 'The lighting's not right.'

'It seems perfectly adequate to me.'

'No, it's too dingy.'

'Look around you, Ms Pointer. The sunlight is cascading through the window and bathing my books in a golden glow.'

'Your eyes have adapted to it, First Lady. It's gloomy.'

'I have to disagree.'

'It'll look like you're standing in front of a wall.'

'That's correct. A wall of my books.'

'Trust me. I'm an expert on these things.' She wasn't. But the First Lady didn't know that.

The First Lady stared at Britt for a few seconds, her face expressionless. Then she spoke, her voice deeper than before. 'You think you know better than I do?'

Britt wasn't sure whether she was expected to reply. But the First Lady's silence made it clear that she was. 'When it comes to writing brilliant books, I don't know better. But when it comes to photos in newspapers, I do know better.' That hadn't come out quite how she'd wanted. Diplomacy never had been her strong point.

The First Lady narrowed her eyes and breathed loudly through her nostrils. She didn't look happy. She didn't even look unhappy. She looked much further along the anger spectrum – beyond furious and possibly heading towards volcanic rage. Britt braced herself for an eruption. And possibly an assault with a self-help book.

'I'm not used to people being quite so direct with me, Ms Pointer.' Her expression softened. 'But I admire a person who stands up for themselves.' She pointed at Britt. 'So, I will listen to you when it comes to photos.' She gestured towards the books. 'And you will listen to me when it comes to self-help guides. Understood?'

'That's a deal.' Britt breathed a mental sigh of relief. 'Shall we get started?' She dug out her digi-pen and pad from her bag and switched them on.

'Of course.' The First Lady settled herself in her chair.

'So, your new book, *Finding the American in You* – give me a short, simple explanation of what it's about.'

A contented smile rippled across the First Lady's face. 'To understand my book, you must first understand that we are all American at heart. All of us. You, me, the ordinary man and woman on the street. Everyone.'

This explanation didn't sound like it was going to be short. Or simple. Or even much of an explanation. Then Britt realised she was frowning. Maybe even sneering. She quickly transformed her expression into one of curiosity. 'That's intensely interesting.'

'It is. You see, Americans have a culture of self-improvement and advancement. They're goal driven. They aspire to better lives than those they have now.' She swivelled her chair so she was gazing at the wall. 'More fulfilling lives – both emotionally and physically. And my new book encourages people to find that drive and desire within themselves.' She swivelled her chair back to face Britt. 'And act on it.'

The British constitution sounded a more stimulating read. But Britt needed to keep the First Lady onside. She forced a smile. 'How fiercely fascinating.'

'I'm glad you think so.' The First Lady reached for a basket on her desk. 'Would you care for a candy?'

Britt wasn't a candy person. But sucking something would at least make it easier to hide her facial expressions. She took one and studied the brightly coloured wrapper. 'Thank you. What are they?'

'American rainbow candies. Seven different flavours. They hit your taste buds one by one, at various speeds.'

Britt rarely saw American candies in Britain. The Americans liked to keep them all for themselves. 'Where did you get these, if you don't mind me asking?' enquired Britt, popping the candy in her mouth.

The First Lady smiled. 'I have an unofficial supplier.'

Someone in high places, thought Britt. The first flavour hit her taste buds. It was sickly honey. She almost gagged.

The First Lady took a candy and then reached for a copy of her book on the desk. 'While we're handing out free gifts, take this.'

Britt took the book and put it in her bag. 'Thank you. I look forward to finding my inner American.'

'When you do, it will open up a whole new world for you.'

Britt doubted that. Anyway, she was stuck in this world for the moment and she needed to raise the subject of the president. 'Can we talk about your husband?'

The First Lady twitched her nose, as if a bad smell had just wafted across her desk. 'Must we?'

'It would look odd if we didn't mention him.'

The First Lady pushed the candy around her mouth for a few seconds. 'I'll be honest with you, Ms Pointer – I'm not a big fan of journalists.'

Britt didn't like the sound of this. Had she been too blunt? Too direct? Her thoughts were interrupted as the second flavour hit her. It was lemon. And she hated lemons.

'I find journalists rude and intrusive.'

'Really?' mumbled Britt, fighting the urge to spit her candy on the floor.

'But you're changing my opinion.'

That was a relief. No. A double relief. The candy was already changing to a slightly less disgusting cherry flavour. 'Thank you,' Britt replied.

The First Lady sat back in her chair. 'You can ask me about my husband.'

Britt wanted to ask if the president had disappeared this morning. But even if it was true, the First Lady would never tell her. At least, not directly. Britt would need to try something more subtle. 'Did you see the president this morning or receive a bleep from him? If so, what did he say?'

'No. I didn't see or hear from him this morning. It's a very busy week for both of us.'

The candy now had a revolting fudge taste. She would just have to ignore it. 'I don't suppose you could bleep him now and ask him for a quote about your new book?'

There was another immediate response. 'He hasn't read it, I'm afraid. He's a busy man.'

'I understand.' Britt wasn't going to give up just yet. 'Maybe you could bleep him and ask for a general quote about your writing?'

'You really need to go through his press office for presidential quotes.'

Those answers weren't much help. In fact, they were no help whatsoever. Britt carried on with the questions. 'Will you see him before Thursday – Independence Day?'

The First Lady stifled a yawn. 'I doubt it. Politics always comes first with Jan.'

'So you don't have any joint engagements planned this week?'

'No, we don't,' sighed the First Lady, her eyes glazing over with boredom.

Britt had one more card to play in this game of presidential poker. 'Your husband cancelled an interview with us this afternoon. It had been in the diary for weeks. We were all very surprised.'

The First Lady's face didn't flicker. 'Presidential engagements are never set in stone. Jan changes his plans when it suits him. I know that from sixteen years of marriage.'

Her heart sank. The First Lady had given nothing away. The emerging taste of bitter coconut in Britt's mouth only added to her misery. A knock on the door interrupted her despair.

'Who is it?' shouted the First Lady. 'I'm busy with a journalist.'

'Security,' replied a familiar voice from behind the door. 'It's urgent.'

The First Lady rolled her eyes. 'Alright. You may enter,' she called.

The same security woman as before opened the door. 'Sorry. Someone needs a word with you, First Lady.'

'Can't it wait? I'm being interviewed.'

'It'll only take a few minutes.'

'What is it that's so urgent?'

'It's your publisher. He's in the hall. He says he's lined up an interview with the *Rise and Shine* programme, tomorrow morning. He needs to confirm with them ASAP that you can do it.'

The First Lady jumped to her feet. 'Of course I can do it!' She turned to Britt. 'My apologies. This won't take long. We'll continue our chat when I get back.' Then she rushed out of the study and the security woman closed the door.

Britt's first instinct was to get up and leave. The trail had quickly gone cold here. But she would have to wait in this study. Presidents might be able to disappear. But journalists halfway through an interview with the First Lady couldn't.

She sat back and stared at the desk in front of her. The candy was now a delicious apple flavour. Britt felt a small rush of pleasure. Whatever chemicals her brain had released kick-started her thoughts. The desk. It might just contain something of value that she could sneak a look at while the First Lady was in the hallway. She checked the ceiling and walls for cameras. She couldn't see any. She stood up. Then wandered around the other side of the desk.

Without even thinking, she pulled at one of the drawers. It was open. But there was nothing inside, except for a collection of old digi-pens and an even bigger collection of dust. She tried a second drawer. It contained more American candies but nothing else. The third drawer she tried was stuck. The fourth one just contained more copies of the First Lady's new book. Britt returned to the third drawer and pulled hard on its handle. It was still jammed. She tried one more time. After a hefty tug, it gave way and the drawer flew open. Inside was something interesting – a folder with the words 'Westminster Private Investigation Agency' on the cover.

Britt listened for approaching footsteps. There weren't any. She opened the thick folder. It became clear within seconds what the contents were – a private investigation into the recent movements of someone called Cherry Blush.

She flicked through dozens of pages of records and photos. There were several snaps of a young woman outside a glass-fronted building. According to the photos' captions, they were pictures of Cherry Blush outside the American Fitness gym in Canary Wharf. There were more photos of the same woman entering the gates of Buckingham Palace.

Britt listened again. There were still no sounds outside. She focused again on the folder. Within a few seconds, she had found another bundle of photos of Cherry outside a townhouse.

There were no captions. But it was clearly a Westminster street. Cherry was wearing dark sunglasses and a hat in all of them. In one of those photos, a man was greeting her at the door. It looked like the president. And you could see Cherry's face clearly. Britt shoved it in her bag and continued sifting through the documents.

Her rummaging was interrupted by distant footsteps. She realised she probably had less than half a minute before the First Lady would be back.

She spread out the wodge of papers, desperately searching for anything else of interest. Some written records caught her eye – regular dates and times of meetings between this woman and the president. They referred to Cherry Blush as the president's personal trainer. Maybe she was more than that? Britt would have to find out.

Britt could hear raised voices outside the door. The voices were growing louder by the second. Britt shoved the papers and photos back in the file and returned it to the drawer. The door began to open. She ran out from behind the desk and threw herself into the chair where she'd been sitting. It rocked back as her weight hit it. But she just managed to keep it under control.

'Forgive me for the interruption,' declared the First Lady, as she entered the room and closed the door. 'Now, where were we?'

Britt needed to cut the interview short. 'Is your publisher still out there?'

'Yes. He's bleeping the *Rise and Shine* people.'

Britt had an idea. 'I've got lots of great quotes from you. I've got the book. And I can get your biography from your publisher. That's all I need for a great feature.'

The First Lady smiled. 'Well, you are the expert, Ms Pointer.'

That was right. Britt was an expert. An expert at uncovering the truth. And she had a feeling she was getting closer to it as every hour passed. The triumphant taste of champagne hit her throat, as the remains of the candy dissolved in her mouth. 'It's been a pleasure, First Lady. I'm sure the book will be a best-seller.'

The First Lady beamed. 'That's very kind of you.'

'And send my best wishes to the president, when you see him.'

'Of course I will ... when I see him.'

Chapter 13

Howie opened his eyes. He felt warm, contented and drowsy. For a minute, he wasn't sure where he was. Then he saw the roaring fireplace and the almost empty pint of Guinness on the table in front of him. And he realised. He was in the upstairs room of the Two Chairmen.

He remembered now. He had popped up here to finish his third pint. It was a cosy little room, unstaffed at lunchtimes. He'd been the only person up here when he arrived. He was the only person up here now. It was perfect peace. So perfect, he must have dozed off for fifteen minutes. It was no disgrace, he told himself. Even James Bond needed the occasional catnap. Admittedly, Bond usually did it after killing bad guys, crashing airplanes and making love to beautiful women. But rushing round London, asking people lots of questions, was still pretty tiring work.

Howie sat up and stretched. What was the time? He took out his bleeper and glanced at the screen. It looked like it was showing 15:49. That couldn't be right. The '5' must be a '2'. He rubbed his eyes and checked again. The bleeper still showed the same time. It must have malfunctioned.

Howie considered tossing the bleeper on the open fire, but resisted the temptation. Instead, he scanned his latest e-comms. There were several marked 'Urgent – CAMS', all from Martha Blake. He read the latest one:

Howie, I've been trying to get hold of you for the last two hours. It's almost 3.30pm now. I can only assume you're busy investigating – rather than enjoying a long lunch while the rest of us run around with empty stomachs. I want to give you a face-to-face briefing on the Central Automated Monitoring System. No other news to report. Martha.

A flush of realisation hit his cheeks. It wasn't his bleeper malfunctioning. It was him. He should never have had that third pint of Guinness. Or the second one. And probably not the first one. Normally, he could handle half a dozen pints and still return to the office and be as productive as usual – sometimes more productive – but this wasn't a normal day. He'd had hardly any sleep. It had been continual stress since his bleeper woke him up at five o'clock. And he'd had a boozy lunch. It was a fatal combination that had led his brain to shut down his system and only reboot it three and a half hours later.

Howie frantically checked what other messages had come in while he'd been dozing. There was one from Maurice Skeets marked 'Super-Urgent'. It begged Howie for more information on the president's secret meetings. Maurice could wait. He didn't have enough material to write a story. Howie knew that. Maurice knew that. Maurice had played this game a thousand times before. He wouldn't expect a response. And no response was exactly what he was going to get.

The next one that caught his eye was from Vice President Zayn Winner:

Hey, Howie. You saved the world yet? Ha, ha! Listen up, buddy. That Daily Democrat journalist, Mina Pritti, bleeped my office. She wants to bring forward the interview with me to 3.45pm. She said it'll give her more time to write it for tomorrow's edition. It totally works for me. If it doesn't work for you, give me a bleep, big guy. Otherwise, the action starts at 3.45pm. See you then! Zayn.

This was a disaster. Assuming the journalist turned up on time, the interview would have started already. Real panic hit him. If Mina Pritti mentioned the president, there would be no one there to jump in and stop Zayn saying something he shouldn't. Maybe Howie could bleep him and tell him to stop the interview until he got there? No. That wouldn't work. Zayn never answered his bleeper. There was only one course of action for Howie to take. He would have to get back to the palace as quickly as he could.

Howie jumped to his feet and flew out of the door. He hurtled down the narrow, twisting, metal staircase two steps at a time. He didn't want to waste a second.

Just before he reached the bottom, he misjudged one of the steps. His right foot slipped and he crashed down onto the floor, hitting it with a thump. It was a heavy impact that took his breath away.

As he lay there, sprawled in a crumpled heap in the tiny entrance hall, a couple on their way out of the downstairs bar stopped. Howie looked up at them. They looked down at him. Howie offered an apologetic smile. They offered contemptuous stares. He tried to summon the breath to ask them to help him up. They shook their heads and tutted before he could say anything. Then they carried on down Dartmouth Street. They think I'm a drunk, thought Howie. He was going to have to help himself.

He struggled to his feet. He took a few moments to catch his breath, ignoring more stares and tutting from customers. Then he took a step forward. And pain shot through his right ankle. He had twisted it. Just what he didn't need.

At least the palace wasn't far away. It was a ten-minute walk. But a fifteen-minute hobble. There would be no point getting a taxi or bleeping for a government car. It would take even longer to get there in the mid-afternoon traffic.

Howie stumbled out of the pub and turned right, towards the Cockpit Steps that led to St James' Park. He had to get to the palace before Zayn finished his interview, so he could try and repair any damage. He would just have to ignore the burning pain in his ankle and press on.

As he limped down the steps, he wondered how he was going to explain all this to Martha Blake. It didn't take him long to realise the answer – he couldn't. He would just have to tell her the truth and face the consequences.

Howie crossed Birdcage Walk into St James' Park. He could hear the pelicans squawking in the distance. They didn't sound happy. It was as if they were yelling at him for falling asleep on the job. And Martha wouldn't be happy either. She would be angrier than all of those pelicans put together.

He staggered on through the park. Halfway through, a large dog ran across his path in a frenzy of excitement. It zig-zagged back and forth, following the scent of some long-gone animal. The creature was probably now asleep in its burrow or den, while the dog ran itself into the ground in pointless pursuit. 'That dog is me,' he thought.

After struggling along its concrete paths, Howie left the park and turned left into The Mall. He could now see Buckingham Palace up ahead. It was a view he had always enjoyed – the spot was far enough away for him to see the building in all its grandeur. But it wasn't a view he was enjoying today. Because it meant he still had a few minutes of ankle-pounding pain to endure.

As he approached the roundabout, Howie gazed up at the palace balcony. He imagined the scene on Thursday morning. Citizens would be gathered in their thousands. The nation would be watching on their digi-screens. All eyes would be on that balcony. But who would be walking out onto it?

The Republican Party, as the party of government, would have to make their presidential nomination by eleven o'clock on Independence Day. Wherever the president was – assuming he was alive – he would have to get back here by then. Otherwise, those third and fourth terms he'd talked about in private with Howie and the vice presidents would never become a reality. His legacy wouldn't be twenty years of stable government. It would be ten years of stable government followed by panic and a million questions. Questions about why Jan Polak wasn't standing again, what was he going to do now and, hey … where the hell is he, by the way? Howie would be the person answering those questions. Or trying to answer them. Or completely failing to answer them because he had absolutely no idea what the hell was going on either.

He swallowed hard. Today was a bad day. But if the president didn't appear on that balcony on Thursday morning, it would be a hundred times worse – for the Government, for the citizens and, most importantly, for Howie. It mustn't happen.

Howie could feel adrenaline start to pump through his veins. As it mixed with the alcohol in his system, a mild euphoria overtook him. Everything became clear. It wasn't a case of *if* he found the president. It was a case of *when* he found the president. He started jogging towards the left-hand gate. He felt no pain now. Two police officers were guarding the gate – one short, one tall. As he got closer, he recognised them. He didn't know them by name, but he knew they would chat all day if he gave them enough encouragement. And Howie had zero time for small talk.

The short officer nodded towards him. 'Afternoon, Mr Pond. How's the boss? Getting ready for the big day, is he?'

'He's fine,' replied Howie, with the bare minimum of politeness. 'Can I get through, gents? I'm in a hurry.'

The tall officer moved to open the gate. 'Certainly, Mr Pond.' As he was about to press a button to open it, he stopped and turned to face Howie. 'But just one question, before I do.'

This pair were as bad as journalists with their 'just one question'. It was usually followed by a dozen follow-up questions. 'Okay. If it's a quick one.'

'Will the American ambassador be popping round for tea and biscuits any time soon?'

'I've no idea.' And it was true. The president's monthly one-to-ones with the American ambassador were private, non-media events. Howie never got involved.

The short officer lowered his voice. 'It's just, Mr Stackshaker promised us a couple of boxes of American jelly queens when he dropped by last week.'

The tall officer tapped his nose and winked knowingly. 'Diplomatic channels.'

'Sorry. I don't know.' Howie pointed at the gates. 'Can I get through?'

The tall officer moved towards the gate again. Then he stopped and turned again. 'One more quick question.'

Howie considered punching the pair on their noses and opening the gate himself. But he restrained himself. 'The final one. I answer it. You open the gate.'

The tall officer nodded. 'We just wondered if you could mention to the president how helpful we'd been to a White House security person. And then he could pass that information on to Mr Stackshaker.'

The short officer grinned. 'Then we might get an extra couple of boxes of jelly queens.'

This sounded worrying. 'What White House security person?'

'American lady,' continued the short officer. 'She was hanging round here this morning. She's doing some security review for their president or something. She had a few questions about our security arrangements.' He turned to his colleague. 'She liked us, didn't she?'

'Reckoned we should be on the digi-screen.'

Howie felt uneasy. Flattery was the weapon of choice for undercover journalists. 'She was definitely an American security person?'

The pair nodded confidently.

Howie wasn't convinced. 'You saw her ID?'

The two officers looked at each other. Then they looked at Howie.

'Well, did you or didn't you?'

The short officer bowed his head. 'She'd, erm … left it at her hotel.'

'That old excuse?' growled Howie. 'Sounds like an undercover journalist to me.'

The tall officer shook a finger. 'I have to disagree. This woman knew intimate details about Mr Stackshaker's home life.'

The short officer took a step forward. 'We work at the embassy sometimes. What she said about the ambassador was spot on, Mr Pond. She weren't no journalist.'

Howie sighed. 'Very briefly, what did she look like?'

'Difficult to say,' replied the tall officer. 'She was wearing dark sunglasses.'

'In this weather?' asked Howie.

The short officer nodded. 'She told us she had very sensitive retinas. It's a genetic thing, apparently.'

This definitely sounded like a journalist. 'What was her name?'

The tall officer wrinkled his brow and looked at his colleague. 'I don't think we got that, did we?'

His colleague shrugged. 'Never came up in conversation.'

Howie bit his lip. 'I don't have a lot of time. Just tell me – did you give her any sensitive information?'

The two officers looked at each other, eyebrows raised. Then they looked at Howie, eyebrows lowered. And they spoke as one. 'No, no, no.'

Howie didn't believe them for one minute. But a negative answer was the one he wanted. He couldn't waste any more time. He walked up to the gate. 'Well, that's fine, then. Open the gates, please.'

The tall officer pressed the button in silence. Howie rushed through the gates and headed towards the palace entrance. He checked the time on his bleeper. It was 4.16pm. Zayn's interview had been running for more than half an hour. Howie hoped he wasn't too late.

Chapter 14

Britt had been loitering outside American Fitness in Canary Wharf for almost twenty minutes now. A steady stream of well-toned bodies had walked, jogged and sprinted through its doors during that time. But none of their faces belonged to the person Britt was hunting.

She peered through the glass front of the building to see if Cherry was in reception. There was no sign of her. But she was definitely still in there. Another personal trainer, on his way out of the building, had confirmed it fifteen minutes ago, before zooming off at ridiculous speed. Britt had thought about marching into reception and demanding to see her. Maybe she could adopt another fake identity? But her gut feeling was that this young woman would be more streetwise than Pellie Cann's victims. A lot more streetwise. It would be better to hang back and track her from a distance.

Two women in American Fitness uniforms suddenly shot out of the building. Britt quickly took out the photo of Cherry she'd obtained from the First Lady's office and checked it. Neither of them looked like the woman in the photo. As quickly as they had appeared, the pair sped off into the crowds. Britt hoped Cherry wouldn't be as fast on her feet.

All this standing around was making her legs ache. She still hadn't recovered from this morning's sprint down The Mall. There was no way she could manage another mad dash through the streets of London. Even a brisk stroll would be hard work.

Britt looked at her bleeper. It was 4.22pm. The clock was ticking. She needed to get back to the office and write her feature on the First Lady's new book by seven. Then she had to get to the Grafton Arms for the gig at eight, so she could probe Herbert the security guy some more.

Cherry, George, Herbert – there wouldn't be much time for anyone else today. But she made a mental note to chat to Howie about his day when he came back from work – assuming he came home at all. If he did, he might be tired and frustrated enough to let something else slip. Howie's traditional post-work rant was a long way off, though. There was plenty more digging to be done before then.

A man in a dark coat, scarf, woolly hat and sunglasses emerged from behind a crowd of suited city workers walking in her direction. At first, he looked like any other middle-aged man heading for an urgent appointment. Then Britt noticed he was looking nervously around him, keeping his head down and glancing towards the gym. His scarf was obscuring his face below the eyes, so he could have been anybody. But there was no sign of Cherry at the moment, so she kept watching him.

The man stopped and muttered to himself. He pulled at his scarf and started to loosen it. As he did so, Britt caught sight of his features for a few seconds. She took a sharp breath. Was that the president? The kinked nose, the full lips and the square jaw – they were unmistakeable, even at a distance of thirty metres or so. She looked to see if anyone else had reached the same conclusion. But everyone else was travelling at a hundred kilometres per hour. To them, he was just another pedestrian getting in their way.

Britt took a few steps closer. The man was tall enough to be the president. He had that distinctive upright stance. He was wearing those trademark shoes. And this was the building where his personal trainer worked – a woman the First Lady suspected was getting a bit more personal than she should be. It must be him.

Questions started racing through Britt's mind. Did the two of them have plans to escape somewhere? It wasn't impossible. She could feel her heart racing and she suddenly felt self-conscious – standing alone outside this gym for no obvious reason. But she needed to stay calm, assess the situation and find out what was going on.

The president started walking again. Britt made a decision. She would follow him into the building at a discreet distance. She edged towards the main doors, keeping one eye on the entrance and one eye on him. But he wasn't going inside. Instead, he stopped at the edge of the concrete plaza.

Of course, thought Britt. The British president isn't going to risk being recognised in a reception area. And someone refusing to remove their hat, scarf and sunglasses would draw attention to themselves. The president was a man of phenomenal intelligence, according to Howie. A man who didn't make mistakes – because he never allowed himself to get into situations where mistakes could be made.

But Britt couldn't just stand around staring at him. She turned around, took a mirror from her bag and pretended she was checking her make-up. She could see his reflection in the glass. For the next few minutes, he paced up and down and looked at his watch – checking all the time to see who was around him.

Britt decided to put the mirror back in her bag and face the entrance to the building again, being careful not to look in the president's direction. If he realised he was being watched, he might cancel his rendezvous. And that would be a disaster.

Two more women wearing American Fitness uniforms left the building. They didn't look like the woman in the photo and the president didn't make a move. They obviously weren't Cherry.

Another few minutes passed. And then Britt saw her. The woman from the photo. Yes. It was definitely Cherry Blush. Her face was unmistakeable. The president was already striding towards her.

Cherry acknowledged the president with a wave. Without slowing down, he took Cherry's arm and they began walking in Britt's direction. The president was already talking animatedly.

Britt turned her back and listened to their approaching conversation.

'Let's make this quick, Cherry.'

'I thought we were going out?'

'No. We won't be going out again.'

'What's that supposed to mean?'

'Keep your voice down! Let's go somewhere less crowded. And don't say anything until we get there.'

'Alright, alright. There's no need to be so mega-miserable.'

The couple hurried past Britt in silence. She allowed them to get a good fifty metres ahead before following them. If they weren't talking, she wouldn't be missing anything.

As Britt followed, she wondered why the president would risk everything for a fling with his personal trainer. He was popular. Probably the most popular leader the country had ever had. Both pre- and post-revolution. But if news of his extra-marital affair emerged before the election, who knows what might happen? British citizens expected their presidents to spend their time running the country. Not running after their personal trainers. Public opinion could turn. It could hand the Democrats victory. And even if he was popular enough to survive, Jan Polak's reputation would never be the same again.

The couple turned right and entered a small park. Britt stopped to watch what they were doing. The pair sat down on a bench and started talking. Britt's instinct was to hold back for now and wait for things to develop. They did. The discussion soon evolved into a heated exchange. So heated, it looked like it might break up at any moment. She decided her best chance was to walk past and try and pick up a snippet of the argument.

As Britt approached, the couple stood up. Cherry was shouting something in her thick London accent – two words. What were they? 'Ask her!' She shouted it again, louder this time. Then she sprinted off in the other direction, even faster than her colleagues had done earlier, leaving the president to shout after her. 'Cherry! Come back!'

It must have been a lovers' argument. Britt's guess was Cherry wanted the president to ask the First Lady for a divorce. But maybe he didn't want to ask that question?

The president sat down on the bench again and started composing a message on his bleeper. Britt seized her opportunity. She walked up to him. Then tried to engage him in conversation. 'Do you mind if I sit here?'

The president didn't reply and kept his head down. Britt sat on the bench anyway. She tried to read the message he was typing, but couldn't make out anything on the bleeper's screen. 'I've had rather a busy day,' she announced, trying to sound cheerful. 'What about you?'

The president completely ignored her. He was completely focused on his bleeper.

Britt wanted to ask so many questions. What's happening with you and Cherry Blush? Did she just ask you to get a divorce? Why did you disappear? When will you reappear? All those and dozens more. Questions whose answers would guarantee her the front-page story she desperately needed. But she knew that was a strategy doomed to failure. He would just run.

Maybe the bleeper was the key to finding out some more information? It must contain a lot of interesting messages between the president and Cherry Blush – and many other people. Britt could grab it and run. Actually, no she couldn't. Her aching legs would give up after ten seconds. She would be caught, arrested and flung into a police cell. Bad idea.

She would have to try and sneak a look at the message he was typing. She stood up. The president was paying her no attention. She leaned over to inspect the bleeper. 'I haven't seen that model before. Is it a Tech-42?' As she did so, all she could make out was the name of the recipient – Maxim. It meant nothing to her.

'Do you mind!' shouted the president, snatching away his bleeper.

'I'm sorry. It's just I have an old Tech-39 and —'

'I don't care,' he snarled, jumping to his feet.

Before Britt could respond, he was gone – heading in the same direction he'd come from. There was no point trying to follow him. He was too fast. But it didn't really matter. She had to get back to the office and write that feature. Britt looked at her own bleeper. It was 4.32pm. She should be able to get to Fulham in forty-five minutes. That would give her an hour and a half to write the article. It would be tight. But she could do it.

She allowed herself a congratulatory smile. In less than a day, she'd gathered some solid evidence for her suspicion that the president was missing. She'd also tracked down the woman with whom the president was having an affair. She had even managed to exchange a few words with the great man himself. And she had done all this while Howie and his cronies ran around like headless royals.

Britt got up and started to make her way to the Metro station. As she walked along, she imagined what the headline of her big story might be. It came to her in a flash. 'We Have Lost The President'. It was simple, memorable and it summed up the situation perfectly. Keys, bleepers, important documents – they were lost. But presidents didn't just slip down the backs of sofas, get left on trains or end up tossed in the rubbish by accident. Countries didn't wake up, bleary-eyed, and forget where they'd left them. Presidents were unlosable. Even when they got assassinated people knew where the body was. But for the first time ever, it had happened – the British Republic had lost its president.

She took a deep breath. She had single-handedly managed to track down Jan Polak. But she wouldn't be informing the police, or anyone else. He would stay missing for now. She needed him to stay missing – for her big story.

Chapter 15

Howie burst through the door of Zayn Winner's office, gasping an apology for his late arrival. But no one accepted it. Because the room was empty.

He stepped outside the door and checked the corridor. There was no sign of Zayn or the *Daily Democrat* journalist. Where were they? Maybe the interview had finished before Howie could get there? Zayn had probably already said something he shouldn't. Mina Pritti might already be planning a story about a missing president. Howie felt nauseous. He sat down at Zayn's desk and composed himself. You could spend whole days roaming the corridors of Buckingham Palace trying to find someone. He only had a few minutes.

Then Howie noticed something – a scribbled note. He read it:

Howie, we're in the State Dining Room, buddy. I thought a red carpet would be appropriate for a Hollywood legend like me. Ha, ha, ha! See you there. Zayn.

It took a few seconds for the full horror to sink in. The State Dining Room? It was where Zayn and his vice-presidential colleagues had been informed of the president's disappearance. It might still show signs of that morning's Code Red crisis meeting – vice-presidential digi-pens or muddy footprints on the carpet. It was common knowledge that it was reserved for the most high-level government meetings. A sharp journalistic mind like Mina's could pick up on any signs of recent activity there. Added to the fact that the president wasn't available for interviews today, it might lead to awkward questions. Questions that a motor-mouth like Zayn was ill-equipped to handle.

Howie dashed along the corridor, as fast as his twisted ankle could carry him. A few minutes later, he was outside the State Dining Room. He was too tired to burst through another set of doors, so he pushed them open. As he entered, he could see Zayn reclining in a chair at the far end of the room, while Mina Pritti peered at him through the lens of a large camera. They were so engrossed in their photoshoot, they didn't notice his arrival.

Photos were always taken at the end of interviews. Howie cursed silently and quickly scanned the table. There were no forgotten digi-pens. Then he looked down at the carpet. No muddy footprints. Martha Blake must have taken care of everything. Of course she had. She always did.

Howie decided to stay where he was. He would try and establish the journalist's mood, before she spotted him in the room. That would give him some clue as to how the interview had gone. If he saw a happy, bubbly journalist that would be bad news. A rude and irritated journalist would be better. That would mean Zayn had – against all odds – stuck to the script. Howie crossed his fingers and listened.

'You're the director here, Mina. How do you want me?'

Mina's face bobbed out from behind the camera. 'I want to try and capture that fun dimension you mentioned earlier.'

'Yeah, the fifth dimension!' laughed Zayn. 'Beyond space, time and Buckingham Palace.'

Howie rolled his eyes. For king's sake, don't mention aliens.

'Do you want my "I've just seen an alien" face? Or my "I've just voted Democrat" face? The second one is scarier.'

Mina giggled. Then her camera flashed. 'That face you pulled right then was perfect.'

'Mega!' roared Zayn, getting to his feet. 'I never like to disappoint an audience.'

Mina nodded in appreciation. 'Thank you so much, Vice President Winner. It's been a total blast.'

'Boom!' yelled Zayn. 'Shake the room!' And he gyrated his hips in the most hideously embarrassing way that Howie had ever seen.

Mina pretended the floor was shaking. 'Easy, vice president. I can feel the earth moving!'

Zayn winked cheekily. 'I bet you say that to all the vice presidents.'

And then they giggled like schoolchildren who'd just been told how babies are made.

Howie sighed. This journalist wasn't just happy. She was positively delirious. It was time for him to step in. 'Sorry, I'm late,' he shouted, as he approached them. 'But then this interview was supposed to take place at five, wasn't it, Mina?'

Mina looked up. Her expression changed to one of polite apology. 'Yes, it was – originally.'

Howie wagged a finger. 'And you shouldn't have rescheduled it without my —'

'Hey, don't go hard on her, buddy,' interrupted Zayn. 'Blame me. I agreed to move it.'

Mina's expression was now one of quiet victory.

Howie strode up to Zayn and glared at him. 'But I didn't agree to it.'

Zayn put his arm round Howie's shoulder. 'I bleeped you, buddy. You didn't bleep back. Then when Mina arrived, we did wait – for a bit. Then we got chatting. And, you know, we got into an interview groove real quick. So we decided to go with the flow.'

Howie shrugged off Zayn's arm. 'You should have gone with the original flow.'

'Maybe I should. But Mina was supposed to be interviewing the president today.' Zayn raised his eyebrows and nudged Howie with his elbow, in the most unsubtle way possible. 'But Jan couldn't make it, could he?'

Howie flicked a glance at Mina. Luckily, she was packing her camera into its case and wasn't watching. But Howie didn't want Zayn mentioning the president again or making any more unsubtle eyebrow or elbow movements. So he changed the subject. 'Did you get what you wanted, Mina?'

'Yes, thank you.' Her expression gave nothing away. But if Zayn had been behaving like this for the whole interview, she would have enough material for a year's worth of stories.

Mina turned to look at Zayn. 'Can I just double-check those film titles again?'

Zayn beamed with pride. 'Sure you can. There was *Alien Invasion*. And *Alien Mutation*. And my personal favourite, *Alien Vacation* – where everyone dies except me.'

'And you played the American president in all of them?'

Zayn adopted an American accent that was so awful, it was almost certainly a capital offence in fifty states. 'Yes, ma'am! I did run the whole show over the Pacific.' He checked himself. 'I mean, over the Atlantic. For all three of them movies.' Zayn returned to his normal voice. 'It was a role I slipped into naturally. I didn't need to act. I was just riding the natural presidential vibe I got inside me and —'

'Right, I think that's about it for today,' interrupted Howie.

Mina cocked her head and gave an inscrutable smile. 'And remind me again why the president couldn't do this interview, Mr Pond. Just so I can add a line to the article.'

'He's attending to important matters of state, which I'm afraid we can't discuss.'

Mina nodded. 'I completely understand.'

Howie hoped she didn't. Or they really would be in trouble. 'This article will be in tomorrow's *Daily Democrat*, yes?'

'Yes. The day before the Republican Party presidential nomination.'

The nomination, yes. Zayn better not have mentioned anything about putting himself forward for the presidency if a vacancy arose. Howie tried not to look concerned. 'It's just a feature, is it?'

'I think I've got enough for a feature with a news angle.'

Howie could feel a lump in his throat. 'And what's the news angle?'

Mina's face showed no emotion. 'The president.'

Howie could feel his heart thumping in his chest. 'And will it be a front-page story?'

'I would think so.' Mina turned to Zayn. 'Unless an alien invasion relegates it to the inside pages.'

Zayn laughed. 'Isn't she great? I can't wait to read it!'

Howie could wait. Preferably a few years – when he would be in another job. But the reality was that, in just over twelve hours, he would wake up to Zayn's grinning face on the front page of Wednesday's *Daily Democrat*.

'I'm going now,' announced Mina. 'Front-page news stories don't write themselves.'

Zayn gestured to the door. 'I'll show you out.'

That was probably a bad idea. It was one last opportunity for Mina to get more off-message quotes from Zayn. But Howie had to speak to Martha Blake as a priority. And, as far as this interview was concerned, the damage was already done. Howie grunted a goodbye and Zayn and Mina crossed the room and headed out of the door.

Howie heaved a sigh of despair. That hadn't gone well. But at least it was out of the way. He took his bleeper out of his pocket and sent Martha a short e-comm, telling her his whereabouts. Five minutes later, she popped her head round the door.

'Howie! I've been looking for you everywhere. Where on earth have you been?'

'Erm … I was off-grid for a while.'

'I bleeped you three hours ago. Come on, I need you in the president's private office right now. Ivan is going to update us on the security camera failure.' She disappeared behind the door and Howie followed her into the corridor.

A few minutes later, they were sitting in the president's private office. Just the two of them.

'Now, while we're waiting, Howie, tell me what you've …' Martha sniffed the air. 'Have you been drinking?'

Howie cleared his throat. 'Yes. But all in the line of duty. A freelance journalist I know, Maurice Skeets, asked to meet me at the Two Chairmen.'

Martha rolled her eyes. 'I should have known.'

'I had to be there. He claimed to have details of secret meetings between Jan and three high-flyers.'

'Who were they?'

'First one was Sky Eastern, chairwoman of Eastern Oil. Maurice had a conspiracy theory about a secret deal between her and the president. He's read a company letter about some test drilling they want to do in British waters. That's the only hard evidence he's got, though.'

'Sounds like guesswork. The second name?'

'Olga Frik. Her firm manufactures the auto-techs. Maurice reckons she and Jan had a long lunch.'

'Well, I hope she was paying. What was the journalist's angle?'

'He didn't have one. Just the fact her firm supplies the auto-techs.'

'That could be considered a crime in itself. What's the last name?'

'A Russian, Petra Putinov. Her company supplies the Government with a few military parts. Maurice said she and Jan had a meeting.'

'That sounds more interesting.'

'Yeah. But they're a multinational. They make loads of other stuff. Maurice is just guessing again. That was it.'

'So it took him three hours to tell you three names with barely anything to back up his suspicions?'

'Ah. Not exactly.' Howie would have to come clean. 'I dozed off. After three pints of Guinness. And a steak-and-ale pie.'

'I admire your honesty. If not your culinary choices.'

'When I woke up, I rushed straight here for the *Daily Democrat* interview. Zayn brought it forward without my permission. It's just finished.'

'And how did that go?'

'I only caught the end of it. He came out with some dumb things while I was there. He'll have come out with even more dumb things when I wasn't there. We'll find out just how dumb tomorrow.'

'I see,' sighed Martha. 'What about the First Lady?'

'I didn't have much time with her. I told her the situation. She seemed pretty calm about it.'

'When did she last see Jan?'

'She met with him on Saturday for lunch. But wouldn't tell me what they discussed.'

'No?'

'She insisted it was personal stuff. And she had no idea where Jan was.'

'And you believed her?'

'No reason not to.'

'Did you get a sense of anything going on in the background that should worry us?'

Howie remembered the discussion about America. 'This book she's written is an open love letter to the New States. I asked her if she'd ever consider moving there. She said it had never been an option. So she hadn't given it any thought.' A possibility hit Howie like a train. So hard, he had to take a sharp breath. 'But if Jan wasn't around … maybe it would be an option.'

Martha wrinkled her forehead. 'Divorce is usually an easier option than disposing of your spouse, Howie.'

'For ordinary citizens, yeah. But if you're the wife of a president, it's not so easy.'

'What do you mean?'

'I mean citizens like their leaders to be married. And stay married. Divorce is a sign of failure. Presidents don't get divorced.'

'This is 2044. Not 1944.'

'Yeah. But Jan's core voters are the Eastern Europeans who came here after Amerigration. They make up thirty per cent of the population now – hard workers with more traditional family values than the natives.'

Martha considered his analysis and then delivered her verdict. 'I'm still not convinced the First Lady would take matters into her own hands. Whether that's by kidnap, murder or whatever. Who would she employ to do it, for a start?'

'I don't know.' Howie paused to think. 'Maybe I'm reading too much into a self-help book.'

'I think you are. But let's keep all this in mind.' Martha looked him in the eyes. 'Where did you go after that? Straight to the pub?'

'No. The First Lady pointed me in the direction of Jan's personal trainer, Cherry Blush. She suspects Cherry and Jan are having an affair.'

'Jan?' exclaimed Martha. 'Well, he might have the energy but he hasn't got the time.'

'That's exactly what I thought. Anyway, I went to see Miss Blush at her gym in Canary Wharf. And she denied having a relationship with the president.'

'Do you think she was telling the truth?'

'She was convincing. So, yeah. I do. And that was it, as far as my meeting with Cherry Blush was concerned. Then I went to the Two Chairmen.' Howie didn't want to discuss his pub visit again, so he changed the subject. 'Any news from the security search?'

Martha shook her head. 'There are still some rooms that need to undergo a full examination. But they've all been walked through, and there's no sign of him.'

'What about Oskar? Have you spoken to him since the Code Red crisis meeting?'

'No. He's a work in progress.' A flicker of a smile crossed Martha's face. 'I've had one piece of luck. The American ambassador's office called to cancel our meeting. It's fortunate because the Americans always seem to sniff out this kind of crisis pretty quickly. So not having to spend an hour with Clinton Stackshaker, watching every word I said, was a bonus.'

'That reminds me. Two policemen at the gate told me there was an American security woman asking questions this morning.'

Martha stopped. 'Really? Who was she?'

'The officers didn't get her name. She told them she was working on a security review for the American president.'

'And what was she asking about?'

'She wanted to know about palace security arrangements. The officers denied telling her anything.' Howie shook his head. 'Not sure I believe them. But the police don't know about the Code Red crisis, so they can't have told her about that.'

'Sounds suspicious to me.'

'Yeah. I think she might have been an undercover journalist. She had no ID.'

'Don't tell me this has been leaked to the media already?'

'Maybe. Or someone at the crisis meeting has been talking about it afterwards and been overheard. It's not impossible.'

'Who would be that stupid?'

Howie shrugged. He had no idea. There were too many possible suspects to choose from.

There was a knock on the main door.

'Come in!' shouted Martha.

Ivan Bonn entered the room, followed by one of the auto-techs.

As soon as the robot detected Howie and Martha, it swivelled its head and fired a laser in their eyes. 'Good afternoon, Martha Blake. Good afternoon, Howard Pond.'

Momentarily dazzled, Martha snapped her eyelids shut. 'Can we turn it off – preferably permanently?'

'No. It's still processing. Data. Lots of it.' Ivan looked down and patted the auto-tech. 'Aren't you, Brian?'

The auto-tech replied in a tinny voice. 'Brian has downloaded the CAMS data. Brian is now processing it to determine the cause of the CAMS shutdown. Please wait for Brian's readout.'

Martha sighed loudly. 'So we still don't know what happened with the cameras?'

Ivan looked worried. 'No. Not yet. Waiting for Brian.'

Martha glared at the auto-tech. 'Brian, how long have we got to wait?'

'Brian is calculating the estimated readout time.'

Everyone waited. After thirty seconds of silence, Martha turned to Ivan. 'I hate to sound impatient, but I don't have all day.'

The robot bleeped. 'Please be patient, Martha. Brian does not like to be rushed.'

Martha folded her arms. 'And this is what you call a helpful auto-tech? I'd hate to be dealing with an unhelpful one.'

Howie tutted. 'Can't you get another one of these things to check it out, Ivan?'

'Sorry, can't. Others malfunctioned. Overnight. Only Brian still works. Don't understand how —'

The auto-tech interrupted. 'Brian reporting. You will wait forty-eight hours for the CAMS readout. Brian apologises for the delay. Brian hopes this does not spoil your Tuesday.'

Martha growled in frustration. 'So we won't get a readout until late Thursday afternoon and all Brian's friends have malfunctioned. This is ludicrous!'

Howie had an idea. 'Hang on. Could someone have done this deliberately?'

Ivan narrowed his eyes. 'Please clarify.'

'I mean, could someone have messed around with the auto-techs' systems?'

Ivan blinked rapidly for a couple of seconds. 'You mean hackers?'

'Maybe. I don't know.'

Martha turned to Ivan. 'Can you check if any of the auto-techs have been tampered with?'

Ivan went pale. 'Don't do actual Tech.'

'Oh, no,' sighed Martha. 'I forgot.'

Howie glanced down at Brian. 'Let's just ask it. Brian, did any humans access your systems last night?'

'Humans access Brian's systems all the time, Howard.'

Howie turned to Ivan. 'Do these things keep a log of who they deal with?'

'They should. Seven days' worth. Dates. Times. Names.'

'Access your logs, Brian,' ordered Howie. 'Who did you interact with last night?'

'Brian had to erase all logs. Brian had to free up memory for the CAMS data download.'

Howie sighed. 'Okay. Let's try another question. Can you be reprogrammed?'

'Brian is an intelligent system. Therefore Brian can be reprogrammed.'

At last, the machine was being moderately helpful. 'And have you been reprogrammed recently?'

'As I just told you, Howard, Brian had to erase all logs. This includes reprogramming logs.'

This machine wasn't being helpful.

'I wouldn't waste any more time with it,' snapped Martha.

'One last try,' grumbled Howie. 'Brian, can you access the CAMS system?'

'Brian and all other auto-techs can access CAMS, Howard.'

Martha was getting ratty. 'Just tell us if you accessed the system last night!'

'At the risk of repeating myself for a second time, Martha, Brian has erased all logs.'

'Shut the bloody thing off!' shouted Martha.

Ivan looked nervous again. 'I can't. Auto-techs power themselves.'

Martha jabbed a finger in Brian's direction. 'Can't you just wheel the little dustbin out of here?'

The auto-tech swivelled its head towards Martha and bleeped. 'Brian can tell when he is not wanted.' Then it glided out the door and left.

'I've had enough of temperamental Tech for one day,' huffed Martha.

Howie felt the same. But another idea came to him. 'Ivan, could I go and have a look at the CAMS system now?'

'If you want.'

'Good. I'm not going to let these bloody machines beat us.'

Martha looked grim. 'I fear they already have.'

Howie shook his head. 'Not yet, they haven't.' He had no idea where his new-found confidence with Tech had come from. He just knew that the auto-tech had been hiding something. Machines could be economical with the truth, just as humans could be. After all, they were programmed by humans. 'I'm going to the CAMS control room. And I'm going to find out what happened to that system.'

Martha didn't look convinced. 'You think you can get to the bottom of this?'

Howie thought for a second. James Bond could usually suss out these supercomputers pretty quickly. It shouldn't take long to work out if CAMS had been interfered with. 'Just leave it to me.'

Martha nodded. 'Very well. We've got nothing to lose. Now, I've got some intelligence reports to go through. That'll take at least a couple of hours. I'll pop up to the control room when I've finished.'

Howie checked the clock on the wall. It was 4.44pm. 'That sounds like a plan. Come on, Ivan. You can help me.'

Ivan wrinkled his forehead. 'Me? But —'

'Yes, I know,' interrupted Howie. 'You don't do Tech.' He put his arm around Ivan so he couldn't escape. 'But you can do more Tech than I can.'

'Al-al-alright,' stuttered Ivan. 'I'll come.'

Excellent, thought Howie. It was time for battle. Two men versus one machine. There could only be one winner.

Chapter 16

Britt was back in the newsroom of *The Republican*. It was where she belonged. But she wasn't at her own desk. Her colleague Rosie was still camped there, engaged in some undemanding sub-editing, light reading and office small talk. Britt was sandwiched between two scruffy young interns who smelled like they must have a soap allergy. At least she would be back at her usual desk next week. After she had broken the biggest story this newspaper had ever known – a story about a missing president.

She looked up at her e-terminal. It told her the time was seven o'clock. That was her deadline. Her Cinderella hour. Her editor George was obsessive about deadlines. If he said 7.00pm he meant 7.00pm. He didn't mean 7.01pm, 7.02pm or 7.03pm. Editors were difficult like that. Editors were difficult about everything.

But on this occasion, Britt was okay. She could relax. She had finished the piece with ten minutes to spare. It was a new record for her. Normally, she worked right up to deadline. That was just her way. But the adrenaline had been flowing so freely, her mind had been thinking so clearly, it had pushed her to new levels of productivity.

Her fifteen-hundred-word feature had been delivered. And now she was just waiting for that booming voice to come from the editor's office and summon her. There she would be told whether the great Caesar had given it the thumbs up or the thumbs down. She was pretty confident it would be a thumbs up. It was a good, solid feature with a neat side story about the novel-writing security woman. It was a little clichéd, but that was deliberate. She didn't want to be singled out as a feature-writing star of the future and be banished from the news desk forever. For that reason, she had used a few American spellings that always annoyed George. And been overly descriptive in places. Without those two spoilers, it could probably be labelled an excellent feature.

Britt looked back at George's office door. There were no signs of him emerging. She was starting to get a little worried. This meeting could take a while if George was in an argumentative mood and she really needed to get away soon. The gig at the Grafton Arms started at eight. Britt would need as much time as possible to probe Herbert the security guy for more information. Or rather, Pellie Cann would need as much time as possible.

A voice shouted her name. It wasn't George. It was Rosie. Britt kept her head down and tried to ignore her.

Rosie stood up, so she could see the top of Britt's head. 'Hey, Britt! I hear you interviewed the First Lady today.'

Britt didn't make eye contact. 'You heard right.'

Rosie walked across the room and stood by Britt's desk. 'What's her new book about then? The usual self-help crap, is it?'

Britt looked hopefully towards George's office again, but the door was firmly shut. She turned back and reluctantly glanced up at Rosie. 'It's about finding the American in you. Enjoying life here, like you're living it over there.'

Rosie pulled up a nearby chair and sat down. 'The New States is over-hyped, if you ask me. Internet, social media, mobile phones, instantaneous personal communication connecting people all over the country in a microsecond – all massively over-rated. I prefer a good old face-to-face chat. Don't you?'

Britt stayed silent in the hope that Rosie's good old face-to-face chat would terminate. It didn't.

'You want my opinion, Britt? If the First Lady loves it so much on the other side of the Atlantic, why doesn't she just bugger off there for good?'

'Because she's married to the president of the British Republic.'

'Oh ... yeah.' Rosie laughed. 'I see what you mean. But here's a question – why is he still married to her? When she's out and about with him, she's got a face like a pickled herring. I feel like saying "Cheer up, love. You've got your hands on Britain's most wanted man."' She winked at Britt. 'I'd love to get my hands on him.'

So would a lot of people right now.

Their conversation was interrupted by a shout from George. 'Britt, can we have a word?'

The emperor was calling. It was time to go and find out which direction his thumb was pointing. Britt got up, walked to the office and pushed the half-open door.

George was sitting behind his desk. She closed the door and took a couple of steps forward but didn't sit down. It was a repeat of what had happened yesterday afternoon. The memory sent a tiny shiver through her body.

George gestured to the chair in front of his desk. 'Are you going to sit down?'

'No. I want a quick getaway, if it's bad news.'

'As you wish.' George took a deep breath, slumped back in his chair and fixed his eyes on her. 'This feature, Britt ...' He allowed the words to hang in the air, as if undecided about its merits.

'Just tell me straight.'

'I'd like to know – what's your opinion on it?'

'It's what we agreed, by the deadline.'

'I have to say, it's not what I expected.'

'Just tell me what you think – preferably in fewer than fifty words.'

'I'm sorry. Are you in a rush to get away?'

'Yes.'

'Something to do with that news story of yours, is it? The one that involves the First Lady and others.'

George could read her mind sometimes. So it was best to tell the truth. 'Yes, it is to do with the news story.'

'Okay, fine. Here's what I think of your feature.' He leaned forward. 'It was interesting. I loved the side story about the novel-writing security woman. But a couple of things let it down. First of all, your insistence on American spellings. This is Britain. Not America. And the one thing that we British still have over the Americans is our ability to use the English language correctly.'

'That's a fair point.'

George looked slightly shocked by her reasonableness, but carried on. 'And secondly, you were overly descriptive in places. I don't need to know that the sunlight was cascading through her study window and bathing her books in a golden glow.'

Britt held up her hands. 'You're right. Take it all out.'

George looked even more shocked than before. 'Are you sure you haven't you been taking illegal substances today?'

'Quite sure. Is it in or not?'

George paused to think. Britt hoped she hadn't overdone the American spellings and flowery language. She couldn't be sure until she had received George's final verdict.

He screwed up his mouth. Then cracked his knuckles. Then extended his thumb. It hovered, parallel to the desk. Then he moved it, so it was pointing upwards. 'It's in.'

A wave of relief swept through her body. But there was no time to dwell on her triumph. 'Now, one more thing about my news story.'

'Go on.'

'I'm hoping I might have it for you tomorrow. For a story on Thursday.'

'Thursday is Independence Day. We've got a lot lined up already. Friday would be better.'

No. This story couldn't wait until Friday. That was because Thursday had two possible outcomes. Number one was the president appearing on the palace balcony at eleven o'clock and declaring his intentions. George wouldn't want to run a story about a missing president if he was no longer missing. So that would kill a Friday story. Outcome number two was one of the vice presidents announcing they would be standing as the Republican candidate. In that case, the world's media would be asking a million and one questions about the president's decision not to run for office again. They would want interviews, quotes and statements from him. The pressure would be so great that, within a few hours, the Government would have to admit the truth about the president's disappearance. Her Friday exclusive would be dead by Thursday teatime. No. She had to break the story in Thursday's edition. She took a step forward. 'It's Thursday or nothing.'

George contemplated her demand for a few seconds. 'Am I allowed to ask why?'

'It's a fast-moving story. We need to break it soon. Before somebody else does.'

George picked up a digi-pen on his desk and starting chewing the end of it. 'Is it political?'

Britt didn't flinch. 'Everything is political, George. That's what you're always telling us.'

'Yes, I am. But I hope it's not too political for *The Republican* at such a sensitive time.'

'It's a story that has to be told. If we don't tell it, someone else will.'

George chewed his digi-pen a bit more. 'Just answer me one question. Is it about the Pierogi Pact?'

Ah, yes – the Pierogi Pact. The deal the Polak brothers were supposed to have made in a pierogi bar, fifteen years ago. Jan would stand for two terms and then step aside for Oskar. No one knew if it ever happened. The brothers had always denied it. But the rumours had never gone away.

Britt shook her head. 'It's nothing to do with mythical deals in pierogi bars.'

'That's reassuring.' He was now jabbing his digi-pen towards her. 'If it's political, and it's running on Thursday, I'll need it verified by two independent sources. No. Make that three. And they all have to be working for different organisations.'

This was bullshit. 'Oh, play fair, George —'

'Sorry, but I can't afford a lawsuit. Or the embarrassment of running a political story on Independence Day that turns out to be anything less than one hundred per cent factually correct.'

Britt knew she should try and stay calm. But it was impossible. 'Three independent sources? Are you crazy?! I've got twenty-four hours to nail this.'

'You set the deadline. Not me.'

'If you're going to mess me around, I'll give the story to someone else.'

'You can't. You're contractually obliged to write stories only for *The Republican*. Check your terms and conditions. Give it to someone else, I fire you. And the paper will sue you.'

Britt scowled. He had her in a corner. And he knew it.

'So … do we have an agreement?' asked George.

'Yes,' she muttered. 'We do.'

'Excellent. Now, is there anything else?'

Through her anger, Britt realised there was something else. If her feature was going in tomorrow's edition, Howie would probably read it. And if he saw that she had written it, he would wonder why his journalist girlfriend, who was supposed to be on leave for the rest of this week, had interviewed the president's wife just hours after her husband had gone missing. Howie wasn't stupid. He would know Britt was on to something. Then he would contact George to demand that her investigation be terminated immediately. And knowing George, without an actual story in front of him, without the facts, he would agree. She couldn't risk that happening.

'Just one thing, George. Don't put the feature in my name.'

'Why would I do that?'

'Just do it.'

'I'm your editor. I give instructions. I don't take them.'

'Look, it could ruin my big story if certain people know I spoke with the First Lady. That's all you need to know.'

George thought about her proposal. 'Very well. We'll call you a feature writer.'

Britt hoped it would be the first, and last time, anyone called her that.

Chapter 17

After three hours in the Central Automated Monitoring System's control room, the heat and malfunctioning machinery were starting to overwhelm Howie. But he had to stay. He needed to figure out what exactly had gone wrong with it. Was it sabotage? Had someone wanted to extract the president from the palace – possibly against his will? That was what Howie suspected. Or had it just been a random failure of the cameras that had given the president the opportunity to escape – unmonitored and undetected – to spend some time on his own somewhere?

Howie was doing his best to find some answers. However, so far, he'd only managed to establish that the system's two-thousand-page instruction book had lots of pictures, but very few actual instructions.

Ivan had at least worked out how to switch the system on again – helped by the presence of a large red button with the words 'SWITCH SYSTEM ON' written on it. But every time the digi-screens flickered into life, they displayed a helpful message announcing the system was shutting down again. Ivan had been studying the instructions for what seemed like an eternity but was probably ten minutes. Eventually, he pointed a finger at the large red button. 'Okay. Turn on again.'

'We've done that seven times already,' grumbled Howie, wiping the sweat from his forehead.

Ivan paused. 'Once more?'

Howie blew some air over his face. 'Got any other ideas?'

'No. Don't do actual Tech.'

'So you keep telling me.'

'Your idea to bring me.'

'Just turn it on,' sighed Howie.

'It's hot. Give it five minutes. To cool down.'

Howie was the one who needed to cool down. He took a deep breath. The large intake of hot air hit his lungs and made him cough. Sweat trickled down his back. Down his arms. Down his legs. It was like being in Tech hell.

'Give me those instructions again,' ordered Howie. Ivan tossed them towards him. As Howie went to grab them, they slipped through his sweaty palms and hit the floor. Howie swore and stooped down. As he was about to pick up the book, he noticed that it had fallen open at a page entitled 'Manual shutdown'. Below the heading were some diagrams. They showed a panel that contained single digit numbers from zero to nine and the first six letters of the alphabet. 'Ivan, come here. I want you to look at something.'

Ivan wandered over. He examined the page. 'Manual shutdown. Ah, yes.'

'You actually know about this?' asked Howie, sounding sceptical.

'Standard protocol. Across all systems.'

'You can just shut the system down?'

'With a code. Eight digits.'

Howie pointed at the instruction book. 'Where's that keypad located?'

'Behind you.'

Howie turned around. And there it was – a metre off the ground. Easy to miss. But not hard to find. 'And why are there letters and numbers on it?'

'Hexadecimal. Number system. Base sixteen.'

'What does that mean in English?'

'Sixteen character choices. Not ten. More combinations.'

'Right. So who knows these codes?'

'We got eight auto-techs. In the palace. Each knows one digit. And its position. Code changes. Every twenty-four hours.'

The world of Tech never was straightforward. 'Let's say I wanted to try and crack the code, could I do it?'

'Human couldn't. Four billion-plus combinations. Take centuries.'

'What about an auto-tech?'

'Still take years.'

Despite this news, Howie still had a gut feeling that a machine was behind all this mayhem. 'What about if the auto-techs worked together?'

Ivan looked puzzled. 'They work for us. Not each other.'

'But if one of them wanted to get the other seven digits from the others, could they?'

'Not programmed to.'

This was proving to be hard work. Anything involving Tech always was. 'Could one of them be reprogrammed to do it?'

Ivan looked uneasy. 'In theory. Yes.'

'And could that be why we've got seven non-functioning auto-techs?'

'Possibly,' replied Ivan after a pause. 'Code extraction invasive. Damages systems.'

Howie felt like running outside, punching the air and screaming 'Eureka!' But there was still more Tech detective work to be done. 'My guess is that your friend Brian – as the only functioning auto-tech – got the codes from his mates and shut down this system manually, buggering up his pals in the process.'

'Difficult to prove. System memory wiped. No logs. No camera records.'

'Why did the memory wipe? It's just a shutdown. My e-terminal doesn't wipe when it shuts down.'

'There's an option. Memory wipe.' Ivan paused again. 'You need a code.'

'Eight digits? Same protocol?'

Ivan's face, despite the heat, was starting to lose its colour. 'Y-yes.'

'If I'm an evil genius and I get the shutdown code, I can probably get the memory wipe code, too?'

Ivan's face was a sickly beige now. 'Almost certainly.'

'And can you mess about with this system's restart function or whatever it's called?'

Ivan was whiter than the blank screens above his head. 'Yes, you can.' He gulped hard. 'No code needed. Just Tech know-how.'

'You mean it's something the auto-techs could do?'

'Affirmative, Howard,' croaked Ivan.

The pieces of this Tech puzzle were starting to fall into place. Just then, the door to the control room opened. It was Martha Blake.

'My goodness, it's horrid in here.' Martha left the door open and walked over. 'Tell me quickly before I pass out, have you two had any joy?'

Howie nodded. 'I've got a theory.'

Martha puffed out her cheeks. 'Enlighten me.'

Howie pointed at the keypad. 'I reckon it was manually shutdown from here.'

'You have evidence for that?' asked Martha.

Ivan shook his head. 'No. Just a theory.' He glanced at Howie. His expression was a mix of defiance and desperation. It was one Howie knew well. Vice presidents adopted it whenever they thought blame was coming their way.

Howie wasn't going to let Ivan squash his theory. 'Someone could have programmed an auto-tech to get the codes it needs to shut down the system and wipe the memory, and then disable the restart function. It could do it all from here in one visit.'

Martha wiped her brow. 'That would be worrying, if true.'

Ivan scowled. 'It's guesswork.'

Howie scowled back. 'Highly educated guesswork. And the prime suspect is Brian.'

'Where's the proof?' asked Ivan, sounding personally offended. 'He's top Tech. A great machine. You don't —'

'Thank you, Ivan. You can go home now,' interrupted Martha, with a polite smile. 'Just get back to us if you find out any more.'

Ivan sounded surprised. 'Oh. Right. Don't need me?'

'No. Just Howie.'

'I'll go then.'

Martha held her smile. 'Yes. And keep an eye on Brian. I think Howie could be right about that machine.'

Ivan nodded weakly and left the room without another word.

Martha grabbed Howie by the arm. 'We're leaving, too. We need to be at The Savoy in half an hour. I'll explain why when we get there. First of all, I need to brief you on a few developments.'

This sounded promising.

Martha pulled Howie towards the door. She checked that Ivan had gone. Then they began the short march up the corridor. 'We've identified a person of interest.' She checked they were completely alone. 'I had Oskar Polak followed after this morning's Code Red crisis meeting.'

'You can have vice presidents followed?'

'I can have presidents followed, if it involves the security of the British Republic.'

'Oskar did seem to be a man in a hurry this morning.'

'Yes. He certainly was. That was what aroused my suspicions.' Martha lowered her voice. 'Oskar had three meetings today. The first was with those two other vice presidents that shadow him everywhere. That meeting was over so quickly, we didn't have the chance to find out what it was about. But no matter – the second meeting was much more intriguing. It was a lunchtime rendezvous with a Russian businessman named Viktor Maxim.'

'Maxim – I've heard that name before.'

'You may well have. He's well-connected and ruthless in business. And according to our files, he has suspected criminal connections. Anyway, Oskar and Maxim had lunch at The Savoy. Some "business" was discussed.'

'What kind of business?'

'They didn't go into details. I assumed it was commercial, so I checked the register of vice presidents' interests. But Oskar is one of the few VPs with no entries. If you believe the register, he has no business interests at all.'

Something occurred to Howie. 'You don't think by "business" he might have meant … something more sinister?'

'That did cross my mind.'

Howie's voice was barely a whisper. 'Would Oskar really have his brother kidnapped? Or, you know …' Howie didn't want to say the word. He didn't have to. Martha understood.

'We mustn't jump to any conclusions. But Oskar has always been a very ambitious man. And, if political rumour is to be believed, Jan was never supposed to stand for a third term.'

Yes. The Pierogi Pact. The one subject the president never discussed with Howie. When the president was re-elected, five years ago, Howie had been told to use the same line with the media: 'The president's intentions with regards to a third term will be made clear in the year 2044 on Independence Day. Until then, he will not be commenting on speculation or rumour.' That line had never changed.

Martha continued. 'I haven't told you about Oskar's third and final meeting. It was late afternoon in Canary Wharf. Coincidentally, with a woman you met today – Cherry Blush. It was secretive and short. My agent suggested it could be an argument between two lovers.' She thought for a second. 'Oskar is married, isn't he?'

Howie nodded. 'But the First Lady seemed pretty sure it was Jan having a relationship with Cherry.'

'We can't rule that out completely. But the two men are identical twins. The First Lady, or someone she knows, might have seen Oskar and Cherry together, and assumed it was the president.'

Howie remembered something. 'That was it. Cherry mentioned Maxim's name when I went to see her. He owns the chain of gyms she works for – American Fitness. Just before I left, Cherry was ordered up to Maxim's office to see him. I didn't think it was strange at the time. But why would Maxim want to see one of his personal trainers face-to-face?'

'It would suggest their professional relationship is a close one.'

Howie's overheated brain was having problems processing this information. 'What does this all mean?'

'I suspect it means Oskar isn't telling us everything. And Miss Blush hasn't been telling you everything. They may both have information on the whereabouts of the president. And so might Viktor Maxim. But we don't have any hard evidence.'

'Can't you bring Oskar in for questioning?'

'He wasn't very talkative this morning. He'll be even less so if we formally question him. No. I'd prefer to keep watching him for the moment. You never know. He could lead us to the president.'

Howie nodded his agreement. 'And what about Cherry and Maxim? Are we going to bring them in?'

'I think it's best to keep our distance for the moment. If we make any kind of intervention they could alert Oskar to our interest.'

Martha was right. She was always right. They turned off the corridor and began walking down a flight of stairs. Howie felt his bleeper vibrate in his pocket. 'One second, Martha. It could be important.' He checked the e-comm. 'It's Maurice Skeets. My least-favourite journalist. He's chasing me for an update on the names he provided. I won't get back to him.'

'Ah, yes. The three names. I've got a bit more information on them.'

'Anything interesting?'

'The Russian woman, Petra Putinov, works for Mr Maxim's firm, Maxim International, and reports directly to him. He encourages her to make government contacts at the highest levels. She's met with heads of state from several countries during her career. So it's possible Maxim might have sent her to meet with Jan.'

'What about the other two?'

'Sky Eastern is a colourful character. American. A little eccentric. Throws her company's money at a lot of worthy projects around the world. And a lot of her own money. But for all the public relations work, the company is still hungry for old oil. And according to the information I've seen, they're very good at finding it.'

They reached the bottom of the stairs and made their way towards the main entrance.

Howie put his bleeper back in his pocket. 'Any idea if what Maurice said about Eastern Oil wanting to do some test drilling over here is true?'

'Yes. I've had it confirmed that they're awaiting approval from the British Government. There have been official meetings at just about every level you can imagine for over a year. It's still up in the air. The decision is ultimately for Jan to make.'

'So he might have met with this Sky Eastern for perfectly legitimate reasons?'

'Yes. Unless he was taking a bribe.'

'What?' The idea seemed ridiculous to Howie.

'Why not? One has to keep an open mind about these things. All energy companies pay bribes. And there's no reason why they wouldn't go straight to the top.'

Howie had never contemplated the president being corrupt before. But he'd learnt that nothing was impossible in government.

They walked along in silence for a few seconds. Then Martha spoke. 'There was a third name Maurice gave you – Olga Frik. She works for Auto-Tech Industries. She's the least troublesome of the three names. But she's under pressure to secure a new Tech-support contract with the Government. It accounts for almost half their turnover.'

Something occurred to Howie. 'You don't think someone at Auto-Tech Industries could have sabotaged the auto-techs, do you? Maybe reprogrammed Brian?'

'Why would they do that? It's their Tech. It wouldn't look very good with a contract to be renewed.'

'I know. But they could come in. Fix it all. Tell us that, after five years of using the old models, we need to upgrade to the new ones. That's how Tech works, isn't it? They design everything to bugger up after five years.'

'Hmmm. I hadn't thought of that.' Martha smiled. 'You're getting rather good at these special investigations. But let's focus our attentions on Oskar, Cherry and Mr Maxim for the moment.'

They had reached the main entrance. A car was waiting.

Martha gestured towards the vehicle. 'And now, The Savoy.'

As Howie got into the car, his stomach grumbled. It must be seven hours since his lunch. He hoped this trip to a top restaurant would involve dinner. Maybe even a pudding. He wouldn't have to wait long to find out.

Chapter 18

Britt pushed open the door of the Grafton Arms and looked around. The lights were dimmed in anticipation of the evening's musical entertainment. It was difficult to see much through her dark sunglasses. But she was Pellie Cann this evening. So she had to wear shades. Even if it was a mid-April evening in a badly lit London pub.

It was just before eight. The band who were playing this evening, Super-Mega Electro Thrash, were still setting up on a small stage at the front of the pub. Two towering loudspeakers, with the words 'Warning: Keep Clear' written on them in white capital letters, stood either side of the stage. This was going to be a noisy evening. Still, at least Herbert the security guy would feel confident enough to discuss a Code Red crisis without fear of being overheard. Assuming he showed up, of course.

Britt looked around to see if he was already there, lurking in one of the pub's hidden corners. There was a group of four young people in one of the snugs. But they were all speaking Polish, so weren't of any interest to her. Then she peered over the top of her sunglasses at two twenty-something guys with London accents at the back of the pub. No. Neither of them were Herbert.

She bought herself a tube of cola at the bar and sat down at a table by the wall, close to the stage. From here, she could see who was coming in the front door, but stay in the shadows. And no one was paying her any attention. That was just how Pellie Cann liked it.

A few minutes passed. Half a dozen short-haired men and women in their twenties wearing 'I'm a Super-Mega Electro

Thrasher' T-shirts drifted in and headed for the bar. But Herbert wasn't one of them. Then a blonde woman arrived, wearing sunglasses even bigger than Britt's, and a large hat. She didn't look like a Super-Mega Electro Thrasher. So, out of curiosity, Britt followed her movements.

The new arrival bought a tube of mineral water and sat down at the table next to Britt's. As the woman settled into her seat, she pulled her hat down as far as it would go and pushed her sunglasses to the top of her nose. Then she held her bleeper up to her face and checked the time. Tonight must be the night for secret meetings, thought Britt.

Super-Mega Electro Thrash's shaven-headed lead singer stepped up to the microphone. He mumbled an introduction and the rest of the band burst into deafening life. His bandmates were certainly thrashing at their electronic instruments. But it didn't sound super-mega. Nowhere near. But Britt would have to sit here and endure it. Just like the blonde woman next to her, who was already grimacing and covering her ears with her hands.

Britt was grateful when the sound-spheres and screeching electro-bars came to an abrupt halt at the end of the first song. As the whoops and cheers echoed around the pub, a man Britt recognised walked through the door. It wasn't Herbert or one of Howie's colleagues. It was a journalist. One that Britt had worked with at *The Republican* a few years ago, before he'd gone freelance and on to greater things. His name was Maurice Skeets.

This was bad news. If Maurice saw through Pellie Cann's disguise and started referring to her as 'Britt', it could ruin everything. Herbert would fly away as soon as he sensed any kind of deception. She turned away and put her hand to her face.

As she held her breath, she could hear footsteps walking towards her. They must be Maurice's. She swore before she could stop herself. He must have recognised her.

Britt's body tensed and she waited for Maurice to say her name. But he didn't. He said someone else's name.

'Kaia-Liisa?' he asked, sounding unsure.

Britt snatched a glance at him. He was talking to the blonde woman, who responded with a nod.

Maurice sat down. 'Nice to put a face to a name, at last. So where are we with everything?'

'That's why I wanted to see you in person,' replied the woman. 'Something's happened. Something that makes things difficult.'

The band erupted into deafening life again and Britt turned to face the stage. This time, the song was even worse. Someone was playing a digi-trumpet – possibly for the first time. Hopefully the last.

At the end of the song, there was still no sign of Herbert. Britt was starting to worry that he wasn't going to show up. He'd been desperate for help when they'd met earlier today. Surely he was going to accept Pellie Cann's offer of assistance? He would be a fool to refuse it.

But then Britt thought again. Was it possible that someone else had offered him help? Maybe his uncle Bogdan had sorted everything out? Or maybe Herbert had decided to tell his girlfriend about their planned rendezvous and she'd made it clear that he wasn't going to meet a strange American woman in a pub? Or maybe he was still asleep at home, after his nightmare shift? There was no point guessing. Either Herbert was going to show up or he wasn't. And if he wasn't, there was nothing she could do about it.

As Super-Mega Electro Thrash got ready to blast out their next song, Britt could just about make out the whispered conversation next to her. She was bored. So she listened.

'You can't get me any more info?' asked Maurice.

'No,' replied the woman, as if repeating herself for the tenth time.

'Why not?' he demanded.

'I told you. Something happened at work.'

'What thing?'

'A work thing. And now I've got someone sat in my office watching my every move.'

'Who's that then?'

'A pair of eyes that sees everything. That's all you need to know.' She sighed wearily. 'If I try and get more information right now, I'll get caught. I'll lose my job.'

Maurice's tone was tetchy. 'You want this bloody oil company exposed or don't you?'

'Of course I do. British citizens have a right to know that the Government might allow drilling again. Eastern Oil's new Tech is an environmental disaster waiting to happen. This could have consequences for us and for future —'

'Yeah, yeah,' interrupted Maurice. 'Spare me the sermon. When can you get me more info on the Sky Eastern meetings? And the others?'

'A couple of weeks maybe.'

'A fortnight? Is that the best you can bloody well do?!'

The woman's voice was firm. 'Yes. It is.'

'Then that'll have to do, I suppose,' grumbled Maurice.

The opening bars of the third song blasted from the huge speakers and the last few seconds of the couple's exchange were drowned out. Their conversation had sounded interesting. Maurice had a reputation for big stories that exposed corruption at the highest level. And the woman was obviously one of his well-placed contacts. But Britt had a big story of her own to worry about. She just hoped that her own well-placed contact would be walking through that door any second now.

Maurice got up, grunted a goodbye and left. Two minutes later, at the end of the third song, the woman followed him out of the door.

Britt stayed for the terrible fourth song. And the slightly less terrible fifth song. And the dismal sixth song. By this time, she was thinking of getting up and leaving. It was self-imposed electro-thrash torture.

To Britt's relief, the band's lead singer announced that they were going to take a break. The lights went up. As they did, a familiar face appeared at the door. It was Herbert the security guy.

Britt felt like a dog owner arriving home after a long overseas trip. She waved frantically at Herbert and called his name. He waved back with equal enthusiasm and bounded over – her little Labrador puppy. So full of excitement to see her.

'Sorry I'm late, Pellie,' he panted.

'No problem, Herbie,' replied Britt in an American drawl. 'Great to see you.' She resisted the urge to pat him on the head and tickle his tummy, and let him settle into his chair.

He widened his eyes and lowered his voice. 'I got called back to work.'

Britt's sixth sense told her this wasn't going to be good news. She stifled a frown. 'Oh, yeah?'

'I think everything's been sorted. Well ... from my point of view, at least.'

A hundred different swear words ran through Britt's mind. But none of them seemed to do justice to the news she'd just received.

'Good old Uncle Bogdan,' beamed Herbert. 'He's come to the rescue.'

Just as Britt had suspected. Good old Uncle Bogdan. Pellie Cann wouldn't be needed now.

'You want another drink?' asked Herbert, buzzing with positive energy.

'No, I'm good,' muttered Britt, oozing negative energy.

'Come on, it's a celebration! I'll get you something British. Something alcoholic.'

Before Britt could protest, Herbert had jumped up and was heading towards the bar. She sighed dejectedly. She didn't feel like consuming alcohol. She had won a lot of victories today. But she felt defeated right now. Defeated and exhausted.

Britt checked her bleeper. It was coming up to half past eight. She thought about getting up and leaving. But she didn't. If she could summon up enough energy to play with Herbert for a short while, perhaps he would give her something. A small scrap of information that could help her. It was worth a try. She wouldn't abandon this puppy just yet.

Herbert returned with two tubes of flat, green, cloudy liquid. 'It's a beer called Britain's Finest.'

Britt knew what it was called. Howie drank it sometimes. It was Britain's worst.

Herbert held up his tube. 'I love the stuff. Go on. See what you think.'

Britt needed to play ball, so she sipped her murky drink. It was even more revolting than she'd remembered. She tried not to grimace. 'It's … different.' She forced a laugh. 'But you gotta try everything once!'

Herbert smiled knowingly. 'Yeah, you have.' He moved his chair a little closer to Britt. 'Why don't you take those sunglasses off?' He paused. 'Then I can see your face properly.'

She tilted her head and smiled. 'I have very sensitive retinas, remember?'

'Oh, yeah.' He thought for a second. 'Then maybe we could go somewhere … darker? My pod's not far away. It's only twenty-five square metres but you can squeeze two people in it. If they don't mind, you know …' Herbert swallowed hard. '… being quite close to each other.'

Britt raised her eyebrows. 'It sounds very cosy.'

'It is. And I've got a six-pack of Britain's Finest in the cooler that we could crack open.'

Britt looked Herbert in the eyes. This puppy really wanted to play. 'What about your girlfriend, Herbie?' she asked, with a shrug of the shoulders. 'I mean, won't she mind if I come back to your pod and … you know …' – she leaned in to him slightly – '… crack open Britain's Finest?'

Herbert's face was starting to flush. The puppy was getting over-excited. 'She's, erm … not really my girlfriend. It's a casual thing. We don't live together.'

'Oh, I see,' drawled Britt.

'Anyway, I prefer older women.' He sipped his drink. 'Foreign older women. So shall we drink up and go back to my pod?'

This puppy was turning into a wolf. A very unsubtle and impatient wolf. It was a complete transformation of the sad little creature who had sat here this morning, with its tail between its legs. But Britt could work this to her advantage. It was time to throw him a ball. 'First I need you to tell me if your crisis situation is still Code Red.'

Herbert thought for a few seconds and then nodded.

That was reassuring news. Now it was time to toss the ball a little further. She whispered in his ear. 'We're talking about the main man, yes?'

Herbert looked nervous. 'I don't want to say his name in public. I could say it in private. My pod would be a good place to —'

'Just tell me, Herbie. And then we can, you know …' She breathed heavily in his ear.

Herbie almost dropped his drink. 'Yeah. It's the main man. The big cheese.'

'The big Polish cheese, right?'

'Yeah, yeah.' Herbert was sounding more impatient by the second.

'And he's still missing?'

'Yeah, yeah, yeah. No one knows where the cheese is.'

That was the news she'd wanted to hear. Britt now had confirmation from one reliable source who worked in Buckingham Palace. She needed two more sources. But first she needed to squeeze all the information that she could from Herbert. 'Tell me, Herbie – what was it you did, or didn't do, when you screwed up last night?'

'That doesn't matter. It's all sorted.' He zipped up his jacket. 'Can we go? I've got a three-cheese lasagne in the freezer back at the pod.' He stared into Britt's eyes. 'But it'll need warming up.'

'Don't be so impatient. We got all evening. And all night.'

Herbert's eyes lit up. 'Have we?' If Herbert had a tail, it would have been wagging furiously by now.

Britt's American drawl became more seductive. 'Just answer my question and then we'll go back to your pod.'

Herbert checked no one was listening. 'Okay. I was in the area of the fridge where they keep the big cheese. At about half past ten, I went to one of the master bedrooms to have a little nap. Six hours later, I woke up. I checked on the cheese. It wasn't where it should've been.' He lowered his voice to a whisper. 'Then I checked the camera system. It failed at eleven – every camera inside and outside the fridge. I didn't raise the alarm until five. The cheese was taken out of the fridge during those six hours. We know it's not hidden in a corner somewhere because my uncle has turned that fridge upside down. The cheese is gone.' He shrugged his shoulders. 'I messed up. I know. But once you get into one of those beds, it's hard to get out.' He circled the edge of his drinking tube with his index finger. 'The bed in my pod is a bit like that.'

It was time for Herbert to go walkies. Britt took her digi-pen and pad out of her bag and switched them on. 'Write down your address.'

'Why?' asked Herbert, with a look of disappointment. 'We can go there together.'

'I have to file a report first. You go on ahead and I'll meet you at the pod. But don't worry. It won't take me long and the report won't mention you.' She touched his hand. 'I swear on the life of the president of the New States.'

Herbert gazed at her with a dreamy expression. 'You are a super-mega lady, Pellie Cann.'

And you're a super-mega dumb ass, thought Britt.

Herbert scribbled down his address and handed the digi-pen and pad back to Britt. Then he stood up. 'My six-pack is going to be waiting for you. And my three-cheese lasagne.'

They were going to have a long wait. Super-Mega Electro Thrash were starting to return to the stage for the second half. But Pellie Cann's performance was over.

Herbert moved to the door. 'See you in a bit, Pellie.'

Britt waved and Herbert disappeared out of sight. She waited a moment, to make sure he was far enough away from the pub. Then she got up and left, just as the band were launching into their new song, *Thrash it all night*.

Britt was too tired to thrash anything. She was heading home.

Chapter 19

Howie and Martha were sitting at a table by the window in The Savoy hotel's exclusive Premier Diners restaurant. It was the number-one place for A-list celebrities, top politicians and big-business people to come and enjoy a meal. And Howie was more than enjoying his experience. He'd already consumed a jumbo prawn cocktail and the largest sirloin steak he'd ever seen. He was now patiently waiting to order one of the super-mega-sized desserts, while Martha half-heartedly jabbed a fork at her salmon salad.

Apart from the fabulous food, things hadn't gone as expected at The Savoy. They were here because Martha was sure that Daisy Gray would still turn up for her eight o'clock dinner date with the chief of police. But it was nearly nine now, and neither Daisy nor the chief had set foot inside the restaurant.

Martha dropped her knife and fork on her plate and pushed it away. 'I'm sorry for wasting your time, Howie. But I don't think they're coming.'

'You did tell her to cancel it.'

'I know I did. I also told you to stay sober today.'

Howie looked down at his empty plate. 'Point taken.'

'I'm sorry. That's unfair. Even with your unscheduled afternoon power nap, you did extremely well for a first day. You've obtained some excellent information. I'm impressed.'

'Thanks. But we've still got to try and piece it all together and work out what the bloody hell happened.'

'Yes.' Martha twisted her lip. 'I just hope Vice President Gray hasn't already spilled the beans to the chief of police. If the boys in sky blue get involved, I can't see this staying Code Red confidential for very long.' Martha shook her head. 'I should have got one of my agents to follow her. It's my stupid mistake.'

Howie had a thought. 'Maybe they met up, like they planned, but went somewhere else for dinner?'

Martha's ears pricked up. 'That's possible.'

'Daisy is a pain in the arse, but she's not stupid. She knows how you work. She probably guessed that you, or one of your team, would be here.'

'But there are hundreds of restaurants in London. They could be anywhere.'

'Yeah. But the chief's office is only round the corner. If they did keep the arrangement, I bet they didn't go far.' Howie pointed out of the window. 'The Strand Palace Hotel has a half-decent restaurant. The vice presidents have their Christmas parties there.'

Martha stood up. 'Then what are we waiting for? They should be on their desserts by now.'

Howie was also on his dessert. But he was a special investigator now. And, just like James Bond, he would have to put his own personal interests to one side for the sake of national security. Dessert would have to wait.

Martha gestured to a waiter and asked for the bill. Then she turned to Howie. 'Can you pay with the cash I gave you? It'll save me rummaging through my bag.'

Howie cleared his throat. 'I spent it.'

Martha's voice went up an octave. 'What?! All in the pub? What were you doing? Buying a round of drinks for the whole civil service?'

'No. I, erm … had to pay cash for an appointment to see Cherry Blush. That gym is an expensive place.'

Martha's voice went up another octave. 'Two thousand pounds for an appointment with a personal trainer?! That's downright criminal!'

'It was a complete con. But all legal.'

Martha took a deep breath and her voice returned to normal. 'She's obviously learnt a lot from her employer.'

Howie didn't think it was the right time to mention the five thousand pounds he'd also paid for a month's gym membership on his credit card.

'Don't worry,' sighed Martha. 'I've got cash.' A minute later, the waiter arrived and the bill was paid. Then Martha took Howie by the arm. 'Come on. Let's see if you're right.'

They rushed out of The Savoy, dodged the evening traffic and ran into the Strand Palace Hotel. Once they had located the main restaurant, they started to wander around, ignoring the curious looks from diners. It didn't take them long to find what they were looking for – Daisy Gray and the chief of police at a corner table. Howie could see the chief was eating a chocolate pudding. His stomach rumbled at the sight of it. This special investigating was hungry work. He would kill for one of those puddings right now.

Martha was the first to their table. The couple didn't notice her arrival. Martha coughed and the chief of police looked up. When he saw Martha's face, he stopped eating his pudding and sat back.

'What's the matter, Freddie?' asked Daisy, completely oblivious to Martha's presence. 'You full up already?'

Howie arrived at their table. 'If he can't manage it, I can. Be a shame to waste it.' He was only half-joking.

Daisy jerked her head around. As soon as she saw Howie and Martha, her eyes filled with fear. 'What are you two doing here?'

Martha scowled. 'We might ask you the same question.'

'W–w–we're just having dinner,' stuttered Daisy.

'Last minute change of venue, was it?' asked Martha, her voice dripping with irony.

'We didn't fancy The Savoy,' mumbled Daisy.

Martha was merciless. 'And has anything interesting popped up in conversation, Vice President Gray? Anything work-related, for instance?'

Daisy looked petrified. 'What, y-you mean the w-w-work thing we talked about, this morning?'

Martha bit her lip and nodded.

'Oh, w-well. I might have m-mentioned it.' Daisy forced a laugh and composed herself. 'You know how these things happen. One minute you're choosing the side orders for your main course, the next you're telling a trusted external stakeholder that the president's gone miss —'

'Let's not tell the whole world, eh?' interrupted Howie.

Martha gave Daisy a look that would have wilted a cactus. 'With all due respect, Vice President Gray, I think it's time you left the restaurant and went home.' Martha turned to the chief of police. 'Howie and I will stay here – to see just how much of the work thing you've discussed.'

Daisy stood up. 'R-right. I'll ... I'll get going.'

The chief of police stood up. 'We'll catch up soon, Daisy. Don't worry. I'll smooth everything out here. And pay the bill. Goodnight.'

'Night,' muttered Daisy. She didn't say another word and scurried out of the restaurant without looking back.

The chief of police turned towards Martha. 'That was a little unnecessary, Martha. She's the vice president for homeland security. Not a junior civil servant.'

'Yes. And I am the head of the National Security and Intelligence Service, in case you'd forgotten. And this, Frederick, is a Code Red security matter. So I make the decisions about who knows about it and who doesn't. Vice President Gray has no authority to tell you anything.'

'I respect you deeply, Martha. But you're being overdramatic. I'm the chief of police, not the exiled king of England.' He stood up and turned to Howie. 'I'm sorry. We haven't been introduced. I'm Frederick English, London's chief of police. You can call me Freddie.'

Howie shook his hand. 'The name's Pond. Howie Pond. Presidential spokesperson and, as from today, special investigator.'

Freddie smiled. 'Ah, Howie Pond. Licence to eat chocolate pudding, eh?'

Howie chuckled and gazed down at Freddie's dessert. 'Something like that.' It wouldn't be professional to ask Freddie if he really could finish it. Not yet, anyway.

Martha's nostrils flared. 'I'll continue to call you Frederick, if you don't mind.'

'If formality makes you more comfortable, then please do so. Now, sit down. And we can discuss this work matter.'

Howie pulled up an extra chair and the trio sat down.

Martha didn't waste any time getting to the point. 'How much did she tell you?'

Freddie lowered his voice. 'Vice President Gray told me about your missing person, the ongoing search at the palace and that the National Security and Intelligence Service wants this all to themselves.'

Martha scowled and shook her head. 'I knew it.'

'She told me because she's anxious that everything should be done to locate your missing person. And she believed it to be in the best interests of national security.'

'I make that decision, Frederick.'

'So you say. But that doesn't mean it's always the right decision.'

This was turning into a real heavyweight clash. The only thing that seemed to be stopping them from lunging at each other was the half-eaten chocolate pudding in the middle of the table. Howie had better leave it there for now.

Martha spoke her next words slowly and clearly. 'Read my lips. I don't want the police involved.'

'Why not?' asked Freddie. 'We are the very people who can help you find your missing person. We're the eyes and ears of London.'

'You're also the mouths of London,' snarled Martha. 'Very big ones.'

'If you're just going to insult me, I can head for home right now. Oh. And I'll be alerting my operational commander to your work matter on my way there.'

Martha leaned forward, her voice less aggressive than before. 'Look, Frederick. I cannot afford for this information to reach the public domain in any shape or form. Our missing person is unlikely to be walking the streets of London waiting for one of your foot patrols to wander past him. So for now, we play it my way.'

Freddie mulled over her words. 'Okay. Here's the deal. I won't pass this down the chain for another twenty-four hours. But I can't hang on to it for any longer. Considering who we're talking about, I think I'm being generous.'

Martha paused to think and then responded. 'Forty-eight hours.'

'No, twenty-four hours is my final offer. If I get hauled before a vice-presidential committee in three months' time, it's going to be hard enough to explain a day's delay on my part. I could lose my job for that alone. Police operations are my responsibility. Not yours. If I sit on this for more than twenty-four hours, I'll look incompetent.'

Martha breathed in through her nose and stared at Freddie. 'Alright. Twenty-four hours. That will have to do. But on one condition.'

'What's that?' asked Freddie.

'I want to run some names past you. You tell me if there's anything I should know. And this goes no further than the three of us.'

'Of course, Martha. Anything I can do to help. Fire away.'

'Sky Eastern. Chairwoman of Eastern Oil.'

Freddie's face looked blank. 'Do you have a photo you can show me?'

Martha sighed. 'I don't have photos of anyone. She's American. In her sixties. Wears lots of jewellery.'

'I'm sorry. That doesn't help.'

'Let's move on. How about Olga Frik from Auto-Tech Industries?'

Freddie shook his head. 'No. Her name means absolutely nothing.'

'What about this one – Cherry Blush? She's a personal trainer at American Fitness.'

Freddie chuckled. 'These aren't exactly Britain's most wanted, are they?'

Martha raised her voice. 'Does the name mean anything to you or not, Frederick?'

'Alas, no. Who's next on the list?'

She lowered her voice. 'Viktor Maxim. He's a Russian businessman.'

Freddie looked thoughtful and rubbed his chin. 'Hmmm. Viktor Maxim, you say?'

'Yes. I do say.' Martha waited for a few seconds. 'I can tell it's a name you recognise, Frederick.'

'Your powers of detection are as strong as ever, Martha. I have heard of him. Viktor Maxim is a Russian chap. He owns a large number of businesses. In fact, I believe he bought that American Fitness place you just mentioned.'

Martha half-smiled. 'Yes. He's bought a lot of things. And people, if you believe the rumours.'

Freddie shook his head. 'Personally, I don't. One or two individuals have come forward and made claims about him. Bribery, black-market activities, extortion, kidnap. That sort of thing.'

Howie nearly jumped out of his chair. 'Kidnap?! Who's he kidnapped?'

Freddie laughed off the question. 'No one. It's all unsubstantiated nonsense. He's Russian, a successful businessman and he enjoys a millionaire's lifestyle. A lot of people don't like those three facts. They make false allegations.'

'And you investigate these allegations?' asked Martha.

'When resources allow.'

'So how many times is that?'

'Approximately?'

'Exactly.'

Freddie thought hard. 'Exactly … zero.'

'I knew it!'

'I can't waste time on wild goose chases. It would be irresponsible of me to devote valuable police resources to —'

'Maxim is here this week,' interrupted Martha. 'Did you know that?'

Freddie nodded. 'Yes. I spotted him in The Savoy yesterday evening.'

Martha's expression was becoming more serious. 'You spotted him? Or you met him?'

Freddie chuckled. 'Yes. That's right. We were finalising our plans to kidnap your missing person. Once we've got the ransom, that's it for me. Early retirement. I'll be writing my memoirs. And don't fret – I shall be very kind to you, Martha.'

'I'm glad you find this funny, Frederick.'

Freddie held up his hands. 'Forgive me. I'm being flippant at a time of crisis. And I sense Mr Maxim is a person of considerable interest to you. So let me tell you this – he is not a person of interest to the police. He has never been arrested, charged or convicted of anything in this country.'

Martha's eyes widened and she fixed them on Freddie. 'That might suggest he's being protected.'

'Evidence, Martha. Evidence. Always the starting point of any enquiry. And if you have any evidence for that allegation, I would be more than happy to review it.'

'Do you know Petra Putinov?' asked Martha. 'She works for Maxim.'

'I don't know her. But whenever Maxim has dinner at The Savoy with a woman, it's always the same one. And I've heard the name Petra mentioned. So that's probably her.'

'Was she there with Viktor Maxim on Monday evening, Frederick?'

'Yes. I believe she was.'

'And were they dining with anyone else?'

'I had to leave early. So I can't give you a full list of his dining companions.' Freddie clasped his hands. 'Now, are there any more names you want to run past me? Because I was halfway through a chocolate pudding.'

'No. That's all. You've been moderately helpful.' Martha got up to leave. 'Howie, are you coming with me or staying here?'

Howie's stomach rumbled so loudly, the people at the next table could hear it.

'You'll be staying,' continued Martha. 'Very well. Just don't overdo it. It's going to be another long day tomorrow. And I need you to be firing on all cylinders.'

Howie couldn't remember the last time he'd fired on all cylinders. But he wouldn't worry Martha with that information right now. 'I won't stay long. See you tomorrow morning.'

'No later than seven o'clock,' ordered Martha. 'Earlier if you can.' She turned to Freddie. 'Not a word to anyone for twenty-four hours. Otherwise, I might start focusing some of my organisation's resources at Mr Maxim's wide range of business activities. And his wide network of associates. Understood?'

Freddie sat back in his chair. 'As a leading law enforcer, I would naturally welcome such a far-reaching investigation.' He put his right index finger to his lips. 'But I shall not be breathing a word to anyone for the next twenty-four hours. So there'll be no need to launch any such enquiry.'

'I'm glad to hear it.' Martha took a deep breath. 'For everyone's sake.' Then she turned and strode from the restaurant.

Freddie looked at Martha. Then he looked at Howie. Then Howie looked at the remains of the chocolate pudding.

Freddie laughed. 'Go on, finish it, my friend. I sense your need is greater than mine.'

'You sure?'

'Positive. Be my guest.'

Howie reached over, took Freddie's plate and began scooping the pudding into his mouth.

Freddie smiled. 'I like you, Howie. I know I've only known you for a few minutes. But I have a natural instinct for people. You're a good man. An honest man. Just like myself. And we honest men need to stick together in this dog-eat-dog world of ours.'

Martha obviously had her doubts about Freddie. But Howie's gut feeling was different. He was the kind of guy Howie could spend a couple of hours with at the Two Chairmen after work. He would go with his instincts. 'Sounds good to me, Freddie,' he spluttered, his mouth full of pudding.

'Excellent. Now, I'd like to tap into your brilliant brain about vice-presidential appointments.'

Howie nodded. He was really starting to like Freddie.

'Am I right in thinking that presidents have the power to make such appointments from outside the party?'

Howie finished his last mouthful and then answered. 'The Democrats did it a couple of times. The Republicans haven't yet. But there's nothing to stop them. The president would need to demonstrate that the person had exceptional talent and skill. And it would have to be someone the president trusted, obviously.'

'Obviously.' He leaned in to Howie. 'Let me give you a hypothetical scenario. After the election, the president – whoever that may be – wants to reward a senior official for his outstanding contribution to his profession with a vice-presidential position.' Freddie thought for a moment. 'For example, for services to law enforcement.'

'You mean someone like yourself?'

Freddie's eyes filled with surprise. 'I wasn't thinking of me. It doesn't have to be me. But if it helps you to create a picture in your mind for the purposes of my hypothesis ... yes. Let's say it's me.' Freddie moved his chair a little nearer to Howie. 'How would the appointment process work exactly?'

Before Howie had a chance to reply, Freddie's bleeper made an urgent noise from his top pocket. He fished it out and read his message. 'Just one moment, my friend. It's work.'

'Of course,' replied Howie, imagining himself and Vice President Freddie English, lunching in the Two Chairmen and sharing anecdotes about the incompetence of the other vice presidents.

Freddie got to his feet. 'I'm terribly sorry, Howie, but I'm going to have to dash.'

Howie stood up. 'That's a shame. It's been good to meet you. Hope to see you again sometime.'

'The feeling is mutual.' Freddie handed Howie a small card. 'That's my personal bleeper number. I carry it everywhere. If you get into any bother, don't hesitate to contact me.'

'I will do. Thanks.'

Freddie gave Howie one of the firmest handshakes he'd ever received. 'It's been a pleasure. You're a man like me, Howie Pond. We're men who get things done. Men destined for greater things.' He smiled. 'Men who love a good chocolate pudding.'

Howie grinned. 'We shared a pudding. We're bonded for life.'

'Good man. Goodnight, Howie. Stay safe. And happy hunting.'

Howie waved goodbye. 'See you, Freddie.'

Howie watched Freddie walk up to a waiter, pay his bill in cash and then rush from the restaurant. Howie hoped he'd see him again soon.

It was late now. Britt would be wondering where Howie was. It was time to go back to his pod and get some sleep. Tomorrow would be an important day. Perhaps the most important of his life.

Chapter 20

It was just before ten. Britt was wide awake in bed, waiting for Howie to come home. She had switched off all the pod's light beams. Howie would assume Britt was asleep. That would make him more likely to start telling the cat about his day at work. To help things along, Britt had left a bottle of Howie's favourite whisky and a jug of cola on the kitchen table. He would see them and find it hard to resist having a drink before bedtime. And he was always more chatty after a whisky and cola.

Lying in the darkness, the reality of what she'd just done made her whole body tingle. She had set a trap for her own boyfriend. The man she loved. And who loved her. The man she trusted. And who trusted her. The man she wanted to marry. And who wanted to change the subject whenever she mentioned weddings. The guilt disappeared.

The cat meowed from the kitchen. Britt had fed her thirty minutes ago, so she couldn't be hungry. Howie must be back. She heard the pod's front door slide shut, followed by the flick of a light-beam switch. Then Howie spoke. 'Hello, pussycat. How's your day been? Mine's been pretty eventful.'

This was a promising start. Britt jumped out of bed, crept up to the bedroom door and listened.

'Mum's fed you,' continued Howie. 'That's good. And your Dad's been fed, too. At The Savoy. Yeah. Then at the Strand Palace Hotel. Lucky old Dad, eh?'

Howie had always had a healthy appetite. Sometimes too healthy. But even on his appetite's healthiest days, he'd never visited two top restaurants in one evening. Britt's thoughts were interrupted by the clink of glass. And the sound of a jug being poured. She clenched her right fist and mouthed 'Yes!' Her plan had worked.

'Just a cheeky drink before bedtime. I know I shouldn't. But it is my birthday.'

Britt heard the cat meow again. Howie made a fuss of her. The cat purred. Then there was silence. He was probably enjoying his whisky and cola. Nothing to worry about. Any second now, he would start downloading all the details of his day into his four-legged friend. A minute passed. Then two. But all Britt heard were the sounds of running water and glass being placed on metal. Another pause. Then a cupboard closing. Followed by the final sound – the bedroom door sliding open.

Before Britt had time to dive back under the duvet, Howie had switched on the light beam. He let out a cry of surprise when he saw her standing there. 'Bloody hell! I thought you were asleep.'

That was the idea. She would have to think of something. 'I was,' she yawned, rubbing her eyes and stretching. 'But you woke me up with all that banging in the kitchen. Drinking before bedtime, were you? Don't deny it.'

Howie lowered his head. 'Sorry, B.'

'You look knackered. Busy day at the palace?'

'Oh, erm … yeah,' he mumbled. 'Busy and boring.'

Howie would have normally spent the next few minutes ranting about a dumb vice president, an uncooperative private secretary or a pain-in-the-arse journalist. His days were always busy. But they were never boring. She tried another question. 'Have you had dinner?'

Howie started to get undressed. 'Yeah.'

Britt got back into bed and waited for him to elaborate. Food was his favourite subject. He loved talking about it almost as much as eating it. But that was all he had to say. He just kept taking his clothes off. Britt was tempted to meow, to keep the conversation flowing, but she decided to stick with human communication for the moment. 'What did you eat?'

'I just grabbed a sandwich from the palace canteen.'

He was lying about dinner. He must have been at The Savoy and Strand Palace for a good reason. A work reason. A Code-Red-crisis reason. But he wasn't going to reveal any more details. And he would be asleep in a couple of minutes. She made a split-second decision to drop a bombshell and see his reaction. She got back under the duvet and made herself comfortable. Then she dropped it. 'I saw the president this afternoon.'

Howie froze, just as his suit trousers fell to the floor. He looked shocked. Then he tried to hide his shock with an expression of mild interest. 'Where was that?'

Britt's first instinct was to lie. Canary Wharf wasn't the kind of place she went on a day off. Howie might get suspicious if she told him. But then she thought again. She would sound more convincing if she told him what she'd seen. 'I took a trip to Canary Wharf. Just for something to do. And I saw the president. Not in his official car. But walking down the street. Like an ordinary citizen.'

Howie's forehead wrinkled. 'You definitely saw the president?'

'He was trying to hide his face but I caught a flash of it. I'm certain it was him.' She wouldn't mention Cherry Blush. He might get suspicious.

Howie kicked his trousers from his ankles and began undressing again. 'What time?'

'Late afternoon. A bit before half-four.'

Howie took off his shirt. His stomach showed clear evidence of his recent restaurant trips. 'Where exactly was this?'

'Outside the American Fitness gym.'

Howie nodded, deep in thought. Then his expression changed to one of realisation. Something had clicked in his brain. But he didn't say anything. Instead, he finished undressing and started putting on his pyjamas.

Britt would have to try a new tactic. 'I was thinking of giving the information to our Westminster gossip guy. "President spotted near gym acting suspiciously". I thought I'd warn you in advance.'

Howie almost fell over, as his left leg caught in his pyjama bottoms. 'No, no. Don't do that. I'm busy enough already.'

'It's my job, Howie.'

He put his left hand on the wall and steadied himself. 'But you're off for the rest of this week, aren't you?'

'A journalist is never off duty. Just like police officers. And presidents.'

Howie managed to squeeze into his pyjama bottoms. Then he put on his serious face. 'Listen, B. I'll tell you a secret.'

This could be it. This could be Britt's breakthrough moment. She sat up in bed and listened.

Howie stood tall. His stomach still straining from the day's intake. 'The person you saw wasn't the president.'

His words didn't make sense. 'What do you mean? I saw his face.'

'You saw a face identical to his. You saw his brother Oskar. He had a meeting over there.'

Howie's tone, and his semi-naked body language, suggested he wasn't lying. And if Britt had seen the missing president, wouldn't Howie be probing her? Yes, he would. He would be firing questions at her. Was there anyone with the president? Did he speak to anyone? Where was he heading? Then Howie would be sending urgent bleeps to senior people. Maybe even disappearing out the door to another restaurant. But he wasn't. He was going to bed. So he must be telling the truth.

Howie yawned. 'Forget about that diary story, okay? It was just Oskar. And he always looks suspicious.' He slipped on his pyjama top, switched off the bedroom light beam, got into bed and kissed her. 'Goodnight. I'm up early tomorrow. I'll try not to wake you.'

Britt was in such a state of shock, she couldn't reply. Her investigation was focused on the president. Not his brother. Of course, she knew Jan Polak had an identical twin. Everyone did. But she hadn't even considered the possibility it could be Oskar.

Questions ran through her mind. Why was Oskar meeting the president's personal trainer? Cherry Blush was a beautiful woman and Oskar might have the president's looks but, to put it bluntly, his personality was nowhere near as sparkling. Was he impersonating the president?

Howie was already snoring. But Britt couldn't sleep with all these thoughts running through her mind. Ten minutes passed. She still couldn't believe it. Then she remembered Cherry's parting words to Oskar in the park. 'Ask her!' she had shouted. But Britt realised now. She had misheard. Cherry, in her thick London accent, had probably been yelling 'Oskar!' So Cherry knew exactly who she was meeting. But what kind of meeting was it? A lovers' liaison? Or something more sinister?

If Britt's brain had been a computer, it would have crashed and displayed one of those annoying error messages. She would need time to process all this data and make some kind of sense out of it.

She settled her head on the pillow. Tomorrow would be her big day. The day when she had to secure and write her missing-president story. Britt closed her eyes and tried to clear her mind. She needed to sleep.

Chapter 21

It was 5.57am. Howie was still asleep. It was one of his deepest sleeps ever. And he was having a vivid dream.

He was powering a speedboat towards an island in the middle of a faraway ocean. But this was no carefree holiday in the Caribbean. He was a man on a mission to save the world. Not just that. He was being hunted. And his hunters weren't far behind. He looked back at the three identical boats pursuing him. They were only a hundred metres away now and getting closer every second. It was time for secret agent Howie Pond to show the bad guys who was boss.

He pressed a red button on the console. Smoke spewed from the boat's rear, filling the air with a temporary fog. It was followed by the sound of motors spluttering to a halt and men shouting urgently in foreign languages. Howie accelerated towards the shore. Thirty seconds later, the speedboat mounted the beach and he expertly skidded it to a halt across the virgin sand. He jumped out, adjusted his sunglasses and glanced seawards. The trio of boats were already emerging from the fog. They would be here in less than a minute. No time for a seafood snack. He had to get moving.

Howie sprinted across the narrow beach. On the other side he found a path. It was surrounded by dense undergrowth. But he sensed it led somewhere, so took a chance and followed it. After a few hundred metres, it ended in a rocky cliff face which stretched into the distance on both sides. Howie took a moment to assess his options. He didn't have many. Then he heard the faint shouts of his pursuers behind him. They were already on the path. That meant he only had one choice. He had to go up.

Moments later, he was clambering up the rocks with all the skill of an alpine goat. As he neared the summit, he could hear gunfire beneath him. Bullets were ricocheting around him. But they weren't going to hit him. Because he was Howie Pond. And no one killed Howie Pond.

He reached the top in what seemed like seconds and scrambled to his feet. Was that some kind of low-level entrance in the rocks up ahead? It looked man-made. As he approached, he could see that it was. He crouched down and made his way inside. After a few seconds, the darkness gave way to bright light. He gasped at what he saw. A huge complex spread out below him. An incredible network of walkways, ladders, control rooms and storage units. All guarded by an army of foot soldiers dressed in identical bright orange, bad-guy uniforms. Then Howie realised that immediately below him was a large nuclear warhead. A man was tied to the huge missile. Was it? Yes, it was. The British President Jan Polak. Unconscious but alive. And there was another man, in a white suit, standing nearby. He was waving a gun around. It must be an evil genius, thought Howie. This is his secret island. That's his nuclear warhead. And he'll shortly be pointing it at a major metropolis. I've got to stop him.

The man in the white suit became aware of Howie's presence. He looked up at Howie and screamed in a Russian accent. 'Mr Pond! I've been expecting you! What took you so long?'

'My apologies,' called Howie. 'The road here was a little rocky.'

'I'm glad you haven't lost your sense of humour, Mr Pond,' shouted the man. 'Even if you have lost your president.' He pointed the gun at Jan Polak's head. 'Now climb down here or I put a bullet through his skull right now.'

Howie descended using a metal ladder attached to the internal rock face, being careful not to take his eye off the man. As he reached the bottom, he dusted himself down and addressed his adversary. 'I don't think we've been introduced.'

'I am Maxim. Viktor Maxim.'

Howie offered his hand. 'Pleased to meet you, Mr Maxim.'

Maxim declined the offer of a handshake. 'Forgive me, Mr Pond. But I reserve such gestures for social occasions.'

'We can grab some lunch, if you like. I'm starving.'

'I am hungry only for power,' sneered Maxim.

'Suit yourself. Now you and I need to have a little chat about why you're doing all this.'

Maxim laughed in the way that evil geniuses always do. 'I will tell you … before I kill you!' He walked up to the president and pointed at him. 'I will replace him, and all your other world leaders, with my people. Then I will rule the world!'

'What about the nuclear warhead?'

'Ah, yes. I will show the world my power by launching it at a major metropolis.' Maxim cackled with pleasure. 'And your British president will be attached to it!'

Before Howie could react to this news, the e-alarm in his bedroom went off. He slapped it with his hand to try and stop it bleeping. It didn't. He tried again. It bleeped even louder. He swore at it. That didn't work either. So he staggered to his feet and turned on the bedroom light beam. Britt half-woke up and grumbled at him. He ignored her complaints and located the e-alarm's power cable. Then he yanked it from the wall. And it finally stopped bleeping. Britt three-quarters woke up, swore at him and put her head under the pillow.

Howie sat on the edge of the bed and assessed his physical state. His body ached – especially the ankle he'd twisted yesterday. He felt bloated from Tuesday's big lunch and double dinner engagements. And his back was aching from all that bending down in the security camera control room. He felt like he was eighty-two years old, not forty-two. But he had to get up, grab a quick water-spray, check the newspapers, have breakfast and get to the palace. So he gathered some clean clothes, turned off the light beam and headed for the bathroom.

As the water jets sprayed around his body, he remembered the conversation with Britt, before they'd gone to sleep. It seemed a strange coincidence that she had seen Oskar Polak yesterday. For a few seconds, he wondered if it was too much of a coincidence. Britt was a journalist after all. Could she have been on an assignment to follow the president? Maybe she was working with Maurice Skeets to try and find out more about the secret meetings. No. Skeets worked alone now. He always wanted all the glory for himself. And if Britt had been in Canary Wharf as part of some journalistic investigation, why would she tell Howie what she'd found out? Anyway, she was on leave for the rest of the week. As he stepped out of the water-spray and the air jets in the wall blew over his body, he had reached his conclusion. It was just one of those weird coincidences. There was no point wasting any more time thinking about it.

He got dressed, went into the kitchen and opened the fridge. He was just about to stuff a cream cake into his mouth, when his regular quarter-past-six special deliveries dropped through the letter box – copies of every national daily newspaper. But he was only really interested in one of them. And that was the *Daily Democrat*. He needed to see how much damage Zayn Winner had inflicted on the Government the day before the Republican Party presidential nomination.

Howie scanned the front page. The main headline was about the Democrats' nomination which would be announced in a few weeks' time. He checked the date. It was definitely today's paper. So where was the story? He examined the front page again. This time he spotted a small column of text in the bottom right corner, headlined 'Winner backs a winner'. The opening paragraph read:

> *Vice President Zayn Winner is calling for another encore by Jan Polak, ahead of this Thursday's Republican Party presidential nomination. Winner expects the 'superstar' president to confirm he wants to continue playing the role for another five years. Speaking exclusively to the Daily Democrat, the thirty-nine-year-old movie legend expressed his admiration for the president's performance as the country's leading man.*

There were only two factual inaccuracies in that opening paragraph. Firstly, Zayn wasn't a movie legend. Secondly, he wasn't thirty-nine years old. More like forty-nine years old. But there was nothing wrong with the rest of the introduction. In fact, if Howie was honest with himself, it was pretty positive. But that might just be the first paragraph. He flicked to page two, where the article continued. After being momentarily startled by a huge photo of a grinning Zayn, Howie continued reading:

> *With the president attending to important matters of state on Tuesday, Vice President Winner – who played the American president in the classic Alien Invasion series of films – was effusive in his praise for his leader. 'The man is a superstar,' he claimed. 'He could be a Hollywood actor. He's got the charisma, the talent, the X-factor. He could do anything he wants. But all he wants to do at the moment is win another election and lead this country. The British Republic is his Hollywood. Jan Polak is our superstar.' And even the harshest critic would find it difficult to argue with that.*

Howie scanned the rest of the article. It was all positive. Zayn's new, fun fifth dimension of politics was mentioned. But in a positive way. What else? Zayn was a man of the people. A politician with charisma. A breath of fresh air. Then there was some nonsense about Zayn feeding the ducks in St James' Park every Wednesday morning. That would go down well with the citizens – the duck being the symbol of the revolution. And what was today? Of course. It was a Wednesday. Howie sighed. He would speak to Conor O'Brean in his press office about handling that. But he doubted any journalists would turn up to see Zayn tossing bread to the ducks. No. It wouldn't be a problem. It was a great article.

He read it one more time. Just to make sure he hadn't missed anything. But he hadn't. There was no hint of criticism or sarcasm anywhere. It was incredible. Zayn had performed a minor media miracle. No. A major media miracle. Howie did something he generally didn't manage before consuming breakfast. He smiled. Then it turned into a grin – one even bigger than Zayn Winner's on page two of the *Daily Democrat*. What a fantastic start to the day.

He checked that there were no front-page stories about missing presidents in the other papers. There weren't. So he ate his cream cake and then fed the cat. But he didn't have time for a chat with his feline friend. He put on his coat and headed outside. It was time to find the president.

Chapter 22

The sound of the pod door sliding shut woke Britt for the third time in twenty minutes. But this time she was fully awake. She rolled over and groaned. Her body was telling her she needed more rest. Lots more rest. It had taken her more than two hours to get to sleep after last night's chat with Howie about the president. Or rather, their chat about the president's brother. When she finally did get to sleep, the songs of Super-Mega Electro Thrash haunted her dreams. Not only that, but Britain's Finest had given her chronic indigestion all night. Right now, she felt more exhausted than when she went to bed.

She glanced over at the e-alarm. Its display was blank. Howie must have yanked its plug from the wall again. That meant it wouldn't go off at half past seven as planned. She would have to get up now. Or risk oversleeping and wasting valuable investigation time.

Britt dragged herself across the bed, got to her feet and switched on the bedroom light beam. As she went to press the switch to open the door, she heard a noise. It sounded like an object vibrating. She looked around. It was coming from the pair of trousers that Howie had kicked across the room last night. She wandered over and searched through his trouser pockets. The buzzing got louder and more insistent. And there it was. His work bleeper. She checked the screen:

E-COMM ALERT – CLASSIFIED message from MARTHA BLAKE. Enter your six-digit PIN to view. Have a wonderful Wednesday!

Britt couldn't believe her luck. Her Wednesday could well turn out to be wonderful. She knew this woman, Martha Blake. She had been the head of the security service for the last ten years. And there was something else Britt knew. Howie always used the cat's birthday for PIN numbers.

She typed in the code. The bleeper bleeped. The display reset. Britt held her breath. Then the first part of the e-comm popped up on its screen:

Hello, Howie. Before you make any Wednesday plans, be aware that a nomination meeting has been pencilled in for later today – assuming our missing president hasn't shown up by then. Timing and venue TBC. I'll be chairing. And I want you there for support.

Any feelings of fatigue were already gone from Britt's system. She gave a whoop of delight. This was her second source. She just needed one more. Britt flicked a button to see the second part of the message:

Don't forget your security service ID card. It's your insurance policy. You need to travel with it everywhere. Think of it like 007's licence to kill. Except you don't have a licence to kill anyone – just to interrogate them. We'll catch up when you arrive at the palace.

This was unbelievable. Howie was working for the security service now? No. She must have misunderstood. She read the message again and came to the same incredible conclusion – her boyfriend was now operating on a whole new level. She took a moment to digest this news. Then she realised that she'd better be careful. Britt didn't want to get on the wrong side of the security service. She scrolled to the third and final part of the message:

Delete this e-comm now. Classified e-comms are not PIN-protected once they've been read. Bloody useless things, these bleepers. See you soon. Martha.

This was a problem. Howie would know that someone had read his top-secret e-comm, now it wasn't PIN-protected. And that someone could only be Britt. Any decent bleeper would have had the highest levels of security. But this wasn't a decent bleeper. It was a government bleeper.

Britt accessed the message options. She surveyed the menu. There was an option to convert 'read e-comms' back into 'unread e-comms', if you knew the PIN. Then she heard the front door of the pod slide open again. Howie was back. He must have realised he'd left his bleeper behind.

Britt felt a flush of panic. If Howie caught her reading his e-comms, he would go through the pod roof – probably all the way up to forty-ninth floor. Howie wasn't stupid. He would guess that she was working on a story. And probably guess which story. He would shout and scream at her. Then go straight to the offices of *The Republican* – possibly with Martha Blake alongside him – and have a chat with George. The kind of chat that leads to stories being killed. And journalists being banished to lifestyle features for the rest of their careers. Assuming they still had a career.

The cat meowed from the kitchen. Britt heard Howie greet her. He would be in the bedroom in less than thirty seconds. She felt like shoving the bleeper under the duvet. But as soon as it buzzed again he would be able to find it and then work out she'd accessed it. No. She had to convert the message back to an unread e-comm.

Her fingers felt like sausages as she tried to enter the six digits again. Six digits that had been so easy to remember just a minute ago. And now she wasn't so sure. It felt like she was picking lottery numbers. She entered her first attempt at the code. The bleeper bleeped. The display reset. It wasn't the right one. She had two more chances. And then it would lock. Or possibly self-destruct. But she could hear Howie's footsteps in the kitchen. She would only have one more chance.

Britt entered a six-digit code. The bleeper bleeped. The display reset. This time, the code was accepted and the original e-comm alert appeared on its screen, requesting Howie's PIN. The relief almost knocked her from her feet. Then the bedroom door slid open. Britt turned and held out the bleeper in her hand. 'Is this yours?'

Howie walked towards her. 'Ah, my bleeper. Thanks. That's what I came back for.'

She handed Howie his bleeper and glared at him. 'It was buzzing in your trousers like a psychotic bumble bee. It woke me up. Thanks very much.'

'Sorry,' he mumbled. 'It won't happen again.'

He looked genuinely remorseful. Britt's fake indignation seemed to have worked. Then Howie looked at his bleeper and frowned. 'What's the cat's birthday again?'

This could be a cunning test to see if she knew his bleeper PIN. She would play dumb. 'I can't remember my own birthday at the moment.'

Howie stared at her without blinking, in the same way the cat did when it wanted something. 'Come on. Help me out.'

Britt shook her head and leapt back into bed. 'My brain doesn't work before nine. Sorry.'

Howie gave a deep sigh. 'How can I forget the cat's birthday?'

Britt raised her voice. 'You forget everybody else's birthday. You forget mine. Your mother's. You even forget your own. Now buzz off with that bumble bleeper and leave me in peace to sleep.'

Howie did as he was told. A few seconds later, he was gone. For good, this time.

Britt looked up at the ceiling and mouthed the words 'thank you'. The journalistic gods had been on her side this morning. She needed things to stay that way.

Chapter 23

Howie was sitting in the president's private office, staring at his bleeper. He had tried twice to enter his PIN and access Martha's e-comm. But neither attempt had been successful. He only had one more try before it locked him out. And every time he tried to access his other messages, it sent him back to the log-in page. It was infuriating. Martha would be here in a minute. He would look a fool if he hadn't been able to access his own e-comms. If only he could remember the number. It was his cat's birthday. What the hell was it?

The door opened. But it wasn't Martha. It was Brian the bloody auto-tech. Its head swivelled in Howie's direction and fired a laser into his eye, momentarily dazzling him.

'Greetings, Howard Pond,' it announced in its metallic monotone.

'What do you want? I don't need an auto-tech.'

'Brian is not here to serve you, Howard. Brian is here to conduct some checks.'

Howie didn't trust this robot one bit. 'What kind of checks?'

'Diagnostic checks. Brian has restored the Tech network. Brian has been working all night to do so. While you and everyone else was sleeping, I was working, Howard.'

If this machine was looking for sympathy, it had picked the wrong human. 'Working all night were you?' grumbled Howie. 'Like on Monday, eh? When the CAMS system went down.'

The auto-tech's head swivelled back and forth and it made a bleeping noise. 'Brian is not sure what you are insinuating.'

'I'm suggesting you bloody well sabotaged it,' snapped Howie. He wasn't sure if using an indignant tone had any effect on these machines, but he was adopting one any way. 'I went to the CAMS command centre. Someone – or rather, something – shut the cameras down manually.'

Brian's eye pulsed. 'That someone would need an eight-digit code to perform a manual shutdown, Howard.'

'Yeah. And the code's digits are held by you and all your other metal pals. Go on, admit it – you did it.'

'Brian had to erase all logs for the CAMS data download. So Brian can neither confirm nor deny such an allegation.' Its voice jumped an octave. 'However, in the low-probability, hypothetical world where an auto-tech did shut down CAMS, it could only be done with the correct human inputs.' Its voice returned to normal. 'Brian respectfully suggests you keep this in mind when criticising his operations in future.'

Howie wondered if he might be replaced by a machine one day. They were so good at avoiding questions, it was only a matter of time.

Martha Blake rushed through the door. 'There you are. You got my e-comm?'

Howie could feel himself blushing. 'I, erm ... couldn't read it. Bleeper problems.'

'Brian is happy to assist with bleeper problems.'

Howie might be having Tech troubles, but he didn't want this auto-tech going anywhere near his bleeper. It would probably take revenge and send rude e-comms to his entire contacts list. 'No, thanks. I'll sort it out myself.'

'Brian wishes you all the luck in the world with that, Howard.' It moved towards the president's e-terminal. 'Please ignore Brian while he undertakes diagnostic tests.'

Howie did exactly that. He turned to Martha. 'So what did your message say?'

'Oh, yes.' She thought for a second. 'The main point was that there'll be a nomination meeting today. In fact, I've just had it confirmed. It's at four o'clock in the State Dining Room – assuming Jan doesn't surface between now and then. You and I are going to be there. Me chairing. You supporting.'

'Any updates on Jan?'

'Only that we've had no contact from the Americans or anyone else asking where he is. Which is a blessing. What about you? Did the chief of police say anything else, after I left?'

'Not really.' Howie wouldn't mention that he now had Freddie's personal bleeper number. It might start an argument. 'He got a bleep and had to leave.'

Martha sat down. 'I don't trust that man.'

'He seemed like a nice guy. He liked me.'

'That's because you're the president's official spokesperson, Howie. You're exactly the kind of person that Frederick English likes to acquire as a friend. You and vice presidents like Daisy Gray. And he'll go out of his way to do so.' She tutted loudly. 'Talking of vice presidents, what about the Zayn Winner article?'

'Don't worry. It's fine.'

'And there's nothing else to worry about in this morning's newspapers?'

'Doesn't look like it. No leaks to Maurice Skeets or anyone else.'

'What about broadcast media?'

'Nothing, as far as I know.'

'Oh, there was one other thing. The palace e-terminals are all working now. Ivan confirmed in an e-comm that it was unrelated to the CAMS problems. He also informed me that all the other auto-techs are now functioning.' She looked towards Brian. 'Apparently, our little friend over there fixed everything.'

Howie glared at the auto-tech. 'It still won't answer any questions about what it was up to on Monday night.'

'It's a machine, Howie. It's human beings we need to focus on. Which brings me onto some good news. We can now access Jan's official diary. Kaia-Liisa set that up for me, this morning. I trawled through the last six months of appointments.'

'Any interesting names jump out at you?'

'No. There was no mention of the three individuals Maurice Skeets gave you. It doesn't look like Jan met with any of them officially. At least, not recently.'

Ah, yes. The three names. A thought occurred to Howie. Maybe those secret meetings held the key to this mystery? He had an idea. 'Can't we find out if Jan had any unofficial meetings with them? We could ask the security guys. They must track his movements.'

'Good thinking. But the president only has security at the palace. And for official engagements and travel. At other times, it's at his discretion.'

'Oh, well,' sighed Howie. 'We might as well forget about them for now.'

'Don't give up hope just yet. There is someone who might know about Jan's unofficial world.'

The door opened. It was the president's chief private secretary. 'You wanted a word, Martha?'

'Yes, Kaia-Liisa. Howie has had some questions from a journalist about presidential meetings. The president is far too busy at the moment for us to trouble him with a media enquiry. As you oversee his diary, I suggested we ask you.'

Kaia-Liisa didn't say anything. She just shut the door and sat down next to them. Howie would leave this interrogation to Martha. She clearly knew what she was doing.

'Howie's been given three names,' explained Martha. 'All you have to do is tell us if you're aware of the president meeting any of them. Officially or unofficially. Then Howie can formulate a response to the journalist. Understood?'

Kaia-Liisa nodded.

Martha began the questioning. 'First name – Olga Frik, chief executive of Auto-Tech Industries.'

Kaia-Liisa gave the question considerable thought before replying. 'I remember the president asked me for Olga Frik's contact details two or three weeks ago. I obtained them for him. That was the end of my involvement.'

'And did he meet her?'

'Not through official channels.'

'What about unofficial ones?'

'I only know about official business.'

'So you only discuss official engagements?'

'Yes.'

'You never discuss unofficial engagements? For example, ones that might conflict with official engagements?'

'No.'

'Very well. Our next name is Petra Putinov.'

After several more seconds of thinking, Kaia-Liisa shook her head. 'No.'

'The name means nothing to you at all?'

'Nothing.'

Martha frowned. 'Maybe we'll have more luck with the last name. Sky Eastern – the chairwoman of Eastern Oil.'

Brian swivelled his head in their direction. 'Brian can see that you are busy and he is disturbing you. Brian will return when the president's office is free.' The auto-tech then glided out of the room.

Howie turned to Martha. 'I don't trust that bloody machine.'

Martha sighed. 'You're in danger of becoming obsessed, Howie.' She turned back to Kaia-Liisa. 'Now, Sky Eastern – did Jan ever meet her?'

Kaia-Liisa responded immediately. 'Yes. The president met Ms Eastern at a charity fundraising event last summer. It was an official engagement. I remember her office calling to confirm that the president would be attending.'

'And there was no more official contact after that?'

'Not through me.'

'And you're not aware of any unofficial contact?'

'It wouldn't come through me.'

'So, just to be clear – you're never aware of any unofficial business whatsoever?'

'No, Martha.'

'Because working in this office, you might overhear something. Or see a scribbled note, for example. Something like that.'

'I can see how someone might think that happens.' Kaia-Liisa paused. 'But it doesn't.'

Martha stared at Kaia-Liisa. The private secretary gazed back at her with the same emotion-free expression she'd maintained throughout the whole conversation. After a few seconds Martha spoke. 'Thank you, Kaia-Liisa. That's everything for now.'

Kaia-Liisa stood up. 'I need to get back to a team meeting.' She turned and walked calmly from the room.

Martha turned to Howie. 'Well, that went well. It was absolutely no use whatsoever.'

Howie got up. 'Well, if it's unofficial, the chances are Kaia-Liisa isn't going to know about it.' He walked over to the large digi-screen on the wall and turned it on. 'The seven o'clock bulletin will be on in a minute. I want to double-check there's nothing running on the news.'

The digi-screen burst into life. It was perfect timing. A female newsreader announced the main headlines. There was nothing political. Not even a mention of preparations for Independence Day. Howie breathed a sigh of relief. 'At least we don't have to worry about the media today.'

After a couple of minutes, the bulletin ended. Then another presenter came on the screen. 'Coming up in the next hour on *Rise and Shine* – have you found the American in you? If not, the new book from the country's First Lady is going to tell us how. She'll be here on the sofa at 7.45am.'

'For king's sake!' shouted Howie. 'What the hell is she doing?! We can't have her going on live digi-screen when we're still at Code Red!'

Martha jumped up. 'You'd better get down to the studios. How far away are they?'

'Half an hour's drive, at least.'

'Take my car. Go on. Go!'

Howie ran from the office. This was really going to bugger up his morning.

Chapter 24

Britt was back in the newsroom at *The Republican*. The digital clock on the wall told her it was 7.30am. She couldn't remember the last time she'd been here this early. But she wished she'd done it more often. The office was unrecognisable from the four-letter chaos that normally greeted her at half past nine every day. In fact, she hadn't even heard a three-letter word since she arrived fifteen minutes ago. Just a two-letter one – 'Hi'. And that had been grunted, not spoken, by two colleagues finishing their night shift.

It was Britt's idea of paradise. No one was paying her any attention. That meant no one asking awkward questions about why she was in the office again on a day off. No one was boring her about their non-functioning Tech. And no one was engaging her in tedious small talk about the outside world. At the moment, the only world Britt cared about was her world – the world of the missing president.

Britt stared at her e-terminal. She had already sketched out a few bullet points for her story:

- Jan Polak last seen at Buck Palace on Monday evening
- Security blunder – private quarters not patrolled
- Security cameras failed
- Code Red crisis launched on Tuesday morning
- Search of palace and grounds found nothing
- Republican presidential nomination due on Thursday

She could feel her heart beating faster. She imagined her colleagues' reaction when they read the story tomorrow. The speechless mouths. The dropped jaws. The disbelieving stares. Hundreds of millions of people around the world would be reacting in the same way. The global news agenda would be focused on the British Republic and the whereabouts of its lost president. All because of one journalist – Britt Pointer. A journalist whose guts, determination and investigative instincts had unearthed the story of the year. No. It would be the story of the decade. Maybe even the story of the century?

She closed her eyes and cleared her mind. She must stay calm. She still needed that third source to confirm the story – someone who wasn't from palace security or the security service. It was far from clear who that was going to be. Not everyone was as dumb as Herbert the security guy. And she wouldn't know the PIN for anyone else's bleeper. That meant it would probably have to be someone in the president's inner circle.

Her thoughts were interrupted by a shrieking voice from behind her. 'Hello, stranger! What are you doing here again on your day off? Boyfriend kicked you out, has he?!'

Britt didn't have to turn around to see who was cackling at her own joke. She could identify that voice from ten kilometres away. It was Rosie Parker.

Britt hunched closer to her e-terminal to obscure the words on the screen. 'I'm working on something for next week.'

'Anything interesting?' asked Rosie, coming alongside Britt to take a closer look.

'Not really.'

'Don't be shy.'

'I told you, it's not interesting,' growled Britt, saving the e-file and closing it down.

Rosie raised her eyebrows theatrically. 'No? I thought I saw the name "Jan Polak" on your screen'. And the words "Buckingham Palace". That sounds interesting to me.'

Britt had to think quickly. Luckily, she'd already drunk a cup of coffee. The neurons fired in her brain and delivered a lightning-fast excuse. 'It was a list of questions from yesterday's interview with the First Lady. I loaded it by mistake.'

'Oh,' sighed Rosie. 'Is that all?' She sat down at Britt's old desk and switched on the e-terminal. 'By the way, your feature on the First Lady is in today's paper. They didn't put your name on it, though.'

George had kept his word. Britt nodded an acknowledgement to Rosie, in the hope that she would stop talking. She didn't.

'I know why you wanted to stay anonymous, Britt.'

She jolted her head sideways, so she could see Rosie's expression. Did she somehow know about Britt's investigation? Had George let something slip? She swallowed hard. Then she spoke in a deadpan voice. 'What do you mean?'

'Come on, Britt. You know what I mean.'

'I'm sorry. I don't.'

'Do I have to spell it out to you?'

'Yes.'

Rosie sighed. 'Dear, oh dear!'

If Rosie didn't answer Britt's question in the next ten seconds, there was a good chance blood was going to be spilled. Britt counted the seconds. One, two, three, four, five, six. Rosie opened her mouth as she reached seven. Britt clenched her fist as she counted eight. Rosie responded on the count of nine.

'You don't want people reading it and knowing it's you,' announced Rosie.

Britt kept her fist clenched. 'What exactly are you saying?'

Rosie half-smiled, half-sneered. 'How can I phrase this?'

'Just say what you've got to say.'

Rosie turned away. 'It was a terrible feature. One of the worst I've ever read. I'm sorry, Britt. That's just my opinion. But I am an expert on these things; I've worked on features before, so my opinion counts.' She gave an insincere smile. 'Better luck next time, eh?'

Britt bit her lip.

Rosie picked up a copy of the *Daily Democrat* on her desk. 'There's a much better feature by Mina Pritti in here. Well, it's news and a feature all rolled into one. It's about that vice president who used to be an actor – Zayn Winner. You should read it. You could pick up a few tips from her.'

Britt bit her lip even harder – so hard, she could taste blood in her mouth.

'Then again, he is a great interviewee,' continued Rosie. 'So open. A people person – like me. If I wasn't stuck in here, I'd be off to St James' Park to help him with those ducks.'

'What ducks?'

Rosie tossed the newspaper over to Britt. 'You've got eyes. Read it yourself. I'm busy with news stuff now.' She bashed her fist on her keyboard. 'Bloody hell, this machine never seems to get going before half nine. It's probably spent too much time working with you, eh, Britt?' Rosie's cackle echoed around the walls – until the other two people on the news desk told her, in words of more than three letters, to keep the noise down.

But Britt didn't hear her colleagues' requests. She was too busy scanning Mina Pritti's article. Rosie was right. Zayn Winner was talkative. He wasn't an ordinary politician. He actually answered journalists' questions.

Britt reached the last few paragraphs. Here was what Rosie had been rambling about – Zayn Winner's Wednesday morning routine of feeding the ducks on the bridge in St James' Park at nine o'clock. Where, according to the article, he would 'gladly pose for photos and sign autographs for his legions of fans'.

An idea entered Britt's head. Maybe Pellie Cann could make another appearance in the park and intercept the Government's most vocal vice president? Why not? It sounded like Zayn Winner would love to meet an American fan.

Rosie got up and walked over to Britt. 'What do you think? Great article, yeah? I might see if I can get a one-to-one with him myself.'

Not before me, you won't, thought Britt.

Rosie picked up the copy of the *Daily Democrat* and walked back to her seat. 'There's a funny story on page five. It's about this woman. She was a tourist, they reckon. There was this traffic jam in Trafalgar Square yesterday and she couldn't cross the road. So she jumped on these three racing cars and caused hundreds of thousands of pounds of damage. Then she ran off towards The Mall. Sounds like your kind of story.' Rosie crinkled her nose in a show of fake sympathy. 'Shame you're not on news any more.'

Britt didn't respond. She had heard the words. But her brain hadn't processed them. Instead, she had been working out if she had time to go back to her pod, get into her Pellie Cann disguise, and get to St James' Park for nine. She did – but only just.

'So who do you think she was, Britt? Must have been a desperate woman to —'

'Not now, Rosie. I've got to go.'

Rosie frowned. 'Oh. Something I said, was it?'

'Yes. It was, actually.' And Britt turned and left for home.

Chapter 25

Howie's government car had been cruising round the Media World industrial estate for the last ten minutes. The *Rise and Shine* studios were here somewhere. But where? It sounded a straightforward question. But it wasn't. Every tall grey building looked like the one before it. Road junctions were identical. Trees were equally spaced. And the storm raging outside wasn't helping the search.

Howie slumped back in the passenger seat and gazed out the window at the charcoal clouds. They were dumping gallons of water in every direction, and showing no signs of stopping. As the drumbeat of water on the car's roof intensified, the driver started up a conversation.

'Interesting feature in *The Republican* today, sir, about the First Lady. Did you read it?'

'In today's paper?'

'Yes, sir. About her new book.'

This was all Howie needed. 'Who was it by?'

'Didn't say.'

Did it mention the president?'

'Once or twice.'

Howie would have to phrase his next question carefully. 'Anything ... newsworthy?'

'Not that I remember, sir.'

That was a relief. But not unexpected. The First Lady tended to reserve her sensible interviews for newspapers. Her less reserved performances were always on digi-screen. More specifically, live digi-screen – a performance that couldn't be edited. Once it was out there, it was out there.

They passed a sign for the studios. But the driver carried on.

'Didn't we just go past the turning?' asked Howie, looking through the rain-soaked rear windscreen.

'The Navi-Tech says it's straight on.'

'But I'm sure there was a sign back there for the studios.'

'Difficult to see in this deluge, sir. The Tech is telling me it's up here on the right. It's one of the new models. It's not often wrong.'

Howie's eyes were old models. But they weren't often wrong either. 'The sign for the studios definitely pointed left.'

'If I ignore the Tech, sir, and you're late because of me, I'll be in hot water. So let's just have a quick look up here, if you don't mind.'

'Alright,' sighed Howie. He checked his bleeper. The stupid thing was still asking him for his six-digit PIN, which he still couldn't remember. It wouldn't even give him the time of day. The digital clock on the driver's dashboard suggested it was 7.38am.

'Is your clock correct?' asked Howie.

'Yes, sir. Give or take a couple of minutes.'

'Fast or slow?'

'Slow, I think.'

That meant it was probably 7.40am. The First Lady would be live on air in five minutes. And here was Howie – once again – at the mercy of a machine.

'No, you were right, sir,' announced the driver, thirty seconds later. 'The Navi-Tech has changed its mind. I should have turned left, where you said. I'm stuck in this one-way loop now. And there's someone behind me. We'll have to go round again.'

That would take another five minutes. Time that Howie didn't have. 'Stop the car,' he ordered. 'I'll go on foot from here.'

'On foot, sir?'

'Yes.'

'You'll get soaked.'

Judging by the intensity of the storm, that was a best-case scenario. 'I know. Just let me out.'

'If you say so, sir.'

The driver brought the car to a halt. Howie flung open the passenger door, jumped out and ran in the direction of the studio, across a muddy patch of grass. As he ran, he remembered the First Lady's previous appearances on the *Rise and Shine* sofa. Each time, she had disclosed sensitive information about the president for cheap publicity and bigger book sales. And the presenters knew exactly how to extract the maximum amount of information from her. The editorial team had probably come in early this morning, to draw up a list of killer questions. Has the president found the American inside him? Is the Royal Family better off staying in Florida? Did the First Lady or president ever date an American? He felt his stomach rumble. It had nothing to do with hunger. It was stress gripping his digestive system.

Howie kept running for what seemed like half an hour, but was actually three minutes. Each step felt heavier as more mud clung to his leather shoes. Each breath became harder as his airways contracted. Each heartbeat thundered louder as his body demanded more oxygen.

A thought sprang into his mind. He was forty-two years old. He shouldn't be doing this. Even James Bond would object to sprinting across muddy grass in his best shoes in a tropical rainstorm. While contemplating this, Howie failed to spot a puddle ahead of him. His left foot landed on it and skidded forward on the saturated ground. The rest of his body could only watch in horror as he lost all control and gravity pulled him downwards. Two seconds later he was flat on his back, gazing up at the clouds as they dumped even more water on him. He could feel mud on his neck, hands and ankles. He didn't have time to fill the air with four-letter words. He peeled himself off the ground and got up. He took a step forward. Then his standing foot gave way. And he fell face first onto the ground.

The mud was everywhere now. In his hair. Up his nose. In his mouth. He pushed his hands into the sodden turf and rocked back on his knees. He looked up at the heavens. The gods were up there somewhere. Having a good laugh at his expense. But he wouldn't let them beat him. His name was Pond. Howie Pond. He was a man on a mission. A very muddy man, but he couldn't let that get in the way of things. He mustn't let the First Lady reach that bright yellow sofa. He leapt to his feet and continued running to the studio entrance, which was now in sight.

A minute later, he was outside the building. There was no security guard, so he dashed straight inside. He'd been here before. He knew where to go.

A receptionist spotted him and gasped in horror. Howie ignored her and ran through reception and up a flight of stairs, leaving a trail of brown footprints behind him. At the top of the stairs he could see the studio's yellow double doors. He shoulder-charged his way in, splattering mud as he did so, and sprinted along the corridor. He spotted a clock on the wall which showed it was 7.41am. What a relief. The car's clock must have been running fast, not slow, otherwise the interview would be about to start. Howie would have two or three minutes to find the First Lady and persuade her to pull out. But it would have to be a quick conversation. Especially as he now looked like one of the Martian mud monsters from Zayn Winner's *Alien Invasion* films.

He carried on down the corridor, drawing astonished looks from everyone who set eyes on him. A couple of people yelled at him. One startled young woman screamed 'They're here! They've come for us! The mud monsters!' But he had no time to explain that he wasn't from Mars. Or a mud monster. Or that he was only coming for one person – the First Lady.

Seconds later, he reached his destination. It was the Green Room. Fortunately, there was just one person sitting in the tiny, glass-walled waiting area. It was the First Lady. She was immersed in her new book and didn't notice him. When he opened the door, she didn't look up. When he walked towards her, she still didn't notice him. But when a blob of mud slopped onto the floor from his jacket, she glanced up. And she froze. Her face filled with fear – just like the people in *Alien Invasion* when they first saw a mud monster.

'It's me, First Lady. It's Howie Pond.'

This news didn't change her expression.

'What the hell happened to you? You look like you've been digging up a dead body.' She raised her eyebrows. 'Not my husband?'

'No, I fell over in some mud.'

'Oh, I see.'

Howie didn't detect any relief in her voice. 'I was in a rush to get here because I don't want you going on that sofa. Your husband is still missing. And you appearing on live digi-screen isn't going to help matters.'

She pointed to a small digi-screen in the corner, which was showing *Rise and Shine* live. 'It's too late now. They've already announced me as the next guest.'

Howie tried to look serious. But it was difficult from behind his muddy face mask. 'You were supposed to inform me about any media bids. You did the *Republican* interview without telling me and now this.'

'My apologies. I'm very forgetful like that.'

It was time to talk tough. 'I don't care what they've announced. You're not going on.'

'I am an experienced media performer. You have nothing to be concerned about.'

Time to talk even tougher. 'Martha Blake sent me here. She told me she doesn't want you doing the interview.'

'Oh, really? Well, I only have your word for that.'

Howie could hear voices in the corridor outside. It wouldn't be long before someone arrived to collect the First Lady and usher her onto the sofa. He had one more chance to persuade her not to do it. It was time to play dirty – even dirtier than the clothes he was wearing. 'You want to know the truth about Cherry Blush?'

The First Lady flinched as he mentioned the name. 'You talked to that girl?'

'Yes, I did. We had a very interesting discussion.'

'Did she admit being involved with my husband?'

'Pull out of the interview and I'll tell you.'

'That sounds like blackmail to me.'

It sounded like blackmail to Howie. But James Bond wouldn't have called it that. What would he have called it? Something witty. 'It's an offer you can refuse, First Lady.'

She looked behind Howie and gestured with her hand at someone in the corridor. Then she turned to him. 'Good. Then I'll refuse it.'

A horrified-looking man in a yellow jumper bearing the words 'Rise and Shine!' burst into the room. 'Security! Where the hell are they?' he screamed. Then he addressed the First Lady. 'I'm so sorry, Your Ladyship. This muddy maniac should never have been allowed inside! I've got three members of staff thinking we're under attack from Martians, the cleaner's going mental ...' He stared at Howie with contempt. '... and this dirty great thing here, whoever he is, got within centimetres of molesting you, our star guest! I'm absolutely mortified!'

Another blob of mud dropped from Howie and hit the floor. 'The name's Pond. Howie Pond. I'm the president's spokesperson and special investigator for the National Security and Intelligence Service. The First Lady can confirm this.'

The man in the yellow jumper took a step back, eyed Howie suspiciously and then turned back to the First Lady. 'Is this true, Your Highness?'

The First Lady stared into Howie's eyes, as if trying to place his face. Then a triumphant smile rippled across her face. 'I've never seen this man before in my life.'

Howie wasn't the only one who could play dirty. But he would have the final word. 'Listen. I've got ID. I can prove it.' He reached for the card in his jacket pocket. But it wasn't there.

'Security!' screamed yellow-jumper man, at the top of his voice. 'Get your lazy arses over here now!'

Panic began to engulf Howie. 'It's in here somewhere.'

A second later, two huge men in security uniforms charged into the room.

'About bloody time, you two! Now, keep this filthy fanatic here until the police arrive.'

The security guards grunted an acknowledgement and fixed their gaze on Howie. There was no point trying to escape. He'd be slammed to the floor in seconds. If he could just find that ID card.

Yellow-jumper man grabbed the First Lady's hand. 'Let's get you out of this mucky madhouse. You're on in sixty seconds, if that's okay, Your Majesty.'

The First Lady smiled. 'The sooner the better.' Then she left the room with her yellow escort, not even bothering to look back.

Howie searched his pockets again. He had his bleeper. He had his wallet. But it didn't contain his security service ID. He must have left it back at the pod.

Five minutes later, a radio crackled in one of the security men's jackets. The man listened to the person on the other end and then spoke to his colleague. 'The boys in light blue are here.'

Howie sighed. This was going to be a long morning.

Chapter 26

Britt was back in St James' Park. Or rather, Pellie Cann was back in St James' Park. She was dressed just as before – raincoat, scarf and huge sunglasses. There hadn't been time to mess around choosing another outfit. Anyway, it felt easier playing the same role in the same clothes. She didn't want to start confusing herself.

From her position on the bridge that crossed the large lake, she surveyed the crowds. She couldn't see any sign of her target, Vice President Zayn Winner. According to the *Daily Democrat* article, this was where the ex-Hollywood star came at nine o'clock every Wednesday morning to feed the ducks. It was a strange thing for a vice president to reveal in an interview. Politicians didn't usually invite contact with citizens unless it was absolutely necessary.

Then a thought occurred to her. Maybe feeding the ducks was part of a plan to show how 'in touch' Zayn was with ordinary citizens? Could he possibly be setting himself up to run as the Republican presidential candidate, if Jan Polak couldn't be found? She would try to probe Zayn on his future plans and find out.

Britt scanned the faces around her. There was still no sign of Zayn. But a small group of people had gathered at the end of the bridge nearest The Mall, possibly in anticipation of his arrival. Britt decided to stay where she was. She would make her move when Zayn set foot on the bridge. Her plan was to charm Zayn and draw him into a chat about the president. It shouldn't be that difficult.

As she gazed at the exotic birds loitering in the water beneath the bridge, she heard a distant voice from behind her. It was a man with an Irish accent. Britt recognised it immediately. She turned around. It was Conor O'Brean – the press officer Pellie Cann had briefly met yesterday in the Grafton Arms. Britt swore so loudly, a passing mother with a young child gave her a dirty look. This was a disaster. The chances of her getting a one-to-one with Zayn were almost zero now. She felt like taking off her sunglasses and throwing them in the lake. But she didn't. There was still some hope. She might be able to grab Zayn for a quick question or two. Perhaps if Conor got distracted?

Britt watched as Zayn and Conor reached the edge of the bridge. By now, a small crowd had formed round them. Autographs were signed. Photos were taken by locals and tourists. After a few minutes, Conor forced a path through the crowd and the pair were now standing on the bridge – just a few metres away from her.

'Can I have everyone's attention, please?' shouted Conor. 'Now, our superstar vice president only has five minutes in his busy schedule to feed our feathered friends. But first of all, good people, do we have any members of the press here?'

No one responded. There were no other journalists here. That was good news.

'Hallelujah!' boomed Conor, so loudly that all the birds within a hundred-metre radius took off and flew out of the park. 'Ah. No birdies. Never mind, ladies and gentlefolk. Vice President Winner will not be deterred. He will now proceed to throw pieces of the best British bread into the murky depths below, for the birdies to enjoy, at their leisure, when we are all gone from this place.' Conor fumbled in his pockets and then turned to Zayn. 'Do you have the bread, sir?'

'No. I gave it to you to put in your rucksack.'

Conor started to go pink. 'Ah. I knew there was something I forgot, sir.' He turned to the fast-dwindling crowd. 'But worry not, dear citizens. There being no birds, and no bread, will not deter the vice president. He will be standing on the bridge and, erm … let me just think.'

Britt took a couple of steps nearer to Zayn. She might just get her chance.

Conor raised a finger, to indicate he'd made a decision. 'He'll just be standing on the bridge looking vice presidential.' He turned to Zayn. 'If you would kindly get yourself in position for a photo, sir. We'll need one, just in case any media want to see you in duck-feeding action.'

Zayn walked forward and stood with his hand on the metal rail, as if he was modelling this spring's new fashions. 'Is this how you want me, Conor?'

'Perfect. Now where's my camera?' Conor began frantically searching in his rucksack.

Britt saw her opportunity. She walked up to Zayn and spoke in a smooth American accent. 'Hi, Vice President Winner! I loved your interview in the paper today.'

Zayn's face lit up. 'You did?'

'I'm from the New States. You're a super-megastar over there. Whenever we talk about actors who played the president, we always think of you first.'

Zayn grinned. 'I always think of me, too.'

Britt casually put her hands on the metal rail. 'I was wondering if you might wanna play the president for real? The British president, I mean.'

He straightened his tie. 'The best actors always want to audition for the best roles. When they're available. It's the same for politicians.'

Britt could see Conor had located his camera. She didn't have much longer. 'And is the role of British president going to become available soon? If so, are you ready to audition?'

Zayn looked thoughtful. Then his eyes widened, as if about to deliver a revelation. Then Conor butted in. 'Sorry, madam, I'm going to have to ask you to step back.'

'Can I just finish my chat with —'

Conor interrupted. 'You're Pellie Cann, aren't you? We met in the pub yesterday.'

This was going to be tricky. 'Erm, yeah … that's me.' Time to change the subject. 'I'm a big fan of the vice president.'

Conor wagged his finger. 'And you were a big fan of my best buddy, Herbert Bogdanowic. And look how that ended – in tears. He bleeped me this morning. Poor fella is in a terrible way. He waited up all night for you. He's devastated. He drank a whole six-pack of Britain's Finest and he had to throw away a perfectly good three-cheese lasagne.' He turned to Zayn. 'I'm sorry, Vice President Winner. I can't have you mixing with troublemakers like her.'

This was all getting a bit surreal. A voice boomed out from beside her. 'Hey, lady!' It was an American accent. A genuine American accent. And it sounded familiar. She turned round. It was the tourist she had encountered in Trafalgar Square yesterday. Her mind flashed back to their conversations about cars and Lord Nelson. Britt had been using her normal accent. Not her American one. This situation had moved from tricky to very tricky.

'I didn't think you was gonna do it!' shouted the American. 'Jump all over them sports cars in Trafalgar Square. But you did!'

Zayn laughed. 'Cool! You can be my stunt double if I do another movie.'

Conor's jaw dropped. 'With respect, sir, this woman is the terror of Trafalgar Square.'

The American whooped with laughter. 'Is that what you guys are calling her?'

Britt wasn't aware that anyone was calling her anything. She was meant to be breaking the news, not making it.

'You're positive it was this woman, sir?' asked Conor.

'Sure is. Saw her with my own two eyeballs. She bounced off those Italian sports cars like they were trampolines. Funniest thing I ever saw!'

Conor was crimson now. 'I read the *Daily Democrat* story. Those beautiful machines. Trampled to death. You showed no mercy! An Italian sports car vandal – the worst kind of criminal!' He looked around and then screamed so loudly, every living creature within earshot scattered for safety. 'Officer, officer! Come quick! I've captured the terror of Trafalgar Square!' He grabbed Britt's arm. She tried to wrestle free but it was impossible. It was like being mauled by a grizzly bear.

'Hey, big guy, go easy on the lady,' shouted the American. 'Your traffic signals screwed up.'

Conor tightened his grip. 'That doesn't mean she can bounce all over the British traffic, sir.'

To Britt's relief, Zayn joined in. 'Give her a break, Conor. She's a big fan of mine.'

'So am I, sir, but that doesn't give me immunity to prosecution for crimes against sports cars.'

The approaching police officer was less than a minute away. Britt tried again to wriggle away from Conor. But it was impossible.

'Come on,' pleaded the American. 'She did what she had to do. Desperate affairs require desperate measures.'

'The words of Lord Nelson himself,' replied Conor, a dreamy look in his eyes. 'One of my historical heroes.' He let go of Britt's arm and saluted. 'England expects that every man will do his duty. And I shall do that duty, by handing this woman over to the authorities.'

The American whispered to her. 'If you're gonna do it, then go and do it! I ain't gonna stop you.'

Britt didn't need a second invitation. She turned and ran from the bridge, in the direction of Birdcage Walk.

'Stop!' cried Conor, from behind her. 'That woman is a fugitive from British justice!'

Conor's shouts, and the laughter of the American tourist, faded into the distance as she headed towards St James' Park

Metro station. The safest place to be right now was back at her pod – where she could plan her next move.

Chapter 27

Howie was sitting alone on a metal bench in a windowless police cell, somewhere in East London. He still couldn't quite believe what had happened to him. For the first time in his forty-two years and one day on the planet, he had been arrested. But this wasn't an everyday arrest. It was an arrest under section 24, subsection 7, of the new Penal Code. Or a 24-7 as it was known. This covered a wide range of offences – everything from stalking and harassment to pro-royal and anti-government activity. The fact Howie's suspected offence came into this category was made clear at his arrest. Mainly in four-letter words. Spoken at high volume. Close to his face.

Other first-time experiences had followed his arrest: being dragged into the back of a police van, being handcuffed, being bundled out of a police van, being processed in a police custody suite and being shoved into a cell. It had been a busy morning. And it wasn't over yet.

The grubby clock on the wall told him it was 11.31am. He'd been sitting here for more than three hours. He had been told that he'd be interviewed about the morning's events, including his close encounter with the First Lady, when an officer became available. But when would that be? He had no idea.

Howie examined himself. He was caked from head to toe in dried mud. And had been stripped of his personal possessions. There were no windows in the cell, just a wall-mounted security camera for the police to monitor his movements. He had no way of communicating with anyone outside the four concrete walls. It was a communication professional's worst nightmare. It was a secret agent's worst nightmare. There was nothing he could do but wait for a police officer to come and collect him for his interrogation. Then he would have to try and talk his way out of here.

More minutes passed. He got up and walked up to the camera. He gazed up at it and waved his hands. 'Hello. Can someone please come and interview me?' There was no response. He tried again, in a louder voice. 'I'm the president's spokesperson and a special investigator for the National Security and Intelligence Service. There's been a misunderstanding. Please can I talk to a police officer urgently?' Still nothing. He tried yelling. 'I want to speak to someone now! Are you listening to me? I don't have time to sit around in a police cell all day!' No response. He walked to the front of the cell to see if the camera would follow him. It didn't. He walked to the back of the cell and pretended to collapse onto the floor. After five uncomfortable minutes sprawled on his stomach, he got up. The camera hadn't moved a millimetre. It probably wasn't even switched on. He sat back down and leaned his head against the wall. No one was watching. No one was listening. He could die of mud poisoning, for all they cared.

After another half an hour, something snapped in Howie's brain. He jumped to his feet, rushed up to the door and screamed. 'I am not a celebrity stalker!' He punched the door. 'I am not a royal renegade!' He kicked the door. 'And I am not a demented Democrat!' He shoulder-charged the door. 'I am Howie Pond. And I am not a 24-7!'

A gruff voice echoed through the room from a speaker behind the camera. 'Mr Pond – or whoever you are. Listen carefully. You will only be told this once. Sit down. And shut up. You're upsetting the other prisoners.'

Prisoners? The realisation hit him. It didn't matter who he was. Or who the police thought he was. He was a prisoner now. And 24-7 prisoners could be held for up to seventy-two hours without charge. He knew this because he had masterminded the Government's media strategy during the new Penal Code's passage into law. Howie had robustly defended the new 24-7 rules, in the face of months of hostile media questions. He'd lost count of the number of times he had replied with the words, 'The innocent have nothing to fear – only the guilty.'

Howie felt a little better. He was innocent. But, then again, he was here on the word of the First Lady. He had no security service – or any other – ID. And he looked like he'd slept in a field. He had everything to fear. If the police didn't believe his story, and the First Lady maintained her pretence – so she could be interviewed by whoever she liked this week without Howie interfering – he could be held without charge for three days.

Then a thought occurred to him. Had the First Lady pretended not to know him for more sinister reasons? Could it be that she didn't want Howie investigating her husband's disappearance? She had been so cool about it yesterday. Maybe she was involved? With the president out of the way, she could make her American dreams a reality. It didn't seem such a stupid idea after this morning's madness. He hoped he was wrong. But he might be right.

Howie sat down again. He was starting to feel weak. He hadn't eaten properly today. Just a cream cake for breakfast. And they hadn't offered him any food at the police station. He forgot about the First Lady and thought back to last night. How ironic that he had been dining with the chief of police. And now he was sitting here, hungry and friendless, in one of Freddie's police cells.

Then he remembered. Freddie had given him a card containing his personal bleeper details. What were his words when he handed it over? Ah, yes. 'If you get into any bother, don't hesitate to contact me.' Howie's body juddered with excitement. He had an escape route. But there was just one problem. Both bleeper and wallet were in a plastic bag in the custody suite. He would have to get access to them.

The cell's automatic door opened and a serious-looking police officer popped his head around it. 'Mr Pond?'

Howie rushed to the door. 'That's me.'

'You look like you've just crawled from a pond.'

'I fell over.'

'Yes. In your rush to kidnap the First Lady of this great nation and hold the entire country to ransom, no doubt.'

Howie was so shocked at the accusation, his tongue wouldn't work.

'Is that a "No comment"?' sneered the officer. 'It usually is with you 24-7s. You could be looking at five years for this.'

Howie's tongue still wasn't working.

'I'll give you some advice,' continued the officer. 'It's better if you confess quickly. It can get very unpleasant in those interview rooms.' He paused. 'The atmosphere, I mean. Very heated. Very stuffy. Very … close.'

Howie was still speechless.

'If you confess in the first fifteen minutes, you get a microwave meal and a fizzy drink. If you maintain your innocence for longer than that, it's bread and tap water. The choice is yours.' The police officer looked Howie up and down. 'We can make it pond water, if you prefer.'

His tongue finally sprang into life. 'I'm innocent!'

The officer chuckled. 'You 24-7s always are. Until the Republic's justice system says otherwise. Now, come on; follow me. We're going to have what's called a "friendly chat".'

Howie didn't move. 'First I need to bleep my solicitor.'

The officer scowled. 'There is no requirement for you to have a solicitor present at the friendly chat stage of our enquiries, Mr Pond. We haven't charged you with anything.' He smiled. 'Yet.'

Fortunately, Howie's knowledge of the updated Penal Code stretched beyond section 24, subsection 7. And while solicitors were not proactively offered at the friendly chat stage, he was perfectly within his rights to ask for one. 'Section 13, subsection 12 of the 2043 Penal Code explicitly states that I am entitled to bleep my solicitor.'

'What makes you such an expert?'

'As I told your colleagues, I work for the president.'

The officer smirked. 'His wife doesn't seem to think so.'

Howie would have to choose his words carefully. Calling the First Lady a liar probably wasn't a good idea in front of this smart-arse. 'She didn't recognise me. I was covered in mud.'

'Who's your solicitor?' grumbled the officer.

'That's my business. But his details are in my wallet. I'll need that and my bleeper, please.'

'Sorry. But all personal possessions must be kept in custody for the duration of your stay with us, Mr Pond.'

'The prisoner must be given access, where those possessions are required to exercise their rights under section 13, subsection 12.'

The officer stared at Howie for a full ten seconds. 'You can forget about that microwave meal. Even if you do confess in the first fifteen minutes.' Then he left the cell and closed the door.

Howie smiled to himself. He would be out of here by lunchtime. Or would he? Before he could send his message, he needed to remember his cat's birthday. What the hell was it?

He sat down on the metal bench and focused his mind. He had to get this right. He only had one more attempt before the bloody thing locked him out. How old was Indie-Day? Five. He was sure of that. So she was born in either 2038 or 2039. And they'd called her Indie-Day because of her date of birth. Britt had chosen the name. It was short for 'Independence Day'. Not the British one. An American one. But which one? The Old States – 4 July – or the New States – 30 March? He remembered that they bought the cat during a heatwave. So it was more likely to be July than March. That meant she would be six this year. Born in 2038. So the PIN was 040738. That sounded familiar. He wasn't a hundred per cent certain. But he would go with it.

The cell door opened again and the police officer walked in. He handed Howie his wallet and bleeper. 'I have to supervise you. And as your supervisor, I'm giving you sixty seconds to perform whatever tasks you need to perform.'

Howie couldn't remember section 13, subsection 12, saying anything about a time limit, but there was no point wasting valuable seconds arguing about it. 'What's the name of this police station?'

'East London 27.'

Howie flicked on the bleeper's screen and read the message:

'E-COMM ALERT – CLASSIFIED message from MARTHA BLAKE. Enter your six-digit PIN to view. It's one more try and then I die!'

Howie punched in the six digits – 0, 4, 0, 7, 3 and 8. He took a breath. Then he pressed the button to confirm his selection. A second later, Martha's message from this morning flashed up. He didn't have time to sigh with relief. Instead, he scrolled down to the bottom, so the machine would think he'd read it, and selected the 'New Message' option. With his other hand, he manoeuvred the chief of police's card out of his wallet and tapped the bleeper code on it into the 'Recipient' box.

'Thirty seconds remaining, Mr Pond.'

Howie's bleeper suddenly felt like a ticking time bomb in his hands. His palms became sweaty. His breathing quickened. His throat went dry. This must be how James Bond felt with half a minute to disable an explosive device, he thought. Only this was probably more stressful.

Howie typed: 'Freddie. It's Howie Pond. President's spokesperson. Need help ASAP. Super-mega urgent.'

'Fifteen seconds.'

Howie wiped his sweaty brow and continued writing his message: 'In cell at East London 27 police station.'

The countdown continued. 'Five, four ...'

Howie selected 'Send Message'. This didn't always work first time. But it better had this time. Or he'd be throwing this bleeper in the Thames – when he eventually got out of here. The bleeper bleeped. The display reset. The message was sent.

'One and zero,' announced the officer, grabbing Howie's bleeper and wallet.

Howie smiled to himself. He'd done it in true Bond style – with just a second to spare.

'If your solicitor isn't here in half an hour, Mr Pond, we'll start without him.'

'Half an hour?' protested Howie. 'Come on, he'll need a bit of time to get here.'

'If you check section 13, subsection 12, you'll find there are no specific time limits stated. It's just a "reasonable period of time". And half an hour, round here, is reasonable.'

Howie sighed. 'Can't you make it an hour? That's reasonable in my book.'

The officer thought about it for a few seconds. 'No. Half an hour.'

This was like dealing with a difficult journalist on a deadline. And he'd handled hundreds of those. So he wasn't giving up just yet. 'Can we meet halfway – forty-five minutes?'

The officer thought about it some more. 'No.'

'What about ten more minutes, eh? Ten minutes is nothing.'

'Well if ten minutes is nothing to you, Mr Pond, I could always reduce it by ten minutes to twenty minutes.' He adopted a smug smile. 'How about that?'

This guy was the Maurice Skeets of the law-enforcement world. Howie would have to admit defeat. 'Okay, okay. Thirty minutes it is.'

'I'm glad we're agreed. Now you must be thirsty after all your exertions this morning. Can I get you something to drink while you're waiting?'

This act of kindness seemed a little out of place. But Howie wasn't going to argue. His throat felt like sandpaper. 'Thanks. I could murder a cup of tea.'

'As long as that's all you'll be murdering. Milk, sugar?'

'Milk, three sugars.'

'Coming right up, Mr Pond,' replied the officer, looking pleased with himself. Then he left the cell and closed the door behind him.

There was nothing left to do. Just wait for his cup of tea. And his chief of police.

Chapter 28

Britt was hurtling eastwards on a Jubilee Line Metro train towards Canary Wharf. The only other passengers in the carriage were a group of American tourists. They looked lost. One of the men turned to her and spoke in a New York accent. 'Excuse me, ma'am. Are we heading in the right direction for that giant dome thing?'

Britt answered in her normal accent. 'Yes. It's North Greenwich station – two more stops.'

'Thank you, ma'am.' The man turned back to his group. Pellie Cann might have engaged him in further conversation. But she was no longer Pellie Cann. She was back to being Britt. That was because she couldn't risk the terror of Trafalgar Square being recognised again. And it was why, after escaping the iron grip of Conor O'Brean in St James' Park, she had continued on to the safety of her pod and changed out of her disguise into a white blouse and slim-fit jeans. It meant Britt was on her own now. It would be up to her, and her alone, to get this story.

After saying goodbye to Pellie, she hadn't headed straight out. Instead, she'd sprawled out on the bed for almost two hours – trying to fit together all the pieces of the puzzle she had collected so far.

The train juddered to a halt in a tunnel outside the next station. The group of tourists stopped talking and there was complete silence. It was a perfect opportunity to run through her conclusions once more, with no interruptions.

The searches of the palace had found no trace of the president. So he must have left on Monday night. Whether he did so voluntarily, or against his will, she didn't know. But whoever managed to mastermind it knew exactly what they were doing. They had to be someone with Tech knowledge, high-speed transport and high-level contacts.

Britt had revisited the interview with the First Lady and considered whether she might be involved in the president's disappearance. But she'd quickly decided that it was very unlikely. Neither a suspected affair with Cherry Blush nor an obvious desire to live in the New States seemed strong enough motives. Britt might be wrong, but her instincts told her otherwise.

Zayn Winner probably wasn't involved either. He wasn't a political heavyweight. He wasn't even a political lightweight. More a featherweight. Yes, he was an opportunist – someone who might be deluded enough to think he could run for president, if the chance came along. But there was no way he was a criminal mastermind who could arrange a presidential kidnap – or worse – to further his political career. He was too dumb. Too nice, even. Anyway, he would never be allowed to run for president. His vice-presidential colleagues simply wouldn't allow it. There were other, much more obvious, candidates for the presidency should Jan Polak not be around to confirm a third term.

Lying on her bed, she had asked herself who could be devious enough to dispose of the president, on either a temporary or permanent basis. A political rival? It was possible. But surely not a Democrat. They were too dull. Too docile. No. It could only be another Republican. Just one name came to mind – Oskar Polak. And then there was the Pierogi Pact between Jan and Oskar – exactly the kind of thing that could create bad blood between brothers. Yes. Oskar was the prime suspect.

Britt had imagined what might go through the mind of a man who had waited so long to be president. The mind of a married man having an affair. That, too, was obvious. Most vice presidents were involved in improper personal or business relationships at some point in their careers. In Britt's experience, only the stupid ones got caught. And Oskar wasn't stupid. Britt's guess was that he was ending his relationship with Cherry because it would be an inconvenience if he were to run for the highest office in the land. And with Oskar holding the sensitive post of vice president for defence, maybe there were other secret relationships to uncover?

Cherry Blush was the person to unlock this mystery. She would know who Oskar's friends were – the movers and shakers he spent his time with. And Oskar would surely have communicated something about his political future to Cherry. Britt would love to know what had been said on that park bench yesterday. Was it the usual break-up script? Or maybe Oskar revealed his true intentions? There was only one way to find out. Track down Cherry Blush and ask her. No. Not just ask her. Interrogate her. And if she didn't want to cooperate, Britt knew exactly what to do – threaten to expose their affair.

'We're moving again, folks!' announced one of the tourists.

The train pulled into Canary Wharf station. It was her stop. She left the train. The platform's digital clocks showed the time as 11:54:20. She rushed up the escalators and out of the station.

Britt then hurried the few hundred metres to American Fitness. She had already bleeped them to confirm Cherry was working there today. How easy it would be to meet with her was another matter. The gym receptionist's e-comm claimed Cherry was fully booked. But this kind of place always said that. Britt would find a way to get to her.

Chapter 29

It had been twenty-five minutes since Howie bleeped Freddie English, requesting his urgent help. But the door to the concrete police cell had remained shut all that time. The only arrival was his cup of tea – pushed through a small flap at the bottom of the door. It had a strange taste. The officer must have let it brew for too long. But badly made tea was the least of his worries. He needed to find a way out of here.

Howie paced up and down the cell. The camera on the wall still wasn't following him, so he wandered up to the door to see if he could hear anything. He pressed his ear against the cold metal. There were no exchanges between police officers about the chief of police arriving unannounced, asking to see the crazy guy covered in dried mud. In fact, there weren't any conversations at all. Just silence, punctuated by the occasional sound of a prisoner screaming in the distance.

Howie swallowed hard. This was getting serious now. If Freddie didn't show up, Howie would soon be dragged into an interrogation room with only bread and tap water to keep him going.

As he walked back to the bench, Howie started to feel odd. He stared at the wall opposite. It seemed to be closing in on him, millimetre by concrete millimetre. He checked the other walls. They were doing the same. Then he examined the ceiling. That was advancing towards him at the same millimetric rate. This couldn't be real. Maybe it was? Could it be a new tactic to obtain confessions from prisoners – the incredible shrinking police cell? Given Howie's experience of police procedure so far, that didn't seem such a crazy idea.

Howie staggered to the centre of the cell. It felt like the safest place to be. He stood tall and shouted. 'Get back! My name is Pond. Howie Pond. And no one kills Howie Pond!' He wasn't sure why he said it. But it did the trick. The walls and ceiling began retreating to their original positions. Seconds later, he felt light-headed and closed his eyes. When the dizziness subsided, he opened them again. He stared at the cell's grey walls. And he realised he had no idea where he was or why he was here. For a full thirty seconds, his mind was a complete blank.

Then his whole body juddered and everything came back to him. But his head and limbs felt heavy. He sat down on the bench and slumped against the wall. His blood-sugar levels must be low. It was the only explanation. Tiredness hit him like a slap in the face.

As he drifted into sleep, images from last night's dream flashed into his mind. The boat chase, the beach escape, the rock climb, the secret complex, the captured president, the evil genius. They spun round his mind in a carousel of confusion. Then he heard a voice from beyond his dream world. 'Howie, old chap, what's going on?'

Howie's eyes flicked open. He looked awake. But he was still deep in his dream state. 'It's Maxim,' he mumbled.

'What do you mean?' asked the voice.

Howie heard the question and responded. 'He's the evil genius who's got the president.'

The voice became louder. 'What are you talking about? Have you discovered new evidence?'

Howie's eyes were still wide open. But all he could see was Maxim pointing a gun at the president and threatening to put a bullet in his head. 'He's going to kill the president!' shouted Howie. Then he took a breath. 'He wants to replace him.'

'My God, this is treason!' gasped the voice.

Howie's eyes blinked three times and he rejoined reality. He became aware of a person sitting next to him. He turned to look at his face. It was a man. But it wasn't any of the police officers he'd encountered today. It was the chief of police. 'Freddie,' he gasped with relief. 'You came.'

'Of course I came. I'm a man of my word.'

Howie still wasn't himself, but having Freddie next to him was making him feel better. 'The police think I'm a 24-7. They locked me in here for nearly four hours. They're going to interrogate me.'

'Don't worry. I saw you on the security camera and confirmed who you are. I explained that you would have been at the studios on business and the First Lady probably didn't recognise you, seeing as you currently resemble a mud monster from Mars.'

'She knew who I was,' growled Howie. 'She just wanted me out of the way, so she could do that bloody interview. She's the one who should be arrested!'

'We are where we are. You being arrested brought me to your rescue. And that may be a fortuitous chain of events for your good self.'

'How do you mean?'

'All will become clear. Now, in a minute I'll take you up to the custody suite and we'll get you de-arrested.' Freddie looked into Howie's eyes. 'But first, you look a little peculiar. Are you in good health?'

'I need to eat. Can we go somewhere?'

'Yes. I'm taking you to a place you'll be familiar with – The Savoy.'

Howie wasn't sure whether he should have a full lunch break, after all the time he'd wasted sitting in this cell. But it would be rude to decline the offer. 'The Savoy it is.'

'But in light of what you've just told me about the president's disappearance, Howie, I'm going to ask someone else to join us.'

Howie was confused. He couldn't remember telling Freddie anything. He must have forgotten in all the confusion. 'What do you mean?'

'I mean it's time that I used my contacts to get you in the same room as the number-one suspect in the president's disappearance.'

The number-one suspect. Yes. Who was that? Howie wasn't sure. Better not to get into a long discussion about it. That would only delay lunch. 'Okay. That sounds good.'

Freddie stood up. 'All I ask is that when your missing person is back where he belongs, you inform him of my pivotal role in helping you with your mission.'

'Of course I will.'

'And whatever you do, don't breathe a word of this to Martha Blake. If she knows I'm helping you – even if it is on a personal level, rather than an official level – we'll both get an ear-bashing. And we don't want that.'

Howie nodded. He would accept Freddie's offer of help and keep his involvement a secret from Martha. 'Yep. Let's work together on this.'

Freddie smiled. 'Good man. Now, you can't go to The Savoy in that state. But don't fret. I've arranged a clean set of clothes.'

Howie wasn't sure he wanted to leave here looking like a teenage drug dealer. 'It's not one of them synth all-in-ones you stick the real criminals in, is it?'

Freddie laughed. 'On the contrary. It's a better suit than the one you're wearing. Much better. The finest Italian silk. We keep a spare at every station. Just in case any high-profile clients like yourself need a bit of assistance. We usually charge, of course, but in your case, consider it a freebie.'

'You're a lifesaver.'

'I like to think so. Now, let's get you discharged, water-sprayed, changed and out of here. There are two sirloin steaks at The Savoy with our names on them.'

Howie stood up. He was feeling better now. Maybe that funny spell was because of something he ate? He looked down at his cup of tea. Or more likely, something he drank. Yes. The reason for the police officer's generosity was clear now. Howie's tea had been spiked in an effort to disorientate him before his interrogation. Luckily, he'd only taken a couple of sips, so its effects had been limited. But it was still outrageous. He thought about mentioning it to Freddie. But he decided against it. It would just cause more hassle for both of them.

They got up and left the cell. Twenty minutes later, they were leaving the police station and jumping in a taxi. Next stop – The Savoy.

Chapter 30

Britt walked forward to the American Fitness reception desk. The receptionist nodded and beamed a huge smile at her.

'Good morning, madam. Are you a member?'

Britt didn't smile back. Partly because she'd been waiting twenty minutes. Partly because smiling politely didn't come naturally to her. And partly because this wasn't going to be a polite request. 'No. I'm here to see Cherry Blush.'

'I'm afraid Miss Blush is fully booked today. Would you like to leave a message?'

'I won't be leaving any messages. I need to see her now.'

The receptionist's smile didn't flicker. 'That won't be possible, madam. Only our Premium Club members can demand to see Miss Blush at their convenience. Membership starts from £5,000 a month, if you would like to —'

'I don't need the marketing brochure,' interrupted Britt. 'It's a personal matter.'

'Then I would suggest you contact Miss Blush about that matter in her own personal time.'

Britt leaned her forearms on the desk and dropped her voice an octave. 'Contact Miss Blush. Tell her someone is in reception. And tell her it's someone who needs to see her urgently.'

The receptionist thought about Britt's request for a few moments, while maintaining her smile. 'And you are?'

Staying anonymous was always the best option in this kind of situation. If it all went wrong, at least your adversaries only knew your face. 'Miss Smith.'

'You have ID, Miss Smith?'

'No, I'm sorry.'

'Then I am sorry. I can't help you.'

Battling against receptionists was always difficult. They were veterans of customer combat. Getting past their defensive line was often impossible, even for an investigative journalist as experienced as Britt. But she had planned for this. She was ready with another line of attack. One that would lure Cherry out of the safety of her consulting room and into the reception area itself. 'Tell Miss Blush that I'm a friend of Oskar.'

'Oskar who?'

'Just Oskar.'

The receptionist's smile was cracking. 'Is he a member?'

'I've no idea. It's not important.'

'Does this Oskar work here?'

'No,' sighed Britt. 'Just make the call.'

The receptionist stopped smiling. 'What is it that you want exactly, madam?'

'That's between me and Miss Blush. Now stop wasting my time and give her the message.'

'And what if I don't?'

Britt's response was immediate. 'Then Cherry Blush won't thank you when I inform her that she had the opportunity to see me right now. But you failed to make a simple call to alert her to that fact.'

They stared at each other for a full ten seconds. Neither spoke. Neither blinked. Neither breathed. Like two warriors about to engage in hand-to-hand combat. Then Britt decided it was time to fake a retreat. 'Fine. Have it your way.' She turned in the direction of the exit.

'Alright,' snapped the receptionist. 'I'll do it.'

Britt swung round. 'Thank you.'

'But if Miss Blush says she doesn't want to see you, you will be asked to leave. If you don't do it voluntarily, I'll call security. Understood?'

Britt nodded. The receptionist gave her a filthy look and then spoke into an intercom. 'A woman is here to see you, Miss Blush.'

'Hi, honey!' trilled Cherry from the intercom. 'You sure about that? All my appointments are fellas today.'

'This woman doesn't have an appointment. She said she's a friend of someone called Oskar. I don't know if that means anything to you.' There was no response. 'Cherry, are you still there? I said she's a friend of —'

Cherry's voice sounded flatter. 'Still here, sweetie. What's the lady's name?'

'She gave her name as Miss Smith. But she doesn't have any ID. She wants to talk to you right now. It's a personal matter.'

'Oh, r-r-right,' stuttered Cherry. 'It's a bit tricky at the mo. I'm with someone. Let me think about how I'm gonna do this.'

As several seconds ticked by, a thought occurred to Britt. After Cherry's secret meeting with Oskar Polak yesterday, she might be wondering if the 'friend of Oskar' was more than just a friend. A wife, maybe. One who'd just discovered her husband had been having an affair with Cherry. A wife who wasn't here on a social visit.

Britt issued one more instruction to the receptionist. 'Tell her I'm not a relative. Definitely just a friend of Oskar.'

The receptionist reluctantly relayed the message via the intercom.

'Okay,' sighed Cherry. 'I'll be straight out.'

Within sixty seconds, Cherry had arrived at reception. She looked flustered. Frightened even.

The receptionist flicked her eyes in Britt's direction. 'This is the woman.'

Cherry's eyes scanned Britt – her face, hair, clothes and shoes – desperately searching for some clue about the identity of this friend of Oskar. But Britt could tell from Cherry's wrinkled forehead that she couldn't find one. 'I haven't got long. I'm with a client.'

'It won't take more than a few minutes,' replied Britt. But she wasn't sure if it was true. It would depend on Cherry's reaction to what she had to say. If things went well, Cherry would play along and answer her questions. And Britt had lots of those. On the other hand, she had already witnessed Cherry take swift flight from one stressful situation. She hoped she wouldn't see a repeat performance today.

Cherry checked the people in the reception area. Then she took a couple of steps towards Britt. Their faces were only a few centimetres away from each other. 'I don't wanna talk here,' she whispered. 'Let's step outside.' Then she turned to the receptionist. 'If anyone asks where I am, honey, just say I've popped out for painkillers.'

Cherry gestured to Britt to follow her and they left the building. They turned right and walked the short distance to the edge of the concrete plaza. There were still people coming and going. But it was private here.

'Who are you?' demanded Cherry, her voice a mix of panic and confusion.

'I didn't want to say who I really was in front of your colleague. I'm actually Britt Pointer.' She fished out her ID and showed it to Cherry. 'I'm a journalist.'

Cherry tried not to react as she examined the card. But Britt could see the fear in her eyes. 'A journalist?'

'Yes. And I'm doing an investigation into Oskar Polak. A man you're very familiar with.'

Cherry was lost for words for a moment. Then she swallowed hard and responded. 'What's that supposed to mean?'

Britt was now in control. 'It means you've been having an affair.'

Cherry tried to laugh off the accusation. It was unconvincing. 'You got it wrong. Me and Oskar are just good friends.'

'I saw you here together yesterday. You met in secret. Went to the park around the corner. Sat on a bench. Had a heated conversation. Then you yelled his name and ran off. I presume because he gave you bad news. I'm guessing he dumped you.' Britt took a breath. 'Am I right?'

Cherry swallowed hard again. 'Like I told you, we're just good friends. He was … he was just telling me we couldn't meet up that evening coz he was busy with something. I forget what.'

'He came all the way out to Canary Wharf to tell you he was too busy to see you?'

'Yeah. Oskar's really considerate like that.'

'He couldn't just bleep you?'

'I work very long hours. Sometimes with no breaks. I don't always get time to check my bleeper.'

'Really?'

'Yeah, really.'

This young woman was proving almost as tough an adversary as her colleague in reception. But, as with that battle, a new angle of attack should set Britt on the road to victory. 'I'm writing a story. But I'm not interested in your relationship with Oskar Polak.'

'No?' replied Cherry, sounding surprised. 'What are you interested in, then?'

'I'm interested in Oskar Polak's relationships with other people. People with power and influence.'

Cherry frowned. 'Sorry. Can't help you. When we met up, it was only ever the two of us.'

Britt sighed. 'If I don't get the information I want – for the story I want – I'll have to write about your relationship with Oskar Polak. Because that's all I have at the moment.'

Cherry's tone was more aggressive now. 'But you only seen us in the park. You got bugger all evidence. You're bullshitting me!'

'You're wrong. I have this.' Britt reached into her bag. She pulled out the photo she had obtained from the First Lady's office – a photo of Cherry Blush outside a Westminster townhouse, with Oskar Polak standing at the door. She showed it to Cherry. 'It's one of many. A private investigator has been following you.'

Cherry's mouth dropped in horror and her breathing became quicker. 'Is that who that bloke was? I thought he was a bloody stalker!' She put her hand on Britt's arm. 'You're not gonna publish it, are you? His wife don't know. We've broken up. It's finished.'

'Why did it finish?' asked Britt, returning the photo to her bag.

'Oskar said it had to finish.'

Britt was getting close to something important. She could feel it. 'Yes. But did he explain why?'

'Something changed. He wouldn't say what. Maybe his wife's ill? Or she was getting suspicious? I dunno. He just said we couldn't carry on. And I was never to say nothing to no one about it.' She heaved a big sigh. 'That didn't last long, did it?'

Britt wasn't going to stop here. 'His other relationships, Cherry. You've got to tell me about those. Who was he meeting recently?'

Cherry thought for a moment. 'Viktor Maxim. He was the only one he ever mentioned.'

Maxim? Where had Britt heard that name before?

'He's the Russian bloke who owns this place,' continued Cherry. 'And a lot of other places.' She looked around to check no one was listening. 'Don't say I told you, for king's sake. But they're very friendly. Oskar likes to keep it top secret. He says it's all hush-hush because he's a top politician and Maxim is a big businessman. People might jump to the wrong conclusions.'

Britt remembered that name now – Maxim. It was the name on the screen when she caught a glimpse of Oskar's bleeper. Her heart started to beat faster. 'What other businesses does this Maxim run?'

'You name it, he runs it. Sports, food, drink, Tech.' Her voice dropped to a whisper. 'Even guns and rockets and stuff. I know, coz Oskar told me once, when he'd had too much red wine.'

The defence industry? That was full of shady characters and dodgy deals. And Oskar was the vice president for defence. No wonder he wanted to keep his relationship with Maxim a secret.

'Did Oskar get you the job as the president's personal trainer?' asked Britt.

'No. American Fitness contacted the palace with an offer of a free personal trainer a couple of years ago. The president accepted. Maxim asked me to do it. He said it would be good PR to have someone like me in the palace. And I could keep all the fees.'

An idea came to Britt. 'Did Maxim encourage you to make contacts at the palace?'

'Yeah, he did. The president introduced me to Oskar not long after I started. And we, you know … got friendly pretty quickly.' She checked that no one could overhear them. 'I was worried at first. So I told Maxim about it. I didn't want to lose my job because of some fling with a married politician. But he weren't bothered. Actually, he was dead chuffed about it. He told me to bring Oskar here and I introduced them.'

'So Maxim knew about your affair?'

'Yeah. I didn't tell Oskar that, though. Maxim told me not to.'

This information was solid gold. Mr Maxim had clearly been making big efforts to make contacts at the centre of government – contacts he could leverage in the future for his own gain.

Britt's thoughts turned to Oskar's presidential ambitions. 'Did Oskar say anything about his political future?'

'He never wanted to talk politics. I tried a few times. But he weren't interested.'

There was no reason to doubt that. So, if Britt was going to confirm what she suspected – that Oskar was lining himself up to take over the presidency – she would have to speak to the man himself.

Cherry took a tentative step towards the gym entrance.

'I'm not finished yet,' growled Britt. It was time to engineer a meeting with Vice President Polak and see what he had to say for himself. 'Do you have Oskar's bleeper number?'

'Yeah. Course.'

'Then bleep him and ask him to meet you today.'

Cherry moved closer to Britt. 'I think I've helped you enough for one day, don't you?'

'Bleep him now and tell him to meet you at one o'clock in Trafalgar Square.'

'Trafalgar Square? Why do I have to schlepp all the way over there?!'

'It's closer to the palace. They'll be lots of crowds. No one will know who you are.'

'But it'll take half the afternoon to get there and back. I've got clients!'

'Cancel the clients.'

Cherry rolled her eyes. '"Cancel the clients," she says, like I'm a bloody hairdresser having a duvet day. My clients don't like being messed around. They're important people.'

'More important than Oskar Polak?' Britt paused for a few seconds. 'More important than you?'

Cherry screwed up her eyes, as if trying to wish herself into a parallel universe where Britt didn't exist. Then she opened them again. Britt was still here. She could see the disappointment in Cherry's face.

Cherry heaved a huge sigh. 'Okay. But it'll be a waste of time. He don't wanna see me again. I'm not even supposed to contact him.'

'Just tell him a journalist has contacted you about your relationship with him. Say you need to speak with him ASAP. Face-to-face. But don't tell him I'm going to be there.'

Cherry took out her bleeper. 'Trafalgar Square, one o'clock, yeah?'

'By the fountain nearest The Mall.'

Cherry tapped out the message. They stood in silence for a short while. Then Oskar's reply came.

'He'll be there,' confirmed Cherry, with a glum expression.

'Excellent. Now we'll go back inside. You'll inform your colleague in reception that you're cancelling all appointments until further notice. You will say this is for personal reasons. You won't enter into any further discussion about it. You won't mention who I really am. You won't scream or shout or call security.' She patted her bag. 'Because I have the photographic evidence. Then we'll come back outside and grab a taxi. And we'll meet Oskar, as arranged.'

Cherry said nothing. She just scowled and headed back inside the building. Britt followed. She was in control now. And she was getting closer and closer to the truth.

Chapter 31

Howie and Freddie had discussed a wide range of subjects since they'd arrived at The Savoy's Premier Diners restaurant. But the missing president hadn't been mentioned once. It was almost as if they had been transported to a parallel universe – one where Jan Polak had been up since five o'clock, preparing an Independence Day speech in his private office, while Howie and Freddie were enjoying an afternoon in each other's company. Howie was more relaxed and at ease than he could ever remember. Maybe it was the dodgy tea he'd drunk in the police cell? Or being in Freddie's company? Maybe a mixture of the two? Whatever it was, it felt good.

'When is this contact of yours joining us?' asked Howie.

'Should be here any minute,' replied Freddie, finishing his glass of red wine.

Howie chewed his last piece of sirloin steak. 'So is he a friend of yours?'

'More of an acquaintance. A contact I've acquired.'

'You told him a special investigator would be here?'

'No. I just invited him for lunch.'

'And he dropped everything?' Howie chuckled. 'Did you say you were paying?'

Freddie smiled. 'I told him that it was in his best interests to be here. And when the chief of police tells you that it's in your best interests to be somewhere, it generally means it's in your best interests to be there.'

They both laughed. Freddie even made Code Red crises feel like fun.

Howie loosened the belt on his new suit a notch. 'You said this guy was the number-one suspect?'

'After what you told me, yes.'

Howie didn't want to look like a fool. But he had to ask. 'Remind me what I told you.'

Freddie chuckled. 'Oh, come on. Don't be coy. It was the first thing you said in the police cell. I know you blurted it out in the heat of the moment – and probably weren't authorised to tell me – but you named a name. And, with my connections, I can bring that name to you.'

Howie tried to remember whose name he had mentioned. But he couldn't. Then his stomach grumbled. 'Do you think we'll have time for dessert?'

Freddie looked across the restaurant. 'Alas, no. Here he is now.'

Howie looked up. A tall man with a crooked nose and high cheekbones was marching towards them in a perfectly tailored white suit that probably cost more than Howie's entire wardrobe. The man didn't look pleased. When he reached their table, the man stopped. He looked at Howie with suspicion and growled at him. 'I see you have already eaten.' He turned to Freddie. 'So why have you dragged me here, Mr English?'

'This is special investigator Howie Pond from the National Security and Intelligence Service,' explained Freddie, gesturing towards Howie. 'He needs to ask you some questions in relation to a matter of national security.'

The man's prickly response was instant. 'Perhaps you have confused me with someone else, Mr Pond? Because I am not the right person to be discussing British national security.'

Howie wasn't sure if this man was the right person. He still had no memory of giving a name to Freddie. But here was the alleged number-one suspect in the president's disappearance presenting himself to Howie for questioning. And the only question that popped into Howie's mind was 'Who the hell are you?' Howie wasn't going to make the mistake of actually asking that question. That could ruin his chances of getting any valuable information from this suspect. And, more importantly, it could make him look like a complete idiot. No. Howie would act tough. Just like 007 when he needed to extract information from the bad guys. And despite currently knowing nothing about the man standing in front of him, years of watching Bond films told Howie that this was, most definitely, a bad guy.

'Sit down,' ordered Howie. 'I don't have much time.'

The man stood motionless.

'I said sit down,' barked Howie. 'Unless you want the chief of police to give you a guided tour of the Westminster police cells.'

The man stared wide-eyed at Freddie. 'I see. Mr English is your back-up.' He took a step towards Freddie and breathed in through his nose. 'I know him well. And he is a wise choice as a friend, Mr Pond.'

Freddie flashed a worried look at Howie. 'I think I'll let you take it from here, old chap.' He jumped up, banged his leg against the table and winced with pain. 'I've done my bit. It's your jurisdiction now.'

Before Howie could respond, Freddie was hobbling across the floor to the safety of a table on the other side of the restaurant. It was a little unexpected. But Freddie was right. It was Howie's jurisdiction. Freddie had given him enough help.

The man sat down. 'So, Mr Pond, what is this matter of national security that has interrupted my day? Is your king flying back from Florida with his ladies-in-waiting?' He laughed a hollow laugh.

Howie didn't acknowledge the attempt at humour. Instead, he picked up the wine bottle from the table, poured the remainder of its contents into his own glass and took a sip.

'I see you're drinking the house red,' sneered the man.

'Yes. I find too much Château Mouton Rothschild dulls the palate.' The man was visibly taken aback at this observation. It was actually a line from the last Bond movie ever made – *The Spy Who Wined and Dined Me* – but, fortunately, the man didn't realise this. Howie now had his full attention. 'To go back to your question, as it's a matter of national security, the details are classified.'

The man muttered something in a foreign language. Howie ignored it and continued. 'All you need to know is that I am a special investigator.'

'So you're a secret agent?'

Howie puffed out his chest. 'Some people might call me that.'

The man sat back and crossed his arms. 'And other people might call you something else.'

'And what do I call you?' asked Howie, in a flash. This could be it. He would get the man's name.

The man leaned forward. 'You can call me what you like, Mr Pond. Just get on with it.'

Howie took another sip of house red, to mask his disappointment at not getting a name. Then he washed the wine around his mouth for a few seconds, to make the point that he was the one in charge of timings. The pause was also long enough for Howie to realise that questioning someone whose identity he still didn't know would be difficult. Very difficult. 'Can I ask if you've ever met the British president?'

The man thought about his answer before replying. 'Not Jan Polak. But I met his predecessor – Michael Short.'

This sounded interesting. 'In what circumstances?'

'A Democratic Party fundraiser for the 2029 election. A long, long time ago.'

'So you made political donations?'

'I did that year.'

'What about President Short's re-election campaign in 2034?'

The man forced a smile. 'I never bet on a loser, Mr Pond.'

'So you backed a winner – Jan Polak?'

'No, I made no contributions to his campaigns.'

'But did you offer to make a donation?'

The man narrowed his eyes. 'It's so long ago, I really can't remember.'

This man reminded Howie of himself at press briefings – confidently batting away tricky questions with carefully worded answers. Howie pressed on. 'What's your opinion of Jan Polak's ten years in power?'

'I'm not a political commentator, Mr Pond.'

'Let me put it another way – would you like to see him stand for a third term? Or would you like to see someone else leading this country?'

The man sighed and stared at the ceiling. 'I do not have a strong opinion either way.'

What next? Howie didn't want to spend too much time talking about the president. The man might get suspicious. He would move on to someone else. The president's brother was the first person who came to mind. 'Do you know Oskar Polak?'

The man rolled his eyes. 'Are you going to run through every member of the president's family? Because I am a very busy man.'

Howie sensed he was on to something. So he narrowed his eyes in the way James Bond often did when interrogating bad guys. 'Do you know him or not?'

The man took a long, slow breath through his nose. Then he shook his head, as if this was a ridiculous waste of his time.

'Tell me if you know Oskar Polak,' growled Howie. 'This is a matter of national security. Failure to answer my question truthfully will be interpreted as you failing to cooperate.' He leaned in towards the man and another line from *The Spy Who Wined and Dined Me* flashed into his mind. 'And that option simply isn't on tonight's menu.'

'Yes, alright. I know him,' gabbled the man.

'How well?'

'Quite well.'

'Do you meet with him regularly?'

'We meet for lunch or dinner, from time to time.'

'And what do you discuss?'

'Things,' sighed the man.

'What kind of things?'

'All kinds of things.'

'Government things?'

The man's frustration spilled over into his voice. 'I work across many industries, Mr Pond. Oskar Polak has responsibility for government policy in many areas relevant to those industries. And so there is a legitimate, mutually beneficial, flow of information between us.' The man took a deep breath. 'That is all.'

Finally Howie was getting somewhere. This man was some kind of big businessman. And, in Howie's experience, big businessmen usually met senior politicians when profits were involved. His firm must be doing some kind of business with the Government. He would try and confirm it. 'Are you a supplier to the Government?'

'Only on a small scale.'

'But you're looking to expand your market share over here?'

The man rolled his eyes. 'That is the general idea of business, Mr Pond.'

Howie had an idea. 'And what's the name of your business?' If he knew that, he could probably figure out who this guy was.

The man shook his head in disbelief. 'It's the international business that bears my name, of course.'

So much for that bright idea. Howie could see his interviewee was getting tetchy and itching to leave. He looked across the restaurant. Freddie was paying no attention to what was happening at Howie's table. Instead he had pulled up his trouser leg and was inspecting a bruise on his right shin. If the man wanted to leave, Freddie wasn't going to be in a position to stop him. Howie needed to ask some killer questions. But he was feeling less relaxed now. Whatever magic was in that tea was wearing off. And there was no Freddie nearby to make him feel at ease. He was on his own now.

'Do you come here often?' asked Howie. It was a stupid question. But he couldn't think of anything else.

'Yes. But I'm struggling to understand what that has to do with British national security.'

So was Howie. His mind was a bit of a mess at the moment.

'You can ask one more question,' sneered the man. 'Then I have to leave.'

The only one that came to mind was an even more stupid question about the quality of the sirloin steaks. But before Howie could think of anything else, a waiter interrupted them.

'Can I get you anything to eat or drink, Mr Maxim?'

'Not now,' snapped the man. 'I'm busy.'

Howie almost hit the ceiling. This was Viktor Maxim. A man with suspected criminal connections. A man who had lunch with Oskar Polak yesterday in this very restaurant. He knew what question to ask. 'When did you last meet with Oskar Polak?'

The man leaned forward and put his hands on the table. His eyes seemed to flash a warning to Howie – don't pursue this line of enquiry or you might end up falling through a trapdoor into a shark-infested pool below. 'I can't remember.'

He was lying. 'You're sure you didn't meet him this week?' asked Howie.

Maxim stood up. 'Positive. Now, I abandoned an all-day meeting to be here and I need to get back.' He cocked his head and looked puzzled. 'I have no idea what relevance your questions had to British national security, but I trust you'll conclude that I have no part to play in whatever it is that's concerning you. Goodbye.' He stormed off towards the exit and passed Freddie, who was completely oblivious to everything except the bruise on his leg.

Howie looked at the clock. It was almost one. The Republican Party nomination meeting was only three hours away. He sighed. There would be no time for dessert. He'd have to grab an ice cream on the way back to the office.

Chapter 32

Britt was back in Trafalgar Square, standing in the shadow of Nelson's column. Her eyes were fixed on Cherry Blush, who was perched on the edge of the fountain nearest The Mall, a few metres away. They were both scanning the crowds for Vice President Oskar Polak. But Big Ben had chimed its one o'clock bong almost ten minutes ago. Oskar was late.

Britt kept her cool and carried on searching. She knew Oskar would come. He had to come. He couldn't afford to risk having the details of his affair with his brother's personal trainer splashed across the front pages on Independence Day – a day when he could be announcing himself as the Republican Party's presidential candidate.

But she had a nagging worry. Oskar might just play dumb. She couldn't assume he would reveal his political ambitions or confirm his brother's disappearance. He was a skilled political operator. A man used to dealing with difficult questions under pressure.

Her confidence wobbled. If she couldn't get the evidence she needed for her story – what then? Another story? Maybe she would write something about Oskar's affair and offer that to her editor? It would interest some people, for sure. But it wouldn't interest George. There was no public-interest angle. Cherry Blush wasn't a senior civil servant, top politician or anyone else that might make the affair an error of judgement. It was just an affair. And it had ended – privately and discretely. Anyway, Cherry had told her about Oskar and Maxim's regular meetings. That made her a secondary source for the purposes of Britt's big story and meant she had a duty to keep Cherry out of it. No.

Britt's salvation could only be an article headlined 'We Have Lost The President'.

Britt pushed the doubts to the back of her mind and looked across at Cherry. They hadn't spoken since they'd arrived twenty minutes ago. But that was deliberate. Britt wanted to keep her distance for the moment. Oskar mustn't suspect that Cherry was with someone. He might get spooked and run. Britt had to play it carefully. She had to be patient. She had to let the rat come to the trap.

She looked around, just in case the American tourist from yesterday had returned to Trafalgar Square. There was no sign of him. Britt felt a pang of disappointment. She could have used some back-up. Still, at least Lord Nelson was here. It was a silly thought but it made her smile. She looked up at him. There he was. Still looking in the direction of The Mall. Oskar would probably be walking down it right now.

A second later, a seagull that had been perching on Nelson's head took off. It soared into the air, in the direction of The Mall, then did a one hundred and eighty degree turn towards The Strand. It proceeded to dive bomb a man in a smart suit who was holding an ice cream and walking straight towards her. As the man battled with the bird, she realised his face was familiar. But it wasn't Oskar Polak.

The man dropped the ice cream in the middle of a pedestrian crossing and ran to the sanctuary of the main square. She could see his face clearly now. No. It couldn't be? It was. Oh, no. It was Howie. He mustn't see her with Cherry. He'd know who Cherry was. He was a secret agent now. He'd get suspicious. Britt would have to disappear for a short while. But hang on. Even if he just saw Cherry it would be bad news. He would engage her in conversation. Ask why she was here. Probably even bore her with his story of a near-death experience with a seagull. And that, too, would scare Oskar away.

As the consequences of this nightmare scenario began to play out in her mind, Britt spotted another man coming towards the square from The Mall. It couldn't be? Not right this second? But it was. Those features. The coat, hat, scarf and sunglasses. That furious walk. They were unmistakeable. It was Oskar Polak. As soon as Oskar saw Howie, the vice president would turn round and head straight back to the palace. This was a nightmare within a nightmare.

Britt swore at her luck. It was luck which had served her well for a day and a half, but which was now balancing things out by dropping her in this dire situation. It was time to take emergency action. Or, as Lord Nelson would have said, more desperate measures.

Britt looked across at Cherry. She wasn't paying her any attention. She had also seen Oskar in the crowd. Her gaze was fixed on his approaching figure – her body frozen. Howie was walking west. If he carried on for another fifteen seconds, he would walk straight past Cherry. Britt had to act now. She ran towards Howie, so she was between him and Cherry. 'It's me!' she gushed, giving him a hug. 'What a coincidence!'

Howie stopped. 'I've just been attacked by a bloody great seagull! It was the size of a small child. The cheeky bugger nearly took my head off – and made me drop my ice cream.'

Britt put her arm round Howie, changing his direction of travel to the north. 'I saw it all. That's how I spotted you. Poor you.'

Howie looked surprised. Britt didn't blame him. Sympathy wasn't an emotion she displayed regularly.

'Are you feeling alright?' asked Howie.

'Great!' chirped Britt, glancing over her shoulder. She could see that Oskar was about to use one of the pedestrian crossings that led to the square. She jolted her head back to face Howie, before he started staring in the same direction. 'I'm just having a wander round. I was bored at home. You heading back to the palace?'

'Yeah. Can't stop. People to see. You know how it is.'

Britt did know how it was. Howie would probably be rushing back to update Martha Blake. If Britt had had a few spare seconds, she would have asked him where he'd just been.

And why he was wearing such an expensive suit. But she had no time. So she kissed him on the cheek and gabbled a goodbye. 'I'll see you back at the pod.' She pointed towards the north end of the square. 'That way will be quicker. The traffic lights aren't working on The Mall side.'

Howie frowned. 'They look like they're working to me.'

Britt adopted the confident tone of a traffic-signal expert. 'They're out of sequence.'

Howie looked towards the crossing where Oskar was waiting. Before he had time to focus on any of the faces, Britt gave him a helping push towards the northern steps. 'Best not to risk it, if you're in a hurry.' They waved to each other and Howie headed off. She waited a moment. He didn't look back. Britt rushed back to the safety of Nelson's column and took up her place again. She puffed out her cheeks in relief. That was close.

A few seconds later, Oskar crossed the road and walked towards Cherry, who was still as stationary as the square's bronze lions. Oskar stopped a couple of metres from Cherry and turned his back to her. He covered his mouth. He was asking a question – probably 'Which bloody journalist is poking their nose into our business?' Cherry didn't respond. She just turned and looked at Britt, as if paralysed from the neck down. Time for action. Britt strode towards Oskar and stopped just in front of him. 'Oskar Polak?'

'Who's asking?' snapped Oskar.

'Britt Pointer from *The Republican*. I'm the journalist Cherry mentioned in her bleep. The one who's been asking questions about your relationship.'

Oskar's facial muscles contorted. His jaw stiffened. His lips might even have trembled a fraction.

Britt's tone was firm and uncompromising. 'I don't have much time. And I imagine you don't either. Shall we get down to business?'

Oskar glared at Cherry. 'You've the brains of a princess, bringing this woman here.'

'I don't want to be in the papers,' croaked Cherry. 'Just speak to her.'

Oskar turned back to Britt. 'Where's your ID?'

Britt plucked it from her pocket and held it up to his face.

Oskar lowered his voice and leaned in to Britt. 'I am the person you think I am. But there appears to have been a ... misunderstanding.'

'I don't think so.'

'Miss Blush and I are just good friends. We share interests. Film, the theatre, keeping fit. That type of thing.'

Britt responded with a burst of rapid-fire statements. 'You met Miss Blush yesterday afternoon outside American Fitness in Canary Wharf at around 4.20pm. You were wearing the same clothes and sunglasses as you are now. You went to a park bench nearby, where you broke off the affair. Miss Blush screamed your name and ran off. I came and sat next to you. I commented on your bleeper. You were sending a message. You didn't want to be interrupted. You jumped up and disappeared into the crowds.'

Oskar stared at her. 'Quite the detective, aren't we, Miss Pointer? But tell me one thing. Does your editor know you've been stalking a government vice president?'

'I'm an investigative reporter. It's what I do.'

A smug look crept across Oskar's face. 'But your investigations yesterday revealed what? That two good friends met up and had an argument? That's hardly the concrete evidence national newspaper editors require.'

Britt reached into her bag and pulled out the photo of Cherry Blush outside a Westminster townhouse, with Oskar standing at the door. 'I forgot to mention this.'

Oskar studied the photo and took a sharp intake of breath. Then he breathed out and responded. 'One photo proves nothing. Miss Blush sometimes pops round to my Westminster residence for coffee and a chat. There's no crime in that.'

'That's just one of a hundred photos. Taken in various locations. At various times.'

'Who took these?' demanded Oskar.

'A private detective agency. They've been tracking you for weeks.'

'I told you some weirdo was following me,' moaned Cherry. 'But you told me not to be so bloody stupid.'

Oskar sat down on the edge of the fountain and looked up at Britt. 'What do you want from me?'

Britt sat down next to him. 'Your relationship with Miss Blush isn't what I'm really interested in. I'm working on a much bigger story. One that you can help me with, vice president.'

'And what's that?' asked Oskar, sounding unenthusiastic.

'It's government-related. For your ears only. I just need you to answer a few questions.'

'And if I don't cooperate?'

Britt inspected the photo and then slipped it back in her bag. 'I think you know the answer to that.'

Oskar rubbed his chin and thought for a few seconds.

'What's there to think about?' urged Cherry. 'I don't want my love life splashed all over the front pages. My granny will have a bloody heart attack!'

'You're blackmailing me, Miss Pointer,' growled Oskar. 'And I don't like being blackmailed.'

Britt thought the b-word might come up. But she was prepared. 'Not at all. I have a factually accurate story that I can run with. But I would rather spend my time and energy on something much bigger. Help me with that, and the other story will disappear. I promise you.'

'And how do I know you're not just going to publish both stories?'

'If I screwed people over all the time, I wouldn't be where I am today.'

Oskar didn't look completely convinced. Possibly because he'd got where he was today by screwing people over all the time.

Britt continued. 'If you've read my articles you'll know I've never written a trashy, tabloid story in my life. And I don't really want to start this week.' She took a step closer to him. 'So help me.' She glanced over at Cherry. 'Help all of us.'

Cherry looked hopefully at Oskar. 'You gonna help her then?'

'Yes,' sighed Oskar. 'I don't really have any choice.'

Cherry stood up. 'I can go then?'

Britt nodded. 'Yes. I don't need you any more.'

'You and him both,' spluttered Cherry, before turning and striding away towards the Metro station.

Oskar watched Cherry disappear down the Metro steps. Then he turned to Britt. 'Let's make it quick.'

Britt was happy to oblige. 'Where's the president?'

Oskar's eyes narrowed. 'What do you mean?'

'You know what I mean. Just answer the question.'

'I don't know. I'm not my brother's keeper.'

'That's because no one knows. He's gone missing.'

Oskar snorted. 'Missing? Don't be so ridiculous.'

'The palace security cameras failed at eleven o'clock on Monday evening. He hasn't been seen since. A Code Red crisis has been declared.'

Oskar laughed it off. 'Who told you that pile of old nonsense?'

'A protected source that works at the palace.'

'I'm sorry to disappoint you. But you've been misinformed.'

'I've also seen a classified bleep from Head of National Security and Intelligence Martha Blake confirming your brother's disappearance.'

'Well, whatever you saw – and misunderstood – it wasn't sent to me.'

'Why don't you bleep Jan? We'll see if he responds.'

'He's a very busy man. Presidents normally are. It could take hours for him to respond.' He clasped his hands. 'Now, I've answered your questions. I suggest we bring this discussion to a close. So everyone can … move on from all this.'

Oskar's defensive manoeuvres were even more impressive than she'd feared. Britt clearly wasn't going to get confirmation of the president's disappearance during this little chat. But she wasn't finished yet. 'Okay. But for your information, I have confirmed sources; there's nothing to stop me writing my missing-president story.' Nothing except George's insistence on a third source. But Oskar didn't know that. 'It will speculate about who might succeed your brother if he isn't around for the Republican nomination tomorrow.'

Britt hoped Oskar would probe further. And he did. 'Will it mention me in that context?'

'No.'

Oskar's eyebrows nearly took off. 'Why ever not?'

'Haven't you read this morning's *Daily Democrat*? There's an interview with Zayn Winner. Lover of life. Man of the people. Feeder of ducks. He's the obvious successor.'

Oskar exploded into a hushed rage. 'Zayn Winner?! There are members of the Royal Family with more brain cells than him. You're not seriously going to propose the best vice president for the job is a washed-up Hollywood halfwit? That's just absurd!'

'Who then?' asked Britt, with fake uncertainty.

Oskar attempted a warm smile. He failed miserably. 'If what you say about my brother disappearing is true – and I'm not saying it is – then I would be the obvious choice to succeed him. I have the skills, personality and experience for the job.' He waited for Britt to acknowledge this fact. She didn't. He continued anyway. 'Others may have more ... popular appeal, but it could be dangerous to set the citizens' thoughts running in that direction. It might gain a momentum that could damage the real candidate's chances. So, if you're going to write this piece tomorrow – despite everything I've told you about it not being true – I would suggest you name me as the best choice to replace Jan. Do you understand my meaning?'

Britt understood his meaning all right. Oskar was planning to run for president. And he wanted the media on his side from the start. If her missing-president story suggested a charismatic former film star would be the Republic's next leader, it could create expectations in the twelve hours between the first edition of Thursday's *Republican* hitting the news stands at eleven o'clock tonight and the big announcement tomorrow. She could visualise the Independence Day crowds outside the palace on Thursday morning. Traditionally, they chanted the president's name as they waited. But, as the news spread of Britt's story, they would stop chanting Jan Polak's name. They would start chanting Zayn's name. Then Oskar would appear on the balcony. It would be like turning up at the West End premiere, only to see the understudy in the leading role. It would be the worst possible start to Oskar's presidential campaign. And they both knew it. Which meant she could use it to get some more information out of Oskar.

'I could change my viewpoint on a possible successor,' suggested Britt. 'I would just need to know one thing.'

'What's that?'

'If the president wasn't going to stand again, for whatever reason, when and where would the vice presidents select the Republican Party's candidate?'

His reply was instant. 'On the record, I couldn't possibly say. Off the record, four o'clock this afternoon in the State Dining Room.'

Britt nodded. Martha Blake's classified e-comm to Howie had mentioned a nomination meeting sometime today. So it looked like Oskar was telling the truth for once. 'Would there be any way I could find out the result of such a meeting before eleven tomorrow morning?'

Oskar shook his head. 'No. The need for secrecy is written into the constitution. Revealing the name beforehand to anyone outside of the meeting would be a breach of a vice president's constitutional duties. And that kind of breach wouldn't look good on anyone's CV. Especially someone who was running for president.'

Britt thought about mentioning Maxim. But then she thought again. Maxim wasn't central to her story. And Oskar might alert Maxim to Britt's interest if she did. The last thing she needed on the most important day of her journalistic career was an angry Russian on her case. No. Her story would focus on the president's disappearance and his possible successor.

Oskar stood up. He smiled like a fox who'd just been invited inside by a family of overweight chickens. 'I believe we have an understanding.'

'Yes. We do.'

'Then I shall get back to my business. And you can get back to yours. Then tomorrow … well, who knows what tomorrow will bring.'

A front page, thought Britt. About you and your brother.

Chapter 33

Howie was just a couple of minutes away from the gates of Buckingham Palace. With any luck, that annoying pair of police officers wouldn't be on duty. After his close encounter with a seagull and the pointless detour Britt had sent him on, he didn't need any more hold ups. At least he was now on The Mall, looking towards the palace and the balcony that would be the focus of the nation's attention tomorrow morning. As he gazed up at it, he felt his bleeper vibrate in his trouser pocket. He pulled it out. The name on the e-comm wasn't one that filled him with joy. It was Maurice Skeets. Again. Another unwanted distraction. He read his message:

Howie, you've gone quiet. Anything else you want to tell me about those meetings? I've heard there's someone in the president's office this week. A pair of eyes that sees everything. Someone checking up on King Jan, are they? Making sure he doesn't sneak off for any more secret meetings, eh? Why don't you let me know? Put your side of the story, before it leaks out and this whole thing blows up. Bleep me. Maurice.

Howie stopped. A pair of eyes who sees everything? He must mean Martha. But Maurice didn't give her name. And Howie knew Maurice well. If he had known the name, he would have been upfront about it. That could only mean one thing. Maurice had been talking to someone inside the palace. A source who didn't want to give Martha's name for some reason.

His thoughts were interrupted when a man overtook him on the pavement. A man who looked just like the president from behind. He put away his bleeper and rubbed his eyes. Could that really be him? Could Jan Polak have returned from wherever he'd been for the last day and a half and be returning to Buckingham Palace, as if he'd just popped out for a sandwich? He called out. 'Hey, Jan! Is that you? It's me, Howie.'

The man stopped and turned. 'No, it's not Jan. It's Oskar. And I'm in a hurry.'

Howie couldn't turn down this opportunity to speak to Oskar face-to-face. 'Wait a second,' he shouted and hurried the twenty metres to where Oskar was standing. 'I've got something to ask you.'

Oskar curled his lip. 'If it's a media enquiry, I'm not interested.'

'No. It's a Howie Pond enquiry.'

'Then be quick.'

'The nomination meeting at four – I just wondered if you'll be putting your name forward if Jan doesn't show up.'

Oskar pouted his annoyance. 'What business is that of yours?'

'I'll have to deal with the media fallout tomorrow,' explained Howie. 'If Jan's not around, I'll have to work with that individual on statements, press briefings, that kind of thing. And if that person eventually becomes president, we'll probably be working together.' Probably, in that Howie had more experience and talent for the job than anyone else in the civil service. But that didn't always count for much when it came to the vice presidents' way of thinking.

Oskar clasped his hands. 'I'll be honest with you, Howie. Whichever vice president is chosen – whether that's myself or someone else – I doubt very much they will want you as their media mouthpiece.'

'With respect, I'm not a mouthpiece. I'm a comms professional with fifteen years' experience as a presidential spokesperson and head of comms. And after ten years in power, the majority of media are still very supportive of your brother. That doesn't happen by accident.'

'Yes. But you're very much Jan's man. The rest of us have our own ideas about media and communications. New ideas.'

Uninformed ideas. Simplistic ideas. Dangerous ideas. He'd heard them all hundreds of times before. Howie puffed out his chest. 'I'll be presidential spokesperson and head of comms until someone in authority tells me otherwise.'

'I know. But you deserve a rest after all you've done. A little gardening leave, perhaps, after the election. And in the longer term, well ... I have someone lined up to replace you.'

An uncharacteristic slip by Oskar. Howie wasn't going to let this pass. 'So you will be standing for president, if Jan doesn't come back.'

Oskar wrinkled his forehead. 'I didn't say that.'

'You said you had someone lined up. The president appoints the spokesperson. No one else.'

Oskar hesitated for a second. 'What I meant was, should one of the vice presidents be forced to stand as a result of my brother's absence, I shall be proposing a fresh start. A new presidential spokesperson and head of comms.' He breathed in and stood tall. 'For a bright new era in the British Republic's history.'

'You got anyone particular in mind?'

'It'll be someone from the private sector. Someone with a more international CV.'

An idea popped into Howie's head. 'This someone – have they been recommended?'

'They've been highly recommended. So you've no need to worry.'

Howie could feel the hairs on the back of neck standing up. He knew the answer to his next question. But he was going to ask it anyway. 'Who's recommended them?'

'That is confidential. I really must get back —'

'Is it one of Viktor Maxim's people, by any chance?' interrupted Howie.

Oskar was momentarily struck dumb. Then he croaked a reply. 'How did you know that?'

'Call it an educated guess.'

Oskar took a step towards Howie. His voice was threatening. 'I'll ask you one more time. How did you know?'

Howie realised he'd gone too far. There was no way he could tell Oskar the truth. His educated guess was the result of intelligence operations that were still ongoing. They mustn't be jeopardised. 'I bumped into Mr Maxim at lunch today. I was at The Savoy.'

Oskar didn't look convinced. 'You were at The Savoy?'

'Yeah. The Premier Diners place. That's why I'm wearing this suit.'

'Yes. It's not like you to present yourself so well.' Oskar thought for several seconds. 'So you know Mr Maxim?'

'I was with a friend who knew him.'

'Who was this friend?'

If Howie mentioned it was the chief of police, Oskar would get suspicious. 'A Russian guy I went to university with,' lied Howie. That sounded just about plausible. 'He introduced us. I mentioned I worked for Jan. Viktor mentioned you and he were acquainted. That was it.'

Oskar pondered Howie's response. His expression suggested he was hovering halfway between belief and disbelief. After ten seconds of forehead-wrinkling and lip-twisting, Oskar replied. 'I didn't know Mr Maxim was in town this week. If I have a window in my busy schedule, I shall speak to him about your replacement.'

That wasn't true. Oskar had had lunch with Maxim yesterday. But Howie didn't challenge him. He needed to avoid any more confrontation. 'So I'm out of a job in the summer, if you're in charge?'

Oskar smirked. 'It would seem that way. But I wouldn't worry.' Oskar lowered his voice and half-smiled. 'You'll be taken care of, Mr Pond.'

Howie shivered. Oskar had sounded just like a James Bond villain. He should have responded with a witty one-liner – just like the world's greatest secret agent would have done. But his mind was blank. And for the first time in his short security service career, he felt afraid. Afraid that Oskar Polak might want people like Howie Pond to disappear if he became president.

Oskar turned and walked purposefully towards the palace gates. Howie let him go ahead, so there was a safe distance between them. Their next meeting would be at four o'clock in the State Dining Room. Howie suddenly had a bad feeling about the nomination meeting – a gut instinct that something was going to go horribly wrong. He tried to put the thought to the back of his mind. He needed to stay positive.

After a few minutes, he started walking towards the palace gates. The two officers he'd encountered yesterday were there. Of course they were. Why did he think it was going to be any different? He walked up to the left-hand gate and greeted them. 'Afternoon, officers. Could you do the honours and let me through, please?'

The tall officer was sucking a sweet, and had to push it to the side of his mouth before replying. 'One moment, sir. My rainbow candy is just transitioning.'

The short officer also had something in his mouth. 'Is it caramel?' he asked his colleague, as if pondering the meaning of life itself.

'I do believe it's our old friend fudge.'

Howie coughed. 'Any chance I could get through, chaps?'

The short officer made a disturbing sucking noise. 'He's right, you know. It is fudge.'

The tall officer smacked his lips. 'They're amazing, these candies. Gift from the American ambassador. Which reminds me, have you seen Mr Stackshaker since we last spoke?'

'No,' sighed Howie. 'I haven't. He's a very busy man. And so am I.'

'I don't doubt that, sir,' replied the tall officer. 'I can see from the look in your eye that you're a man on a mission. Something top secret, no doubt. Almost certainly of vital national importance.'

'We'd better not hold him up,' added the short officer. 'He's probably got to save the world by teatime!'

You're not far from the truth, Howie thought, as the officers convulsed in laughter. While the pair recovered their composure, Howie thought of something else. 'Tell me, has that security woman from Washington been back since yesterday morning?'

'Not as far as we're aware, sir. And the other lads haven't said anything.'

'Good. If she or anyone else comes sniffing round here again, talking about palace security, be as unhelpful as possible.' He nodded towards the gate. 'Now, if you wouldn't mind?'

The tall officer walked up and pressed the button. 'Don't worry. You can trust us, sir.'

Howie doubted that this pair could keep their mouths shut for five minutes. But he didn't have time to worry about it. As he hurried towards the palace, just one thing was on his mind. He needed to speak to Martha – to talk about the president, Oskar, Maxim, the First Lady and Maurice Skeets. That was a lot to discuss. And with less than three hours until the nomination meeting, there wouldn't be much time to do it.

Chapter 34

Britt was still sitting on the edge of the same fountain in Trafalgar Square. There was no Oskar. No Cherry. No Howie. Just her. And strangers all around. Tourists, workers, students and others. People she could see. But didn't see. Deep in thought, her mind was focused on only one thing – the imminent nomination meeting. One that could change her life. And shape the future of the British Republic. A meeting that would take place just a short distance away. But there was one big problem. It was a meeting she wasn't invited to. And Buckingham Palace wasn't an easy place to gatecrash.

Without even trying, her mind created a picture of the scene in the State Dining Room at four o'clock. The fifty vice presidents would be sat round the edges of the ridiculously long table – whispering, watching, and wondering. All asking the same questions. Where's Jan Polak? Is he alive or dead? If he's alive, is he coming back? If he's not coming back, who'll replace him? Will it be me? Or him? Or her? And the question that every single man and woman in that room would be asking themselves – what does all this mean for me? Yes. Without a leader, self-interest would be king.

She imagined the meeting starting. The first item on the agenda would be an update on the search for the president. Hopefully, Jan Polak was still missing. If so, that would be confirmed for the benefit of everyone in the room – including any hidden journalists. Potential candidates would then put themselves forward. Each would deliver a short speech, stating their credentials. Voting would then take place and continue until a winner emerged. And, barring an appearance from Jan

Polak between then and eleven o'clock the following morning, the winning candidate would appear on the balcony of Buckingham Palace to inform British citizens that he or she – and not Jan Polak – was the Republican Party candidate for that summer's elections.

It was clear now. The State Dining Room at four o'clock was the only place and time to get a third source that no one could argue with – not even George. And she had to be there if she wanted to learn the identity of the nominated candidate. It would probably be Oskar. But in the unlikely event that it wasn't, she would know who it was. Her story of the century would be one hundred per cent true. No misguided speculation. Pure fact. The stuff of which journalistic dreams are made.

'You must be there,' she told herself. Yes. She would find a way. She had less than three hours, but she would get into that room before everyone arrived and eavesdrop on that meeting. Then make her escape.

She held her breath, as her brain processed that possibility. To anyone with a nanogramme of sense, it was a crazy idea. But, as the stone admiral above would say, desperate affairs require desperate measures. And what would George say? She imagined standing in his office, having just outlined her plan. His response would be something like:

> *So, Britt. You're going to penetrate Buckingham Palace security the day before Independence Day, waltz into a top-secret meeting in one its most iconic rooms and find a curtain to hide behind. And when you're done, you're going to waltz straight out again, wave everyone goodbye and then file the story. I'm sorry, but it's not just mission impossible. It's mission insanity.*

She hated to admit it. But the George inside her head was right. The backs of her legs were starting to feel numb on the cold concrete. She needed to stretch them. She got up and started walking in the direction of St James' Park, for no other reason than it would bring her nearer the palace. But no nearer to getting inside it.

Even if she could get inside the palace, how would she find the State Dining Room before all those vice presidents? Where would she hide from sight to listen to proceedings – would it really be behind a curtain, as the George inside her head had suggested? And how was she going to walk out of the palace without being wrestled to the ground, arrested or worse?

She allowed her mind to rest and concentrated on navigating the road safely. She passed under Admiralty Arch – just as she had done yesterday morning. But this time, she was proceeding at a more leisurely pace. There was no rush. She had no real idea what she was doing. But it felt better than just sitting doing nothing.

Instead of continuing down The Mall, Britt decided to go into the park and head towards the lake. As she arrived, a large pelican screeched. It was staring at her and flapping its wings. It's probably hungry, she thought. Howie got like that sometimes. Or maybe this bird was trying to tell her some lost secret of the universe that it was doomed to carry for all eternity. The meaning of life, perhaps? Well, one thing was sure. Life would have no meaning for her if she was banished to the features desk. Moving to another newspaper wasn't an option either. All the editors knew George. His grumpiness was legendary. They wouldn't want to get in his bad books by taking her on as a news reporter. No. As things stood, she would soon be turning into a feature creature.

The pelican screeched again. As it tried to communicate its secrets, yesterday's meeting with Herbert the security guy popped into her head. Or rather, Pellie Cann's meeting with Herbert. That boy was so gullible. How had someone like him got a job in Buckingham Palace security? Then she remembered. He was the nephew of the head of security. Now there was a man who could give her access to the palace. If only she could find a way to persuade Bogdan Bogdanowic to let her in. That was a stupid thought. She didn't even know Bogdan. Or how to get hold of him. Britt's whole body heaved a sigh so loud, it drew stares from the people standing near her. It would be impossible.

Britt stared at the pelican. It had settled down on the grassy bank, buried its beak in its wing, and readied itself for an afternoon nap. You lucky prince, she thought. Such an easy life. You can take a nap any time you want. Watching the bird ready itself for sleep jogged her memory. It was so obvious. Why hadn't she thought of it before? The pelican wasn't the only creature who enjoyed his naps. Herbert the security guy did, too. On Monday night, in particular. The night that the president went missing. What had he told her in the pub? It was 'all sorted'. Yes. After Uncle Bogdan had stepped in. She didn't know exactly what Uncle Bogdan had done, but it would have involved lying. And why had he lied? She knew why. Not just to protect his nephew. Herbert's failure was, ultimately, his failure. Bogdan had sorted everything to protect himself. Self-interest was everyone's king in a Code Red crisis. Yes. He had covered up his nephew's negligence. Protected himself from blame. Rescued the family name from an unwanted entry in the history books. And that made him vulnerable.

Britt collected her thoughts. Bogdan couldn't be her third source. Both he and his nephew Herbert, who was her first source, worked for palace security. And George wanted three people from different organisations to confirm the story. And anyway, Britt wanted to know the winner of the nomination vote and Bogdan wouldn't be any help with that. But she could use him in another way.

In just a few seconds, she had formulated a plan. She was going back to those palace gates. But this time, not as Pellie Cann. She would be returning as Britt Pointer. There would be no need for any disguise. She made her way out of the park and headed back along The Mall to Buckingham Palace.

Within five minutes she was a short distance from the gates. It would be the second time in two days that she had to fool the police standing outside them. It wasn't always easy to do. But it was easy if you approached the right officers. And she could already see two familiar silhouettes in the distance. One tall. One short. As she got nearer, she could see their faces. Yes. It was definitely them. Both chatting. Both laughing at their own jokes.

'Excuse me officers,' she called in her normal voice. 'Do you have a moment?'

The tall officer smiled. 'I think we have a moment, madam.' He turned to his colleague. 'Don't you?'

The short officer checked his watch. 'You're in luck. Tea break's not for five minutes yet.'

Ah. Tea break wasn't far away. In Britt's experience, police officers only postponed tea breaks for major emergencies. She didn't have much time. 'I need your help. It's about a woman you spoke to yesterday morning. You'll remember her – she was American, wore large sunglasses and claimed she worked in Washington in presidential security. She didn't give her name. She had no ID.'

'Doesn't ring any bells, I'm afraid,' replied the tall officer, avoiding eye contact.

'Nope,' added the short officer, staring at his boots. 'It weren't us.'

Britt thought for a second. Maybe these two realised their mistake after their encounter with Pellie Cann and were staying tight-lipped? Or maybe someone found out about it and told them to keep their mouths shut. Either way, she would have to increase the pressure. 'I understand you pointed her in the direction of an individual named Herbert Bogdanowic. He works in palace security.'

Both officers shook their heads.

Britt tried again. 'Well, listen to this. She wasn't American. And she doesn't work in security.' She took a breath. 'In fact, she's a journalist for *The Republican*. And I believe she may be planning to gain access to the palace this afternoon – using information she obtained from Herbert Bogdanowic – to gatecrash a top-secret meeting about the future of this country.'

The officers' jaws dropped. Colour drained from their cheeks. But no words came from their gaping mouths.

She went into bullshit mode. 'I'm a patriot. It's Independence Day tomorrow. And whatever her story is – whether it's true or untrue, it doesn't matter – I don't want the citizens of this nation waking up to a story that could bring down this Government. Because that's what will happen if we don't stop her.'

The officers were still speechless. What was the magic ingredient she needed? Ah, yes. Self-interest. She took a step towards them and whispered. 'It wouldn't just be the Government this woman would bring down. It would be anyone who crossed her path in the last forty-eight hours – and that includes you two.'

The short officer sprang into life. 'And how come you know all this?'

'I'm a journalist. I work with her.'

'Would you mind showing us some ID, madam?' asked the tall officer, his tone cautious.

'I'm Britt Pointer and I work for *The Republican*,' she announced, flashing her ID.

Both officers spoke as one. 'You're that bloody journalist!'

'I know. And I know my recent investigation lost some of your friends their jobs. But they were corrupt. You're not. You just happened to be tricked by one of the most deceptive, most deadly journalists in the country.'

'Deadly?' croaked the tall officer. 'What do you mean by that?'

'She has a licence to kill. But she doesn't kill people.' Britt took a step forward and whispered in a sinister voice. 'She kills reputations. Kills careers. And there's a hell of a lot of collateral damage along the way.'

The tall officer loosened his collar with his hand. 'What's this ... killer's name?'

It would be better to use a real name. There was a chance they might check. And the name that came to mind was perfect. 'Rosie Parker. She's on the news desk. You can confirm it with our editor, if you like. His name is George Smith. But whatever you do, don't mention me if you speak to him. I'm doing this as a patriot. Not as a journalist.'

The short officer gulped. 'I've seen that Rosie Parker's name in the paper. Nosey Parker, I call her.'

The tall officer wiped a drop of sweat from his brow. 'Yes. And George Smith is her boss. I know because I wrote a letter to him earlier this year. A complaint about his journalists' constant harassment of police officers.' He then whispered something in his colleague's ear. His colleague whispered back.

'Well, gentlemen? Are you going to help me?'

The officers exchanged serious glances and then nodded.

'Good. I need you to contact Bogdan Bogdanowic. He and I need to talk. So we can stop Rosie Parker from bringing down the Government.'

The tall officer barked at the short officer. 'Find Mr Bogdanowic! Get him out here!'

'And if he won't come?' asked the short officer.

'Tell him this is a matter of life and death. There's a killer on the loose! And she must be stopped!' He took a dramatic breath. 'And if that means we miss our tea break, that is a sacrifice we shall have to make for our country!'

The short officer didn't reply. He just opened the gate and ran towards the palace entrance.

Britt felt butterflies in her stomach. She, too, could be entering those gates very soon.

Chapter 35

Howie was back in the State Dining Room. It wasn't being used between now and four, so it was the best place to meet Martha Blake and tell her about the extraordinary events of his morning and early afternoon. Well, not all of them. He'd have to leave out any reference to the chief of police rushing to his rescue and then arranging a meeting with Viktor Maxim. But that shouldn't be difficult. Howie was a senior government comms professional. An ability to be economical with the truth was an essential requirement for the job.

As he inspected the room's fireplace, chandeliers and portraits, Howie realised he was in exactly the same spot as yesterday morning – at the top of the table, with its huge expanse of oak stretching out before him. It was probably where he would be sitting in two hours' time, when he and Martha attended the nomination meeting. The room was quiet now. No birds were singing outside. Motorists were taking a break from honking at each other on the streets. Vice presidents weren't screaming at civil servants in the corridor. It was an old-world cliché, traditionally trotted out by press officers when a big story was about to break, but this really did feel like the calm before the storm. And not just a storm – more like a force ten hurricane.

He closed his eyes and imagined he had been transported two hours into the future. This room would be buzzing with excitement and expectation. The vice presidents would be choosing the new Jan Polak. Or rather, choosing the next-best thing to Jan Polak. No one could follow in that man's footsteps, as far as Howie was concerned. Jan was a legend. The most intelligent, receptive, switched-on politician he had ever come across. He just hoped he would come across him again. Because he was starting to become concerned for the president's safety. Especially after today's unpleasant encounters with Viktor Maxim and Oskar Polak.

The main door opened and Martha appeared. 'Ah, you're here. Good. Let's get started.' She took a step forward. Then stopped. 'Hang on a moment. You're wearing a different suit.'

Howie cursed under his breath. He had forgotten about his quick change at the police station. 'Don't mention Freddie,' he told himself and mumbled a response. 'I fell in some mud on my way to the studios. I had to change.'

Martha examined his new office wear. 'It looks new.'

Howie fiddled with his tie. 'Erm … yeah. It's quite new.'

Martha walked over and peeled a sticker from the collar. 'It's brand new. It's still got the import sticker on it.'

Howie tried not to look guilty. But failed. 'Oh, erm … has it? I hadn't noticed.'

Martha examined the sticker. 'This says it was part of a bulk order of a thousand.' She looked deep into his eyes. 'Is there something you're not telling me, Howie?'

'I was given it.' He paused. 'After I fell over.'

'Someone just gave you that suit?'

'Yeah, that's right.' He was just on the boundary between being economical with the truth and lying. He would have to be careful. 'Someone gave it to me.'

'And who was this someone?' asked Martha.

Howie needed to try and change the subject, before he crossed the line. 'I forget now.' He clapped his hands together. 'Right. Shall we get down to business?'

Martha peered down at him. 'You're acting very strangely.'

'It's been a strange couple of days.'

Martha paused just long enough for Howie's cheeks to flush bright pink. It was no good trying to play games with her. She knew he was hiding something.

'Tell me everything that happened today,' demanded Martha. 'Including how you got that finest Italian silk suit.'

Howie shuffled in his seat. 'It's a long story.'

'Then give me the synopsis,' she ordered, sitting down.

Howie sighed. He wasn't looking forward to this. 'Right. I was arrested at the *Rise and Shine* studios.'

Martha's head jolted back, as if she'd just received a mild electric shock. 'Arrested?! For what exactly?'

'Harassing the First Lady. She was so desperate to get on that bloody show, she pretended she didn't know me.' He raised his eyebrows. 'Either that or she was involved in Jan's disappearance and wanted me out of the way.'

'I think that's unlikely. You're not the only person looking into it. She would know that.'

'Yeah. I suppose so.' Howie sighed. 'Anyway, to get back to the story, they all thought I was some kind of lunatic stalker. I got carted off to the local police station.'

'Oh, for goodness sake. What about your special investigator's ID?'

Howie looked away. 'Erm … I left it back at the pod.'

Martha's eyes cartwheeled. 'What did I say in my e-comm, this morning? Don't forget your ID. It's your insurance – your get-out-of-jail-free card.'

Howie wasn't enjoying this. But it was his own fault for forgetting the cat's birthday. 'I had bleeper problems, remember?'

'Well, everyone else's bleeper is working alright.' Martha sighed. 'How much time did you waste at the police station?'

'About four hours, I reckon. I was arrested as a suspected 24-7. So they didn't exactly roll out the red carpet.'

'You were arrested as a 24-7 and you were out in four hours? How the hell did you manage that? You should still be there.'

'After I told them who I was, they said I could go. And they gave me this suit – for free.' That wasn't a lie. He just hadn't mentioned Freddie.

Martha frowned. She didn't look at all convinced. 'I'm sorry to doubt you, Howie, but 24-7s don't talk their way out of police stations. And they most certainly don't receive free suits on their way out.'

Howie smiled hopefully. 'There's a first time for everything.'

'Yes. You're quite right.' Martha gave Howie a fierce stare. 'And this is the first time you've tried to be economical with the truth with me. I'm not a journalist. I'm the head of the National Security and Intelligence Service. Now tell me how you got out of there.'

He would have to come clean. 'Okay. I had some help.'

'Was it divine intervention? Because no one helps a 24-7.'

'It was the earthly kind, actually.' He swallowed hard. 'The chief-of-police kind.'

Martha took one of the longest, loudest, breaths through her nose that Howie had ever witnessed. 'I'm not angry. I'm just disappointed.' A second later she corrected herself. 'No, actually I am angry. And I'm not just disappointed. I'm extremely disappointed, Howard.'

She had called him Howard. That was a bad sign. 'I know what you said about him, but I bleeped him for help. And he came straight away.'

Martha crossed her arms. 'How did you know his bleeper number?'

'He gave it to me at The Savoy last night, after you left.'

'I see. And now you are in his debt. Like so many other high-profile, connected people in this city.' She shook her head. 'You've compromised your position.'

'No, no. Nothing is compromised. In fact, he didn't just get me out of that hellhole. Freddie then arranged a meeting with one of the people that we think could be linked to the president's disappearance.'

'Who's that?'

'Viktor Maxim. Freddie and I met him at The Savoy not long ago.'

Martha put her head in her hands. 'This gets worse.'

'Before you have me thrown in the Tower, just let me say this. It's not Maxim's connection to Freddie English you need to worry about. It's Maxim's connections to Oskar Polak.'

'What do you mean?'

'Maxim met Oskar on Tuesday. We know that. But I got Maxim to admit that he and Oskar meet up regularly to exchange information.'

Martha cocked her head. 'What kind of information?'

'Industry stuff. Current government policy. "A mutually beneficial exchange", Maxim called it. All legal – so he says. Anyway, I asked if he'd met with Oskar this week. He denied it.'

'He's a liar.'

'Exactly. And another thing – he's made at least one political donation in the past. Michael Short's first campaign. That tells me Maxim is a man who wants connections to the centre of government.'

'That was a long time ago.'

'Yeah, but he claimed he couldn't remember if he tried to give money to Jan's campaigns. But of course he bloody remembered. He just wasn't telling me. He probably got knocked back by Jan's campaign team. They know a businessman trying to buy influence when they see one.'

'But what's his motive for getting close to Oskar?' asked Martha, sounding more alarmed by the second.

'He's a government supplier. Only small scale. But he confirmed he's looking to expand. And what are the biggest contracts we award?'

'Tech contracts?'

'No. Defence contracts. Maxim has got interests in that industry. Maurice Skeets told me. And who's in charge of defence? Step forward, Vice President Oskar Polak.'

'But the president makes the ultimate decision on defence contracts.'

'Only major contracts. Oskar might have already helped him win some smaller ones. But if Oskar becomes the main man …

well, then he would make the big decisions. And a winning bid to provide defence services would be worth hundreds of millions of pounds in extra business to Mr Maxim. Maybe even billions.'

Martha looked thoughtful. 'You may well be right.'

'There's more. I bumped into Oskar on the way back to the palace. We had a little chat. Now that's a man planning for a world without Jan Polak as president. He's definitely going to be putting his name forward this afternoon.'

'Perhaps that's what Oskar's first meeting was about yesterday – the one with the two vice presidents whose names I can never remember.'

Howie nodded. 'It's got to be.'

'Oskar Polak has been a busy boy.'

'Even busier than you think. He's lined up a replacement for me.'

'You mean someone closer to him?'

Howie nodded. 'And our friend Maxim. I don't know my replacement's name. But I asked Oskar if they worked for one of Maxim's companies.'

'That was risky. He might think we're on to him.'

'Don't worry. I told him Maxim and I were introduced by a mutual friend and Maxim mentioned their relationship. He just about believed it. But listen to this – Oskar said he had no idea Maxim was in town this week.'

'So they're both denying Tuesday's meeting ever took place? This isn't sounding good. Those two are planning something.'

'Yeah. It's like they knew Jan was going to disappear.'

Martha sat in silence for a half a minute, while she digested everything Howie had told her. Then she gave her assessment. 'You've reached a very reasonable conclusion, Howie.'

She was calling him Howie again. This was a good sign. Then his bleeper buzzed. He rummaged in his trouser pocket. 'Sorry, Martha. I'll turn it off.'

'No. See who it is.'

Howie checked his bleeper. 'It's that bloody Maurice Skeets again. He's a pain in the arse.' Then Howie remembered Maurice's earlier bleep. And he had an idea. 'Where's Kaia-Liisa? We need an urgent word with her.'

'She's in the president's private office. But why bother her again? She told us nothing useful this morning.'

'I think she might be Maurice's source.'

Martha looked at Howie in disbelief. 'Kaia-Liisa? Don't be so silly. She's a career civil servant. Efficient, trusted, reliable. You must be mistaken.'

'Maurice told me there's a pair of eyes that sees everything in the president's office. That means you. But he didn't give me your name.'

'Why is that so strange?'

'If it was one of the vice presidents feeding him stuff, they would have told him it was you. Why wouldn't they? But if that source was someone inside the president's office – someone who dealt with the president's daily business and was being watched by that pair of eyes – then they wouldn't be so free with their information. It's all about self-interest.'

'You're the expert on these things, but I'm still not sure it's something we should be pursuing today.'

'Let's say Kaia-Liisa is the source. Then maybe she knows more about those secret meetings than she told us. Okay, Maurice didn't have a lot of detail, but maybe Kaia-Liisa didn't tell him the whole story? Or maybe Maurice knows more than he's letting on? I don't know.'

Martha frowned. 'That's a lot of maybes.'

'I know. But if we can get more out of her, it might give us a clue about where Jan might be. If we don't confront her, we won't know.'

She considered his suggestion. 'It wouldn't do any harm, I suppose.'

'Then let's do it. Let's find the leak and plug it.'

Martha stood up and nodded. 'Yes. Let's do it.'

Chapter 36

Britt had been waiting twenty minutes for Bogdan Bogdanowic to emerge with his police escort. He was the only man who could give her the access to the palace she so desperately needed. Where the hell was he? She started to wonder if he was going to show up at all. And if he did, maybe he would say her plan was just too crazy and refuse to cooperate. Even worse, he could accuse Britt of blackmail and contact the police. That could end in a trip to a police cell. She had only experienced that joy once during her journalistic career and it wasn't something she wanted to repeat. It was five years ago. Back then, she'd been released after a couple of hours, after explaining she was a journalist. But now, with the new 24-7 rules and her reputation for exposing police corruption, that wouldn't be so easy.

Then a stupid thought entered her head – had the president been arrested? Was he trapped in a police station somewhere, trying to persuade some dumb police officer that he was the leader of the British Republic? Could they have confused him with his brother Oskar? Now there was a man who needed to be locked up. As a rule, Britt tried not to make judgements about politicians. But over the past day or so, she had developed an intense dislike for the president's twin brother. While getting her story was the priority, it would be an added bonus if she could ruin his chances of becoming president.

'I think that's them now, Miss Pointer,' announced the tall police officer. He waited a few moments until their faces came into view. 'Yes. It's definitely my colleague with Mr Bogdanowic.'

As they approached, Britt could see that Bogdan was a huge Rottweiler of a man – the total opposite of his Labrador-puppy nephew. She would have to take care when handling this particular Bogdanowic breed. If she wasn't careful, she could easily get mauled.

The left-hand gate opened. The short officer marched Bogdan out to where Britt was standing and gestured towards him. 'This is Mr Bogdanowic.'

Bogdan didn't speak. He just snarled.

'Thank you, officers,' replied Britt, realising that getting rid of them was her next priority. It was never a good idea to have police witnesses when you were blackmailing someone. 'Now, I don't want to take up any more of your valuable time. I can handle things from here.'

'You sure about that, madam?' asked the tall officer, sounding worried.

Britt nodded. 'You carry on with whatever it was you were doing, before I interrupted you.'

The short officer turned to his colleague. 'We weren't really doing nothing, were we? We can walk you to the entrance, if you like, and —'

'Officers!' Bogdan barked, so loudly that he made Britt and the officers jump. 'This my business. Not yours. So go.'

The officers reluctantly turned around and walked towards their colleagues on the central gate. As Britt watched them trudge away, she gave a silent cheer. She was now alone with the man who held the key to Buckingham Palace. All she had to do was persuade him to put it in the lock and open the door.

Bogdan's top lip curled upwards to reveal a large set of yellowing teeth. 'You are … journalist?'

Britt took a step back. Just in case Bogdan decided to bite her. 'My name is Britt Pointer. I work for *The Republican*.' She showed him her ID. 'We need to chat.'

Bogdan inspected the card. Then he looked her up and down, as if assessing which of her bones he wanted to chew first. 'One of your colleagues trying to break into palace, yes?'

It was time to reveal her real motives and see if Bogdan was going to play ball. 'That's not true. I just told the officers that to get you out here.'

Bogdan's nostrils flared. His eyes bulged. And the veins in his neck throbbed. Then he took a step towards her. 'Then why I here?'

His words sounded more of a threat than a question. Britt felt genuine fear. But she stood her ground. 'I know about your Code Red crisis.'

Bogdan glanced backwards, as if checking for escape routes. 'I not understand.'

Britt looked around. There was no one within fifty metres of them, so she raised her voice. 'I know the president went missing from the palace on Monday night.'

Bogdan glared at her but didn't speak.

'Your nephew, Herbert, works as a security guy. He fell asleep on Monday night in one of the master bedrooms. The camera system went down at eleven, but he didn't wake up until six hours later. So it didn't get reported until 5.00am.'

Bogdan gave a long, guttural growl, as if warning her not to go any further. Britt ignored it and continued. 'You covered up for your nephew's incompetence. I know because Herbert admitted it to a woman he met in the park yesterday.'

Bogdan flashed one of his canine teeth. 'What woman?'

'An American security expert called Pellie Cann.'

'I never heard of this woman. She talking horseshit.'

'It was me. An identity I used to get the information.'

'My nephew not talk to strangers in parks about security matters.'

'Oh, he does. And then he agrees to meet those strangers in pubs, buys them a tube of Britain's Finest and invites them back to his pod for a three-cheese lasagne. I didn't go, of course. But he gave me his address – 190,872 Revolution Towers in Battersea.'

Bogdan cursed in a foreign language. Then he returned to English. 'So, you writing story about missing president?'

'Of course I'm writing a story,' snapped Britt, in an attempt to show the Rottweiler who was boss. 'I'm a journalist. Why else would I be here?' It seemed to work. Bogdan's shoulders dropped in submission and his snarl disappeared.

'What you want from me?' asked Bogdan, with dread in his voice.

'I want you to get me into the palace.'

Bogdan chuckled. 'That not possible.'

'Then you and your nephew will be on the front page of *The Republican* tomorrow. I hope you both have good CVs. Because you'll be looking for alternative employment. And before you ask, that's not a threat. It's a fact.'

'It sound more than threat. It sound like blackmail.'

'It's not blackmail. It's a business arrangement.'

'And what your business in Buckingham Palace?'

'A meeting in the State Dining Room at four o'clock. A Republican Party nomination meeting.'

Bogdan rubbed his chin. 'That sound like important meeting.'

'Yes. Get me in there before everyone else turns up, so I can listen to the whole thing. If you do that, I'll forget all about your nephew's six-hour nap and your cover-up. And whatever happens – even if I'm discovered before, during or after the meeting – I won't reveal your involvement in getting me inside.'

Bogdan eyeballed her for a full ten seconds. 'How can I trust you?'

'I'm a journalist. We always protect the identity of those who help us. Just like you protected your nephew.'

Bogdan twisted his mouth. 'It will be difficult.'

Britt felt her heart beating in her ears. Her mouth was dry. And her legs felt weak. 'I need an answer now. Yes or no?'

Bogdan took a deep breath. 'Yes. I do it.'

Britt wanted to scream with joy. But she remained calm. 'Then we have a business arrangement, Mr Bogdanowic?'

'Yes. We have business arrangement.'

'Excellent. Now, the meeting doesn't start for nearly two hours. I don't want to be in that room any longer than I have to. What time will everyone start arriving?'

'Vice presidents' offices close to State Dining Room. So earliest they probably start arriving is 3.50pm.'

'Okay. Meet me at half past three at this gate.' Britt pointed at the two police officers they'd been talking with, just moments ago. 'Speak with those two. Ask them to be here at the same time, so they can buzz me through. You then escort me to the State Dining Room. That's all you have to do. I'll find my own way out.'

Bogdan nodded in acknowledgement.

'Go and speak to the officers now,' ordered Britt. 'I want to see you do it.'

Without a word, Bogdan turned and started to make his way over to them. Britt allowed herself a smile. The rabid Rottweiler was now her obedient poodle.

Once she could see Bogdan instructing the police officers, she began walking towards The Mall and contemplated grabbing a coffee in Piccadilly. But then she realised she would need a more suitable outfit than a blouse and slim-fit jeans if she was going to walk the corridors of Buckingham Palace without raising suspicion.

Britt had enough time to take a cab home, make a quick change and taxi it back here for half three. She smiled to herself. Everything was going to plan.

Chapter 37

Howie drummed his fingers on the State Dining Room's oak table until the noise started to annoy him. He'd been waiting fifteen minutes for Martha to return with Kaia-Liisa. The president's office was just round the corner. Martha's round trip should have taken a maximum of five minutes. Why was it taking so long? Howie was starting to get worried.

He leaned back in his chair and pondered the possibilities. Kaia-Liisa might be refusing to cooperate. She had answered their questions about presidential meetings just a few hours ago. Being hauled in for a repeat performance would set alarm bells ringing. She could easily find some excuse not to come here. Or make a quick exit from the president's office with false promises of an imminent return. But no. Martha would have foreseen that. She wouldn't tell Kaia-Liisa what this was about until all three of them were in this room. There must be some other reason for the delay. What could it be?

Howie searched his mind for an answer. After a minute of deep thought, he came up with an idea. Perhaps Kaia-Liisa was enjoying a long lunch with Maurice Skeets? It was entirely possible that she could have worked out that the president had gone missing. Kaia-Liisa was an intelligent woman. Yes, Martha had told her that the president was away on official state business and the Code Red crisis plan was being reviewed. But that wouldn't explain the increased security activity around the palace. She must have her suspicions.

Howie felt nauseous at the thought of the missing-president story being fed to Maurice Skeets. He checked his bleeper. There were no new messages from Maurice. Not yet, at least. He was tempted to turn it off. But not reading his e-comms had already caused him enough trouble today, so he kept it on and stuffed it back in his trouser pocket.

Another couple of minutes passed. Still no sign of Martha or Kaia-Liisa. With nothing else to do, Howie decided to treat himself to a long, loud stretch. The physical exertions of the last day and a half had taken a heavy toll on his body. In fact, he couldn't remember feeling this knackered in a long while. James Bond probably went to the gym between missions. But Howie had no time for rowing, running or weight machines. Only coffee machines. And even the strongest espresso wasn't going to cure his current aches and pains.

Another sixty seconds dragged by. His muscles were still aching. So he stretched even longer and louder than before. As he raised his arms above his head, he felt a muscle spasm in his shoulder. As he twisted to grab the affected area, something clicked in his back. 'I'm getting old,' he groaned to himself.

The door opened. Kaia-Liisa walked in first. She appeared calm as she nodded at him and sat down. But Howie could see fear in her eyes. He'd seen the same fear in many civil servants over the years. Usually when they had been summoned to a meeting with the president to explain why something they should have done hadn't been done. Or why they'd done it at the wrong time. Or why they'd done something they weren't supposed to do in the first place.

Martha followed a few moments later, holding some kind of book. She shut the door and sat down, making sure that she was closer to the door than Kaia-Liisa.

Howie couldn't resist asking. 'What took you so long?'

Martha turned to Howie and spoke in a matter-of-fact voice. 'Kaia-Liisa has located the president's personal diary. I was looking through it.'

Howie didn't know the president kept a personal diary. He had assumed that personal engagements would have been entered in Jan's official diary. In fact, taking time out from presidential duties was so rare for Jan, Howie was surprised he even kept a personal diary. But the president's chief private secretary knew about it. 'You never mentioned a personal diary, Kaia-Liisa.'

'It's not something I've come across before.'

'Why has it suddenly turned up now?' asked Howie.

'I was being proactive,' explained Kaia-Liisa. 'I was trying to find out more about those meetings we discussed.'

Howie doubted that Kaia-Liisa was being proactive for his and Martha's benefit. It was much more likely for her own benefit. Possibly so she could provide Maurice Skeets with additional information. 'How did you find it?'

'I was searching the office for clues, when I noticed a key to one of the president's private drawers was still in the lock. I opened it and found the diary. I was just about to come and find one of you when Martha came in.' The corners of her mouth turned upwards for a second, then returned to their former position. 'Such a coincidence.'

'Unbelievable,' replied Howie, with a hint of sarcasm.

Kaia-Liisa cocked her head and examined Howie's face, as if looking for some physical confirmation of his disbelief. But there was none. He would keep her guessing a little longer. The more pressure she was under, the more she would reveal when she finally cracked.

Martha patted the diary. 'It was a very interesting read.'

'Any mention of the three names the journalist gave us?' asked Howie.

Martha flicked through its pages. 'Jan met privately with Sky Eastern three times. Twice with Olga Frik. And just once with Petra Putinov. All in the last six weeks or so.'

Howie stared at Kaia-Liisa. It was time to put her under more pressure. 'Does that sound right to you?'

Kaia-Liisa stared back. 'I didn't have time to examine the entries.' She turned to Martha. 'Would you mind if we moved on to whatever it is that you brought me here to discuss? It's just I have a backlog of presidential submissions to read through.

With the Independence Day holiday tomorrow, I have to process them all before I leave the office today.'

Martha smiled. 'What we wish to discuss with you is exactly what we're discussing now – the secret meetings.'

Kaia-Liisa adopted a wide-eyed, confused expression. 'I don't understand. I told you everything I know, this morning. You have the president's personal diary. What more is there to discuss?'

Howie took over the interrogation. 'Plenty. We need to find out who's feeding information to this journalist. Not just so we can plug the leak. We need to know everything they know about the meetings in that diary.'

Kais-Liisa's lips hardly moved as she spoke. 'I'm afraid I can't help you with that.'

'Oh, I think you can,' continued Howie. 'This private drawer that contained the diary – is today the first time you've found it unlocked?'

'Yes.'

'So you've never seen a key in that lock before?'

'No.'

'And you've never seen the diary anywhere else in the president's office?'

'Never.'

Howie assessed his interviewee's demeanour. The fear in her eyes was growing. 'Then who else could have had access to Jan's personal diary, Kaia-Liisa? Because whoever's been talking to the journalist must have seen it.'

'I have no idea.'

Howie looked at Martha. She gave the faintest of nods. The signal was clear. It's in your hands now, agent Pond. Finish the job. 'I've had a lot of communication with this journalist lately, Kaia-Liisa. His source is very well-placed within Buckingham Palace.'

Kaia-Liisa didn't respond.

Howie leaned forward. 'His name is Maurice Skeets.' Howie watched for a reaction. Kaia-Liisa was doing everything in her power to appear calm. But he could see a tendon in her neck tense. Almost as if a noose had tightened around it. 'I'll be honest with you, I've never trusted Maurice.'

Kaia-Liisa blinked rapidly but was otherwise motionless.

'And I wouldn't trust him to protect his sources. I'll give you an example. If I offered him a massive exclusive, in exchange for the name of this palace source, he'd give it to me. He might grumble a few platitudes about journalistic ethics at first. But if I told him who I suspected his source was, and I was right, they would be no use to him any more. And Maurice can always find another source.'

Kaia-Liisa wrinkled her forehead. 'Why are you telling me this, Howard?'

'Well, we have a good idea who this person is. And we think they work in the president's private office.'

Kaia-Liisa's face was pale now. Howie could see her hands trembling slightly. 'And you want me to try and find out who it is?'

She was pretty smart, this private secretary. But Howie was smarter. It was time to go for the kill. 'Let's cut the bullshit. We know it's you.'

Kaia-Liisa jerked her head to look at Martha, as if expecting Martha to jump to her defence. She didn't.

Howie lowered his voice. 'If you don't tell me all you know in the next five minutes, I'll be bleeping my friend the chief of police. And informing him that we have a suspected 24-7 in the president's office.'

Martha stood up. 'I wouldn't recommend being arrested for a 24-7 offence, Kaia-Liisa. Things can get rather unpleasant.'

Howie nodded. 'You'd be lucky to see the outside world again before the weekend.'

Kaia-Liisa tried to stop herself sobbing, but the muscle contractions were too strong. She covered her mouth with her hand. Her stifled sobs were all that filled the room for a few seconds. No words of denial. Just sobs.

'I'm afraid that your career in the civil service is over, Kaia-Liisa,' announced Martha. 'But we don't want you to go to prison. It wouldn't be good for anyone.'

Kaia-Liisa froze for a few seconds. Then she burst into floods of tears. 'Please forgive me!'

'Why did you do it?' asked Martha.

Kaia-Liisa composed herself. 'The meetings with Sky Eastern – I'm certain it was about old oil and the application for test drilling. She came here, late one evening, when I was working late. The president didn't know I was still here. I was in the corridor and I overheard them talking.'

'Talking about what?' asked Howie.

'About oil platforms. About secret locations.' She wiped her eyes and then launched into a passionate monologue. 'After everything the president promised about not going back to old energy! He's going to approve the test drilling. I know it. Sky Eastern has probably filled his head with promises of huge tax windfalls. But it's all lies. They don't care about finding oil in British waters. They just want to test their new Tech.' She gasped for air and continued. 'But why should we British be the guinea pigs? Why should we play little brother to the Americans' big brother all the time?' She put her head in her hands. 'I can't believe it. After all he promised the citizens five years ago, when he was re-elected. "Out with the old energy, and in with the new." Those were his words. He lied to us! And that's why I gave the information to a journalist. I wanted his lies exposed for all the world to see.' She burst into tears again.

Martha handed Kaia-Liisa a tissue. 'And what about the other meetings?'

Kaia-Liisa took the tissue and blew her nose. 'I don't know anything about the Auto-Tech Industries woman. I swear on the president's life.'

'And the Russian woman?' asked Martha. 'We need to know about her.'

'I don't know what that was about. All I know is that it was arranged by his brother, Oskar.' She choked back a tear. 'He came into the office a couple of weeks ago. They were having a loud conversation in the private meeting room. I heard them arguing. Oskar was shouting about having already arranged a meeting for Jan with Petra Putinov and how it would look bad for him if it didn't happen. Then Oskar stormed out.'

Martha thought for a moment. 'Any other unofficial meetings you were aware of?'

Kaia-Liisa bowed her head and stared at the red carpet. 'No. That's everything.'

Howie moved closer to Kaia-Liisa. 'You sure about that? Because you haven't been very truthful with us, up till now.'

Tears were streaming down Kaia-Liisa's cheeks now, faster than her tissue could catch them. 'That's ... that's all I know.'

There was one last question Howie needed to ask. 'Have you told Maurice Skeets anything about the president being away from the palace for the last couple of days?'

Kaia-Liisa looked confused. 'No. Why would I?'

Howie stared into her terrified eyes. 'You told him about Martha being in your office. You didn't give her name, but you told him a pair of eyes that sees everything was watching over you.' He lowered his voice. 'What else did you tell him?'

'N-n-nothing,' stuttered Kaia-Liisa. 'I wanted him to stop harassing me for more information. I thought he was going to write the story weeks ago. But he kept coming back. Wanting more and more details.' She choked back another tear. 'It wasn't supposed to be like this.'

Howie was satisfied that Maurice Skeets wouldn't be contacting him about a missing president. He looked over at Martha. 'I'm finished with her.'

Martha took Kaia-Liisa's arm. 'So am I. Time to escort you from the building.'

'Will you be calling the police?' asked Kaia-Liisa, her voice cracking.

Martha shook her head.

'But you cut off all contact with Maurice Skeets,' added Howie. 'And any other journalists. Dealing with them is my job. Not yours.'

Kaia-Liisa closed her eyes and gave the faintest of nods.

'Human Resources will be in touch about the termination of your employment,' announced Martha. 'If you haven't already resigned by then.'

Kaia-Liisa began to sob again. Martha ushered her out before she could flood the room with tears.

Howie watched the door close on Kaia-Liisa and her civil service career. In a few months, he might also be gone. He groaned at the thought of all the contact with Human Resources it would mean. All the impenetrable e-forms, gigabytes of guidance and badly written e-comms. It was enough to drive a presidential spokesperson to early retirement. But Howie didn't want to dwell on this possibility any longer. He had enough to worry about with all the chaos the nomination meeting would bring.

Fed up with sitting on his backside for most of the day, Howie decided to stretch his legs and walk to the other end of the room. As he strolled across the red carpet, he began to wonder if the president really would go back on his promise about old energy. It would be strange if he did. Jan Polak was a man of principles. No business or individual, however big or powerful, had ever received a favour from him. Neither did Jan accept unsolicited cash or gifts from the outside world. Dodgy deals and dubious donations might characterise the rest of European politics, but not here. Not in post-revolution Britain.

Howie stopped by one of the huge windows and stared out at the world beyond. Had Sky Eastern really influenced the president? He tried to think of a situation where the president's principles might be tested. A situation where he might be tempted to prioritise his own needs over and above those of his political party, his government or even his country. Howie stood thinking for a full five minutes. But he couldn't think of anything. And oil exploration – why that of all industries? It didn't make any sense.

He didn't notice the main door being pushed open very slowly. Only when the large figure of Bogdan Bogdanowic appeared in the corner of his eye did he snap out of his daydream and turn to face the door. 'Bogdan,' he shouted, as he walked back to his seat. 'Any news on the president?'

Bogdan looked surprised to see him. 'No news on president.'

'Do you need to search this room?' asked Howie.

'Erm, well … n-n-no, I don't,' stuttered Bogdan, sounding unsure. 'You have meeting in here now?'

'Just with Martha Blake. And we've got another one at four with the vice presidents, so we could be here all afternoon.'

Bogdan suddenly looked worried. 'I change mind. I need to do security check for 4.00pm meeting.'

Howie sighed. 'Make your mind up.'

Bogdan was still looking concerned. 'If vice presidents there, I need to do check. I not know this until you say.'

'Okay, okay.'

'I need you out by 3.45pm for security check.' Bogdan bowed his head. 'Sorry if this problem, Mr Pond. But room must be clear then.'

There was something about Bogdan's behaviour that made Howie suspicious. Bogdan wasn't usually concerned about whether security procedures caused Howie, or anyone else, any inconvenience. Perhaps he'd been on a training course recently. It was the only explanation. Howie nodded his agreement.

Bogdan nodded back, turned and hurried out of the room.

A few minutes later, Martha was back. 'That's the leak plugged.' She walked over to Howie. 'What are your thoughts on all that Sky Eastern business?'

'It doesn't add up. I don't see why he would approve test drilling in British waters. New energy was always part of his vision for the future.'

'Money is the only thing that I could think of.'

'Jan isn't driven by money. Or even power – not in itself. I know it sounds like a cliché, but that's Jan. That's why people love him.'

Martha sighed. 'None of it makes much sense. Even if Eastern has got some kind of hold over him – financial or otherwise – that doesn't help explain his disappearance.'

'Maybe it's a red herring. My gut feeling is it's Oskar and Maxim we've got to worry about.'

'Yes. Mine, too.'

'What are we going to do between now and the big meeting?' asked Howie. 'We don't have much time.'

'I think a little research is required. And you can help me.'

Howie's heart sank. 'It doesn't involve using an e-terminal, does it?'

Martha put her hand on his shoulder. 'No, it doesn't. Now, come on. I want to double-check the British constitution for loopholes that might buy us some more time. We can read it together.'

Howie groaned. That didn't sound like much fun.

Chapter 38

Britt had rushed home, put on a new outfit, and dashed back to central London. She was now only one hundred metres from the Buckingham Palace gates. They were beginning to feel like a second home. She checked her bleeper. It was 3.28pm. Bogdan would be here any minute. Those two police officers should then let her through the gates without too much fuss. Bogdan would take her inside the palace and escort her to the State Dining Room. Britt would find a suitable hiding place, wait for the meeting to start and then listen for confirmation that the president was still missing – preferably from someone other than Martha Blake, as her bleep to Howie was already one of Britt's sources. But there would be dozens of people at that meeting. It shouldn't be a problem. She would also be able to hear the results of the nomination voting. Once the meeting was over and its participants had returned to their offices, she would escape the palace, rush to her desk and write the story for tomorrow's edition of *The Republican*. George would have to reverse his decision to shunt her on to features. Everything would go back to normal.

Her thoughts were interrupted by the squeak of her knee-high red leather boots. She hadn't worn them in years and had forgotten what a high-pitched racket they made when they rubbed together. She had rescued them from the back of her wardrobe for one reason only – they matched the dark-red coat, sweater and trousers she was currently wearing. Even her tinted glasses had dark-red rims. Her single-colour ensemble wasn't a fashion statement. It was her attempt at camouflage. Britt had once visited Buckingham Palace on a school trip, and she remembered the State Dining Room's carpet, walls and curtains were all red. The same shade of red that she was wearing today. If a collar, sleeve or boot popped out from behind the curtain – or wherever she was hiding – it would reduce her chances of being spotted.

Britt felt an adrenaline rush as she realised how close she was to achieving her goal. But she knew there was a possibility that things might not go to plan. In fact, they could go seriously wrong. If she was spotted the police would be called. She would be arrested as a 24-7 and dragged to a police station. It could be days before she saw daylight again. She spoke aloud to herself. 'Be calm. Be cool. Be careful.'

After a few minutes, she checked her bleeper again. It was 3.35pm. Bogdan was late. There was no sign of him in the distance. Unfortunately for her, he wasn't a man who moved quickly. That meant it was unlikely she would set foot inside the palace until at least twenty to four. Bogdan had said the vice presidents would start arriving from about ten to. From what she could remember from her school trip, the State Dining Room was on the other side of the palace from the main entrance. It would take several minutes, if not more, to walk there. She wouldn't be able to run once she was inside. That would draw attention and she didn't want that. She needed to get to that room before anyone else. Time was going to be very tight.

Britt stared at the gates ahead of her. The two police officers were standing by the left-hand gate awaiting her arrival. She had deliberately held back, to avoid getting into a long conversation with them. But then she had a thought. Maybe she could persuade them to let her through now? Then she could meet Bogdan right outside the palace entrance and save herself two or three valuable minutes. It was worth a try. She walked up to them. They didn't recognise her, so she reintroduced herself. 'Hello again, officers. It's that bloody journalist again.'

The tall officer shook his head. 'Please, madam. Don't use language like that to describe yourself.'

'We don't think of you as that bloody journalist no more,' added the short officer. 'Not even a journalist. You're just a normal human being. Like what we are.'

'One who's got the country's best interests – and our interests – at heart, madam.'

As Britt began to speak, the short officer spoke over her. 'But that other bloody journalist, Rosie Parker – she won't be on our Christmas card list.'

The tall officer frowned. 'Definitely not. I know I'm an officer of the law, but if I ever come face-to-face with that fraud again, I can tell you now, madam. I will not be responsible for my actions.'

'You ain't seen him when he's angry. There was a French school trip here on Sunday. Kids were climbing all over the railings. Chaos it was.'

'It was like the storming of the Bastille, madam.'

The police officers carried on with their story. But Britt wasn't listening. She had noticed Bogdan moving towards them at a speed that didn't seem possible for a man of his size. Within half a minute, he had reached the other side of the gate.

'Sorry,' gasped Bogdan, through the railings. 'Held up ... meeting.'

The tall officer raised a hand. 'Greetings, Mr Bogdanowic. Let us just finish this story and we'll be right with you.'

Britt didn't like the look of Bogdan. His face was sweaty, his skin pale and his breathing heavy. The last thing she needed was him collapsing – it would be game over for her. And possibly game over for Bogdan, judging by the state of him. 'Take a few deep breaths, Bogdan. I'll get them to open the gate.' She turned to the police officers and spoke urgently. 'I need to get through now.'

The short officer was so engrossed in his storytelling, he didn't hear. 'So these French schoolkids are running riot. Then who suddenly appears? Our old friend the American ambassador, Clinton Stackshaker, with some American woman who was covered in jewellery.'

'Tell me another time,' urged Britt.

The short officer nodded towards his colleague. 'Me and him didn't have a chance to say nothing to these two VIPs. We were too busy being given the run around by those little French terrors.'

'We're still good physical specimens, madam. But not as young as we used to be.'

'No, really,' insisted Britt. 'I don't have time for this.'

The tall officer smiled. 'It'll only take a moment. You wait till he gets to the punchline.'

Britt felt like beating them to the punchline – with her right fist. Before she could protest, the short officer had launched back into the story.

'So the ambassador yells something at them in French. They stop what they're doing, jump off the railings and run off towards the park. Like they just seen a ghost.'

Bogdan bent down and put his hands on his knees. 'We … need to go.'

The tall officer took up the story. 'So I asked the ambassador what it was he said to them. And you'll never guess.'

'I don't care,' hissed Britt.

Bogdan sat down on the ground. 'I not feel too good.'

The tall officer waved a hand towards Bogdan. 'Be with you in a moment, sir.' He turned to Britt. 'He told them, in French, that he was the king. And his well-dressed lady friend was the queen. And if they didn't get off his railings in the next five seconds, he'd have them all thrown in the Tower of London!'

The officers roared with laughter, as Bogdan started wheezing loudly.

Britt spoke in a firm voice. 'That was a fascinating tale, gentlemen. Now let me through those gates.'

'We got loads more stories like that,' replied the short officer, patting his colleague on the back. 'We could write a book, couldn't we, Charlie?'

'That is correct, Charlie. Things are never dull outside these gates.'

Britt's patience had run out. 'Things will get a lot livelier, if you don't open those gates in the next five seconds.'

The officers looked at each other, then at her – unsure whether her anger was genuine.

'For king's sake, let me through!' snapped Britt. 'Or I swear, I will put you pair of Charlies on the front page of *The Republican* tomorrow. And once your bosses read about your big mouths and loose tongues, the only gates you'll be standing in front of will be the ones in your gardens, while you're suspended awaiting disciplinary hearings.'

Both the officers' mouths opened. For a change, not a word came from either of them. The tall officer took a deep breath through his nose. Then he marched indignantly to the button that opened the gate and pressed it.

Britt half-smiled, half-grimaced. 'Thank you.'

The officers turned to each other, shook their heads and spoke as one. 'Bloody journalist.'

The gate opened and Britt hurried towards Bogdan. She needed to check if he was still in a fit state to escort her inside the palace. He was back on his feet, but puffing urgently on an inhaler. 'Are you alright to get going, Bogdan?'

'I think so,' he croaked, patting his chest.

Britt checked her bleeper. It was 3.40pm. The vice presidents would start arriving in about ten minutes and she wasn't even in the palace. 'How long will it take to get to the State Dining Room, once we're in there?'

'After security … not long.'

She had forgotten that there would be some sort of airport-style security to get through. And Howie had mentioned last week that the palace had just opened up for visitors again. She would just have to hope that she didn't get stuck behind a group of rioting French schoolchildren. 'How long will security take?'

Bogdan didn't reply. He just waved his hand rapidly. She assumed it meant that security wouldn't be a problem, rather than a sign that he was about to collapse, die and ruin her chances of getting to that meeting.

They started walking slowly towards the palace entrance. They had only travelled twenty metres when Bogdan stopped to take another blast on his inhaler. But his medication didn't seem to be helping much. This continued for the whole journey to the entrance – every twenty metres or so, he took another puff. And he wasn't sounding any better.

Britt had to say something. 'I'm sorry you're not well. But if we carry on at this speed, I'm not going to make it.'

'Can't go faster,' panted Bogdan. 'Asthma attack.'

She linked her right arm with his left arm. 'Come on, you can do it.' With all her strength, she pulled Bogdan towards the entrance. It was like dragging a fatally wounded buffalo. But he was starting to move a little bit faster.

Two minutes later, they entered the palace. In front of them was an unmanned security checkpoint – a bag scanner and a single archway for visitors to walk through.

Bogdan reached into his pocket and handed Britt a pass. 'Here. Visitor security pass. You supposed to have someone with you.' He took a huge breath that Britt thought might be his last. 'But I cannot go on.'

'Where are the security people?' asked Britt, desperately looking around for someone to wave her through the machine.

'Must be on break,' wheezed Bogdan.

'I can't wait around. What happens if I just run through that machine?'

'Alarm go off.'

'But you can turn it off?'

'Yes.' Bogdan pointed beyond the archway. 'Button over there. I press. It recognise my hand.'

Britt assessed Bogdan's physical shape. It wasn't good. In fact, it wasn't even bad. It was terrible. So terrible, she wasn't filled with confidence that his hand would reach it before she had been wrestled to the ground by security. 'Are the cameras working now?'

'No. Still trying to fix.'

At least that was something. Britt put her hand on Bogdan's arm. 'I'm going to run through there and you're going to get up, take a deep breath, walk through and press that button to stop the alarm.'

Bogdan took another puff on his inhaler. 'You know where room is?'

'I think so. I can always ask someone.'

'You get caught, they call police. I cannot help.'

'I know.' She checked her bleeper. It was 3.44pm. 'Just push that button.'

Bogdan nodded. 'Your eyes,' he croaked. 'They …'

But Britt didn't have time to listen to compliments. Instead, she ran through the security gate. A second after passing through, an alarm screeched behind her. It reminded her of the pelicans. And Pellie Cann. She had an idea. Maybe it was time for Pellie to put in another appearance. After all, it would be foolish to admit her real name and profession in this situation. Yes. It was time for a final cameo from her American alter ego.

She confidently speed-walked down a corridor, with the alarm still echoing around the walls and ceilings. Then a man appeared in the corridor, right in front of her.

'Is that alarm coming from the entrance?' he asked.

Britt stopped and looked the man in the eyes. 'Sure is,' she replied, in an American drawl. 'A huge guy with a foreign accent is trying to turn it off.'

'Oh, right. That'll be Bogdan. We'd better leave him to it.'

Britt sensed an opportunity. 'My name's Pellie Cann. I'm here for a meeting in the State Dining Room. I got lost.' She flashed her visitor's pass. 'I'm supposed to have someone escorting me and I don't want to break any rules.' She smiled. 'I know what you British are like about your rules.'

The man laughed. 'Rule one – don't break the rules. Rule two – if you do break the rules, make sure you don't get caught.'

Exactly. 'It starts very soon. Could you possibly take me there?'

'No problem.' He offered his hand. 'I'm Bryan. Bryan with a "y".'

'Then let's go, Bryan with a "y"!'

The next three minutes were a blur of corridors, doors and stairs. Britt checked her bleeper one more time. It was 3.48pm. 'Is it nearby?'

'About a minute away. It's up there on the left, just after that big portrait of the president.'

Britt could see the portrait. And she couldn't see anyone else heading towards it. It looked like she would be the first there. At the same moment, the distant alarm stopped screeching. Bogdan had summoned up the strength to get to that button. Hallelujah! Everything was going to plan now. The State Dining Room was just metres away.

And then a strange little robot rolled out of an office, just ahead of her, and moved towards them.

'Oh look, it's my namesake, Brian the auto-tech,' announced Bryan. 'But he's Brian with an "i". A big red eye!' He laughed at his own joke and peered down at the robot. 'Aren't you, Brian?'

The little robot stopped, turned its top half towards Bryan and fired a laser towards his eye. Then it spoke in a tinny voice. 'Greetings, Bryan Burke.' Then its top half swivelled towards Britt and fired a laser at her eye. 'Greetings … unregistered human.'

'She's a visitor,' reassured Bryan. 'I'm escorting her to the State Dining Room for a meeting.'

'Brian has access to all visitors' iris scans. Brian has no record of this visitor's iris scan.'

Her eyes needed to be scanned. That must have been what Bogdan was trying to tell her before she ran though security. She swallowed hard. She wasn't sure if you could bullshit a robot. There was only one way to find out. 'There was some kinda technical hitch with the scanner when I came in,' gabbled Britt, in her fake American accent.

The robot's red eye pulsed. 'Brian is not aware of any Tech issues with security scanners. Brian is only aware of a recent alarm being triggered in the entrance zone.'

Bryan patted the robot on the head. 'Chillax, little fella. That was a false alarm. Bogdan is dealing with it.'

The robot bleeped. 'Brian is only seventeen per cent convinced of that fact. Brian cannot allow this human to proceed. She must return to the entrance zone for iris scanning.'

Britt clenched her buttocks. She had a feeling this stubborn heap of metal was going to ruin everything. Then she heard faint voices behind her. Looking back, she saw a red-haired woman and a man in a super-smart suit about a hundred metres away, walking slowly in her direction. She couldn't make out their faces. But they must be vice presidents. She turned back to face the robot and cursed her luck. She probably had less than a minute to talk herself out of this situation and get to the room. But this robot would be hard to fool. What was she going to say to get rid of it? Her mind went blank. And the voices behind her grew louder.

Then a familiar figure flew out of an office to their left – Conor O'Brean. Britt covered her face with a hand, so he didn't recognise her. But she needn't have bothered. Conor only had eyes for the robot.

'It's one of them little auto-fellas!' cried Conor. 'Sent by the gods to save me!'

The robot swivelled its top half and fired a laser at the man. 'Greetings, Conor O'Brean. Brian is currently dealing with a potential security —'

'This is an emergency,' interrupted Conor. 'I need you to wipe some sensitive messages from my bleeper. They're from a close personal friend in marketing. A close personal lady friend, if you understand my meaning.'

'Brian does not understand your meaning.'

Conor's voice became more urgent. 'Listen, young fella. I left my bleeper on the kitchen table. My wife gets home from work in fifteen minutes. If she sees those messages, my life won't be worth living.'

'Brian has to prioritise all requests. Brian has assessed yours as low priority. Brian will first deal with this unregistered human.'

Conor wasn't taking 'no' for an answer. He moved behind the robot and pushed him towards his office. 'This way, little auto-buddy. It'll only take five earth minutes to save my life.' Conor was at least one hundred kilos, but even he was struggling to move the machine.

'Brian does not like to be handled in a rough manner,' protested the robot, its metallic voice going up an octave. 'Brian has very delicate circuitry.'

Britt saw her chance. 'Bryan, let's give Conor a hand.' Bryan nodded and he and Britt joined the big push. In a few seconds, they had succeeded in pushing the robot into Conor's office. Britt and Bryan stepped back into the corridor. Conor slammed the door shut. The little metal menace was gone.

She glanced back. The man and woman were only forty metres away, but deep in conversation. They weren't paying her any attention. The man's face looked familiar. So did his gorgeous suit. Oh, no. Not again. It was Howie. She needed to get moving. 'Thanks, Bryan,' shouted Britt and she ran towards the door of the State Dining Room.

A few seconds later, she was standing outside it. She opened the wooden door and went in. She was the only person in the room. But that wouldn't be the case for much longer. She looked across at the long curtains. Her heart jumped when she saw they matched her dark-red outfit perfectly. Then it sank, as she realised they were all expertly tied back and would offer no hiding place from the gaze of fifty vice presidents.

Britt frantically looked around. There wasn't anything else to hide behind in this room. She felt herself becoming sweaty with panic. She checked again. No. There was nothing.

She heard voices outside the door. One of them was definitely Howie's. He was about to come in and see her standing there, like a lost child in a very posh restaurant. She rested a hand on the oak table and wondered what he would say when he saw her. Then an idea came to her. There wasn't anything to hide behind. But there was something to hide under.

Britt dived under the table and started crawling towards the centre. As she did so, she heard the door open and Howie's voice.

'It's all clear, Martha. Bogdan's people must have finished the security check. Let's sit down.'

The woman must be Martha Blake. If she discovered Britt hiding under her table, she wouldn't be too happy.

Britt tucked herself into a ball – being careful not to rub her leather boots together – and waited for the meeting to start.

Chapter 39

Howie slumped into his usual chair in the State Dining Room while Martha stood by the table in deep thought. It was clear from her expression that she was a troubled woman. And Howie was a troubled man. He gazed along the table. It would be surrounded by vice presidents in just a few minutes. There would be excited chattering, whispered speculation, passionate speeches, tense voting and, eventually, triumphant celebrations. Whoever it was, it wouldn't be good news for Howie, Martha or the citizens or the country. Only good news for the winner – unless Jan Polak put in an appearance before eleven o'clock tomorrow morning and spoiled their party. But there was nothing to suggest that was going to happen.

Howie turned to Martha. 'That's an hour and a half we'll never get back.'

She nodded and sat down, a glum expression on her face. 'It's disappointing that our constitution is so utterly lacking in loopholes when it comes to presidential nominations. I'd convinced myself we would find some way to postpone this damn meeting if we searched hard enough. But it's one hundred per cent loophole-free.' She put her elbows on the table and rested her head on her hands. 'It's the first time I've ever seen anything that watertight in my life. And of course, it has to be now. When we need more time.'

Howie nodded glumly. While ploughing through the constitution they had discussed the information they'd gathered so far and agreed that Oskar and Maxim were definitely up to something. But there was no hard evidence to link them, or any other human being, to the president's disappearance. There was only that annoying little auto-tech, Brian. And its logs had conveniently been wiped. The chances of finding that evidence before eleven o'clock tomorrow were slim at best. At worst, they were zero.

Then Howie had an idea. 'What about asking the lawyers for advice about the constitutional implications of all this? They're always talking about grey areas in the law.'

Martha shook her head. 'I don't see the point. It all looks pretty black and white to me.'

'Yeah. But we're not lawyers. We could get a couple of the senior solicitors to take a look overnight. See if there's a loophole that we've missed. Something that might buy us time.'

Martha thought about his suggestion. 'I can't see Oskar going for it. He won't want any delays.'

The door opened. Vice presidents began trickling into the room. All chatting to each other. All ignoring Martha and Howie.

'Okay, we'll try it,' whispered Martha. 'I might need you to back me up. If I do, put on a good performance. Use whatever artistic licence you need. Because this isn't a meeting any more. It's a theatre.' She looked him in the eyes. 'A theatre of war.'

They both sat silently as more vice presidents filed into the room and took their places around the table. Howie started to count them. Five minutes later, he had reached forty-six. Then he felt a slap on his back. It was vice president number forty-seven – Zayn Winner.

'Alright, 006-and-a-half?' sniggered Zayn, right in Howie's ear. 'You got your suicide pill ready – in case Jan's evil twin wins the vote?'

'This isn't a laughing matter,' grumbled Howie.

'You see my *Daily Democrat* interview, buddy?'

'Yeah. Mina Pritti did a good job for us.'

Zayn nudged Howie in the ribs. 'It was me that did the good job, my old pal. I should be nominated for an award for that performance.' Zayn winked at Howie. 'Maybe nominated for something even bigger, eh, buddy? Anyway, I'd better sit down, in case this lot think we're getting too friendly. They're not your biggest fans – especially since you became a secret agent. Bit jealous. And, no offence, but I don't want them thinking we're too close. In case I lose votes.' He gave Howie an even harder jab in the ribs. 'Wish me luck, big guy!' Zayn took his seat, grinning like a chimpanzee.

Howie rubbed his side. He hadn't really been listening to Zayn. He was too preoccupied with thoughts of lawyers, the constitution and loopholes. He checked his bleeper. It was 3.59pm. There were three more vice presidents still to arrive. Howie knew what was coming – Oskar Polak's grand entrance.

A minute later, with the distant sound of Big Ben striking four drifting across St James' Park, the missing trio arrived. Oskar entered first – stopping at the top of the table to inflate his chest and straighten his tie. A moment later, the two vice presidents whose names no one could ever remember followed him into the room, shutting the door behind them. Then they hurriedly positioned themselves on either side of Oskar and put their hands behind their backs.

'Honourable colleagues,' boomed Oskar, as if speaking to a stadium full of people. 'Good afternoon to you all. Is everyone here?'

'They're all here,' confirmed Howie. 'I've counted. Now if you and your colleagues would kindly sit down, Martha can begin the meeting.'

Oskar looked down his nose at Howie. 'And what are you doing here? Taking minutes?'

He ignored the urge to jump up and punch Oskar in the face. 'I'm here to make sure I know exactly what happens, Oskar. I don't want to hear it second-hand. From you or anybody else.'

A murmur went around the table. Oskar glared at Howie and then gestured to his companions to walk ahead of him – an order they obeyed without hesitation. One of them pulled out Oskar's chair, at the far end of the table, while the other brushed the seat with a handkerchief. The two vice presidents waited for

Oskar to take his seat. Then they silently sat down either side of him.

'Please proceed,' announced Oskar, with a regal wave of the hand. Then he began nodding, in turn, to all the other vice presidents in the room. Each nod accompanied by a false smile.

Martha stood up. 'Excellent. We have all fifty of you in attendance. So I can begin the meeting.'

Forty-nine pairs of vice-presidential eyes focused on Martha. The exception was Zayn Winner, who seemed to be practising a speech.

'We all know why we're here, so let's not waste time,' declared Martha. 'Unfortunately, after extensive investigations, I have no further news for you on the president's whereabouts. Or, indeed, when he might be returning to us.'

An excited rumble filled the room, sending vibrations pulsing through the wooden table. So powerful, they made Zayn stop talking to himself and pay attention.

Oskar addressed the room. 'My brother is still missing. That leaves us no alternative.' He took a deep breath. 'Let us begin the nomination process.'

Zayn's hands shot into the air. 'Woah, big fella! Don't jump the starting gun. You might get disqualified!'

Oskar stared at Zayn, who responded with a double thumbs up.

Martha ignored the interruptions and continued. 'Now, I don't need to tell you that tomorrow is Independence Day. And it appears that the constitution requires you, vice presidents, to nominate your election candidate for the eleven o'clock announcement on the palace balcony.'

Oskar wrinkled his forehead, glanced theatrically at his two aides, and then bellowed, 'What do you mean "appears"? There's no question about it.'

Martha stayed calm. 'Please, let me finish. The constitution makes it clear that this meeting must be chaired, and overseen, by a senior, non-political, public servant. And as I'm the only person in full possession of all the facts, and who fulfils those criteria, it falls to me to fulfil that role in the best way —'

'Yes, well, it's not about the referee,' interrupted Oskar, grinning with self-satisfaction. 'It's about the players. So can we just get on with it?'

'This referee wants to talk about the current team captain. And I won't allow him to be substituted just yet. No matter how loudly his vice-captains might protest.'

A smattering of nervous laughter was quickly silenced by Oskar's two-man entourage shushing the room. Howie could see Oskar's eyes bulging with indignation. But the president's brother remained silent. Martha was smarter than Oskar. And Oskar knew that. It was in his interests to keep his mouth shut and avoid any more devastating put-downs.

Martha pushed her hands together, as if about to say a prayer. 'So, as official chair of this meeting, I have a proposal for you all to consider. We refer this to a small team of senior lawyers to consider overnight. I want to be one hundred per cent sure that there's no possible way to postpone all this until Jan is safely back with us. The plan would be to reconvene here at half past seven tomorrow morning, listen to their advice, and take it from there.'

Howie could see that most of the vice presidents were shaking their heads – including the Oskar Polak trio.

'We're all here now, let's get it over with!' shouted a grey suit.

'I don't want another bloody early start tomorrow,' moaned a greyer suit.

There was more muttering from half a dozen other vice presidents. Oskar waited until they'd all finished. 'There's your answer.'

Martha tried again. 'The constitution is a very detailed, very dense document. I would suggest that an independent, expert eye is required to give us a definitive view.'

'Are you suggesting that we don't know our own constitution?' shouted a charcoal suit.

Martha looked slightly rattled. 'No. I'm simply suggesting that legal experts take a look at it.'

'Forget it!' cried a graphite suit. 'Those bloody lawyers never give a straight answer.'

Martha took a deep breath. 'If you don't wish to take the legal route, that is your decision, vice presidents. However, may I respectfully request you delay nominating until tomorrow morning for the purposes of my investigations into the president's disappearance?'

There was more muttering around the table.

Martha raised her voice. 'We suspect foul play. That is why we need more time. I didn't want to alarm you until I was in possession of all the facts. But you have left me with no alternative but to inform you of my concerns.'

'Foul play?' scoffed Oskar. 'What nonsense!'

Martha turned her body so she was directly facing Oskar, her eyes like laser beams cutting into metal. 'We have uncovered some rather troubling ... relationships.'

Oskar waved a dismissive hand. 'Whatever are you talking about?'

'I'm going to give you a name, vice presidents, and I want you to raise your arm if you have ever met this individual.' Martha paused for just a second, so no one could confer. 'Russian businessman Viktor Maxim.'

A buzz went around the room. The vice presidents all seemed to know who he was – there were no shrugged shoulders or blank expressions. But there were no arms being raised. Howie stared at Oskar, who was now avoiding eye contact with anyone except his two attendants.

Martha raised her voice. 'Perhaps some of you didn't hear my question. So I'll ask it again. Have any of you ever met Viktor Maxim? I know at least one person in this room has.'

The vice president to Oskar's right raised his arm. 'I may have done, very briefly. I can't remember the exact details. Now, can we proceed to the business of the Republican Party nomination for president?'

Martha's eyes were still focused on Oskar. 'It wasn't you I was thinking of.'

'What was the name again?' asked Oskar.

'Viktor Maxim. He owns a multinational company – Maxim International. It has a diverse portfolio of interests. Including defence – your area of responsibility, Vice President Polak.'

Oskar wasn't a great actor. His attempts to look thoughtful were clumsy. When he finally spoke, it sounded unconvincing. 'Viktor Maxim? Possibly. I attend a lot of meetings. I come across many international businessmen. I can't be expected to remember all their names.' His two associates nodded vigorously. Their acting was even worse.

'If you need any acting lessons, Oskar, just say the word!' shouted Zayn. 'I can give you a discount.' He laughed loudly. A few other vice presidents joined in.

While the laughter echoed round the room, Howie heard a strange squeaking noise. It seemed to be coming from under the table. He looked down. There was no mouse or squeaky floorboard under the carpet. But he somehow knew it wasn't a rodent or a piece of loose wood making the noise. It was something else. It was a sound he'd heard before. But he couldn't remember when or where. Anyway, it wasn't important.

'You should remember his name, Vice President Polak,' insisted Martha, once the laughter had subsided. 'You met him for lunch yesterday at The Savoy. I know because one of my agents witnessed it.'

The room fell silent. Oskar's face drained of colour. His lieutenants glanced anxiously at each other. Howie knew Oskar wanted to scream 'Why have you been following me?' across the room. But he wouldn't. He wouldn't want the whole room to be told if Martha had uncovered the truth about his relationship with Maxim. Instead, Oskar put his hand on his chest and responded. 'Dearest colleagues, my sincere apologies. The stress of the last two days has taken its toll on me. This discussion has jogged my memory. I did indeed bump into Mr

Maxim in The Savoy yesterday. And we did speak for a short time.'

'What did you discuss?' demanded Martha.

Oskar waved a dismissive hand. 'The food, the wine ... possibly the weather.'

'My agent overheard you discussing some "business". What might that be?'

A murmur of speculation echoed round the walls and ceiling. As it did, Howie heard that squeaking noise again. He was just about to bend down and peek under the table, when Oskar jumped to his feet.

'I don't know who this agent was,' snarled Oskar. 'But he sounds no more competent than Mr Pond here. Because he is wrong. I did not discuss any business with Mr Maxim.'

Martha crossed her arms. 'Maxim International is a government supplier of defence goods – albeit on a small scale. Perhaps the business was a future defence contract?'

Oskar jabbed a finger in Martha's direction. 'I am not involved in any improper conduct with regard to defence contracts, with Viktor Maxim or anyone else.'

Nobody spoke for a few seconds. Then Martha pierced the silence. 'Nobody said you were involved in any improper conduct.'

'What's that supposed to mean?!' shrieked Oskar.

'You're the only person who's uttered the words "improper conduct", Vice President Polak. Which might suggest that improper conduct has been playing on your mind somewhat.'

'This is outrageous!' screamed Oskar, his arms flailing. 'My good name is being called into question on the basis of nothing but a chance encounter in a restaurant and a conversation misheard by one of your halfwit agents. If you'd spent more time looking for my brother and less time eavesdropping on my lunches, maybe you would've found him by now.'

Martha looked shocked at Oskar's outburst. 'But vice president —'

'Before this meeting descends into chaos,' interrupted Oskar, 'I propose we move straight to nominations.' He turned to his colleagues. 'Do any of you disagree with my proposal, vice presidents?' He didn't allow enough time for anyone to respond. 'Good. Then we will move to the main business of this meeting.' He attempted a warm smile, which was more of a cold grimace. 'And I would like to put my name forward.'

The vice presidents either side of Oskar spoke as one. 'I'll second that nomination.'

Howie looked over at Martha. Her expression was now one of resignation. It matched Howie's. They had tried to stop this process. But they had failed. They would have to let the meeting run its natural course.

'Now, if anyone else wants to waste their time standing against me, raise your hand in the next ten seconds.' Oskar lowered his voice to a growl. 'But let me make this quite clear. If you do stand against me, there'll be no place for you in my Government. So think carefully.'

Howie bowed his head. He couldn't watch. He counted the seconds. He'd reached nine, when, from the corner of his eye, he saw a hand shoot up. He felt a pang of relief. Then he realised who the hand belonged to. It was Zayn Winner. An unlikely superhero. But no one else was offering to save the world from Oskar Polak.

Zayn grinned at his forty-nine astonished colleagues. 'You've got to be in it to win it!' He turned to Ivan Bonn, sitting next to him, and put an arm round his shoulder. 'You'll second my nomination, won't you, my old buddy?'

Ivan nearly jumped off his seat. 'What's that? Me? Second you?' His head spun towards Oskar. 'Not sure. Have to think.'

Zayn stood up. 'Come on, people. We're not a monarchy any more. We're a Republic.' He made a serious face. 'And we are Republicans. We don't just let the nearest blood relative take over at the palace. Democracy is at the heart of everything we do.'

A handful of vice presidents started nodding. It was odd. For the first time that Howie could ever remember, Zayn actually sounded like a politician. He decided to sit back and watch.

Zayn stood tall. 'Democracy isn't just about the citizens voting. No. It's about politicians exercising their democratic rights when the constitution gives them that opportunity. We should lead by example.' He nodded – as if confirming that everyone was in complete agreement. 'What I'm saying is that we, vice presidents, have a democratic duty to take this to a vote.'

There was a smattering of applause around the table. It was a good speech. Short and to the point. And he had acted in a surprisingly presidential manner. No one mentioned the fact that he seemed to drift in and out of a dodgy American accent.

Zayn put his hand on Ivan's shoulder. 'So, Ivan … I'm asking you as a colleague and as a friend. Will you do me the honour of seconding my nomination? If you do that, I will grant you whatever wish you want when I become president.'

Ivan thought for a few seconds. 'Tech contract. Up for expiry. I like auto-techs. Can we stick with them?'

Zayn raised his hands. 'No problem. You're the Tech-head.'

'Okay. Why not? Let's do it. I second you.'

Zayn ruffled Ivan's hair. 'Good man. And the same goes for any of you here. You back me in the vote and I'll help fulfil your political dreams.'

'And where will the money come from for all this dream-chasing?' huffed Oskar.

'That's easy. We'll cut the defence budget. Your friend Viktor Maxim probably won't be too happy about it. But he's no friend of mine, so who cares?'

'He's no friend of mine either!' snapped Oskar.

Martha stepped forward. 'Vice presidents, I formally declare nominations to be closed. You now have two candidates from which to choose – Oskar Polak and Zayn Winner. In the event that Jan Polak does not return to stake his claim for a third term, one of them will be running as the Republican Party candidate in this summer's election. Now, do either of you wish to say anything else?'

Oskar stood up. 'I won't bother. I'm the only serious candidate. Zayn Winner is unelectable.'

Zayn sat back in his chair. 'Didn't you see my interview in today's *Daily Democrat*, Oskar? I'm a politician with charisma. A breath of fresh air. A man of the people.'

Oskar eyeballed Zayn for several seconds before responding. 'That's your assessment. Mine is that you're a terrible actor and an even worse politician.'

Zayn responded with a cheeky smile. 'Tut, tut. That's not very presidential behaviour, is it now? I think HR run some anger-management training. I'll put your name down.'

Oskar turned up his nose. 'I'm fed up with this childishness. I propose we go straight to a vote.'

'Suits me, buddy. That *Daily Democrat* article said everything for me.'

Martha nodded. 'As you wish.' She took a deep breath. 'This is to be done via a simple show of hands. All those vice presidents in favour of Oskar Polak standing as the Republican candidate, in the absence of Jan Polak, please raise your —'

A loud knock on the door interrupted proceedings.

'This room is occupied,' shouted Martha.

A second knock rang out, louder than the first.

'Whoever it is, get rid of them,' barked Oskar. 'I don't care if it's the exiled king of England, this vote is happening now.'

Daisy Gray grabbed the arm of the vice president to her right. 'Oh my God. You don't think it really is one of the royals coming back, do you? I mean, they never open the door themselves, do they? They always get someone else to do it for them.' The vice president she was holding onto shook her off, so she grabbed the one to her left. 'Maybe they got sick of all that Florida sunshine and they're launching a counter-revolution? I can see it all now. We'll all be thrown in the Tower!' She stood up. 'I'll skip the vote. I'm going to pack my things. I don't want my head on display at Traitor's Gate!'

'You stupid woman!' shouted Oskar. 'Of course it's not the royals. Now keep calm!'

'And carry on?' gabbled Daisy. 'How we can carry on without your brother? He's ten times the man you are, Oskar Polak.' She pointed at Zayn. 'I'm voting for him! He may not be the sharpest tool in the box, but at least he doesn't walk around with a face like a slapped arse all day!'

Zayn whooped with delight. 'Welcome to Team Winner, Daisy! If you fancy a change of scenery after the election, Oskar's job will be up for grabs.'

Daisy's face lit up like a Trafalgar Square Christmas tree. 'Ooh, that'd be lovely.'

Oskar was about to launch into another tirade when there was a third knock on the door. Martha sighed. 'Would you mind opening it and telling them to go away, Howie?'

'No problem. Let's hope it's Bogdan with some good news.'

Martha shook her head. 'I doubt that very much.'

Howie got to his feet and opened the door. Standing before him was a familiar face. It wasn't Bogdan. Or any other member of the security staff. It was someone else. A person who Howie hadn't been expecting to see for a while.

It was such a surprise that Howie froze on the spot. And his tongue stopped working again.

Chapter 40

Britt had been in some tight spots in her career. But hiding under this table, surrounded on all sides by vice presidents, was the tightest one she could ever remember. Hunched forward, with both arms hugging her legs, she had soon developed a painful cramp in her lower limbs. It had forced her to move position a couple of times and caused her boots to squeak. She gritted her teeth and resisted the urge to move again. There was no way she could risk her footwear squeaking again. She had been lucky to escape detection on the first two occasions – the background chatter had probably saved her. But the whole room had gone quiet now. If she made any more high-pitched noises, she would almost certainly be discovered.

Britt wasn't sure why the room had descended into silence. As far as she could make out, the vice presidents were just about to vote. Zayn Winner had surprised her and made a stirring mini-speech. But she doubted it would be enough against Oskar Polak's political reputation.

She closed her eyes and gave a silent cheer. She had her indisputable third source. She had heard Oskar Polak confirm his brother was missing. And she would soon learn the nomination winner. Neither George nor anyone else could deny her this story now. 'We Have Lost The President' would be the five words on everyone's lips tomorrow morning. It would be a headline that would go down in history. She would go down in history. All she had to do now was get out from under this table, get to the offices of *The Republican* and write the story.

The silence was broken by a man's voice coming from the far end of the room. She could just about make it out. 'Hello,

Howie. Is there room for one more at this meeting? If there are no chairs, I don't mind standing.'

The feet, knees and legs around her began moving. There were gasps from some of the vice presidents. Then a door closed.

'Oh my God!' screamed Vice President Daisy Gray.

The man spoke again. 'Please, just keep calm and ... well, carry on.'

That cool, authoritative voice was familiar. Whose was it?

Martha spoke next. 'Can I suggest that the three of us reconvene in your office? We have a lot to discuss.'

'I'd prefer to stay here for the moment, if you don't mind,' replied the man.

This was getting confusing. Britt couldn't hear Howie any more. Oskar had shut up. Daisy had stopped screaming. Even Zayn wasn't talking. When was the vote going to happen?

Howie broke the silence. 'Where have you been, Mr President?'

Britt must have been imagining things. She thought Howie had called the new arrival 'Mr President'. She must have misheard.

'Where have I been? It's a long story. I won't bore you all with the details right now.'

Then Britt heard Martha's voice. 'With respect, Mr President, your absence has caused us a considerable amount of worry. It would be a courtesy to us all if you told us why you left and what you've been doing.'

Britt's whole body shuddered as her brain processed those words. It couldn't be the president. This must be a bad dream. She'd probably nodded off under the table. In reality, Jan Polak was still missing and the nominations vote was already underway. There was no president in the room. Only vice presidents. And a sleeping journalist under the table.

Then she heard the man's voice again. 'All in good time, my dear Martha. I promise you. Now, what has Jan Polak missed while he's been away?'

It was then the truth hit her. This wasn't a bad dream. It was a horrible reality. Jan Polak wasn't lost any more. He was found. That meant he'd be appearing on the Buckingham Palace balcony at eleven tomorrow to announce he was standing for a third term. It also meant this nomination meeting would be abandoned any minute.

What would happen now? She tried to think. Howie, Martha and the president would agree an official story to tell anyone asking awkward questions. 'The president was taking a well-deserved break at a secret location before his big day.' Or something else that was equally vague and untrue. And that would be that. Britt wouldn't be able to salvage anything from the wreckage of her investigation. Not even a lifestyle feature.

Britt kicked out a leg in frustration. The result was a loud squeak as one leather boot skidded over the other. She realised her mistake immediately. All she could do was stay completely still and hope everyone was too distracted by the returning president to bother finding out what was making strange noises under the table. She held her breath.

At the end of the corridor of legs, she saw Howie's face appear, upside down. He was staring directly at her. He seemed to recognise her. She waved and put her finger to her lips, hoping he wouldn't reveal that his journalist girlfriend was hiding under the table. Howie put his finger to his lips and then mouthed 'Stay there'. His head bobbed back up. That was a relief. She had avoided exposure.

But things changed five seconds later. Daisy Gray's head appeared under the table – upside down and staring at Britt like she had just stepped out of a spacecraft and asked to be taken to their leader.

Then Daisy screamed. 'There's a woman under the bloody table! Sat there, listening to us!' Daisy poked her upside-down finger in Britt's direction. 'I recognise her, as well. It's that bloody journalist who got all those police officers sacked. Britt what's-her-name from *The Republican*. She's Howie Pond's girlfriend! Oh my God, he's smuggled her in here!'

'No I haven't!' shouted Howie, his head still under the table.

The president's head now bobbed upside down in front of Britt. 'Another unexpected visitor.'

Then Oskar's head appeared. He said nothing. He just glared.

'Come on, Britt,' Howie sighed. 'Out you come.'

Britt had no choice. She crawled towards Howie's feet, with one thought in her mind – she had lost her story. She could feel her lip trembling. So she bit it. This was no time for tears. She would have to fight hard now. Or she wouldn't just lose her story. She would lose her liberty.

Chapter 41

Howie wasn't sure which had been the bigger surprise – opening the door of the State Dining Room to find President Jan Polak standing there or bending down under the table to find his girlfriend hiding under it. For a second, he wondered if that dodgy tea he'd been given in the police station was still causing him to hallucinate. He peered over the table edge and checked the appearance of everybody else in the room. Apart from their wide eyes and open mouths, they looked relatively normal. As he bent down again and saw Britt crawling towards him, he realised he wasn't seeing things. This was really happening. He climbed under the table. 'One second,' he called out to the people above it. 'I'll help her out.'

Before anyone could object, Howie got down on his knees and shuffled a few metres under the table. 'What the hell are you doing down here?' he whispered to Britt.

'Your Code Red crisis,' she whispered back. 'My exclusive. Now it's buggered.'

Howie had to strain every muscle not to raise his voice. 'How did you find out about that?'

'You told the cat.'

'What?!'

'Yesterday morning, when you were feeding her.'

Howie looked confused. 'How did the cat manage to tell you what I'd told her?'

'I overheard, you prince. You thought I was asleep. But I wasn't.'

Howie looked horrified. 'So I gave you the story?'

'Yes. You did.'

Howie pointed upwards. 'Don't tell them that, for king's sake!'

'Of course I won't.'

'So why were you listening to me talking to the cat?' huffed Howie. He knew it probably wasn't the best time or place to discuss this. But his privacy had been invaded. And so had the cat's. It was a matter of principle.

'You were speaking loudly,' insisted Britt.

'I wasn't speaking loudly!' retorted Howie, through gritted teeth.

'You were.'

'I wasn't. You must have been listening in.'

Martha's voice from above interrupted them. 'Is everything alright down there?'

'She's just got a bit of cramp,' shouted Howie. 'Be with you shortly.' He turned back to Britt. 'Look, you're here now. We need a plan.'

'They're going to call the police, aren't they?'

'Don't panic. I've got an idea.' Howie and Britt wriggled out from under the table and got to their feet. Everyone was watching them – as if they were a circus act about to perform some incredible feat of acrobatics. In fact, that wasn't far from the truth. They would have to perform some breathtaking manoeuvres to escape from this situation with Britt's liberty and Howie's reputation intact. Hopefully his idea would work.

'Howie, is this really your girlfriend?' asked Martha.

'Yes, it is.'

Martha turned to Britt. 'And you're a journalist for *The Republican*?'

Britt nodded. 'I'm an investigative reporter who received a tip-off about the president going missing.'

'Oh dear,' sighed Martha. 'That rather complicates matters.' She glanced at Howie. 'For everyone.'

Howie shook his head and began firing sentences around the room. 'I don't think it does. Britt was just a journalist doing her job. Completely independently of me. While she may have broken a few rules getting in here, I don't think calling the police would be a wise move. We don't want headlines on Independence Day about journalists getting arrested, do we?' He took a quick breath. 'Now, if we agree not to call the police and allow her to leave, I'm sure Britt will drop whatever story she was going to write.'

'How can we trust her?' whined Daisy Gray. 'She's a bloody journalist!'

Howie took a step forward. 'We'll get her to sign a guarantee of non-publication of confidential information obtained at this meeting. If she breaches that, we can take out an injunction. But no one ever breaches them. You can end up in prison.'

Oskar nodded. 'That sounds like a very sensible idea, Mr Pond. Excellent advice from our media expert. I don't think there's any need for further discussion.'

Howie was taken aback at Oskar's positivity. He looked at Britt, who was looking at Oskar, who was looking at Britt.

Martha frowned. 'Let's check with the man in charge first, shall we?' She turned to the president. 'Jan, are you happy with that?'

The president nodded. 'Absolutely. If Howie recommends it, I agree with it.'

Oskar returned to his normal, disagreeable self. 'Now get that bloody journalist out of here. And get her to sign what she's got to sign. Then we can get on with the damn voting.'

Martha nodded. 'Miss Pointer. Please come with Howie and me, and we'll arrange for you to sign a guarantee of non-publication.' She took a step towards the door.

Britt didn't follow. Instead, she pointed a finger at Oskar. 'What did you mean just then – let's get on with the voting? The president is back. So there's no need for it.'

'Just leave,' snarled Oskar, whose expression was growing more uncomfortable by the minute. 'Before we change our minds.'

A look of joy appeared on Britt's face. 'You're not standing for a third term, are you, Mr President?'

The president's expression was non-committal. 'You will find out tomorrow.'

'So what's happening, guys and girls?' asked Zayn. 'Are we doing this vote thing or not?'

Martha looked concerned. 'I've no idea what we're doing. But I do know we shouldn't be discussing it in front of a journalist.'

The president took a step towards Britt. 'I'm sorry, but we can't discuss any more government business in your presence.'

Howie glanced at Britt. She had a look of steely determination in her eyes. He could see she was standing bolt upright – like a soldier about to launch herself at the enemy. And the smile on her face – it was so inscrutable it made The Mona Lisa seem positively hysterical. Howie took a gulp of air. He had seen this cocktail of physical characteristics before – usually when he'd just told Britt that he was too busy to help with the vacuuming or too exhausted to accompany her on a shopping trip. And in that moment, Howie knew beyond doubt – Britt was about to get what she wanted.

Chapter 42

When Britt crawled from under the table, her only thought had been escaping from the State Dining Room as quickly as her stiff legs could carry her. But as soon as she saw the faces of the vice presidents, her journalistic instincts told her something wasn't right. There was no reaction whatsoever from Oskar to his brother's return. All the others were visibly shocked and shaken. She examined Oskar's face again. It was as stern and unfriendly as ever. In fact, he seemed more affected by Britt's appearance than his own brother's – his eyes had widened when she emerged from her hiding place and then quickly narrowed, as if warning her to keep her mouth shut about his private life. Oskar's insistence that the vice presidents move to a vote, together with Jan's suggestion that everyone just 'carry on', didn't add up. What was going on?

Then she realised. Of course – it was the Pierogi Pact. Yes. The president had returned from wherever it was he'd been hiding but he was going to step aside for Oskar. The handover of Republican Party power, from one Polak brother to another, really had been planned all along. And it was happening today.

Britt felt the hope surge through her body like a drug. She might still have a chance of grabbing a front-page story for tomorrow's paper. The headline wouldn't be 'We Have Lost The President'. It would be 'We're Going To Lose The President'. George would love it. But she still had work to do. George would want concrete proof.

'Is there a problem, Miss Pointer?' asked Martha.

Britt didn't answer. She was thinking. What kind of proof would George want? The best kind – official confirmation from the man himself that he wouldn't be standing. There was only one way Britt was going to get that – create a situation. Right here, right now. One that would give her something to bargain with. Then she could get the proof she needed and secure her new story.

'Come on, Britt, let's do the paperwork,' urged Howie. 'Then we can get you out of here.'

Britt took a deep breath. She wasn't going anywhere. 'First of all, I want you all to know something that I've uncovered during my investigation.' She pointed at Oskar. 'This man has been having an affair with a member of the president's staff.'

The vice presidents gasped. Howie and Martha turned to each other and raised their eyebrows.

'Is this true, Oskar?' asked the president, sounding alarmed.

Oskar scowled. 'Of course it isn't. She's lying.'

Britt shook her head. 'No. You're lying. I've met the young woman. I won't reveal her identity because she's now one of my sources. But I can tell you that she doesn't just work for the president. She's directly employed by one of Viktor Maxim's companies. And not just employed – she and Mr Maxim work very closely together.'

'The Russian businessman?' asked the president, sounding worried.

Martha nodded. 'Yes. A very influential businessman. One with suspected criminal connections.'

Criminal connections? That was even better news for Britt. Her confidence grew and she stood as tall as she could without falling over. 'This woman's appointment was arranged by Mr Maxim, seemingly so she could make high-level contacts at the centre of government. She was the bait, if you like. And it seems she caught a big fish.'

Zayn rubbed his hands with glee. 'He looks more like a shark to me!'

Oskar jabbed a finger at Zayn. 'Shut up, you moron!'

Zayn just laughed. 'First rule of presidency – always keep your cool under pressure.'

'Don't you dare tell me what to do!' shouted Oskar, his cheeks flushed.

'And rule number two is – never lose your temper in meetings.'

Oskar looked ready to explode. 'And rule three is don't stick your nose into business that doesn't concern you!'

Zayn shook his head. 'Sorry to correct you, old buddy, but I was quoting those rules from the American president's autobiography. I read it last night. Call it a bit of homework for today's meeting, if you like. And rule three is always know your subject.' He flashed a grin. 'Which you clearly don't.'

Oskar smashed his fist on the table. 'That is enough!'

Britt carried on, showing no fear. 'This young woman has a very close relationship with Mr Maxim. So close, she told him about the affair soon after it began, two years ago.'

Oskar looked incredulous. 'What?!'

'Yes. She told me.' She stared straight into Oskar's eyes. 'And I think you'll agree, that's a very compromising position for a potential president to be in.'

'Don't say another word,' growled Oskar. 'Or I promise you – you'll regret it.'

'Tell me, do you regret dumping your lover yesterday on a park bench, where you could be seen by anyone? And you were seen – by me. Despite your feeble attempt to disguise yourself.' She looked around the room at the other vice presidents. 'And this is the man you want as your new leader?'

The vice presidents exchanged worried glances while Martha whispered hurriedly to the president. Howie was watching Britt. He didn't say anything. But his eyes told her to keep going.

'He also met his lover – or rather, ex-lover – in Trafalgar Square this afternoon. I know. Because I was there.'

Zayn leaned forward. 'Sounds like Oskar's been sorting out his affairs before the big day tomorrow.'

Britt couldn't have put it better herself.

Oskar began to march towards Britt. 'Right, that's enough.'

'What are you doing, Oskar?' asked the president.

'I'm going to personally remove this woman from the room, before she spreads any more filthy lies.'

'Please, keep calm,' urged the president.

Britt smiled triumphantly. 'And I'll carry on, shall I?' She started to walk around the table, so Oskar couldn't catch her.

Oskar was moving quickly. 'I'll make sure you're finished as a journalist!'

'Have you really been playing away, Oskar?' asked Daisy. 'Because the voters won't want a president who can't keep his trousers on.'

'And what's this Martha tells me about you having lunch with Viktor Maxim yesterday?' asked the president. 'Some business was discussed, apparently. What was that?'

Oskar stopped and looked horrified. 'Not my own brother, as well! You're all turning against me!'

Britt came to a halt behind Zayn. 'Mr President, your brother has been meeting Viktor Maxim on a regular basis. But he denied knowing him, moments before you walked into the room.'

'I know lots of people,' shouted Oskar, turning to his brother. 'I can't be expected to remember all their names!'

'Really?' asked Britt, with mock surprise. 'Well, I'm surprised you forgot. Because your ex-lover told me that you and Maxim are "very friendly". But you like to keep it "top secret".'

'I can confirm that Oskar and Maxim meet up regularly, Mr President,' added Howie. 'Maxim told me himself today.'

Oskar made a croaking noise in protest. But nothing intelligible came out of his mouth.

Britt continued. 'My guess is the business they were discussing was the contracts that might come Viktor Maxim's way if Oskar were elected as president. Defence contracts, for example.'

The other vice presidents began glancing nervously at each other.

'She's lying!' screamed Oskar, so loudly it made everyone jump. Everyone except Britt.

Britt stared straight into Oskar's eyes. 'How much has Maxim paid you, Vice President Polak? And how much more do you stand to gain in bribes and kickbacks if you become president?'

Oskar started running towards her. 'I'm fed up listening to this deluded bloody woman!'

Britt was surprised by Oskar's sudden burst of speed. Within a few seconds, he had reached her and grabbed her by the arm. His grip was hard and rough. She cried out in pain.

'Get off her!' yelled Howie, from the other side of the room.

'Oskar, put her down!' shouted the president.

'Oh my God, it's all kicking off!' screamed Daisy.

Oskar twisted Britt into a headlock. There were gasps from the vice presidents. Several of them stood up. But they seemed too scared to tackle Oskar themselves.

Britt wasn't enjoying being manhandled by Oskar Polak. She had wanted to generate a response from him. But not one that involved this level of physical violence. He was a strong man and was really hurting her. If he lost control, he could do her some serious physical damage. And a trip to the hospital would mean she wouldn't be able to write her story.

She tried to scream. But Oskar's arm was too tight around her throat. Britt couldn't breathe. She couldn't break free. She needed someone to save her. Preferably before she lost consciousness.

Chapter 43

Howie couldn't believe what he was witnessing – Oskar Polak was almost choking Britt, while the president, the other forty-nine vice presidents and the head of the National Security and Intelligence Service looked on in horror. Howie didn't react immediately. This wasn't the kind of situation he'd ever had to deal with in a work environment. Or any other environment. He'd seen a few drunken fights outside the Two Chairmen, but nothing like this. This was a vice president physically restraining an undercover journalist. There was no training course in the world that could prepare you for this kind of thing.

'Don't sit around like lemons!' screamed Daisy Gray. 'One of you men do something!'

For once, Daisy was talking sense. Oskar needed to be stopped. Before he strangled the woman Howie loved and was going to marry. Yes – marry. He had put off asking Britt for too long. He was always too preoccupied with work or … well, if he was honest, it was always work. But as they were crawling towards each other, underneath the table, he somehow just knew – this was the woman he wanted to be with for the rest of his life. Under tables, over tables – it didn't matter where. All that mattered was that they were together. Preferably not in any situations like this again, but he didn't want to dwell on that possibility.

Having made this matrimonial decision, Howie suddenly felt a base, animal instinct driving him to action. This room was a jungle. He was its king. Britt was his queen. Oskar was … what was Oskar? He realised he didn't have time for this. Instead, he sprang forward, as quickly as his new designer suit would allow him. 'I'm coming, Britt!' he roared.

'Don't try and stop me, Pond!' snarled Oskar, sounding like a Bond villain who was about to launch a nuclear warhead at a major metropolis.

'Let her go, Oskar!' ordered Howie, as he got within twenty metres of the struggling pair.

'Or you'll do what?'

Howie was fifteen metres away. 'Whatever I have to do.'

'Go on, Howie!' shouted Zayn, as if it was a fight in a school playground. 'Show him who's boss!'

'You talk too much, Pond,' sneered Oskar, jerking Britt's head forward. 'Just like your interfering girlfriend.'

Britt yelped with pain. Howie was still ten metres away and unable to help her. So he just kept running.

'For king's sake, Oskar, you're hurting her!' screamed Daisy.

Ivan Bonn scrambled out of Howie's way. 'Sorry. Can't help. Don't do fights.'

'Put her down, Oskar!" shouted the president, as Howie got within five metres of them.

'Gentlemen, please!' shouted Martha.

Zayn whooped with delight. Ivan kept scrambling. Daisy shrieked. Martha winced. The rest of the vice presidents were either diving for cover or frozen with shock. It was total chaos.

Howie launched himself at Oskar. But the crazed vice president swung Britt in front of himself as a defensive shield and batted Howie away with her body. Britt cried out as Howie bounced off her and fell backwards onto a vice president.

'You dirty coward.' shouted Daisy. 'Don't hide behind a defenceless woman! Fight like a real man!'

Oskar glared at Daisy. Then he flung Britt to the ground, stood tall and puffed out his chest. 'Very well. Let's see what you've got, Mr Pond.'

Was this really happening? Was the president's brother really challenging Howie to a fight in Buckingham Palace's State Dining Room? Howie stumbled to his feet, groaning as he felt his shoulder muscle spasm and something in his back click again. As he staggered to his feet, he realised he wasn't in the best physical shape for a fight right now. And HR had never sent him on a physical combat training course. He stood rooted to the spot, unsure what to do now that Britt was free from Oskar's grasp and his own physical frailties had been exposed.

'You're not a James Bond,' laughed Oskar, in the way evil villains always did when they thought they had 007 at their mercy. 'Not even close. You're a Howie Pond – a pathetic excuse for a secret agent.' He snorted with contempt. 'But you and Mr Bond do have one thing in common.' An evil grin crossed Oskar's face. 'You can't protect your women.'

In that second, Howie forgot about his aches and pains. He swung his right fist so fast that he could only see a flesh-coloured blur as it flew towards Oskar's nose. The blow was so forceful Howie thought his hand was going to go through Oskar's face and come out the other side. It felt like it almost did.

Oskar flew backwards and smashed into the wall. Then he slowly slid down it and hit the floor with a thud, a dazed expression on his face throughout – as if he were the fall guy in one of those old-world cartoons. Everyone in the room gasped.

'Woohoo!' cried Zayn. 'Bang on his hooter!'

'Why didn't you help him, Zayn, you big lump?' shouted Daisy. 'You've been in action movies!'

'Oh. I, erm ... always had a stunt double do that for me.'

As Oskar lay groaning on the carpet, Howie wished that he had a double. But he was doing all his own stunts. And now his right fist was really throbbing. As he rubbed his hand, he knelt down beside Britt. 'Are you okay, B?'

Britt coughed. 'I'll live.'

Howie examined her neck. It looked sore. 'We'd better get you checked out.'

'No.' She struggled for air. 'Must get to the office. Got a deadline.'

'Don't be silly. You're more important than some stupid —'

Howie was interrupted by a painful kick to his right kidney. He hadn't been paying attention. Oskar had sprung to his feet and was now on the attack. Howie crumpled to the floor. Three seconds later, he felt another hard kick. This time to his left buttock. He rolled away from Oskar, before his right buttock came under attack.

As Howie lay clutching his aching left buttock with his non-throbbing left hand, Oskar grabbed Britt around the neck again and pulled her up. 'I'm escorting this interfering little bitch from the premises. And nobody is going to stop me!'

'You're hurting me!' croaked Britt. 'I can't breathe, I can't —'

'Oskar!' yelled the president. 'Have you completely lost your senses?!'

'No!' roared Oskar, a manic look of world domination in his eyes. 'It's about time we treated journalists like the dirt-digging scum they are!'

Martha looked horrified. 'I'm going to call security!'

Oskar dragged Britt along the ground. 'Yes, security. The most sensible thing you've said all afternoon.'

Martha shook her head. 'I meant for you, Oskar.'

The president nodded. 'Yes, Martha. My brother's dangerously out of control. He needs to be restrained. And possibly sedated.'

Oskar was so shocked at hearing these words, he released his grip on Britt. She was too breathless to move more than a few centimetres. So Howie dived on top of her to prevent Oskar taking hold of her again. Howie held his breath and waited for more blows to rain down on his body. But they didn't. Instead, Oskar just stood there, searching for sympathy in the faces of his colleagues.

'Is that what you really think of me?' asked Oskar, sounding hurt.

'I'll tell you what I think – you're a bloody lunatic!' shouted Daisy. 'I'd rather have Viktor Maxim running the country than you.'

Zayn nodded. 'Sounds like Maxim would be running the country if Oskar got the top job.'

The two vice presidents who had been sitting either side of Oskar stood up and walked towards where Howie and Britt were lying on the floor. They offered their hands and pulled Howie and Britt to their feet. Then they looked at Oskar and shook their heads in disgust.

The president broke the silence. 'Yes, Martha. Bleep Mr Bogdanowic. Ask him to escort my brother from the building, confiscate his security pass and alert staff that he isn't to enter the palace again until I say so.'

'Call yourself a brother?' shouted Oskar, striding towards his sibling. 'You promised I could have this chance.' He moved his face to within a centimetre of Jan's. 'You betrayed me!'

The president didn't flinch. 'I'm sorry to say, you betrayed yourself.'

Oskar flung an arm in the air. 'Fifteen years I've waited for this!'

'The Pierogi Pact was never a formal deal, Oskar. We'd drunk three bottles of vodka.'

'I'd accepted that years ago! But then last week, you suddenly turn round – completely out of the blue – and say you might not be standing again.' Oskar was pleading now. 'You gave me hope. Dear brother, don't take that hope away from me. Just because I lost my temper.' He pointed at Britt. 'You'd lose your temper if a bloody journalist came in here, accusing you of improper relationships!'

Daisy stood up. 'You didn't just lose your temper. You lost all bloody control, man!' She pointed at Britt. 'You assaulted her!'

'W-w-what?' stuttered Oskar. 'Don't talk such —'

'Not only that,' interrupted the president. 'You've indulged in an unwise affair with a young woman.'

Oskar opened his mouth to speak.

'Shut up, I'm talking now,' snapped the president. 'This is a woman who, when she's got over the shock of you casting her aside like yesterday's newspapers, could very well sell her story to the media. Before or after the election – it wouldn't matter – you'd be finished.' He shook his head in disbelief. 'And thanks to Miss Pointer, we know Viktor Maxim is aware of this affair. He placed the girl here so some middle-aged fool with his brains in his trousers could compromise himself and his position.'

Oskar hung his head and muttered something under his breath.

The president's tone was firm. 'If you have something to say, Oskar, say it now.'

'I said don't worry. I can make sure the girl doesn't talk.'

The president didn't often get angry. But this was one of those rare occasions. 'You can "sort" it, can you? You've definitely been spending too much time with Viktor Maxim.'

'No. That's not true.'

'You may be my brother, but you really are an idiot.'

'I'm not an idiot!' shouted Oskar defiantly.

'That's exactly what you are. Don't you see? You can't terminate your relationship with Viktor Maxim so easily. You could never be sure he wouldn't leak your affair to the media.' Jan held his head in his hands. 'You were always the one I wanted to hand over the reins of power to – if anything happened to me or I changed my mind about a third term. You knew that. And you still went ahead with your affair. And you fraternised with Viktor Maxim and goodness knows how many others.'

'It was just Maxim,' mumbled Oskar.

'Well, no it wasn't, was it? There was Maxim's number two – Petra Putinov. I can see now why you were so insistent on me meeting her, before I told you I was thinking of stepping down. A wide-ranging discussion about British business you said it would be. But it focused very quickly on the subject of British military contracts. And what Maxim International could do, outside of official channels, to secure them. It wasn't subtle. That was all Mr Maxim's idea, wasn't it?'

Oskar couldn't even bring himself to look at his brother.

'Look me in the eye and tell me that you haven't taken a penny from that man. We're brothers. I'll know if you're lying to me.' Jan didn't get any response. 'Tell me!' he shouted, so loudly it echoed around the room for a couple of seconds.

Oskar's voice was cracking. 'It was just ... some ... consultancy expenses.'

The president was sounding calm again. 'I'm disappointed in you. Not just as a politician. Not just as a vice president in my Government.' He sighed. 'I'm disappointed in you as a brother.'

Oskar's face was pale now. As blood began to drip from his nose, it made it look even paler. He opened his mouth, as if about to deliver one last appeal for mercy. Then he closed his eyes, wiped the blood away with his sleeve and bowed his head. He was a defeated man.

Martha pressed a button on her bleeper and then stepped forward. 'Mr Bogdanowic will be here very shortly.'

Oskar started to cry. No one spoke, as his sobs echoed around the room. They weren't tears of remorse. They were tears of self-pity. And everybody knew it.

Within sixty seconds of Martha sending her bleep, Bogdan had arrived.

'You have emergency?' panted Bogdan.

'Yes,' confirmed Martha. 'Mr Bogdanowic, please remove Vice President Oskar Polak from the building and retrieve his security pass on the way out. He's not to return until the president tells you.'

Bogdan looked confused. Then he pointed at Oskar. 'You want me to remove *him*, chief?'

Martha nodded. 'That's right. It's best if you don't ask any more questions.'

Bogdan noticed Britt. He stared at her for a few seconds but said nothing. Then he turned to Oskar and expanded his considerable chest. 'Vice President Polak, you come with me.' Bogdan gripped Oskar's arm and led him out. As the door closed, there was a buzz of relief around the room.

'Now old misery guts is out the way, I've got a question!' shouted Zayn.

'What's that?' sighed Martha.

'Are we carrying on with the nomination stuff? Or is Jan the man going to stand for a third term? If he's not, we'd better have that vote.'

'Hang on!' shouted a charcoal suit. 'If we are having a vote, I want to put my name forward now!'

'Me, too,' added a granite suit.

Martha intervened. 'I'm afraid nominations are closed. You all had your chance. The rules are quite clear on that point.'

The vice presidents looked at each other, with expressions of concern and surprise.

Zayn leaned his elbows on the table. 'So, Jan, my man – what's the plan?'

'Please don't say you're standing down,' pleaded Daisy.

Howie held his breath. In his mind, he prayed to the gods who'd given him such a bad time lately – please, please give him a break. Let the answer be 'I'm standing again'. Howie didn't want to be Zayn Winner's spokesperson. That would be a nightmare job.

The president hesitated. Then he turned to Britt. 'Will you report what I say in your newspaper tomorrow?'

'Of course, Mr President. I wouldn't be doing my job otherwise.'

The president smiled politely. 'Then, if you wouldn't mind, Miss Pointer, I would prefer that you left the room.'

Howie could see Britt was bruised and battered. But she wasn't beaten. 'If I leave this room now, the story on the front page of tomorrow's Republican will feature your brother, Mr President. It will be a first-hand account of how he assaulted me at a presidential nomination meeting.'

Howie grimaced. That was the kind of front-page story that gave him sleepless nights for weeks.

The president sighed. 'I see. And if I allow you to stay, what will happen to that particular story?'

Britt smiled. 'It will be forgotten forever. And replaced by a story about your political future.'

'Very well,' replied the president. 'Then in the interests of this Government, and of the Republican Party, I will allow you to stay.' He raised a finger. 'But on one condition – that after this meeting, you, Howie and I sit down and agree what exactly is being printed in *The Republican* tomorrow.'

Howie wasn't sure if Britt would agree to being told what could and couldn't go in her story. She was a journalist with principles. And Howie would never have asked for such a favour in a million years. This could be a tough decision for her.

Britt's response was lightning quick. 'As it's such an important issue for the future of this nation, and to ensure everything is one hundred per cent accurate, I am happy to agree to that condition. The story will confirm your decision on whether you will be standing for a third term – including a direct quote from yourself.'

Howie nodded to the president. 'Sounds like a fair deal to me, Jan. I'm happy with that.'

The president smiled. 'You drive a hard bargain, Miss Pointer. But there's nothing in the constitution to say I can't speak to the media about the Independence Day announcement before I make it. So we have a deal.'

Martha turned to the president. 'Then tell us your decision, Jan.'

The president clasped his hands. 'I have always wanted to lead this great country for as long as I am physically, and mentally, able to do so.' He paused. 'But a few weeks ago, I received the most extraordinary offer. And it caused me to reflect on my future.'

'Oh, no! Don't tell us you're going, Jan!' shouted Daisy, tears forming in her eyes. 'Everyone will be gutted if you do. Not just us, but the citizens, as well. And what about the Americans? They'll go crazy. They'll probably send the royals back over here, as a punishment.'

The president smiled. 'If I was to accept it, you wouldn't need to worry about that happening. It was the Americans who made me the offer.'

'Have they offered to make you a movie star, Jan?' asked Zayn, with a stupid grin.

The president laughed. 'No, they haven't. The offer was in relation to a major project they've been working on.'

'What project?' asked Daisy.

'Allow me to explain. It's a huge, self-contained offshore community in American territorial waters that will bring together the brightest minds from around the globe.' The president began pacing up and down. 'The Americans call it "State 51". But it will be much more than that. It will be a community which will look for new solutions to some of the global problems facing the New States, and its international partners, in the twenty-first century and beyond.'

Howie didn't want to say it, but State 51 sounded like one of those desert islands where Bond villains were always hiding. With one exception – it would be a place where the good guys, and not the bad guys, lived. At least, that would be the theory.

'Why's it offshore, Mr President?' asked Britt.

'I hadn't planned on this being a question and answer session. But … I suppose I owe you all a full explanation.' He stopped pacing up and down. 'It's offshore for two reasons. The first is security. The second is space – the environment will be able to expand, or contract, over time.'

Howie had read about the idea of an ocean-based community. It had never really appealed to him – he felt seasick if he spent too long under the water-spray. But he could see the advantages. As well as offering security and space, it wouldn't be difficult to construct. Deep-sea structures weren't anything new. The energy industry, for example, had been using them for years. Then his brain made a connection. 'Has this environment got anything to do with oil platforms, Jan?'

The president nodded. 'Yes. Eastern Oil is providing the technology – it will be a network of interconnected platforms, much like they use in the oil industry. But it will be adapted to suit our needs. In fact, their chairwoman is also putting some of her own money into the project. Along with a few others.'

Things were finally starting to make sense. The meetings with Sky Eastern had been about State 51 – not test drilling in UK waters.

The president continued. 'I've been in discussions with the American ambassador – who has been my main point of contact on this – and Sky Eastern. In fact, the three of us have just returned from an overseas trip.'

'So that's where Clinton Stackshaker has been,' whispered Martha to Howie.

'Where were you?' asked Zayn. 'Hollywood? The Big Apple?'

'I can't tell you where I was. For the simple reason that I don't know myself. It was somewhere out at sea – a mini version of State 51 that the Americans have created. I wanted to see it with my own eyes. And I did.' He took a breath. 'It was remarkable. The only problem was, the state-of-the-art private aircraft which got us there developed a fault after landing. Then we had quite a storm. It knocked out the comms links for 36 hours. So we were stuck there for some considerable time.'

'We thought you'd been kidnapped,' shouted Daisy. 'The cameras buggered up, so no one knew what the hell had happened.'

The president looked at Vice President Ivan Bonn. 'My apologies. But to ensure I left the palace undetected via one of the evacuation tunnels, I disabled the security cameras with the help of my auto-tech friend, Brian.'

Ivan looked astonished. 'Brian is top Tech. Must have reprogrammed. How? Needs Tech knowledge.'

'Yes. I had a little bit of training from a person with rather a lot of auto-tech know-how. But I can't say more than that.'

Howie knew who – Olga Frik. All three people on Maurice Skeet's list had had a part to play in this bizarre story of a missing president and his scheming vice-presidential brother.

But, unluckily for Maurice, he wouldn't be the one getting a story out of it. The irony of it all made Howie laugh silently in his head. It couldn't happen to a nicer journalist.

'Cameras still down,' confirmed Ivan. 'System won't restart.'

The president looked embarrassed. 'Ah, that's my fault. Brian was programmed to restore the system on my return. That was meant to be the early hours of Tuesday morning. But don't worry. Once Brian knows I'm back, he'll restore everything to its former glory.' He smiled. 'He's a very clever little robot.'

Howie was just about to suggest that Brian be given an extended period of shutdown as a reward, but he wasn't quick enough.

'Why all the secrecy?' asked Britt.

'The Americans were very clear – no one could know about my trip until I was back in Buckingham Palace. Oskar and the First Lady were aware that I was considering not standing for a third term. I told them both a few days ago. But I swore them to secrecy.'

That explained the First Lady's and Oskar's indifference to the president's disappearance. They must have assumed it was all part of the plan. And the president's possible third-term U-turn must have been the subject of the private conversation between him and the First Lady at the weekend – the one she wasn't willing to discuss with Howie. Yes. And it also explained Oskar's rush to get back from his Paris defence summit. As well as the swift termination of his affair. All the pieces of the jigsaw were clicking into place now.

The president continued. 'I was extremely impressed with what I saw. And I had a lot of time to think – and talk – about it while we were stranded there. And I've come to a decision …'

Everyone in the room held their breath.

'I am going to accept the Americans' offer to be the leader of State 51. To be the person in charge of its policies, research programme and long-term strategy. They will announce it at eleven o'clock tomorrow. At the same time that the new

Republican Party candidate steps onto the palace balcony to declare themselves.'

Whispered conversations began to break out around the table. They were quickly silenced when the president clapped his hands together. 'That's enough from me. Time for the vote, I think. The nominees were Oskar and who else?'

All eyes in the room turned to Zayn Winner. The vice president pointed both index fingers at himself and grinned. 'You're looking straight at him, Jan, baby!'

The president nodded. 'I see. Well, I'm glad that someone was brave enough to put themselves forward. And I'm pleased to see it's someone who's used to being in the public eye.' The president turned to Martha. 'It's over to you.'

Martha stepped forward. 'So ... all those in favour of Oskar Polak becoming the Republican Party candidate, please raise your hands.'

No vice-presidential hands went up in the air.

Martha took a deep breath. 'All those in favour of Zayn Winner, please raise your hands.'

A few seconds passed. Then Ivan and Daisy raised their hands, followed by a few others. Then Oskar's two friends raised theirs. Then the remaining vice presidents reluctantly thrust their hands in the air.

Martha counted the hands. 'That's everyone in agreement. I can formally declare Zayn Winner as the Republican Party's candidate for the 2044 presidential election. Congratulations, Vice President Winner.'

Zayn sat with his arms crossed, looking supremely smug. 'Once a Winner, always a Winner!'

The vice presidents started to get up, wander over to Zayn and offer their congratulations.

'This is going to be fun,' whispered Britt to Howie.

'No,' grumbled Howie. 'This is going to be a total bloody disaster.'

Britt kissed him on the cheek. 'By the way, thanks for saving me, Mr Pond. How can I ever repay you?'

'You could marry me,' replied Howie softly, so only Britt could hear him.

Britt's eyes lit up like fireworks. 'You're joking, right?'

'No. I'm not joking. I could do with a couple of weeks' honeymoon just to get out of this lunatic asylum.'

'You always were a romantic. Where's the ring?'

'Still in the jeweller's shop. But at least I'm wearing a decent suit.'

'You bought it specially for the occasion?'

'No. I got it free after I was wrongly arrested for attempting to kidnap the First Lady from a television studio. My other one was completely covered in dried mud because I went arse-over-tit on the grass. Twice.'

'I see. You've had another boring day at the office, then?'

'Yeah, completely forgettable.' Howie laughed. Then his mind really did go blank. 'What were we talking about?'

'You asked me to marry you.'

'Oh, yeah. Sorry, B.' This wasn't how Howie had imagined his proposal. Although, thinking about it, he wasn't sure he'd ever imagined it at all. 'Let's start again.' He took a deep breath. 'Britt Pointer ... will you marry me?'

Britt's eyes filled with a look of steely determination. She stood bolt upright. And an inscrutable smile swept across her face. 'Yes,' she whispered. 'You big, dumb prince.'

This would have been the point in a James Bond film when he and Britt retired to the privacy of one of the royal bedrooms, kissed, and the final credits would roll. But that wasn't going to happen. This movie wasn't finished just yet.

Zayn shouted from behind the throng of vice presidents. 'Hey, Martha! When I win, do I get to keep Howie as my spokesperson?'

'I don't see why not. Unless the president has plans to poach him for State 51?'

Working for the Americans on a glorified oil rig sounded preferable to having to clear up Zayn's media mess for five years. Even if he would feel seasick the whole time. Howie gazed at the president with eyes of hope. It was hope bordering on desperation.

'I would love to bring Howie with me. But the Americans have their own media and publicity team. In any case, I wouldn't want to deprive this great nation of such a dedicated and loyal public servant.'

'Actually, I was thinking of retiring early,' announced Howie. 'Living in the country … on a farm. Or something.'

'What?!' cried Zayn. 'You're only in your fifties. You're in the prime of your life.'

Howie frowned. 'I'm forty-two, actually.'

'That's great news – even more years left in you than I thought! And listen – I still want you do all your secret agent stuff for Martha. I'm not planning on going missing, or anything like that.' He thought for a second. 'Well, I might disappear down the West End for a few hours, every now and then. Just because you're president doesn't mean you can't have a social life, does it? No. But if I ever do go missing – down the West End, on an oil rig, wherever – I want you to be the one who comes and finds me.'

Martha gave Zayn a bemused look. 'Let's hope it never comes to that. We don't want to get a reputation for losing our presidents, do we?'

'No. I mean, if I was president, and you lost me, they'd probably be some kind of revolution. The people love Zayn. And Zayn loves the people. But not as much as he loves Howie the media maestro over there.' He looked at his colleagues. 'You people don't appreciate what he does. But I do. He has those journalists in the palm of his hand. Look at him – one of them just kissed him on the cheek. That's how much they love him. And I really love this guy. He's a living legend.'

Howie had to admit – it did feel good to be appreciated.

Zayn winked at him. 'Well, what's it going to be, my not-so-old buddy?'

Howie was probably going to regret this. 'Okay' he sighed. 'I'll stay on as presidential spokesperson if you win the election.'

Zayn punched the air. 'Yes! You and me – the dream team! The media love Zayn. It'll be the easiest job in the world.'

Somehow Howie doubted that. 'We'll see. But if I'm going to be your spokesperson, I'm not sure I can keep up with the intelligence work. It's a lot harder than James Bond makes it look. I spent three hours in a police cell this morning, for reasons I'd rather not discuss. I nearly broke my ankle yesterday, falling down a flight of stairs. I was even dive-bombed by a seagull at lunchtime in Trafalgar Square. I'm lucky to still be here.' Howie shook his head. 'No. I'd better get out of this secret agent game, before one of the bad guys chucks me in a piranha-infested swimming pool.'

Martha smiled in the way that people always do when they're about to give you bad news. 'Ah, yes. I was going to have a word with you about that. Those additional employment conditions you signed yesterday – we didn't fully understand the implications.'

'What do you mean?' asked Howie, the panic already rising within him.

'There's a minimum period of service in the National Security and Intelligence Service. It's twelve months. So you still have a little time yet to serve.'

Howie knew he should have read those bloody terms and conditions. 'Can't I just resign from the service?'

'You can. But there's a twelve-month notice period.'

Howie closed his eyes. 'Of course there is.'

Martha walked up to him and put her hand on his arm. 'But listen, Howie. Don't worry. I'll only call on you if we ever have another Code Red crisis. And that's not likely to happen again in the next twelve months, is it?'

Howie sighed. Somehow he just knew. Something was going to happen.

Other novels by Paul Mathews:

We Have Lost The Pelicans
We Have Lost The Coffee
We Have Lost The Chihuahuas
We Have Lost The Plot
***We Have Lost* series**

An Accidental Royal Kidnap
The Royal Wedding Saboteurs
Royal Wedding in Vegas
***Royally Funny* series**

A Very Funny Murder Mystery
The Blood Moon Of Doom
To Kill A Shocking Bard
***Clinton Trump Detective Genius* series**

Discover more about Paul Mathews and his super-mega novels by visiting his website at www.quitefunnyguy.com and signing up for his Very Funny Newsletter

P.S. Robots and humans are both welcome!

Printed in Great Britain
by Amazon